MATT COWAN'S HORROR DELVE:

13 QUESTIONS WITH RAMSEY CAMPBELL

GOODWOOD

ALLEN K. '95

MATT COWAN'S
HORROR DELVE:

WELCOME TO HORROR DELVE,
A SPECTER-HAUNTED PLACE DEDICATED TO THE CELEBRATION OF ALL THINGS THAT RESIDE WITHIN THE SUPERNATURAL HORROR REALM!

I'm Matt Cowan, a lifelong fan of the uncanny with a hopeless addiction to buying horror anthologies. I've been writing over at my Horror Delve website (Horrordelve.com) for several years now, examining selected stories by featured authors, reviewing the occasional novel and putting together annual suggested reading lists for Halloween and Christmas. Basically, whatever horror-related subject catches my eye is potential fodder for the *Delve*. This column will function in similar fashion but will be unique and exclusive to *Nightmare Abbey*.

With introductions out-of-the-way, we come to the subject of this inaugural issue of *Nightmare Abbey*. As noted above, I read a lot of horror fiction and have discovered several authors whose work I find consistently exemplary along the way. Classic examples include M. R. James, Algernon Blackwood, Edith Wharton, E. F. Benson and William Hope Hodgson. I don't limit my tastes to authors from bygone eras either, as many modern horror writers also rank amongst my favorites: Reggie Oliver, Jo Kaplan (Joanna Parypinski), Thomas Ligotti, Simon Kurt Unsworth, and Anna Taborska, for instance. That being said, there is one author whom I personally consider to be the greatest of all time, Ramsey Campbell. I first encountered his work back in 1989 when I bought a book titled *Ancient Images* in a mall bookstore. It was a bit of a blind choice at the time but proved a fateful one, as its discovery would set the course of my reading life from that point onward. Since then, I've read a ton more of Ramsey's work (both short stories and novels) and have never once been disappointed.

So, how does one sum up Ramsey Campbell's stellar career? He published his first short story in 1962 at the of age 17 and didn't stop there. He has since produced hundreds of short stories, over two dozen story collections, and well over thirty novels; edited numerous anthologies, and won more awards than any writer in the field, including British Fantasy Awards, World Fantasy Awards, The Bram Stoker Award, The World Horror Grand Master Award, The Horror Writer's Association's Lifetime Achievement Award, and The Living Legend Award of The International Horror Guild. Three of his novels, *The Nameless, Pact of the Fathers,* and *The Influence,* have been adapted to film in Spain. In short, Ramsey Campbell is unquestionably an icon of the genre and I'm honored he agreed to answer some questions for us here today.

NIGHTMARE ABBEY

Summer 2022 ❶

SPECIAL RAMSEY CAMPBELL ISSUE

COVER IMAGE: VIRGIL FINLAY ☠ **ILLUSTRATIONS: ALLEN KOSZOWSKI**
EDITOR AND PUBLISHER: TOM ENGLISH

Nightmare Abbey (Volume #1, Summer 2022) is published semi-annually by Dead Letter Press and is copyright © Tom English and Dead Letter Press, PO Box 134, New Kent, VA 23124-0134. All rights reserved, including the right to reproduce this book, or portions thereof, in any form including but not limited to electronic and print media, without written permission from the publisher.

www.DeadLetterPress.com   ISBN-13: 979-8-9862307-0-2

DEAR ABBEY

MY DEAR ABBEY... MY DEAR NIGHTMARE ABBEY.
Many sleepless nights have I wandered your haunted corridors, heard the unearthly chanting of my cowled brothers and sisters—the keepers of unholy tales of terror—and witnessed their bizarre rituals.

My dear Abbey, even in my daylight hours you hide me within your crumbling, ancient vaults; veiled by shadows and cloistered in mystery; silent as the grave and timeless.

WELCOME TO MY NIGHTMARE

Old dark houses and stormy nights; secret passageways and hidden chambers; fog-shrouded streets and spectral figures; ghost ships and haunted seas; ancient curses and satanic rituals; creeping shadows and things that go bump in the night. Things both seen and unseen, real or imagined, that chill the soul and thrill the heart. The adventurous reader will discover these and other such horrors, in *Nightmare Abbey*.

Not to mention a few hundred starving rats, a vengeful cat, and a black dog that's not necessarily of the four-legged variety.

Please excuse this bout of purple prose and puffery, but these scribblings are mostly true: I do spend the better part of my days and nights here in the abbey ... sweeping the floors ... dusting the relics ... feeding the hellish creature chained up in the bell tower....

WHY *NIGHTMARE ABBEY*? AND WHY NOW?

Long story, the telling of which I'll make as brief as possible.

I started Dead Letter Press around 2005, when I launched a series of ultra-limited, laser-printed, hand-stapled chapbooks reprinting classic tales of vampirism. If memory serves, I produced close to two dozen *Classic Vampires Revisited* booklets, over a period of two and a half years—with subtitles such as: *A Botanical Nightmare*; *A Fearful Feasting*; and *A Consuming Passion* —before growing weary of the series. I found the Literary Vampire had become a pain in the neck, and I was ready to move on.

Early in 2008, I published a limited-edition hardcover anthology called *Bound for Evil: Curious Tales of Books Gone Bad*, featuring scary stories about the occasionally pernicious power of books. I felt well qualified to edit an anthology on the subject, having been at the mercy of thousands of bound volumes for years, buying them with money I could ill-afford to spend, collecting and cataloguing them, constantly dusting and protecting them. Always searching for others of their kind. Never satisfied. Never able to rest. Never... Well, now I *am* exaggerating. But I do love books. Old books, in particular. This may be the main reason I started publishing those fat chapbooks in the first place: I was like a wino who fancied seeing his own family label on the bottle.

Chateau Anglais.

Only I came up with a better name: Dead Letter Press; a combination of two ideas connected to the antiquarian fiction I loved. I wanted to showcase such writers as Henry

James, Charles Dickens, Edgar Allan Poe, and Nathaniel Hawthorne—the great men of *English Letters*. All long gone, of course, but never to be forgotten; their works, especially their weird tales, like "dead letters" to modern readers. (I have also published a few French, Spanish and Russian tales along the way—translated, of course. But I do confess my limitations and apologize for my interest mainly in English writers; but then, English *is* my first language. You can blame my parents for this.)

My second thought was of *letterpress*, a method of printing dating back to the 15th century, and the Gutenberg Bible, named for the German inventor and publisher Johannes Gutenberg. (The letterpress process prints pages by pressing sheets of paper against a surface covered with raised, inked letters.) I wouldn't be using letterpress printing—thank God for home computers and laser printers—but I liked the association with the past. And so, Dead Letter Press was christened.

But as much as I enjoy antiquarian ghost stories and such classic pulp magazines as *Weird Tales*, I wanted to branch out and host contemporary writers with my publishing house. I did this by including both new stories and old favorites in *Bound for Evil*. (Included in its 800 pages are tales by Ramsey Campbell and dozens of other great writers.) And to my amazement, the resultant book was a finalist for the Shirley Jackson Award (for Best Anthology, 2009).

And then what happened? Not much, until about 2016, when I caught the publishing bug again. I was missing all those great science fiction magazines that flooded the newsstands throughout the 1950s and '60s, as well as the creepy SF movies that kept me up late nights when I was a kid.

Voila! Black Infinity was born. This thick book/magazine hybrid features spooky SF stories, both old and new, and photo-illustrated articles on fantastic cinema and TV. It's published roughly twice a year, and I say *roughly* because getting out each new volume leaves me beat. *Am I happy now?*

After reading (almost exclusively) tons of stuff for eight fat volumes of *Black Infinity*—and as soon as I finish typing this, I'll begin work on the ninth—I started longing for a good ghost story; a bit of old-fashioned horror; fiction that relies on atmosphere, a mounting sense of dread, and the amazing power of suggestion to chill the reader's heart. Not the frequently violent and bloody horror popular today, but rather the suspenseful tales of terror published in such magazines as *Strange Tales* or *Unknown*, or in those great 1970s paperback novels—the kind drugstores used to sell. Or new stories by writers who understand what makes classic horror fiction so timeless.

Stephen King once wrote, and I'm paraphrasing, *if you can't scare the reader, then go for the gross-out.* I like King's fiction, but never appreciate being grossed out. And I doubt I'm alone in my sentiments, which may answer the *why* of *Nightmare Abbey*.

I chose *that* title after several hours of Internet research, during which I discovered most of my best word combinations—I had a list of about 32 killer titles—had already been claimed. I didn't care to share my magazine's title with a computer game or a heavy metal rock band, so I finally settled on borrowing the title of Thomas Love Peacock's 1818 Gothic novel, in which the author good-naturedly poked fun at the horror genre and several of the prevailing literary trends of his day. The title, I hope and believe, will conjure memories of antiquarian ghost stories; of mad monks, ancient rites, and haunted ruins; of both undead creatures and psychological terrors; of hidden fears that invade the reader's nights and haunt his days. In keeping with the best in terrifying, old-fashioned storytelling, *Nightmare Abbey* sounds entirely appropriate.

ASSEMBLED HERE are several of the scariest tales of yesterday and today, a mix of "literary" horror, gothic terror, Jamesian ghost stories, and classic weird tales; illustrated tributes to two icons of classic horror in film and television; and a new interview with a grandmaster of the terror tale.

Welcome to *our* nightmare.

Tom English
New Kent, VA

13 QUESTIONS WITH RAMSEY CAMPBELL:

Horror Delve (HD): Greetings, Ramsey!
(1) What initially sparked your love for the horror genre?

Ramsey Campbell (RC): We could argue it was the first fiction to terrify me—an uncanny *Adventures of Rupert Bear* when I was coming up to two years old, or George MacDonald's *The Princess and the Goblin* a couple of years later. Both contain scenes I take to have been designed not to scare their youthful audience too unbearably, but for me this simply meant they showed enough to suggest far worse, especially when I lay awake in the dark. Retrospectively they look like stages in the process that led me to my first adult tales of terror when I was six, *50 Years of Ghost Stories*. I was sufficiently literate to read the Edith Wharton tale ("Afterward") and to be appropriately unnerved. The tale that crawled into bed with me, however, was "The Residence at Whitminster", specifically the Jamesian images of the little hand that reaches out of the drawer and the insectoid feelers that grope over their victim's face in an unlit room. Once I recovered to some extent I wanted to repeat the experience or seek out similar. I take this to separate the horror aficionado from the rest of humanity.

2

HD: You have cited several vintage horror authors *(H. P. Lovecraft and M. R. James for example)* as early influences on your writing. Can you tell us about some of the classic stories which made a big impact on you?

Campbell: It was Lovecraft who gave me an example to emulate and a focus to employ, though I'd already had a feeble go at imitating Machen's manner and then, in another abandoned sally, John Dickson Carr's. *"The Colour Out of Space", "The Call of Cthulhu", "The Dunwich Horror"*—all these overwhelmed me with a sense of the cosmic when I was fourteen and set me off on my own literary trek, though my early unrevised attempts were closer to the florid mode of *"The Hound"*. *"The Willows"* haunted me and still does, and *Midnight Sun* was one of my bids to incarnate my admiration. *"The White People"* is incomparably insidious in its use of folklore and of the naïve voice, both of which have influenced quite a number of my stories. I found Philip K. Dick's "Upon the Dull Earth" thoroughly unnerving. *The October Country* of Bradbury, Matheson's *I Am Legend*—these too were among my first loves in the field, and Leiber's "Smoke Ghost" was as crucial a turning point in my work as it certainly was in the field of urban supernatural horror.

3

HD: Two of your novels, *Ancient Images* and *The Grin of the Dark*, involve the search for suppressed movies. Are there any real-life films that served as your inspiration?

Campbell: For *Ancient Images*, in a general sense horror movies that were hard to find—*Murder by the Clock*, for instance, which was cited by William K. Everson but remained virtually impossible to see until the internet came to the rescue. There was also the experience I and others had of hearing Mario Bava's *La Maschera del Demonio*[1] enthused about by lucky viewers at the National Film Theatre, only to learn that the British film censor had refused it a certificate (it remained unseen here for eight years and then for a while was released with obvious cuts). Behind *The Grin of the Dark* we may glimpse forgotten (if no longer) early film comedians such as the extraordinary Charley Bowers—admired

---

[1] Released in English as *Black Sunday* (1960).

Barbara Steele in
La Maschera del Demonio
(The Mask of the Demon)

by André Breton, no less—but I should explain that my original concept involved a silent serial of the kind directed by Feuillade and Lang, called *The Sixth Face of the Spider* (unless that would have been the title of the novel). The notion of a comedian seemed more productive, but I may yet return to the original idea.

4

HD: Your novels have featured a wide range of intriguing subjects, from psychic dreaming in *Incarnate*, to fairy folklore in *The Kind Folk*, to Liverpool's hidden histories in *Creatures of the Pool,* to name a few. What sort of research methods do you employ in preparation for a new project?

Campbell: I confess that the backgrounds and foundations of the first two were pretty well entirely made up, but *Creatures of the Pool* was a different matter. I wanted to write a novel drawing on Liverpool traditions and the odder aspects of its history, not to mention its legends and reports of the uncanny, and for fifteen years or so I picked up every rare book about the city I could find. I find research of this kind a real stimulus, because I always discover surprising material I can incorporate. Because the research for that novel was spread over such a period, I'm often unsure which of my notes are simple transcriptions or summaries and which are imaginative developments or even invented. I'm now in the position of any innocent reader who can't distinguish what's genuine from what isn't in that

book. If any of it turns into local legend, I'll be delighted. There have also been occasions when I've invented a legend or tradition and then looked for actual collaborative evidence. In each case I've been unnerved by how much evidence I've found to back up a pure invention. It makes me (if possible) even more skeptical of conspiracy theories.

5

HD: 2018 saw the publication of the final book in your excellent *The Three Births of Daoloth* trilogy. What was it like writing a trio of connected novels as opposed to single, self-contained ones, and is that something you would consider doing again in the future?

Campbell: I'm very much of the view that a story should take the form the material dictates, and so for years I resisted my old friend and publisher Pete Crowther's suggestion that I should write a trilogy around the Brichester Mythos (just as decades earlier, and for the same reason, I'd needed some persuading to write a

ILLUSTRATED BY RANDY BROECKER

VISIONS *from* BRICHESTER

RAMSEY CAMPBELL

Ramsey Campbell
FAR AWAY & NEVER

DMR

novella for Debbie Beale at Legend). I didn't want to write a massive novel and then split it into three volumes—I wanted a reason for those. At last it occurred to me to follow the central characters and their antagonists through most of their lives, and show how an originally secretive cult might over the decades grow in power and come into the open, even gaining public acceptance for its apparently innocuous activities. I found writing it and returning to the characters in two subsequent years gathered creative energy in a way I haven't often experienced, and I was moved as they aged and came to their end. I can't imagine writing another one, since I have no themes in mind that require more than a single volume.

6

HD: The collection *Far Away and Never* brings us eight of your sword and sorcery stories. I became a big fan of your Ryre the swordsman tales as a result. What did you use for inspiration when you were writing them, and do you think you might ever return to the genre?

Campbell: To be brutally honest, the inspiration was the relative lack of markets for horror fiction in the early 1970s. My old friend and agent Kirby McCauley urged me to diversify, and so I tried writing science fiction, almost none of which was any good, before giving sword and sorcery a go. The first of the series, *"The Sustenance of Hoak"*, was picked up by Andy Offutt. He rightly felt it was overlong, and so I cut it by about thirty percent without losing any significant material. When his publishers asked for a second anthology he suggested I should revive Ryre, and we went for four volumes. The termination of the series ended my ideas along those lines, and I've had none since.

7

HD: Of your own work do you have any particular favorites?

Campbell: *Needing Ghosts* remains one,

RAMSEY CAMPBELL

NEEDING GHOSTS

because it virtually wrote itself and challenged me to keep up with the stream of ideas. I do like the trilogy—it seems to epitomise much of what I try to do. I've a perverse affection for "Again", surely my purest horror tale.

8

HD: What aspects of embarking on a new short story or novel most excite you?

Campbell: There's the moment of getting a good idea whose potential is immediately apparent, though that's by no means true of all of the notions that present themselves. There's the pleasure of seeing how it develops, though often enough that's preceded by a period in psychological limbo, where nothing about the story—characters, events, settings and much else—seems clear. Still, for me perhaps the greatest pleasure is being taken by surprise by the narrative, which happens when (as very frequently) I let it develop organically rather than forcing it to conform to a preconceived plot. Indeed, I try to surprise myself every day in the course of a first draft by writing something I didn't know I was going to write until it presented itself. Lastly, I have fun rewriting, the more thoroughly and unsparingly the better.

9

HD: You've had such an amazing career. Could you share some advice for new writers?

Campbell: We all have an optimum period of creativity each day, and it's worth beginning work then if you possibly can. Mine is from about six in the morning until noon or so. Don't be too eager to feel you've exhausted your creative energy for the day, but if you sense you're close to doing so, then don't squeeze yourself dry: better to know what the next paragraph is going to be and start with that next time. Scribble down a rough version of it rather than risk forgetting it. Always have a rough idea of your first line or lines before you sit down to write, and then you won't be trapped into fearing the blank page. If you must take a day or more out from a story, break off before the end of a scene or a chapter, to give yourself some impetus when you return. Always carry a notebook (or a phone with that function) for ideas, glimpses, overheard dialogue, details of what you're about to write, developments of work in progress. If an idea or something larger refuses to be developed, try altering the viewpoint or even the form: if it won't grow as a short story, it may be a poem. Sometimes two apparently unproductive ideas may be cross-fertilized to give you a story. Then again, you may not be ready technically or emotionally to deal with an idea, and it can improve with waiting. What else can I tell you? Only to write. Surprise us, astonish us. Enjoy your work. Above all, don't despair. The frustration you will inevitably experience sometimes, the feeling that you don't know

Dana Andrews in Jacques Tourneur's 1957 film *Night of the Demon* (aka *Curse of the Demon*)

how to write, may be the birth pangs of something genuinely new. I know I still suffer that experience every time I write a story. Believe me, it's preferable to playing it safe with a formula.

10

HD: Is there a horror element or creature in literature or film which is a particular favorite of yours? (I, for example, have an affinity for faceless creatures/entities.)

Campbell: The aspiration towards awe, which I find in tales such as "The Willows" and "The Colour out of Space". I've made a few feeble leaps in its direction.

James Stewart in Alfred Hitchcock's 1958 film *Vertigo* (Universal Pictures)

11

HD: What do you do to relax when you are not writing?

RC: Watch films of every kind, listen to classical (for want of a better term) music, read (sometimes but very far from exclusively) horror.

12

HD: Are there some films you can suggest which you think fans of your work would enjoy?

RC: I hope some of my favourites may appeal to folk. *Night of the Demon* remains my top horror film, with which I fell in love at the age of fourteen (one of the first horrors I ever saw, since the British censor's certificate barred anybody apparently under sixteen from nearly every horror movie). *Vertigo* is Hitchcock's most beautiful and disturbing work, and repays repeated viewings, while the recent UHD release is a revelation. Buñuel's *Los Olvidados*[2] overwhelmed me in my midteens and demonstrated how extreme realism could tip into surrealism, incidentally influencing my choice of a writing route. *Last Year in Marienbad* convinced me that an enigma can be more satisfying than any explanation. Several of David Lynch's films—*Fire Walk with Me, Lost Highway, Mulholland Dr*—take me to the very edge of visceral terror.

13

HD: Can you talk about any current projects you are working on?

RC: I've completed a new novel of cosmic terror, *Fellstones*, which is scheduled by Flame Tree for September, and the latest—a supernatural one, *The Lonely Lands*—is waiting to be reread in first draft. My collected columns from *Video Watchdog* will come from Electric Dreamhouse with a substantial introduction as *Ramsey's Rambles*, and I'm close to completing a 70,000-word study of the *Three Stooges* for the same publisher.

> *Now let me say thank you to Matt!*
> *His interviews are where it's at.*
> *Such interrogation*
> *Produces elation—*
> *In tribute I'll take off my hat.*

Ramsey's Website can be found at: **RAMSEYCAMPBELL.COM**

---

[2] 1950 Mexican teen crime drama (trans: *The Forgotten Ones*), aka *The Young and the Damned*.

THE OXFORD COMPANION TO ENGLISH LITERATURE DESCRIBES RAMSEY CAMPBELL AS "BRITAIN'S MOST RESPECTED LIVING HORROR WRITER." He has been given more awards than any other writer in the field, including the Grand Master Award of the World Horror Convention, the Lifetime Achievement Award of the Horror Writers Association, the Living Legend Award of the International Horror Guild and the World Fantasy Life-time Achievement Award. In 2015 he was made an Honorary Fellow of Liverpool John Moores University for outstanding services to literature. Among his novels are *The Face That Must Die, Incarnate, Midnight Sun, The Count of Eleven, The Darkest Part of the Woods, The Overnight, Secret Story, The Grin of the Dark, Thieving Fear, Creatures of the Pool, The Seven Days of Cain, Ghosts Know, The Kind Folk, Think Yourself Lucky, Thirteen Days by Sunset Beach, The Wise Friend, Somebody's Voice* and *Fellstones*. His Brichester Mythos trilogy consists of *The Searching Dead, Born to the Dark* and *The Way of the Worm*. His collections include *Waking Nightmares, Ghosts and Grisly Things, Told by the Dead, Just Behind You, Holes for Faces, By the Light of My Skull* and a two-volume retrospective roundup (*Phantasmagorical Stories*) as well as *The Village Killings and Other Novellas*. His non-fiction is collected as *Ramsey Campbell, Probably* and *Ramsey Campbell, Certainly*, while *Ramsey's Rambles* collects his video reviews, and he is working on a book-length study of the Three Stooges, *Six Stooges and Counting*. *Limericks of the Alarming and Phantasmal* is a history of horror fiction in the form of fifty limericks. His novels *The Nameless, Pact of the Fathers* and *The Influence* have been filmed in Spain, where a television series based on *The Nameless* is in development. He is the President of the Society of Fantastic Films.

Ramsey Campbell was born in Liverpool in 1946 and still lives on Merseyside with his wife Jenny. His pleasures include classical music, good food and wine. His web site is at www.ramseycampbell.com

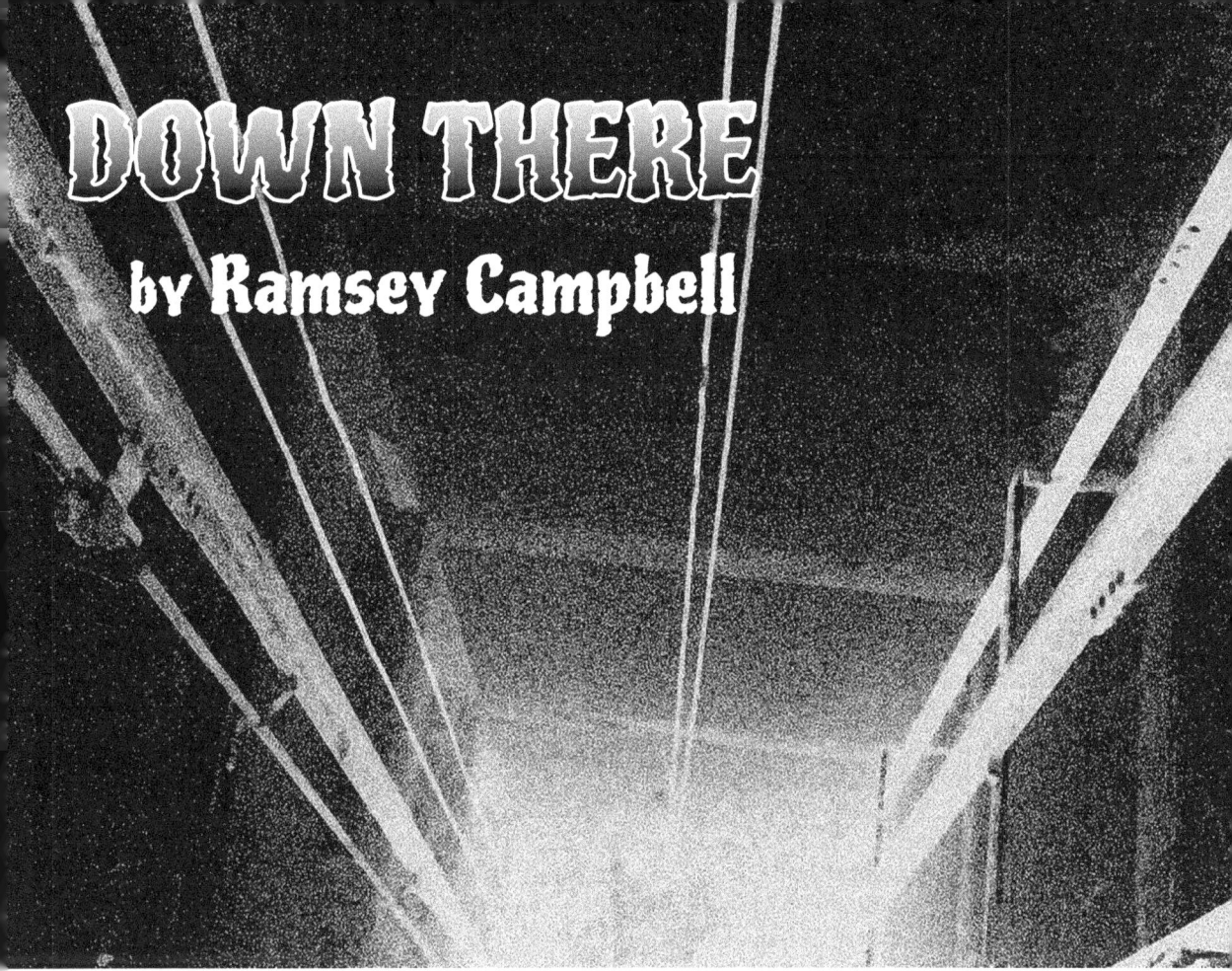

DOWN THERE

by Ramsey Campbell

"HURRY ALONG THERE," Steve called as the girls trooped down the office. "Last one tonight. Mind the doors."

The girls smiled at Elaine as they passed her desk, but their smiles meant different things: just like you to make things more difficult for the rest of us, looks like you've been kept in after school, suppose you've nothing better to do, fancy having to put up with him by yourself. She didn't give a damn what they thought of her. No doubt they earned enough without working overtime, since all they did with their money was squander it on makeup and new clothes.

She only wished Steve wouldn't make a joke of everything: even the lifts, one of which had broken down entirely after sinking uncontrollably to the bottom of the shaft all day. She was glad that hadn't happened to her, even though she gathered the sub-basement was no longer so disgusting. Still, the surviving lift had rid her of everyone now,

including Mr Williams the union representative, who'd tried the longest to persuade her not to stay. He still hadn't forgiven the union for accepting a temporary move to this building; perhaps he was taking it out on her. Well, he'd gone now, into the November night and rain.

It had been raining all day. The warehouses outside the windows looked like melting chocolate; the river and the canals were opaque with tangled ripples. Cottages and terraces, some of them derelict, crowded up the steep hills towards the disused mines. Through the skeins of water on the glass their infrequent lights looked shaky as candle flames.

She was safe from all that, in the long office above five untenanted and two basements. Ranks of filing cabinets stuffed with blue Inland Revenue files divided the office down the middle; smells of dust and old paper hung in the air. Beneath a fluttering fluorescent tube protruding files drowsed, jerked awake. Through the steamy window above an unquenchable radiator, she could just make out the frame where the top section of the fire escape should be.

"Are you feeling exploited?" Steve said.

He'd heard Mr Williams's parting shot, calling her the employers' weapon against solidarity. "No, certainly not." She wished he would let her be quiet for a while. "I'm feeling hot," she said.

"Yes, it is a bit much." He stood up, mopping his forehead theatrically. "I'll go and sort out Mr Tuttle."

She doubted that he would find the caretaker, who was no doubt hidden somewhere with a bottle of cheap rum. At least he tried to hide his drinking, which was more than one could say for the obese half-chewed sandwiches he left on windowsills, in the room where tea was brewed, even once on someone's desk.

She turned idly to the window behind her chair and watched the indicator in the lobby counting down. Steve had reached the basement now. The letter *B* flickered, then brightened: he'd gone down to the sub-basement, which had been meant to be kept secret from the indicator and from everyone except the holder of the key. Perhaps the finding of the cache down there had encouraged Mr Tuttle to be careless with food.

She couldn't help growing angry. If the man who had built these offices had had so much money, why hadn't he put it to better use? The offices had been merely a disguise for the sub-basement, which was to have been his refuge. What had he feared? War, revolution, a nuclear disaster? All anyone knew was that he'd spent the months before he had been certified insane in smuggling food down there. He'd wasted all that food, left it there to rot, and he'd had no thought for the people who would have to work in the offices: no staircases, a fire escape that fell apart when someone tried to paint it—but she was beginning to sound like Mr Williams, and there was no point in brooding.

The numbers were counting upwards, slow as a child's first sum. Eventually Steve appeared, the solution. "No sign of him," he said. "He's somewhere communing with alcohol, I expect. Most of the lights are off, which doesn't help."

That sounded like one of Mr Tuttle's ruses. "Did you go right down?" she said. "What's it like down there?"

"Huge. They say it's much bigger than any of the floors. You could play two football games at once in there." Was he exaggerating? His face was bland as a silent comedian's except for raised eyebrows. "They left the big doors open when they cleaned it up. If there were any lights I reckon you could see for miles. I'm only surprised it didn't cut into one of the sewers."

"I shouldn't think it could be any more smelly."

"It still reeks a bit, that's true. Do you want a look? Shall I take you down?" When he dodged towards her as though to carry her away, she sat forward rigidly and held the arms of her chair against the desk. "No thank you," she said, though she'd felt a start of delicious apprehension.

"Did you ever hear what was supposed to have happened while they were cleaning up all the food? Tuttle told me, if you can believe him." She didn't want to hear; Mr Tuttle had annoyed her enough for one day. She leafed determinedly through a file, until Steve went up the office to his desk.

For a while she was able to concentrate. The sounds of the office merged into a background discreet as muzak: the rustle of papers, the rushes of the wind, the buzz of the defective fluorescent like an insect trying to bumble its way out of the tube. She manoeuvred files across her desk. This man was going to be happy, since they owed him money. This fellow wasn't, since he owed them some.

But the thought of the food had settled on her like the heat. Only this morning, in the room where the tea-urn stood, she'd found an ancient packet of Mr Tuttle's sandwiches in the waste bin. No doubt the packet was still there, since the cleaners were refusing to work until the building was made safe. She seemed unable to rid herself of the memory.

No, it wasn't a memory she was smelling. As she glanced up, wrinkling her nostrils, she saw that Steve was doing so too. "Tuttle," he said, grimacing.

As though he'd given a cue, they heard movement on the floor below. Someone was dragging a wet cloth across linoleum. Was the caretaker doing the cleaners' job? More likely he'd spilled a bottle and was trying to wipe away the evidence. "I'll get him this time," Steve said, and ran towards the lobby.

Was he making too much noise? The soft moist dragging on the floor below had ceased. The air seemed thick with heat and dust and the stench of food; when she lit a cigarette, the smoke loomed reprovingly above her. She opened the thin louvres at the top of the nearest window, but that brought no relief. There was nothing else for it; she opened the window that gave onto the space where the fire escape should be.

It was almost too much for her. A gust of rain dashed in, drenching her face while she clung to the handle. The window felt capable of smashing wide, of snatching her out into the storm. She managed to anchor the bar to the sill, and leaned out into the night to let the rain wash away the smell.

Nine feet below her she could see the fifth-floor platform of the fire escape, its iron mesh slippery and streaming. The iron stairs that hung from it, poised to swing down to the next platform, seemed to dangle into a deep pit of rain whose sides were incessantly collapsing. The thought of having to jump to the platform made her flinch back; she could imagine herself losing her footing, slithering off into space.

She was about to close the window, for the flock of papers on her desk had begun to flap, when she glimpsed movement in the unlit warehouse opposite and just below her. She was reminded of a maggot, writhing in food. Of course, that was because she was glimpsing it through the warehouse windows, small dark holes. It was reflected from her building, which was why it looked so large and puffily vague. It must be Mr Tuttle, for as it moved she heard a scuffling below her, retreating from the lifts.

She'd closed the window by the time Steve returned. "You didn't find him, did you? Never mind," she said, for he was frowning. Did he feel she was spying on him? At once his face grew blank. Perhaps he resented her knowing, first that he'd gone down to the sub-basement, now that he'd been outwitted. When he sat at his desk at the far end of the office, the emptiness between them felt like a rebuff. "Do you fancy some tea?" she said, to placate him.

"I'll make it. A special treat." He jumped up at once and strode to the lobby.

Why was he so eager? Five minutes later, as she leafed through someone's private life, she wondered if he meant to creep up on her, if that was the joke he had been planning behind his mask. Her father had used to pounce on her to make her shriek when she was little—when he had still been able to. She turned sharply, but Steve had pulled open the doors of the out-of-work lift shaft and was peering down, apparently listening. Perhaps it was Mr Tuttle he meant to surprise, not her.

The tea was hot and fawn, but little else. Why did it seem to taste of the lingering stench? Of course, Steve hadn't closed the door of the room off the lobby, where Mr Tuttle's sandwiches must still be festering. She hurried out and slammed the door with the hand that wasn't covering her mouth.

On impulse she went to the doors of the lift shaft where Steve had been listening. They opened easily as curtains; for a moment she was teetering on the edge. The shock blurred her vision, but she knew it wasn't Mr Tuttle who was climbing the lift cord like a fat pale monkey on a stick. When she screwed up her eyes and peered into the dim well, of course there was nothing.

Steve was watching her when she returned to her desk. His face was absolutely noncommittal. Was he keeping something from her—a special joke, perhaps? Here it came; he was about to speak. "How's your father?" he said.

It sounded momentarily like a comedian's catch-phrase. "Oh, he's happier now," she blurted. "They've got a new stock of large print books in the library."

"Is there someone who can sit with him?"

"Sometimes." The community spirit had faded once the mine owners had moved on, leaving the area honeycombed with mines, burdened with unemployment. People seemed locked into themselves, afraid of being robbed of the little they had left.

"I was wondering if he's all right on his own."

"He'll have to be, won't he." She was growing angry; he was as bad as Mr Williams, reminding her of things it was no use remembering.

"I was just thinking that if you want to slope off home, I won't tell anyone. You've already done more work than some of the rest of them would do in an evening."

She clenched her fists beneath the desk to hold on to her temper. He must want to leave early himself and so was trying to persuade her. No doubt he had problems of his own—perhaps they were the secret behind his face—but he mustn't try to make her act dishonestly. Or was he testing her? She knew so little about him. "He'll be perfectly safe," she said. "He can always knock on the wall if he needs anyone."

Though his face stayed blank his eyes, frustrated now, gave him away. Five minutes later he was craning out of the window over the fire escape, while Elaine pinned flapping files down with both hands. Did he really expect his date, if that was his problem, to come out on a night like this? It would be just like a man to expect her to wait outside.

The worst of it was that Elaine felt disappointed, which was absurd and infuriating. She knew perfectly well that the only reason he was working tonight was that one of the seniors had to do so. Good God, what had she expected to come of an evening alone with him? They were both in their forties—they knew what they wanted by now, which in his case was bound to be someone younger than Elaine. She hoped he and his girlfriend would be very happy. Her hands on the files were tight fists.

When he slammed the window she saw that his face was glistening. Of course it wasn't sweat, only rain. He hurried away without looking at her, and vanished into the lift. Perhaps the girl was waiting in the doorway, unable to rouse Mr Tuttle to let her in. Elaine hoped Steve wouldn't bring her upstairs. She would be a distraction, that was why. Elaine was here to work.

And she wasn't about to be distracted by Steve and his attempts at jokes. She refused to turn when she heard the soft sounds by the lifts. No doubt he was peering through the lobby window at her, waiting for her to turn and jump. Or was it his girlfriend? As Elaine reached across her desk for a file she thought that the face was pale and very fat. Elaine was damned if she would give her the satisfaction of being noticed—but when she tried to work she couldn't concentrate. She turned angrily. The lobby was deserted.

In a minute she would lose her temper. She could see where he was hiding, or they were: the door of the room off the lobby was ajar. She turned away, determined to work, but the deserted office wouldn't let her; each alley between the filing cabinets was a hiding-place, the buzz of the defective light and the fusillade of rain could hide the sound of soft footsteps. It was no longer at all funny. He was going too far.

At last he came in from the lobby, with no attempt at stealth. Perhaps he had tired of the joke. He must have been to the street door: his forehead was wet, though it didn't look like rain. Would he go back to work now, and pretend that the urn's room was empty? No, he must have thought of a new ruse, for he began pacing from cabinet to cabinet, glancing at files, stuffing them back into place. Was he trying to make her as impatient as he appeared to be? His quick sharp footsteps seemed to grow louder and more nerve-racking, like the ticking of the clock when she was lying awake, afraid to doze off in case her father needed her. "Steve, for heaven's sake, what's wrong?"

He stopped in the act of pulling a file from its cabinet. He looked abashed, at a loss for words, like a schoolboy caught stealing. She couldn't help taking pity on him; her resentment had been presumptuous. "You didn't go down to find Mr Tuttle just now, did you?" she said, to make it easier for him.

But he looked even less at ease. "No, I didn't. I don't think he's here at all. I think he left hours ago."

Why must he lie? They had both heard the caretaker on the floor below. Steve seemed determined to go on. "As a matter of fact," he said, "I'm beginning to suspect that he sneaks off home as soon as he can once the building's empty."

He was speaking low, which annoyed her: didn't he want his girlfriend to hear? "But there's someone else in the building," he said.

"Oh yes," she retorted. "I'm sure there is." Why did he have to dawdle instead of coming out with the truth? He was worse than her father when he groped among his memories.

He frowned, obviously not sure how much she knew. "Whoever it is, they're up to no good. I'll tell you the rest once we're out of the building. We mustn't waste any more time."

His struggles to avoid the truth amused and irritated her. The moisture on his forehead wasn't rain at all. "If they're up to no good," she said innocently, "we ought to wait until the police arrive."

"No, we'll call the police once we're out." He seemed to be saying anything that came into his head. How much longer could he keep his face blank? "Listen," he said, his fist crumpling the file, "I'll tell you why Tuttle doesn't stay here at night. The cleaners too, I think he told them. When the men were cleaning out the sub-basement, some of the food disappeared overnight. You understand what that means? Someone stole a hundred-weight of rotten food. The men couldn't have cared less, they treated it as a joke, and there was no sign how anyone could have got in. But as he says, that could mean that whatever it was was clever enough to conceal the way in. Of course I thought he was drunk or joking, but now..."

His words hung like dust in the air. She didn't trust herself to speak. How dare he expect her to swallow such rubbish, as if she were too stupid to know what was going on? Her reaction must have shown on her face; she had never heard him speak coldly before. "We must go immediately," he said.

Her face was blazing. "Is that an order?"

"Yes, it is. I'll make sure you don't lose by it." His voice grew authoritative. "I'll call the lift while you fetch your coat."

Blind with anger, she marched to the cloakroom at the far end of the office from the lobby. As she grabbed her coat the hangers clashed together, a shrill violent sound which went some way towards expressing her feelings. Since Steve had no coat, he would be soaked. Though that gave her no pleasure, she couldn't help smiling.

The windows were shaking with rain. In the deserted office her footsteps sounded high-pitched, nervous. No, she wasn't on edge, only furious. She didn't mind passing the alleys between the cabinets, she wouldn't deign to look, not even at the alley where a vague shadow was lurching forward; it was only the shadow of a cabinet, jerked by the defective light. She didn't falter until she came in sight of the lobby, where there was no sign of Steve.

Had he gone without her? Was he smuggling out his girlfriend? They weren't in the room off the lobby, which was open and empty; the overturned waste bin seemed to demonstrate their haste. The doors of the disused lift shaft were open too. They must have opened when Steve had called the other lift. Everything could be explained; there was no reason for her to feel that something was wrong.

But something was. Between the two lift shafts, the call-button was glowing. That could mean only one thing: the working lift hadn't yet answered the call. There was no other exit from the lobby—but there was no sign of Steve.

When she made herself go to the disused lift shaft, it was only in order to confirm that her thought was absurd. Clinging to the edges of the doorway, she leaned out. The lift was stranded in the sub-basement, where it was very dim. At first all she could distinguish was that the trapdoor in its roof was open, though the opening was largely covered by a sack. Could anything except a sack be draped so limply? Yes, for it was Steve, his eyes like glass that was forcing their lids wide, his mouth gagged with what appeared to be a torn-off wad of dough—except that the dough had fingers and a thumb.

She was reeling, perhaps over the edge of the shaft. No, she was stumbling back into the foyer, and already less sure what she'd glimpsed. Steve was dead, and she must get out of the building; she could think of nothing else. Thank God, she need not think, for the working lift had arrived. Was there soft movement in the disused shaft, a chorus of sucking like the mouthing of a crowd of babies? Nothing could have made her look. She staggered away, between the opening doors, into total darkness.

For a moment she thought she'd stepped out into an empty well. But there was a floor underfoot; the lift's bulb must have blown. As the door clamped shut behind her, the utter darkness closed in.

She was scrabbling at the metal wall in a frantic bid to locate the buttons—to open the doors, to let in some light—before she controlled herself. Which was worse: a quick descent in the darkness, or to be trapped alone on the sixth floor? In any case, she needn't suffer the dark. Hurriedly she groped in her handbag for her lighter.

She flicked the lighter uselessly once, twice, as the lift reached the fifth floor. The sudden plunge in her guts wasn't only shock; the lift had juddered to a halt. She flicked the lighter desperately. It had just lit when the doors hobbled open.

The fifth floor was unlit. Beyond the lobby she could see the windows of the untenanted office, swarming with rain and specks of light. The bare floor looked like a carpet of dim fog, interrupted by angular patches of greater dimness, blurred rugs of shadow. There was no sign of Mr Tuttle or whoever she'd heard from above. The doors were closing, but she wasn't reassured: if the lift had begun to misbehave, the least it could do would be to stop at every floor.

The doors closed her in with her tiny light. Vague reflections of the flame hung on the walls and tinged the greyish metal yellow; the roof was a hovering blotch. All the lighter had achieved was to remind her how cramped the lift was. She stared at the doors, which were trembling. Was there a movement beyond them other than the outbursts of rain?

When the doors parted, she retreated a step. The fourth floor was a replica of the fifth—bare floors colourless with dimness, windows that looked shattered by rain—but the shuffling was closer. Was the floor of the lobby glistening in patches, as though from moist footsteps? The doors were hesitating,

she was brandishing her tiny flame as though it might defend her—then the doors closed reluctantly, the lift faltered downwards.

She'd had no time to sigh with relief, if indeed she had meant to, when she heard the lobby doors open above her. A moment later the lift shook. Something had plumped down on its roof.

At once, with a shock that felt as though it would tear out her guts, she knew what perhaps she had known, deep down, for a while: Steve hadn't been trying to frighten her—he had been trying not to. She hadn't heard Mr Tuttle on the fifth floor, nor any imaginary girlfriend of Steve's. Whatever she had heard was above her now, fumbling softly at the trapdoor.

It couldn't get in. She could hear that it couldn't, not before the lift reached the third—oh God, make the lift be quick! Then she could run for the fire escape, which wasn't damaged except on the sixth. She was thinking quickly now, almost in a trance that carried her above her fear, aware of nothing except the clarity of her plan—and it was no use.

The doors were only beginning to open as they reached the third when the lift continued downwards without stopping. Either the weight on its roof, or the tampering, was sending it down. As the doors gaped to display the brick wall of the shaft, then closed again, the trapdoor clanged back and something like a hand came reaching down towards her.

It was very large. If it found her, it would engulf her face. It was the colour of ancient dough, and looked puffed up as if by decay; patches of the flesh were torn and ragged, but there seemed to be no blood, only greyness. She clamped her left hand over her mouth, which was twitching uncontrollably, and thrust the lighter at the swollen groping fingers.

They hissed in the flame and recoiled, squirming. Whitish beads had broken out on them. In a way, the worst thing was the absence of a cry. The hand retreated through the opening, scraping the edge, and a huge vague face peered down with eyes like blobs of dough. She felt a surge of hysterical mirth at the way the hand had fled—but she choked it back, for she had no reason to feel triumphant. Her skirmish had distracted her from the progress of the lift, which had reached the bottom of the shaft.

Ought she to struggle with the doors, try to prevent them from opening? It was too late. They were creeping back, they were open now, and she could see the sub-basement.

At least, she could see darkness which her light couldn't even reach. She had an impression of an enormous doorway, beyond which the darkness, if it was in proportion, might extend for hundreds of yards; she thought of the mouth of a sewer or a mine. The stench of putrid food was overwhelming, parts of the dark looked restless and puffy. But when she heard scuttling, and a dim shape came darting towards her, it proved to be a large rat.

Though that was bad enough, it mustn't distract her from the thing above her, on the lift. It had no chance to do so. The rat was yards away from her, and darting aside from her light, when she heard a spongy rush and the rat was overwhelmed by a whitish flood like a gushing of effluent. She backed away until the wall of the lift arrested her. She could still see too much—but how could she make herself put out the flame, trap herself in the dark?

For the flood was composed of obese bodies which clambered over one another, clutching for the trapped rat. The rat was tearing at the pudgy hands, ripping pieces from the doughy flesh, but that seemed not to affect them at all. Huge toothless mouths gaped in the puffy faces, collapsed inwards like senile lips, sucking loudly, hungrily. Three of the bloated heads fell on the rat, and she heard its squeals above their sucking.

Then the others that were clambering over them, out of the dark, turned towards her. Great moist nostrils were dilating and vanishing in their noseless faces. Could they see her light with their blobs of eyes, or were they smelling her terror? Perhaps they'd had only soft rotten things to eat down here, but they were learning fast. Hunger was their only motive, ruthless, all-consuming.

They came jostling towards the lift. Once, delirious, she'd heard all the sounds around her grow stealthily padded, but this softness was far worse. She was trying both to stand back and to jab the lift-button, quite uselessly; the doors refused to budge. The doughy shapes would pile in like tripe, suffocating her, putting out the flame, gorging themselves on her in the dark. The one that had ridden the lift was slithering down the outside to join them.

Perhaps its movement unburdened the lift, or jarred a connection into place, for all at once the doors were closing. Swollen hands were thumping them, soft fingers like grubs were trying to squeeze between them, but already the lift was sailing upwards. Oh God, suppose it went straight up to the sixth floor! But she'd found the ground-floor button, though it twitched away from her, shaken by the flame, and the lift was slowing. Through the slit between the doors, beyond the glass doors to the street, a street-lamp blazed like the sun.

The lift's doors opened, and the doughy face lurched in, its fat white blind eyes bulging, its avid mouth huge as a fist. It took her a moment prolonged as a nightmare to realise that it had been crushed between lift and shaft—for as the doors struggled open, the face began to tear. Screaming, she dragged the doors open, tearing the body in half. As she ran through it she heard it plump at the foot of the shaft, to be met by a soft eager rush—but was fleeing blindly into the torrent of rain, towards the steep maze of unlit streets, her father at the fireside, his quiet vulnerable demand to know all that she'd done today.

💀 💀 💀

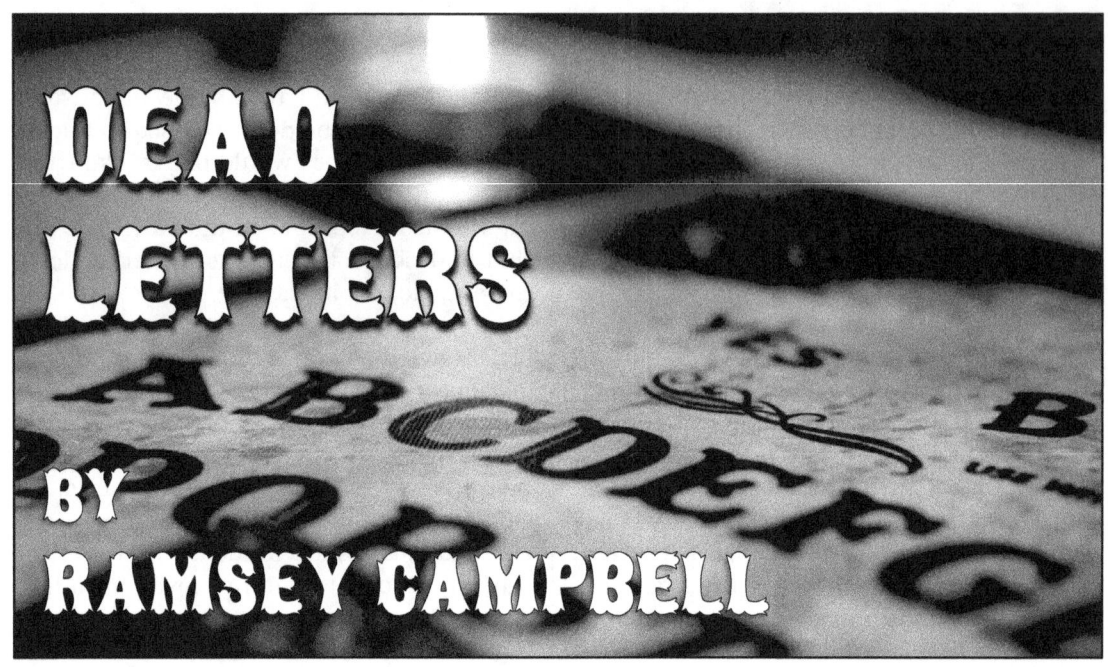

DEAD LETTERS

BY RAMSEY CAMPBELL

THE SÉANCE WAS BOB'S IDEA, OF COURSE. We'd finished dinner and were lighting more candles to stave off the effects of the power cut when he made the suggestion. "What's the point? The apartment's only three years old," Joan said, though in fact she was disturbed by this threat of a séance in our home. But he'd brought his usual bottle of Pernod to the dinner party, inclining it toward us as if he'd forgotten that nobody else touched the stuff, and now he was drunk enough to believe he could carry us unprotesting with him. He almost did. When opposition came, it surprised me as much as it did Bob.

"I'm not joining in," his wife Louise said. "I won't."

I could feel one of his rages building, though usually they didn't need to be provoked. "Is this some more of your stupidity we have to suffer?" he said. "Don't you know what everyone in this room is thinking of you?"

"I'm not sure you do," I told him sharply. I could see Stan and Marge were embarrassed. I'd thought Bob might behave himself when meeting them for the first time.

He peered laboriously at me, his face white and sweating as if from a death battle with the Pernod. "One thing's sure," he said. "If she doesn't know what I think of her, she will for the next fortnight."

I glared at him. He and Louise were bound for France in the morning to visit her relatives; the tickets were poking out of his top pocket. We'd made this dinner date with them weeks ago—as usual, to relieve Louise's burdens of Bob and of the demands of her work as a nurse—and as if to curtail the party Bob had brought their flight date forward. I imagined her having to travel with Bob's hangover. But at least she looked in control for the moment, sitting in a chair near the apartment door, away from the round dining table. "Sit down, everybody," Bob said. "Before someone else cracks up."

From his briefcase where he kept the Pernod he produced a device that he slid into the middle of the table, his unsteady hand slipping and almost flinging his toy to the floor. I wondered what had happened in the weeks since I'd last seen him, so to lessen his ability to hold his drink; he'd been in this state when they arrived. As a rule he contrived to drink for much of the day at work, with little obvious effect except to make him more unpleasant to Louise. Perhaps alcoholism had overtaken him at last.

The device was a large glass inside which a small electric flashlight sat on top of another glass. Bob switched on the flashlight and pressed in a ring of cork that held the glasses together while Marge, no doubt hoping the party would quieten down, dealt around the table the alphabet Bob had written on cards. I imagined him harping on the séance to Louise as he prepared the apparatus.

"So you're not so cool as you'd like me to think," he said to her, and blew out all the candles.

I sat opposite him. Joan checked the light switch before taking her place next to me, and I knew she hoped the power would interrupt us. Bob had insinuated himself between Stan and Marge, smacking his lips as he drained his bottle. If I hadn't wanted to save them further unpleasantness I'd have opposed the whole thing.

A thick scroll of candle smoke drifted through the flashlight beam. Our brightening hands converged and rested on the glass. I felt as if our apartment had retreated now that the light was concentrated on the table. I could see only dim ovals of faces floating above the splash of light; I couldn't see Louise at all. Silence settled on us like wax, and we waited.

After what seemed a considerable time I began to feel, absurdly perhaps, that it was my duty as host to start things moving. I'd been involved in a few séances and knew the general principles; since Bob was unusually quiet I would have to lead. "Is anybody there?" I said. "Anyone there? Anybody there?"

"Sounds like you've got a bad line," said Stan.

"Shouldn't you say here rather than there?" Marge said.

"I'll try that," I said. "Is anyone here? Anybody here?"

I was still waiting for Stan to play me for a stooge again when Bob's hand began to tremble convulsively on the glass. "You're just playing the fool," Joan said, but I was no more certain than she really was, because from what I could distinguish of Bob's indistinct face I could see he was staring fixedly ahead, though not at me. "What is it? What's the matter?" I said, afraid both that he sensed something and that he was about to reveal the whole situation as an elaborate joke.

Then the glass began to move.

I'd seen it happen at séances before, but never quite like this. The glass was making aimless darting starts in all directions, like an animal that had suddenly found itself caged. It seemed frantic and bewildered, and in a strange way its blind struggling beneath our fingers reminded me of the almost mindless fluttering of hands near to death. "Stop playing the fool," Joan said to Bob, but I was becoming certain that he wasn't, all the more so when he didn't answer.

Then the glass made a rush for the edge of the table, so fast that my fingers would have been left behind if our fingertips hadn't been pressed so closely together that they carried each other along. The light swooped on the letter I and held it for what felt like minutes. It returned to the centre of the table, drawing our luminous orange fingertips with it, then swept back to the I. And again. I. I. I.

"Aye aye, Cap'n," Stan said.

"He doesn't know who he is," Marge whispered.

"Who are you?" I said. "Can you tell us your name?"

The glass inched toward the centre. Then, as if terrified to find itself out in the darkness, it fled back to the I. Thinking of what Marge had said, I had an image of someone awakening in total darkness, woken by us perhaps, trying to remember anything about himself, even his name. I felt unease: Joan's unease, I told myself. "Can you tell us anything about yourself?" I said.

The glass seemed to be struggling again, almost to be forcing itself into the centre. Once there it sat shifting restlessly. The light reached toward letters, then flinched away. At last it began to edge out. I felt isolated with the groping light, cut off even from Joan beside me, as if the light were drawing on me for strength. I didn't know if anyone else felt this, nor whether they also had an oppressive sense of terrible effort. The light began to nudge letters, fumbling before it came to rest on each. MUD, it spelled.

"His name's mud!" Stan said delightedly.

But the glass hadn't finished. R, it added.

"Hello Mudr, hello Fadr," Stan said.

"Murder," Marge said. "He could be trying to say murder."

"If he's dead he should be old enough to spell."

I had an impression of bursting frustration, of a suffocated swelling fury. I felt a little like that myself, because Stan was annoying me. I'd ceased to feel Joan's unease; I was engrossed. "Do you mean murder?" I said. "Who's been murdered?"

Again came the frustration, like the leaden shell of a storm. Incongruously, I remembered my own thwarted fury when I was trying to learn to type. The light began to wobble and glide, and the oppression seemed to clench until I had to soothe my forehead as best I could with my free hand. "Oh my head," Marge said

"Shall we stop?" said Joan.

"Not yet," Marge said, because the light seemed to have gained confidence and was swinging from one letter to another. POISN, it spelled.

"Six out of ten," Stan said. "Could do better."

"Shut up, Stan," Marge said.

"I beg your pardon? You're not taking this nonsense seriously? Because if that's what we're doing, deal me out."

The glass was shuddering now and clutching letters rapidly with its beam. "Please, Stan," Marge said. "Say it's a game, then. If you sit out now you won't be able to discuss it afterwards."

DSLOLY, the glass had been shouting. "Poisoned slowly," Stan translated. "Very clever, Bob. You can stop it now."

"I don't think it is Bob," I said.

"What is it then, a ghost? Don't be absurd. Come on then, ghost. If you're here let's see you."

I heard Marge stop herself saying "Don't!" I felt Joan grow tense, felt the oppression crushed into a last straining effort. Then I heard a click from the apartment door.

Suddenly the darkness felt more crowded. I began to peer into the apartment beyond the light, slowly in an attempt not to betray to Joan what I was doing, but I was blinded by the glass. I caught sight of Stan and knew by the tilt of his head that he'd realised he might be upsetting Louise. "Sorry, Louise," he called and lifted his face ceilingward as he realised that could only make the situation worse.

Then the glass seemed to gather itself and began to dart among the letters. We all knew that it was answering Stan's challenge. We held ourselves still, only our exhausted hands swinging about the table like parts of a machine. When the glass halted at last we'd all separated out the words of the answer. WHEN LIGHT COMS ON, it said.

"I want to stop now," Joan said.

"All right," I said. "I'll light the candles."

But she'd gripped my hand. "I'll do it," Stan said. "I've got some matches." And he'd left the table, and we were listening to the rhythm he was picking out with his shaken matches as he groped into the enormous surrounding darkness, when the lights came on.

We'd all heard the sound of the door but hadn't admitted it, and we all blinked first in that direction. The door was closed. It took a few seconds for us to realise there was no sign of Louise. I think I was the first to look at Bob, sitting grinning opposite me behind his empty bottle of Pernod. My mind must have been thinking faster than consciously, because I knew before I pulled it out that there was only one ticket in his pocket, perhaps folded to look like two by Louise as she laid out his suit. Bob just grinned at me and gazed, until Stan closed his eyes.

MEETING THE AUTHOR

By RAMSEY CAMPBELL

I **WAS YOUNG THEN. I WAS EIGHT YEARS OLD.** I thought adults knew the truth about most things and would own up when they didn't. I thought my parents stood between me and anything about the world that might harm me. I thought I could keep my nightmares away by myself, because I hadn't had one for years—not since I'd first read about the little match girl being left alone in the dark by the things she saw and the emperor realising in front of everyone that he wasn't wearing any clothes. My parents had taken me to a doctor who asked me so many questions I think they were what put me to sleep. I used to repeat his questions in my head whenever I felt in danger of staying awake in the dark.

As I said, I was eight when Harold Mealing came to town. All my parents knew about him was what his publisher told the paper where they worked. My mother brought home the letter she'd been sent at the features desk. "A celebrity's coming to town," she said, or at least that's what I remember her saying, and surely that's what counts.

My father held up the letter with one hand while he cut up his meat with his fork. "'Harold Mealing's first book *Beware of the Smile* takes its place among the classics of children's fiction,'" he read. "Well, that was quick. Still, if his publishers say so that's damn near enough by itself to get him on the front page in this town."

"I've already said I'll interview him."

"Robbed of a scoop by my own family."

My father struck himself across the forehead with the letter and passed it to me. "Maybe you should see what you think of him too, Timmy. He'll be signing at the bookshop."

"You might think of reviewing his book now we have children writing the children's page," my mother added. "Get some use out of that imagination of yours."

The letter said Harold Mealing had written "a return to the old-fashioned moral tale for children—a story which excites for a purpose." Meeting an author seemed an adventure, though since both my parents were journalists, you could say I already had. By the time he was due in town I was so worked up I had to bore myself to sleep.

In the morning there was an accident on the motorway that had taken the traffic away from the town, and my father went off to cover the story. Me and my mother drove into town in her car that was really only big enough for two. In some of the streets the shops were mostly boarded up, and people with spray paint who always made my father angry had been writing on them. Most of the town worked at the toy factory, and dozens of their children were queueing outside Books & Things. "Shows it pays to advertise in our paper," my mother said.

Mrs Trend, who ran the shop, hurried to the door to let my mother in. I'd always been a bit afraid of her, with her pins bristling like antennae in her buns of hair that was black as the paint around her eyes, but her waiting on us like this made me feel grown up and superior. She led us past the toys and stationery and posters of pop stars to the bookshop part of the shop, and there was Harold Mealing in an armchair behind a table full of his book.

He was wearing a white suit and bow tie, but I thought he looked like a king on his throne, a bit petulant and bored. Then he saw us. His big loose face that was spidery with veins started smiling so hard it puffed his cheeks out, and even his grey hair that looked as if he never combed it seemed to stand up to greet us. "This is Mary Duncan from the *Beacon*," Mrs Trend said, "and her son Timothy who wants to review your book."

"A pleasure, I'm sure." Harold Mealing reached across the table and shook us both by the hand at once, squeezing hard as if he didn't want us to feel how soft his hands were. Then he let go of my mother's and held on to mine. "Has this young man no copy of my book? He shall have one with my inscription and my blessing."

He leaned his elbow on the nearest book to keep it open and wrote "To Timothy Duncan, who looks as if he knows how to behave himself: best wishes from the author." The next moment he was smiling past me at Mrs Trend. "Is it time for me to meet the little treasures? Let my public at me and the register shall peal."

I sat on the ladder people used to reach the top shelves and started reading his book while he signed copies, but I couldn't concentrate. The book was about a smiling man who went from place to place trying to tempt children to be naughty and then punished them in horrible ways if they were. After a while I sat and watched Harold Mealing smiling over all the smiles on the covers of the books. One of the children waiting to have a book bought for him knocked a plastic letter-rack off a shelf and broke it, and got smacked by his mother and dragged out while nearly everyone turned to watch. But I saw Harold Mealing's face, and his smile was wider than ever.

When the queue was dealt with, my mother interviewed him. "A writer has to sell himself. I'll go wherever my paying public is. I want every child who will enjoy my book to be able to go into the nearest bookshop and buy one," he said, as well as how he'd sent the book to twenty publishers before this one had bought it and how we should all be grateful to his publisher. "Now I've given up teaching I'll be telling all the stories I've been saving up," he said.

The only time he stopped smiling was when Mrs Trend wouldn't let him sign all his books that were left, just some in case she couldn't sell the rest. He started again when I said goodbye to him as my mother got ready to leave. "I'll look forward to reading what you write about my little tale," he said to me. "I saw you were enjoying it. I'm sure you'll say you did."

"Whoever reviews your book won't do so under any coercion," my mother told him, and steered me out of the shop.

That evening at dinner my father said "So how did it feel to meet a real writer?"

"I don't think he likes children very much," I said.

"I believe Timmy's right," my mother said. "I'll want to read this book before I decide what kind of publicity to give him. Maybe I'll just review the book."

I finished it before I went to bed. I didn't much like the ending, when Mr Smiler led all the children who hadn't learned to be good away to his land where it was always dark. I woke in the middle of the night, screaming because I thought he'd taken me there. No wonder my mother disliked the book and stopped just short of saying in her review that it shouldn't have been published. I admired her for saying what she thought, but I wondered what Harold Mealing might do when he read what she'd written. "He isn't entitled to do anything, Timmy," my father said. "He has to learn the rules like the rest of us if he wants to be a pro."

The week after the paper printed the review we went on holiday to Spain, and I forgot about the book. When we came home I wrote about the parts of Spain we'd been to that most visitors didn't bother with, and the children's page published what I'd written, more or less. I might have written other things, except I was too busy worrying what the teacher I'd have when I went back to school might be like and trying not to let my parents see I was. I took to stuffing a handkerchief in my mouth before I went to sleep so they wouldn't hear me if a nightmare woke me up.

At the end of the week before I went back to school, my mother got the first phone call. The three of us were doing a jigsaw on the dining table, because that was the only place big enough, when the phone rang. As soon as my mother said who she was, the voice at the other end got so loud and sharp I could hear it across the room. "My publishers have just sent me a copy of your review. What do you mean by saying that you wouldn't give my book to a child?"

"Exactly that, Mr Mealing. I've seen the nightmares it can cause."

"Don't be so sure," he said, and then his voice went from crafty to pompous. "Since all they seem to want these days are horrors, I've invented one that will do some good. I suggest you give some thought to what children need before you presume to start shaping their ideas."

My mother laughed so hard it must have made his earpiece buzz. "I must say I'm glad you aren't in charge of children any longer. How did you get our home number, by the way?"

"You'd be surprised what I can do when I put my mind to it."

"Then try writing something more acceptable," my mother said, and cut him off.

She'd hardly sat down at the table when the phone rang again. It must have been my imagination that made it sound as sharp as Harold Mealing's voice. This time he started threatening to tell the paper and my school who he was convinced had really written the review. "Go ahead if you want to make yourself look more of a fool," my mother said.

The third time the phone rang, my father picked it up. "I'm warning you to stop troubling my family," he said, and Harold Mealing started wheedling: "They shouldn't have attacked me after I gave them my time. You don't know what it's like to be a writer. I put myself into that book."

"God help you, then," my father said, and warned him again before cutting him off. "All writers are mad," he told us, "but professionals use it instead of letting it use them."

After I'd gone to bed I heard the phone again, and after my parents were in bed. I thought of Harold Mealing lying awake in the middle of the night and deciding we shouldn't sleep either, letting the phone ring and ring until one of my parents had to pick it up, though when they did nobody would answer.

Next day my father rang up Harold Mealing's publishers. They wouldn't tell him where Harold Mealing had got to on his tour, but his editor promised to have a word with him. He must have, because the phone calls stopped, and then there was nothing for days until the publisher sent me a parcel.

My mother watched over my shoulder while I opened the padded bag. Inside was a book called *Mr Smiler's Pop-Up Surprise Book* and a letter addressed to nobody in particular. "We hope you are as excited by this book as we are to publish it, sure to introduce Harold Mealing's already famous character Mr Smiler to many new readers and a state-of-the-art example of pop-up design" was some of what it said. I gave the letter to my mother while I looked inside the book.

At first I couldn't see Mr Smiler. The pictures stood to attention as I opened the pages, pictures of children up to mischief, climbing on each other's shoulders to steal apples or spraying their names on a wall or making faces behind their teacher's back. The harder I had to look for Mr Smiler, the more nervous I became of seeing him. I turned back to the first pages and spread the book flat on the table, and he jumped up from behind the hedge under the apple tree, shaking his long arms. On every two pages he was waiting for someone to be curious enough to open the book that little bit further. My mother watched me, and then she said "You don't have to accept it, you know. We can send it back."

I thought she wanted me to be grown-up enough not to be frightened by the book. I also thought that if I kept it Harold Mealing would be satisfied, because he'd meant it as an apology for waking us in the night. "I want to keep it. It's good," I said. "Shall I write and say thank you?"

"I shouldn't bother." She seemed disappointed that I was keeping it. "We don't even know who sent it," she said.

Despite the letter, I hoped Harold Mealing might have. Hoped! Once I was by myself I kept turning the pages as if I would find a sign if I looked hard enough. Mr Smiler jumped up behind a hedge and a wall and a desk, and every time his face reminded me more of Harold Mealing's. I didn't like that much, and I put the book away in the middle of a pile in my room. After my parents had tucked me up and kissed me good night, early because I was starting school in the morning, I wondered if it might give me nightmares, but I slept soundly enough. I remember thinking Mr Smiler wouldn't be able to move with all those books on top of him.

My first day at school made me forget him. The teacher asked about my parents, who she knew worked on the paper, and wanted to know if I was a writer too. When I said I'd written some things she asked me to bring one in to read to the class. I remember wishing Harold Mealing could know, and when I got home I pulled out the pop-up book as if that would let me tell him.

At first I couldn't find Mr Smiler at all. I felt as if he was hiding to give me time to be scared of him. I had to open the book still wider before he came up from behind the hedge with a kind of shivery wriggle that reminded me of a dying insect. Once was enough. I pushed the book under the bottom of the pile and looked for something to read to the class.

There wasn't anything I thought was good enough, so I wrote about meeting Harold Mealing and how he'd kept phoning, pretty well as I've written it now. I finished it just before bedtime. When the light was off and the room began to take shape out of the dark, I thought I hadn't closed the pop-up book properly, because I could see darkness inside it that made me think of a lid, especially when I thought I could see a pale object poking out of it. I didn't dare get up to look. After a while I got so tired of being frightened I must have fallen asleep.

In the morning I was sure I'd imagined all that, because the book was shut flat on the shelf. At school I read out what I'd written. The children who'd been at Books & Things laughed as if they agreed with me, and the teacher said I wrote like someone older than I was. Only I didn't feel older, I felt as I used to feel when I had nightmares about books, because the moment I started reading aloud I wished I hadn't written about Harold Mealing. I was afraid he might find out, though I didn't see how he could.

When I got home I realised I was nervous of going to my room, and yet I felt I had to go there and open the pop-up book. Once I'd finished convincing my mother that I'd enjoyed my day at school I made myself go upstairs and pull it from under the pile. I thought I'd have to flatten it even more to make Mr Smiler pop up. I put it on the quilt and started leaning on it, but it wasn't even open flat when he squirmed up from behind the hedge, flapping his arms, as if he'd been waiting all day for me. Only now his face was Harold Mealing's face.

It looked as if part of Mr Smiler's face had fallen off to show what was underneath, Harold Mealing's face gone grey and blotchy but smiling harder than ever, straight at me. I wanted to scream and rip him out of the book, but all I could do was fling the book across my bed and run to my mother.

She was sorting out the topics she'd be covering for next week's paper, but she dropped her notes when she saw me. "What's up?"

"In the book. Go and see," I said in a voice like a scream that was stuck in my throat, and then I was afraid of what the book might do to her. I went up again, though only fast enough that she would be just behind me. I had to wait until she was in the room before I could touch the book.

It was leaning against the pillow, gaping as if something was holding it open from inside. I leaned on the corners to open it, and then I made myself pick it up and bend it back until I heard the spine creak. I did that with the first two pages and all the other pairs. By the time I'd finished I was nearly sobbing, because I couldn't find Mr Smiler or whatever he looked like now. "He's got out," I cried.

"I knew we shouldn't have let you keep that book," my mother said. "You've enough of an imagination without being fed nonsense like that. I don't care how he tries to get at me, but I'm damned if I'll have him upsetting any child of mine."

My father came home just then, and joined in. "We'll get you a better book, Timmy, to make up for this old rubbish," he said, and put the book where I couldn't reach it, on top of the wardrobe in their bedroom.

That didn't help. The more my mother tried to persuade me that the pop-up was broken and so I shouldn't care about not having the book, the more I thought about Mr Smiler's face that had stopped pretending. While we were having dinner I heard scratchy sounds walking about upstairs, and my father had to tell me it was a bird on the roof. While we were watching one of the programmes my parents let me watch on television a puffy white thing came and pressed itself against the window, and I almost wasn't quick enough at the window to see an old bin-liner blowing away down the road. My mother read to me in bed to try and calm me down, but when I saw a figure creeping upstairs beyond her that looked as if it hadn't much more to it than the dimness on the landing, I screamed before I realised it was my father coming to see if I was nearly asleep. "Oh dear," he said, and went down to get me some of the medicine the doctor had prescribed to help me sleep.

My mother had been keeping it in the refrigerator. It must have been years old. Maybe that was why, when I drifted off to sleep although I was afraid to in case

anything came into my room, I kept jerking awake as if something had wakened me, something that had just ducked out of sight at the end of the bed. Once I was sure I saw a blotchy forehead disappearing as I forced my eyes open, and another time I saw hair like cobwebs being pulled out of sight over the footboard. I was too afraid to scream, and even more afraid of going to my parents, in case I hadn't really seen anything in the room and it was waiting outside for me to open the door.

I was still jerking awake when the dawn came. It made my room even more threatening, because now everything looked flat as the hiding places in the pop-up book. I was frightened to look at anything. I lay with my eyes squeezed shut until I heard movements outside my door and my father's voice convinced me it was him. When he inched the door open I pretended to be asleep so that he wouldn't think I needed more medicine. I actually managed to sleep for a couple of hours before the smell of breakfast woke me up.

It was Saturday, and my father took me fishing in the canal. Usually fishing made me feel as if I'd had a rest, though we never caught any fish, but that day I was too worried about leaving my mother alone in the house or rather, not as alone as she thought she was. I kept asking my father when we were going home, until he got so irritable that we did.

As soon as he was in his chair he stuck the evening paper up in front of himself. He was meaning to show that I'd spoiled his day, but suddenly he looked over the top of the paper at me. "Here's something that may cheer you up, Timmy," he said. "Harold Mealing's in the paper."

I thought he meant the little smiling man was waiting in there to jump out at me, and I nearly grabbed the paper to tear it up. "Good God, son, no need to look so timid about it," my father said. "He's dead, that's why he's in. Died yesterday of too much dashing about in search of publicity. Poor old twerp, after all his self-promotion he wasn't considered important enough to put in the same day's news."

I heard what he was saying, but all I

could think was that if Harold Mealing was dead he could be anywhere—and then I realised he already had been. He must have died just about the time I'd seen his face in the pop-up book. Before my parents could stop me, I grabbed a chair from the dining suite and struggled upstairs with it, and climbed on it to get the book down from the wardrobe.

I was bending it open as I jumped off the chair. I jerked it so hard as I landed that it shook the little man out from behind the hedge. I shut my eyes so as not to see his face, and closed my hand around him, though my skin felt as if it was trying to crawl away from him. I'd just got hold of him to tear him up as he wriggled like an insect when my father came in and took hold of my fingers to make me let go before I could do more than crumple the little man. He closed the book and squeezed it under his arm as if he was as angry with it as he was with me. "I thought you knew better than to damage books," he said. "You know I can't stand vandalism. I'm afraid you're going straight to bed, and think yourself lucky I'm keeping my temper."

That wasn't what I was afraid of. "What are you going to do with the book?"

"Put it somewhere you won't find it. Now, not another word or you'll be sorry. Bed."

I turned to my mother, but she frowned and put her finger to her lips. "You heard your father."

When I tried to stay until I could see where my father hid the book, she pushed me into the bathroom and stood outside the door and told me to get ready for bed. By the time I came out, my father and the book had gone. My mother tucked me into bed and frowned at me, and gave my forehead a kiss so quick it felt papery. "Just go to sleep now and we'll have forgotten all about it in the morning," she said.

I lay and watched the bedroom furniture begin to go flat and thin as cardboard as it got dark. When either of my parents came to see if I was asleep I tried to make them think I was, but before it was completely dark I was shaking too much. My mother brought me some of the medicine and wouldn't go away until I'd swallowed it, and then I lay there fighting to stay awake.

I heard my parents talking, too low for me to understand. I heard one of them go out to the dustbin, and eventually I smelled burning. I couldn't tell if that was in our yard or a neighbour's, and I was too afraid to get up in the dark and look. I lay feeling as if I couldn't move, as if the medicine had made the bedclothes heavier or me weaker, and before I could stop myself I was asleep.

When I jerked awake I didn't know what time it was. I held myself still and tried to hear my parents so that I'd know they hadn't gone to sleep and left me alone. Then I heard my father snoring in their room, and I knew they had, because he always went to bed last. His snores broke off, probably because my mother had nudged him in her sleep, and for a while I couldn't hear anything except my own breathing, so loud it made me feel I was suffocating. And then I heard another sound in my room.

It was a creaking as if something was trying to straighten itself. It might have been cardboard, but I wasn't sure, because I couldn't tell how far away from me it was. I dug my fingers into the mattress to stop myself shaking, and held my breath until I was almost sure the sound was ahead of me, between me and the door. I listened until I couldn't hold my breath any longer, and it came out in a gasp. And then I dug my fingers into the mattress so hard my nails bent, and banged my head against the wall behind the pillow, because Harold Mealing had risen up in front of me.

I could only really see his face. There was less of it than last time I'd seen it, and maybe that was why it was smiling even harder, both wider and taller than a mouth ought to be able to go. His body was a dark shape he was struggling to raise, whether because it was stiff or crippled I couldn't tell. I could still hear it creaking. It might have been cardboard or a corpse, because I couldn't make out how close he was, at the end of the bed and big as life or standing on the quilt in front of my face, the size he'd been in the book. All I could do was bruise my head as I shoved the back of it against the wall, the furthest I could get away from him.

He shivered upright until his face was

above mine, and his hands came flapping towards me. I was almost sure he was no bigger than he'd been in the book, but that didn't help me, because I could feel myself shrinking until I was small enough for him to carry away into the dark, all of me that mattered. He leaned towards me as if he was toppling over, and I started to scream.

I heard my parents waken, far away. I heard one of them stumble out of bed. I was afraid they would be too late, because now I'd started screaming I couldn't stop, and the figure that was smaller than my head was leaning down as if it meant to crawl into my mouth and hide there or drag what it wanted out of me. Somehow I managed to let go of the mattress and flail my hands at him. I hardly knew what I was doing, but I felt my fist close around something that broke and wriggled, just as the light came on.

Both my parents ran in. "It's all right, Timmy, we're here," my mother said, and to my father "It must be that medicine. We won't give him any more."

I clenched my fist harder and stared around the room. "I've got him," I babbled. "Where's the book?"

They knew which one I meant, because they exchanged a glance. At first I couldn't understand why they looked almost guilty. "You're to remember what I said, Timmy," my father said. "We should always respect books. But listen, son, that one was bothering you so much I made an exception. You can forget about it. I put it in the bin and burnt it before we came to bed."

I stared at him as if that could make him take back what he'd said. "But that means I can't put him back," I cried.

"What've you got there, Timmy? Let me see," my mother said, and watched until I had to open my fist. There was nothing in it except a smear of red that she eventually convinced me was ink.

When she saw I was afraid to be left alone she stayed with me all night. After a while I fell asleep because I couldn't stay awake, though I knew Harold Mealing was still hiding somewhere. He'd slipped out of my fist when I wasn't looking, and now I'd lost my chance to trap him and get rid of him.

My mother took me to the doctor in the morning and got me some new medicine that made me sleep even when I was afraid to. It couldn't stop me being afraid of books, even when my parents sent *Beware of the Smile* back to the publisher and found out that the publisher had gone bankrupt from gambling too much money on Harold Mealing's books. I thought that would only make Harold Mealing more spiteful. I had to read at school, but I never enjoyed a book again. I'd get my friends to shake them open to make sure there was nothing inside them before I would touch them, only before long I didn't have many friends. Sometimes I thought I felt something squirming under the page I was reading, and I'd throw the book on the floor.

I thought I'd grown out of all this when I went to college. Writing what I've written shows I'm not afraid of things just because they're written down. I worked so hard at college I almost forgot to be afraid of books. Maybe that's why he kept wakening me at night with his smile half the height of his face and his hands that feel like insects on my cheeks. Yes, I set fire to the library, but I didn't know what else to do. I thought he might be hiding in one of those books.

Now I know that was a mistake. Now you and my parents and the rest of them smile at me and say I'll be better for writing it down, only you don't realise how much it's helped me see things clear. I don't know yet which of you smilers Harold Mealing is pretending to be, but I will when I've stopped the rest of you smiling. And then I'll tear him up to prove it to all of you. I'll tear him up just as I'm going to tear up this paragraph.

THE HORROR AT CHILTON CASTLE

By Joseph Payne Brennan

Art by Allen Koszowski

I HAD DECIDED TO SPEND A LEISURELY SUMMER IN EUROPE, concentrating, if at all, on genealogical research. I went first to Ireland, journeying to Kilkenny, where I unearthed a mine of legend and authentic lore concerning my remote Irish ancestors, the O'Braonains, chiefs of the Ui Duach in the ancient kingdom of Ossory. The Brennans (as the name was later spelled) lost their estates in the British confiscation under Thomas Wentworth, Earl of Stafford. The thieving Earl, I am happy to report, was subsequently beheaded in the Tower.

From Kilkenny I travelled to London and then to Chesterfield in search of maternal ancestors: the Holborns, Wilkersons, Searles, etc. Incomplete and fragmentary records left many great gaps, but my efforts were moderately successful, and at length I decided to go farther north and visit the vicinity of Chilton Castle, seat of Robert Chilton-Payne, the twelfth Earl of Chilton. My relationship to the Chilton-Paynes was a most distant one, and yet there existed a tenuous thread of past connection and I thought it would amuse me to glimpse the castle.

Arriving in Wexwold, the tiny village near the castle, late in the afternoon, I engaged a room at the Inn of the Red Goose—the only one there was—unpacked and went down for a simple meal consisting of a small loaf, cheese and ale.

By the time I had finished this stark and

yet satisfying repast, darkness had set in, and with it came wind and rain.

I resigned myself to an evening at the inn. There was ale enough and I was in no hurry to go anywhere.

After writing a few letters, I went down and ordered a pint of ale. The taproom was almost deserted; the bartender, a stout gentleman who seemed forever on the point of falling asleep, was pleasant but taciturn, and at length I fell to musing on the strange and frightening legend of Chilton Castle.

There were variations of the legend, and without doubt the original tale had been embroidered down through the centuries, but the essential outline of the story concerned a secret room somewhere in the castle. It was said that this room contained a terrifying spectacle which the Chilton-Paynes were obliged to keep hidden from the world.

Only three persons were ever permitted to enter the room: the presiding Earl of Chilton, the Earl's male heir and one other person designated by the Earl. Ordinarily this person was the Factor of Chilton Castle. The room was entered only once in a generation; within three days after the male heir came of age, he was conducted to the secret room by the Earl and the Factor. The room was then sealed and never opened again until the heir conducted his own son to the grisly chamber.

According to the legend, the heir was never the same person again after entering the room. Invariably he would become sombre and withdrawn; his countenance would acquire a brooding, apprehensive expression which nothing could long dispel. One of the earlier earls of Chilton had gone completely mad and hurled himself from the turrets of the castle.

Speculation about the contents of the secret room had continued for centuries. One version of the tale described the panic-stricken flight of the Gowers, with armed enemies hot on their flagging heels. Although there had been bad blood between the Chilton-Paynes and the Gowers, in their desperation the Gowers begged for refuge at Chilton Castle. The Earl gave them entry, conducted them to a hidden room and left with a promise that they would be shielded from their pursuers. The Earl kept his promise; the Gowers' enemies were turned away from the Castle, their murderous plans unconsummated. The Earl, however, simply left the Gowers in the locked room to starve to death. The chamber was not opened until thirty years later, when the Earl's son finally broke the seal. A fearful sight met his eyes. The Gowers had starved to death slowly, and at the last, judging by the appearance of the mingled skeletons, had turned to cannibalism.

Another version of the legend indicated that the secret room had been used by medieval earls as a torture chamber. It was said that the ingenious instruments of pain were yet in the room and that these lethal apparatuses still clutched the pitiful remains of their final victims, twisted fearfully in their last agonies.

A third version mentioned one of the female ancestors of the Chilton-Paynes, Lady Susan Glanville, who had reputedly made a pact with the Devil. She had been condemned as a witch but had somehow managed to escape the stake. The date and even the manner of her death were unknown, but in some vague way the secret room was supposed to be connected with it.

As I speculated on these different versions of the gruesome legend, the storm increased in intensity. Rain drummed steadily against the leaded windows of the inn and now I could occasionally hear the distant mutter of thunder.

Glancing at the rain-streaked panes, I shrugged and ordered another pint of ale.

I had the fresh tankard halfway to my lips when the taproom door burst open, letting in a blast of wind and rain. The door was shut and a tall figure, muffled to the ears in a dripping greatcoat, moved to the bar. Removing his cap, he ordered brandy.

Having nothing better to do, I observed him closely. He looked about seventy, grizzled and weather-worn, but wiry, with an appearance of toughness and determination. He was frowning, as if absorbed in thinking through some unpleasant problem, yet his cold blue eyes inspected me keenly for a brief but deliberate interval.

I could not place him in a tidy niche. He

might be a local farmer, and yet I did not think that he was. He had a vague aura of authority, and though his clothes were certainly plain, they were, I thought, somewhat better in cut and quality than those of the local countrymen I had observed.

A trivial incident opened a conversation between us. An unusually sharp crack of thunder made him turn towards the window. As he did so, he accidentally brushed his wet cap onto the floor. I retrieved it for him; he thanked me; and then we exchanged commonplace remarks about the weather.

I had an intuitive feeling that although he was normally a reticent individual, he was presently wrestling with some severe problem which made him want to hear a human voice. Realizing there was always the possibility that my intuition might, for once, have failed me, I nevertheless babbled on about my trip, about my genealogical researches in Kilkenny, London, and Chesterfield, and finally about my distant relationship to the Chilton-Paynes and my desire to get a good look at Chilton Castle.

Suddenly I found that he was gazing at me with an expression which, if not fierce, was disturbingly intense. An awkward silence ensued. I coughed, wondering uneasily what I had said to make those cold blue eyes stare at me so fixedly.

At length he became aware of my growing embarrassment. "You must excuse me for staring," he apologized, "but something you said...." He hesitated. "Could we perhaps take that table?" He nodded towards a small table, which sat half in shadow in the far corner of the room.

I agreed, mystified but curious, and we took our drinks to the secluded table.

He sat frowning for a minute, as if uncertain how to begin. Finally he introduced himself as William Cowath. I gave him my name and still he hesitated. At length he took a swallow of brandy and then looked straight at me. "I am," he stated, "the Factor at Chilton Castle."

I surveyed him with surprise and renewed interest. "What an agreeable coincidence!" I exclaimed. "Then perhaps tomorrow you could arrange for me to have a look at the castle?"

He seemed scarcely to hear me. "Yes, yes, of course," he replied absently.

Puzzled and a bit irritated by his air of detachment, I remained silent.

He took a deep breath and then spoke rapidly, running some of his words together. "Robert Chilton-Payne, the Twelfth Earl of Chilton, was buried in the family vaults one week ago. Frederick, the young heir and now Thirteenth Earl, came of age just three days ago. Tonight it is imperative that he be conducted to the secret chamber!"

I gaped at him in incredulous amazement. For a moment I had an idea that he had somehow heard of my interest in Chilton Castle and was merely "pulling my leg" for amusement in the belief that I was the greenest of gullible tourists.

But there could be no mistaking his deadly seriousness. There was not the faintest suspicion of humor in his eyes.

I groped for words. "It seems so strange—so unbelievable! Just before you arrived, I had been thinking about the various legends connected with the secret room."

His cold eyes held my own. "It is not legend that confronts us; it is fact."

A thrill of fear and excitement ran through me. "You are going there—tonight?"

He nodded. "Tonight. Myself, the young Earl—and one other."

I stared at him.

"Ordinarily," he continued, "the Earl himself would accompany us. That is the custom. But he is dead. Shortly before he passed away, he instructed me to select someone to go with the young Earl and myself. That person must be male—and preferably of the blood."

I took a deep drink of ale and said not a word.

He continued. "Besides the young Earl, there is no one at the Castle save his elderly mother, Lady Beatrice Chilton, and an ailing aunt."

"Who could the Earl have had in mind?" I enquired cautiously.

The Factor frowned. "There are some distant male cousins residing in the country. I have an idea he thought at least one of them might appear for the obsequies. But not one of them did."

"That was most unfortunate!" I observed.

"Extremely unfortunate. And I am therefore asking you, as one of the blood, to accompany the young Earl and myself to the secret room tonight!"

I gulped like a bumpkin. Lightning flashed against the windows and I could hear rain swishing along the stones outside. When feathers of ice stopped fluttering in my stomach, I managed a reply.

"But I … that is … my relationship is so very remote! I am 'of the blood' by courtesy only, you might say. The strain in me is so very diluted."

He shrugged. "You bear the name. And you possess at least a few drops of the Payne blood. Under the present urgent circumstances, no more is necessary. I am sure that the old Earl would agree with me, could he still speak. You will come?"

There was no escaping the intensity, the pressure, of those cold blue eyes. They seemed to follow my mind about as it groped for further excuses.

Finally, inevitably it seemed, I agreed. A feeling grew in me that the meeting had been preordained, that somehow I had always been destined to visit the secret chamber in Chilton Castle.

We finished our drinks and I went up to my room for rainwear. When I descended, suitably attired for the storm, the obese bartender was snoring on his stool, in spite of savage crashes of thunder which had now become almost incessant. I envied him as I left the cosy room with William Cowath.

Once outside, my guide informed me that we would have to go on foot to the castle. He had purposely walked down to the inn, he explained, in order that he might have time and solitude to straighten out in his own mind the things which he would have to do.

The sheets of heavy rain, the strong wind and the roar of thunder made conversation difficult. I walked Indian-fashion behind the Factor, who took enormous strides and appeared to know every inch of the way in spite of the darkness.

We walked only a short distance down the village street and then struck into a side road, which very soon dwindled to a footpath made slippery and treacherous by the driving rain.

Abruptly the path began to ascend; the footing became more precarious. It was at once necessary to concentrate all one's attention on one's feet. Fortunately, the flashes of lightning were frequent.

It seemed to me that we had been walking for an hour—actually, I suppose, it was only a few minutes—when the Factor finally stopped.

I found myself standing beside him on a flat, rocky plateau. He pointed up an incline which rose before us. "Chilton Castle," he said.

For a moment I saw nothing in the unrelieved darkness. Then the lightning flashed.

Beyond high battlemented walls, fissured with age, I glimpsed a great square Norman castle with four rectangular corner towers pierced by narrow window apertures which looked like evil slitted eyes. The huge, weathered pile was half-covered by a mantle of ivy which appeared more black than green.

"It looks incredibly old!" I commented.

William Cowath nodded. "It was begun in 1122 by Henry de Montargis." Without another word he started up the incline.

As we approached the castle wall, the storm grew worse. The slanting rain and powerful wind now made speech all but impossible. We bent our heads and staggered upwards.

When the wall finally loomed in front of us, I was amazed at its height and thickness. It had been constructed, obviously, to withstand the best siege guns and battering rams which its early enemies could bring to bear on it.

As we crossed a massive, timbered drawbridge, I peered down into the black ditch of a moat, but I could not be sure whether there was water in it. A low, arched gateway gave access through the wall to an inner, cobblestoned courtyard. This courtyard was entirely empty, save for rivulets of rushing water.

Crossing the cobblestones with swift strides, the Factor led me to another arched gateway in yet another wall. Inside was a second, smaller yard, and beyond spread the ivy-clutched base of the ancient keep itself.

Traversing a darkened, stone-flagged passage, we found ourselves facing a ponderous door, age-blackened oak reinforced with pitted bands of iron. The Factor flung open this door and there before us was the great hall of the castle.

Four long, hand-hewn tables with their accompanying benches stretched almost the entire length of the hall. Metal torch brackets, stained with age, were affixed to sculptured stone columns which supported the roof. Ranged around the walls were suits of armor, heraldic shields, halberds, pikes and banners—the accumulated trophies and prizes of bloody centuries when each castle was almost a kingdom unto itself. In flickering candlelight, which appeared to be the only illumination, the grim array was eerily impressive.

William Cowath waved a hand. "The holders of Chilton lived by the sword for many centuries."

Walking the length of the great hall, he entered another dim passageway. I followed silently.

As we strode along, he spoke in a subdued voice. "Frederick, the young heir, does not enjoy robust health. The shock of his father's death was severe—and he dreads tonight's ordeal, which he knows must come."

Stopping before a wooden door embellished with carved fleurs-de-lis and metal scrollwork, he gave me a shadowed, enigmatic glance, and then knocked.

Someone enquired who was there and he identified himself. Presently a heavy bolt was lifted and the door opened.

If the Chilton-Paynes had been stubborn fighters in their day, the warrior blood appeared to have become considerably diluted in the veins of Frederick, the young heir and now Thirteenth Earl. I saw before me a thin, pale-complexioned young man whose dark sunken eyes looked haunted and fearful. His dress was both theatrical and anachronistic: a dark green velvet coat and trousers, a green satin waist-band, flounces of white lace at neck and wrists.

He beckoned us in, as if with reluctance, and closed the door. The walls of the small room were entirely covered with tapestries depicting the hunt or medieval battle scenes. A draught of air from a window or other aperture made them undulate constantly; they seemed to have a disturbing life of their own. In one corner of the room there was an antique canopy bed; in another a large writing table with an agate lamp.

After a brief introduction which included an explanation of how I came to be accompanying them, the Factor enquired if his Lordship was ready to visit the chamber.

Although he was wan in any case, Frederick's face now lost every last trace of color. He nodded, however, and preceded us into the passage.

William Cowath led the way; the young Earl followed him, and I brought up the rear.

At the far end of the passage, the Factor opened the door of a cobwebbed supply room. Here he secured candles, chisels, a pick and a sledgehammer. After packing these into a leather bag which he slung over one shoulder, he picked up a faggot torch which lay on one of the shelves in the room. He lit this, then waited while it flared into a steady flame. Satisfied with this illumination, he closed the room and beckoned for us to continue after him.

Nearby was a descending spiral of stone steps. Lifting his torch, the Factor started down. We trailed after him, wordlessly.

There must have been fifty steps in that long, downward spiral. As we descended, the stones became wet and cold; the air, too, grew colder, but the cold was not of the type that refreshes. It was too laden with the smell of mold and dampness.

At the bottom of the steps we faced a tunnel, pitch-black and silent.

The Factor raised his torch. "Chilton Castle is Norman, but is said to have been reared over a Saxon ruin. It is believed that the passageways in these depths were constructed by the Saxons." He peered, frowning, into the tunnel. "Or by some still earlier folk."

He hesitated briefly, and I thought he was listening. Then, glancing round at us, he proceeded down the passage.

I walked after the Earl, shivering. The dead, icy air seemed to pierce to the pith of my bones. The stones underfoot grew slippery with a film of slime. I longed for more light, but there was none save that cast by the flickering, bobbing torch of the Factor.

Partway down the passage he paused, and again I sensed that he was listening. The silence seemed absolute, however, and we went on.

The end of the passage brought us to more descending steps. We went down some fifteen and entered another tunnel which appeared to have been cut out of the solid rock on which the castle had been reared. White-crusted nitre clung to the walls. The reek of mold was intense. The icy air was fetid with some other odor which I found peculiarly repellent, though I could not name it.

At last the Factor stopped, lifted his torch and slid the leather bag from his shoulder.

I saw that we stood before a wall made of some kind of building stone. Though damp and stained with nitre, it was obviously of much more recent construction than anything we had previously encountered.

Glancing round at us, William Cowath handed me the torch. "Keep a good hold on it, if you please. I have candles, but...."

Leaving the sentence unfinished, he drew the pick from his sling bag and began an assault on the wall. The barrier was solid enough, but after he had worked a hole in it, he took up the sledgehammer and quicker progress was made. Once I offered to take up the hammer while he held the torch, but he only shook his head and went on with his work of demolition.

All this time the young Earl had not spoken a word. As I looked at his tense white face, I felt sorry for him, in spite of my own mounting trepidation.

Abruptly there was silence as the Factor lowered the sledgehammer. I saw that a good two feet of the lower wall remained.

William Cowath bent to inspect it. "Strong enough," he commented cryptically. "I will leave that to build on. We can step over it."

For a full minute he stood looking silently into the blackness beyond. Finally, shouldering his bag, he took the torch from my hand and stepped over the ragged base of the wall. We followed suit.

As I entered that chamber, the fetid odor which I had noticed in the passage seemed to overwhelm us. It washed around us in a nauseating wave and we all gasped for breath.

The Factor spoke between coughs. "It will subside in a minute or two. Stand near the aperture."

Although the reek remained repellently strong, we could at length breathe more freely.

William Cowath lifted his torch and peered into the black depths of the chamber. Fearfully, I gazed around his shoulder.

There was no sound, and at first I could see nothing but nitre-encrusted walls and wet stone floor. Presently, however, in a far corner, just beyond the flickering halo of the faggot torch, I saw two tiny, fiery spots of red. I tried to convince myself that they were two red jewels, two rubies, shining in the torchlight.

But I knew at once—I *felt* at once—what they were. They were two red eyes and they were watching us with a fierce, unwavering stare.

The Factor spoke softly. "Wait here."

He crossed towards the corner, stopped halfway and held out his torch at arm's length. For a moment he was silent. Finally he emitted a long, shuddering sigh.

When he spoke again, his voice had changed. It was only a sepulchral whisper. "Come forward," he told us in that strange, hollow voice.

I followed Frederick until we stood at either side of the Factor.

When I saw what crouched on a stone bench in that far corner, I felt sure that I would faint. My heart literally stopped beating for perceptible seconds. The blood left my extremities; I reeled with dizziness. I might have cried out, but my throat would not open.

The entity which rested on that stone bench was like something that had crawled up out of hell. Piercing, malignant red eyes proclaimed that it had a terrible life, and yet that life sustained itself in a black, shrunken, half-mummified body which resembled a disinterred corpse. A few moldy rags clung to the cadaver-like frame. Wisps of white hair sprouted out of its ghastly grey-white skull. A red smear or blotch of some sort covered the wizened slit which served it as a mouth.

It surveyed us with a malignancy which was beyond anything merely human. It was impossible to stare back into those monstrous red eyes. They were so inexpressibly evil, one felt that one's soul would be consumed in the fires of their malevolence.

Glancing aside, I saw that the Factor was now supporting Frederick. The young heir had sagged against him, staring fixedly at the fearful apparition with terror-glazed eyes. In spite of my own sense of horror, I pitied him.

The Factor sighed again, and then he spoke once more in that low, sepulchral voice.

"You see before you," he told us, "Lady Susan Glanville. She was carried into this chamber and fettered to the wall in 1473."

A thrill of horror coursed through me; I felt that we were in the presence of malign forces from the Pit itself.

To me, the hideous thing had appeared sexless, but at the sound of its name, the ghastly mockery of a grin contorted the puckered, red-smeared mouth.

I noticed now for the first time that the monster actually was secured to the wall. The great double shackles were so blackened with age, I had not noticed them before.

The Factor went on, as if he spoke by rote. "Lady Glanville was a maternal ancestor of the Chilton-Paynes. She had commerce with the Devil. She was condemned as a witch but escaped the stake. Finally her own people forcibly overcame her. She was brought in here, fettered, and left to die."

He was silent a moment and then continued. "It was too late. She had already made a pact with the Powers of Darkness. It was an unspeakably evil thing and it has condemned her issue to a life of torment and nightmare, a lifetime of terror and dread."

He swung his torch towards the blackened, red-eyed thing. "She was a beauty once. She hated death. She feared death.

And so she finally bartered her own immortal soul—and the bodies of her issue—for eternal earthly life."

I heard his voice as in a nightmare; it seemed to be coming from an infinite distance.

He went on. "The consequences of breaking the pact are too terrible to describe. No descendant of hers has ever dared to do so, once the forfeit is known. And so she has bided here for these nearly five hundred years."

I had thought he was finished, but he resumed. Glancing upwards, he lifted his torch towards the roof of that accursed chamber. "This room," he said, "lies directly underneath the family vaults. Upon the death of the Earl, the body is ostensibly left in the vaults. When the mourners have gone, however, the false bottom of the vault is thrust aside and the body of the Earl is lowered into this room."

Looking up, I saw the square rectangle of a trap-door above.

The Factor's voice now became barely audible. "Once every generation Lady Glanville feeds—on the corpse of the deceased Earl. It is a provision of that unspeakable pact which cannot be broken."

I knew now—with a sense of horror utterly beyond description—whence came that red smear on the repulsive mouth of the creature before us.

As if to confirm his words, the Factor lowered his torch until its flame illuminated the floor at the foot of the stone bench where the vampiric monster was fettered.

Strewn about the floor were the scattered bones and skull of an adult male, red with fresh blood. And at some distance were other human bones, brown and crumbling with age.

At this point, Frederick began to scream. His shrill, hysterical cries filled the chamber. Although the Factor shook him roughly, his terrible shrieks continued, terror-filled, nerve-shaking.

For moments, the corpse-like thing on the bench watched him with its frightful red eyes. It uttered sound finally, a kind of animal squeal which might have been intended as laughter.

Abruptly then, and without any warning, it slid from the bench and lunged towards the young Earl. The blackened shackles which fettered it to the wall permitted it to advance only a yard or two. It was pulled back sharply; yet it lunged again and again, squealing with a kind of hellish glee which stirred the hair on my head.

William Cowath thrust his torch towards the monster, but it continued to lunge at the end of its fetters. The nightmare room resounded with the Earl's screams and the creature's horrible squeals of bestial laughter. I felt that my own mind would give way unless I escaped from that anteroom of hell.

For the first time during an ordeal which would have sent any lesser man fleeing for his life and sanity, the iron control of the Factor appeared to be shaken. He looked beyond the wild lunging thing towards the wall where the fetters were fastened.

I sensed what was in his mind. Would those fastenings hold, after all these centuries of rust and dampness?

On a sudden resolve he reached into an inner pocket and drew out something which glittered in the torchlight. It was a silver crucifix. Striding forward, he thrust it almost into the twisted face of the leaping monstrosity which had once been the ravishing Lady Susan Glanville.

The creature reeled back with an agonized scream which drowned out the cries of the Earl. It cowered on the bench, abruptly silent and motionless, only the pulsating of its wizened mouth and the fires of hatred in its red eyes giving evidence that it still lived.

William Cowath addressed it grimly. "Creature of hell! If ye leave that bench 'ere we quit this room and seal it once again, I swear that I shall hold this cross against ye!"

The thing's red eyes watched the Factor with an expression of abysmal hatred which no combination of mere letters could convey. They actually appeared to glow with fire. And yet I read in them something else—fear.

I suddenly became aware that silence had descended on that room of the damned. It lasted only a few moments. The Earl had finally stopped screaming, but now came something worse. He began to laugh.

It was only a low chuckle, but it was somehow worse than all his screams. It went on and on, softly, mindlessly.

The Factor turned, beckoning me towards the partially demolished wall. Crossing the room, I climbed out. Behind me the Factor led the young Earl, who shuffled like an old man, chuckling to himself.

There was then what seemed an interminable interval, during which the Factor carried back a sack of mortar and a keg of water which he had previously left somewhere in the tunnel. Working by torchlight, he prepared the cement and proceeded to seal up the chamber, using the same stones which he had displaced.

While the Factor labored, the young Earl sat motionless in the tunnel, chuckling softly.

There was silence from within. Once, only, I heard the thing's fetters clank against the stone.

At last the Factor finished and led us back through those nitre-stained passageways and up the icy stairs. The Earl could scarcely ascend; with difficulty the Factor supported him from step to step.

Back in his tapestry-paneled chamber, Frederick sat on his canopy bed and stared at the floor, laughing quietly. With horror I noticed that his black hair had actually turned grey. After persuading him to drink a glass of liquid which I had no doubt contained a heavy dose of sedative, the Factor managed to get him stretched out on the bed.

William Cowath then led me to a nearby bedchamber. My impulse was to rush from that hellish pile without delay, but the storm still raged and I was by no means sure I could find my way back to the village without a guide.

The Factor shook his head sadly. "I fear his Lordship is doomed to an early death. He was never strong and tonight's events may have deranged his mind ... may have weakened him beyond hope of recovery."

I expressed my sympathy and horror. The Factor's cold blue eyes held my own. "It may be," he said, "that in the event of the young Earl's death, you yourself might be considered...." He hesitated. "Might be considered," he finally concluded, "as one somewhat in the line of succession."

I wanted to hear no more. I gave him a curt goodnight, bolted the door after him and tried—quite unsuccessfully—to salvage a few minutes' sleep.

But sleep would not come. I had feverish visions of that red-eyed thing in the sealed chamber escaping its fetters, breaking through the wall and crawling up those icy, slime-covered stairs....

Even before dawn I softly unbolted my door and, like a marauding thief, crept shivering through the cold passageways and the great deserted hall of the castle. Crossing the cobbled courtyards and the black moat, I scrambled down the incline toward the village.

Long before noon I was well on my way to London. Luck was with me; the next day I was on a boat bound for the Atlantic run.

I shall never return to England. I intend always to keep Chilton Castle and its permanent occupant at least an ocean away.

"The Horror at Chilton Castle" first appeared in Brennan's self-published 1963 collection, Scream at Midnight.

Prolific American writer Joseph Payne Brennan (1918–1990) was once described as "a gentle, soft-spoken, modest man" who was "most comfortable with his wife (Doris) and his dog (Chaucer)." Stephen King further described Brennan as "a master of the unashamed horror tale."

Over the course of fifty years Brennan published hundreds of stories—the majority of which are horror or fantasy—and even more poems. In 1957 he launched his own magazine, Macabre, *to "work for the revival" of* Weird Tales *while encouraging and providing an outlet for both new and established writers.* Macabre *ran for 23 issues, ceasing publication in 1976.*

THREE SKELETON KEY

By George G. Toudouze

MY MOST TERRIFYING EXPERIENCE? Well, one does have a few in thirty-five years of service in the Lights, although it's mostly monotonous routine work—keeping the light in order, making out the reports.

When I was a young man, not very long in the service, there was an opening in a lighthouse newly built off the coast of Guiana, on a small rock twenty miles or so from the main land. The pay was high, so in order to reach the sum I had set out to save before I was married, I volunteered for service in the new light.

Three Skeleton Key, the small rock on which the light stood, bore a bad reputation. It earned its name from the story of the three convicts who, escaping from Cayenne in a stolen dugout canoe, were wrecked on the rock during the night, managed to escape the sea but eventually died of hunger and thirst. When they were discovered, nothing remained but three heaps of bones, picked clean by birds. The story was that the three skeletons, gleaming with phosphorescent light, danced over the small rock, screaming....

But there are many such stories and I did not give the warnings of the old-timers at the *Isle de Sein* a second thought. I signed up, boarded ship, and in a month I was installed at the light.

Picture a gray, tapering cylinder welded to the solid black rock by iron rods and concrete, rising from a small island twenty-odd miles from land. It lay in the midst of the sea, this island, a small, bare piece of stone, about one hundred fifty feet long, perhaps forty wide. Small, barely large enough for a man to walk about and stretch his legs at low tide.

This is an advantage one doesn't find in all lights, however, for some of them rise sheer from the waves, with no room for one to move save within the light itself. Still, on our island, one must be careful, for the rocks were treacherously smooth. One misstep and down you would fall into the sea—not that the risk of drowning was so great, but the waters around our island swarmed with huge sharks that kept an eternal patrol around the base of the light.

Still, it was a nice life there. We had enough provisions to last for months, in the event that the sea should become too rough for the supply ship to reach us on schedule. During the day we would work about the light, cleaning the rooms, polishing the metalwork and the lens and the reflector of the light itself, and at night we would sit on the gallery and watch our light, a twenty-thousand-candle power lantern, swing its strong, white bar of light over the sea from the top of its hundred-twenty-foot tower.

Some days, when the air would be very clear, we could see the land, a threadlike line to the west. To the east, north, and south stretched the ocean. Landsmen, perhaps, would soon have tired of that kind of life, perched on a small island off the coast of South America for eighteen weeks, until one's turn for leave ashore came around. But we liked it there, my two fellow tenders and myself—so much so that, for twenty-two months on end with the exception of shore leaves, I was greatly satisfied with the life on Three Skeleton Key.

I HAD JUST RETURNED from my leave at the end of June, that is to say mid-winter in that latitude, and had settled down to the routine with my two fellow-keepers, a Breton by the name of Le Gleo and the head keeper Itchoua, a Basque some dozen years or so older than either of us.

Eight days went by as usual; then on the ninth night after my return, Itchoua, who was on night duty, called Le Gleo and me, sleeping in our rooms in the middle of the tower, at two in the morning. We rose immediately and, climbing the thirty or so steps that led to the gallery, stood beside our chief.

Now, ships were a rare sight in our waters, for our light was a warning of treacherous reefs, barely hidden under the surface and running far out to sea.

Consequently, we were always given a wide berth, especially by sailing vessels, which cannot maneuver as readily as steamers.

No wonder that we were surprised at seeing this three-master heading dead for us in the gloom of early morning. I had immediately recognized her lines, for she stood out plainly, even at the distance of a mile, when our light shone on her.

She was a beautiful ship of some four thousand tons, a fast sailer that had carried cargoes to every part of the world, plowing the seas unceasingly. By her lines she was identified as Dutch-built, which was understandable, as Paramaribo and Dutch Guiana are very close to Cayenne.

Watching her sailing dead for us, a white wave boiling her bows, Le Gleo cried out, "What's wrong with her crew? Are they all drunk or insane? Can't they see us?"

Itchoua nodded soberly, looked at us sharply as he remarked: "See us? No doubt —if there *is* a crew aboard!"

"What do you mean, Chief?" Le Gleo had started, turned to the Basque. "Are you saying that she's the *Flying Dutchman*?"

His sudden fright had been so evident that the older man laughed:

"No, old man, that's not what I meant. If I say there's no one aboard, I mean she's derelict."

Then we understood her queer behavior. Itchoua was right. For some reason, believing she was doomed, her crew had abandoned her. Then she had righted herself and sailed on, wandering with the wind.

The three of us grew tense as the ship seemed about to crash on one of our numerous reefs, but she suddenly lurched with some change of the wind, the yards swung around and the derelict came clumsily about and sailed dead away from us.

In the light of our lantern she seemed so sound, so strong, that Itchoua exclaimed impatiently: "But why the devil was she abandoned? Nothing is smashed, no sign of fire—and she doesn't sail as if she were taking water."

Le Gleo waved to the departing ship:

"Bon voyage!" he smiled at Itchoua and went on. "She's leaving us, chief, and now we'll never know what—"

"No, she's not!" cried the Basque. "Look! She's turning!"

As if obeying his words, the derelict three-master stopped, came about, and headed for us once more. And for the next four hours the vessel played around us—zig-zagging, coming about, stopping, then suddenly lurching forward. No doubt some freak of current and wind, of which our island was the center, kept her near us.

Then suddenly, the tropic dawn broke, the sun rose and it was day, and the ship was plainly visible as she sailed past us. Our light extinguished, we returned to the gallery with our glasses and inspected her.

The three of us focused our glasses on her poop, saw standing out sharply, black letters on the white background of a life-ring, the stenciled name: *Cornelius de Witt, Rotterdam.*

We had read her lines correctly, she was Dutch. Just then the wind rose and the *Cornelius de Witt* changed course, leaned to port and headed straight for us once more. But this time she was so close that we knew she would not turn in time.

"Thunder!" cried Le Gleo, his Breton soul aching to see a fine ship doomed to smash upon a reef. "She's going to pile up! She's gone!"

I shook my head: "Yes, and a shame to see that beautiful ship wreck herself. And we're helpless."

There was nothing we could do but watch. A ship sailing with all sail spread, creaming the sea with her forefoot as she runs before the wind, is one of the most beautiful sights in the world—but this time I could feel the tears stinging my eyes as I saw this fine ship headed for her doom.

All this time our glasses were riveted on her and we suddenly cried out together: "The rats!"

Now we knew why this ship, in perfect condition, was sailing without her crew aboard. They had been driven out by the rats. Not those poor specimens of rats you see ashore, barely reaching the length of one foot from their trembling noses to the tip of their skinny tails, wretched creatures that dodge and hide at the mere sound of a footfall.

No, these were ships' rats, huge, wise creatures, born on the sea, sailing all over the world on ships, transferring to other, larger ships as they multiply. There is as much difference between the rats of the land and these maritime rats as between a fishing smack and an armored cruiser.

The rats of the sea were fierce, bold animals. Large, strong and intelligent, clannish and sea-wise, able to put the best of mariners to shame with their knowledge of the sea, their uncanny ability to foretell the weather.

And they are brave, these rats, and vengeful. If you so much as harm one, his sharp cry will bring hordes of his fellows to swarm over you, tear you, and not cease until your flesh has been stripped from the bones.

The ones on this ship, the rats of Holland, are the worst, as superior to other rats of the sea as their brethren are to the land rats. There is a well-known tale about these animals.

A Dutch captain, thinking to protect his cargo, brought aboard his ship—not cats—but two terriers, dogs trained in the hunting, fighting and killing of vicious rats. By the time the ship, sailing from Rotterdam, had passed the Ostend light, the dogs were gone and never seen again. In twenty-four hours they had been overwhelmed, killed and eaten by the rats.

At times, when the cargo does not suffice, the rats attack the crew, either driving them from the ship, or eating them alive. And studying the *Cornelius de Witt*, I turned sick, for her small boats were all in place. She had not been abandoned.

Over her bridge, on her deck, in the rigging, on every visible spot, the ship was a writhing mass—a starving army coming toward us on a vessel gone mad!

Our island was a small spot in that immense stretch of sea. The ship could have grazed us, passed to port or starboard with its ravening cargo—but no, she came for us at full speed, as if she were leading the regatta at a race, and impaled herself on a sharp point of rock.

There was a dull shock as her bottom stove in, then a horrible crackling as the three masts went overboard at once, as if cut down with one blow of some gigantic sickle. A sighing groan came as the water rushed into the ship; then she split in two and sank like a stone.

But the rats did not drown. Not these fellows! As much at home in the sea as any fish, they formed ranks in the water, heads lifted, tails stretched out, paws paddling. And half of them, those from the forepart of the ship, sprang along the masts and onto the rocks in the instant before she sank. Before we had time even to move, nothing remained of the three-master save some pieces of wreckage floating on the surface and an army of rats covering the rocks left bare by the receding tide.

Thousands of heads rose, felt the wind, and we were scented, seen! To them, we were fresh meat, after possible weeks of starving. There came a scream, composed of innumerable screams, sharper than the howl of a saw attacking a bar of iron, and in the one motion, every rat leaped to attack the tower!

We barely had time to leap back, close the door leading to the gallery, descend the stairs and shut every window tightly. Luckily the door at the base of the light, which we never could have reached in time, was of bronze set in granite and was tightly closed.

The horrible band, in no measurable time, had swarmed up and over the tower as if it had been a tree, piled on the embrasures of the windows, scraped at the glass with thousands of claws, covered the lighthouse with a furry mantle, and reached the top of the tower, filling the gallery and piling atop the lantern.

Their teeth grated as they pressed against the glass of the lantern room, where they could plainly see us, though they could not reach us. A few millimeters of glass, luckily very strong, separated our faces from their gleaming, beady eyes, their sharp claws and teeth. Their odor filled the tower, poisoned our lungs, and rasped our nostrils with a pestilential, nauseating smell. And there we were, sealed alive in our own light, prisoners of a horde of starving rats.

THAT FIRST NIGHT, the tension was so great that we could not sleep. Every moment, we felt that some opening had been made, some window given way, and that our horrible besiegers were pouring through the breach. The rising tide, chasing those of the rats which had stayed on the bare rocks, increased the numbers clinging to the walls, piled on the balcony—so much so that clusters of rats clinging to one another hung from the lantern and the gallery.

With the coming of darkness we lit the light and the turning beam completely maddened the beasts. As the light turned, it successively blinded thousands of rats crowded against the glass, while the dark side of the lantern room gleamed with thousands of points of light, burning like the eyes of jungle beasts in the night.

All the while we could hear the enraged scraping of claws against the stone and glass, while the chorus of cries was so loud that we had to shout to hear one another. From time to time, some of the rats fought among themselves and a cluster would detach itself, falling into the sea like a ripe fruit from a tree. Then we would see phosphorescent streaks as triangular fins slashed the water—sharks, permanent guardians of our rock, feasting on our jailers.

The next day we were calmer, and amused ourselves teasing the rats, placing our faces against the glass which separated us. They could not fathom the invisible barrier which separated them from us, and we laughed as we watched them leaping against the heavy glass.

But the day after that, we realized how serious our position was. The air was foul; even the heavy smell of oil within our stronghold could not dominate the fetid odor of the beasts massed around us. And there was no way of admitting fresh air without also admitting the rats.

In the morning of the fourth day, at early dawn, I saw the wooden framework of my window, eaten away from the outside, sagging inward. I called my comrades and the three of us fastened a sheet of tin in the opening, sealing it tightly. When we had completed the task, Itchoua turned to us and said dully:

"Well—the supply boat came thirteen days ago, and she won't be back for twenty-nine." He pointed at the white metal plate sealing the opening through the granite. "If that gives way"—he shrugged—"they can change the name of this place to Six Skeleton Key."

The next six days and seven nights, our only distraction was watching the rats whose holds were insecure fall a hundred and twenty feet into the maws of the sharks—but they were so many that we could not see any diminution in their numbers.

Thinking to calm ourselves and pass the time, we attempted to count them, but we soon gave up. They moved incessantly, never still. Then we tried identifying them, naming them.

One of them, larger than the others, who seemed to lead them in their rushes against the glass separating us, we named "Nero"; and there were several others whom we had learned to distinguish through various peculiarities.

But the thought of our bones joining those of the convicts was always in the back of our minds. And the gloom of our prison fed these thoughts, for the interior of the light was almost completely dark, as we had to seal every window in the same fashion as mine, and the only space that still admitted daylight was the glassed-in lantern room at the very top of the tower.

Then Le Gleo became morose and had nightmares in which he would see the three skeletons dancing around him, gleaming coldly, seeking to grasp him. His maniacal, raving descriptions were so vivid that Itchoua and I began seeing them also.

It was a living nightmare, the raging cries of the rats as they swarmed over the light, mad with hunger; the sickening, strangling odor of their bodies—

True, there is a way of signaling from lighthouses. But to reach the mast on which to hang the signal, we would have to go out on the gallery where the rats were.

There was only one thing left to do. After debating all of the ninth day, we decided not to light the lantern that night. This is the greatest breach of our service, never committed as long as the tenders of the light are alive; for the light is something sacred, warning ships of danger in the night. Either

the light gleams, a quarter hour after the sun goes down, or no one is left alive to light it.

Well, that night, Three Skeleton Light was dark, and all the men were alive. At the risk of causing ships to crash on our reefs, we left it unlit, for we were worn out—going mad!

At two in the morning, while Itchoua was dozing in his room, the sheet metal sealing his window gave way. The chief had just time enough to leap to his feet and cry for help, the rats swarming over him.

But Le Gleo and I, who had been watching from the lantern room, got to him immediately, and the three of us battled with the horde of maddened rats which flowed through the gaping window. They bit, we struck them down with our knives—and retreated.

We locked the door of the room on them, but before we had time to bind our wounds, the door was eaten through, and gave way, and we retreated up the stairs, fighting off the rats that leaped on us from the knee-deep swarm.

I do not remember to this day, how we managed to escape. All I can remember is wading through them up the stairs, striking them off as they swarmed over us; and then we found ourselves, bleeding from innumerable bites, our clothes shredded, sprawled across the trapdoor in the floor of the lantern room—without food or drink.

Luckily, the trapdoor was metal set into the granite with iron bolts.

The rats occupied the entire light beneath us, and on the floor of our retreat lay some twenty of their fellows, who had gotten in with us before the trapdoor closed, and whom we had killed with our knives. Below us, in the tower, we could hear the screams of the rats as they devoured everything edible that they found. Those on the outside squealed in reply, and writhed in a horrible curtain as they stared at us through the glass of the lantern room.

Itchoua sat up, stared silently at the blood trickling from the wounds on his limbs and body, and running in thin streams on the floor around him. Le Gleo, who was in as bad a state (and so was I, for that matter), stared at the chief and me vacantly, started as his gaze swung to the multitude of rats against the glass, then, suddenly began laughing horribly:

"Hee! Hee! The Three Skeletons! Hee! Hee! The Three Skeletons are now *six* skeletons! *Six* skeletons!"

He threw his head back and howled, his eyes glazed, a trickle of saliva running from the corners of his mouth and thinning the blood flowing over his chest. I shouted to him to shut up, but he did not hear me, so I did the only thing I could do to quiet him—I swung the back of my hand across his face.

The howling stopped suddenly, his eyes swung around the room, then he bowed his head and began weeping softly, like a child.

OUR DARKENED LIGHT had been noticed from the mainland, and as dawn was breaking the patrol was there, to investigate the failure of our light. Looking through my binoculars, I could see the horrified expression on the faces of the officers and crew when, the daylight strengthening, they saw the light completely covered by a seething mass of rats. They thought, as I afterward found out, that we had been eaten alive.

But the rats had also seen the ship, or had scented the crew. As the ship drew nearer, a solid phalanx left the light, plunged into the water and, swimming out, attempted to board her. They would have succeeded, as the ship was hove to, but the engineer connected his steam to a hose on the deck and scalded the head of the attacking column, which slowed them up long enough for the ship to get underway and leave the rats behind.

Then the sharks took part. Belly up, mouths gaping, they arrived in swarms and scooped up the rats, sweeping through them like a sickle through wheat. That was one day that sharks really served a useful purpose.

The remaining rats turned tail, swam to the shore and emerged dripping. As they neared the light, their comrades greeted them with shrill cries, with what sounded like a derisive note predominating. They answered angrily and mingled with their fellows. From the several tussles that broke out, it seemed as if they resented being ridiculed for their failure to capture the ship.

But all this did nothing to get us out of our jail. The small ship could not approach, but steamed around the light at a safe distance, and the tower must have seemed fantastic, some weird, many-mouthed beast hurling defiance at them.

Finally, seeing the rats running in and out of the tower through the door and the windows, those on the ship decided that we had perished and were about to leave when Itchoua, regaining his senses, thought of using the light as a signal. He lit it and, using a plank placed and withdrawn before the beam to form the dots and dashes, quickly sent out our story to those on the vessel.

Our reply came quickly. When they understood our position, how we could not get rid of the rats, Le Gleo's mind going fast, Itchoua and myself covered with bites, cornered in the lantern room without food or water, they had a signalman send us their reply.

His arms swinging like those of a windmill, he quickly spelled out: "Don't give up, hang on a little longer! We'll get you out of this!"

Then she turned and steamed at top speed for the coast, leaving us little reassured.

She was back at noon, accompanied by the supply ship, two small coast guard boats, and the fireboat—a small squadron. At twelve-thirty the battle was on.

After a short reconnaissance, the fireboat picked her way slowly through the reefs until she was close to us, then turned her powerful jet of water on the rats. The heavy stream tore the rats from their places, hurled them screaming into the water where the sharks gulped them down. But for every ten that were dislodged, seven swam ashore, and the stream could do nothing to the rats within the tower. Furthermore, some of them, instead of returning to the rocks, boarded the fireboat and the men were forced to battle them hand-to-hand. They were true rats of Holland, fearing no man, fighting for the right to live!

Nightfall came, and it was as if nothing had been done, the rats were still in possession. One of the patrol boats stayed by the island; the rest of the flotilla departed for the coast. We had to spend another night in our prison. Le Gleo was sitting on the floor, babbling about skeletons; and as I turned to Itchoua, he fell unconscious from his wounds. I was in no better shape and could feel my blood flaming with fever.

Somehow the night dragged by, and the next afternoon I saw the tug, accompanied by the fireboat, come from the mainland with a huge barge in tow. Through my glasses, I saw the barge was filled with meat.

Risking the treacherous reefs, the tug dragged the barge as close to the island as possible. To the last rat, our besiegers deserted the rock, swam out and boarded the barge reeking with the scent of freshly cut meat. The tug dragged the barge about a mile from shore, where the fireboat drenched the barge with gasoline. A well-placed incendiary shell from the patrol boat bombarded them with shrapnel from a safe distance, and the sharks finished off the survivors.

A whaleboat from the patrol boat took us off the island and left three men to replace us. By nightfall we were in the hospital in Cayenne. What became of my friends?

Well, Le Gleo's mind had cracked and he was raving mad. They sent him back to France and locked him up in an asylum, the poor devil. Itchoua died within a week; a rat's bite is dangerous in that hot humid climate, and infection sets in rapidly.

As for me—when they fumigated the light and repaired the damage done by the rats, I resumed my service there. Why not? No reason why such an incident should keep me from finishing out my service there, is there?

Besides—I told you I liked the place— to be truthful, I've never had a post as pleasant as that one, and when my time came to leave it forever, I tell you that I almost wept as Three Skeleton Key disappeared below the horizon.

💀 💀 💀

French author Georges-Gustave Toudouze's classic terror tale "Three Skeleton Key" first appeared in English in the January 1937 issue of Esquire. *The story was adapted by screenwriter James Poe for the CBS radio drama* Escape, *first airing on November 15, 1949. By popular demand Poe's adaptation was performed twice again on* Escape: *in 1950, with Vincent Price playing the story's narrator; and in 1953. Price repeated the role for two more performances, in '56 and '58, on* Suspense *(also on CBS Radio).*

Although Toudouze (1877–1972) wrote on a wide variety of topics, including French naval history, and penned several adventure novels, he is mostly remembered today for "Three Skeleton Key."

Want more rats? Of course you do! After all, rats need love too. And you wouldn't want to hurt their furry little feelings, would you? Well then, read on.

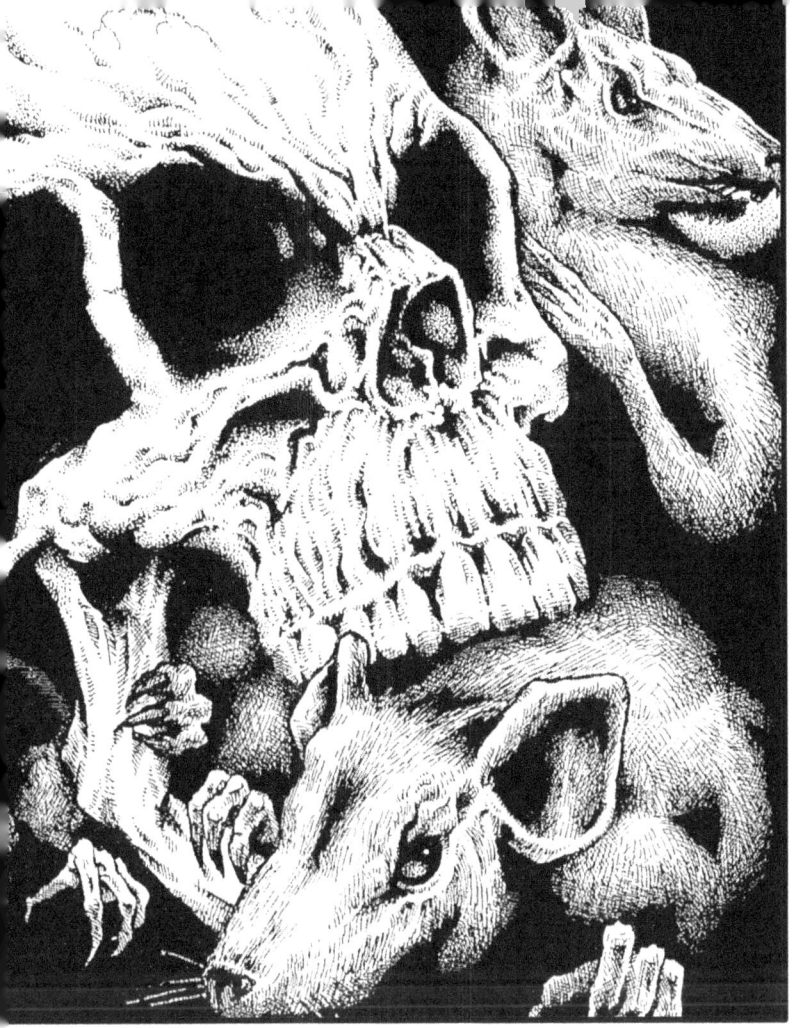

THE GRAVEYARD RATS

By
Henry Kuttner

Illustrated by
Allen Koszowski

O LD MASSON, THE CARETAKER OF ONE OF SALEM'S OLDEST AND MOST NEGLECTED CEMETERIES, had a feud with the rats. Generations ago they had come up from the wharves and settled in the graveyard, a colony of abnormally large rats, and when Masson had taken charge after the inexplicable disappearance of the former caretaker, he decided that they must go. At first he set traps for them and put poisoned food by their burrows, and later he tried to shoot them, but it did no good. The rats stayed, multiplying and overrunning the graveyard with their ravenous hordes.

They were large, even for the *mus decumanus*, which sometimes measures fifteen inches in length, exclusive of the naked pink and grey tail. Masson had caught glimpses of some as large as good-sized cats, and when, once or twice, the gravediggers had uncovered their burrows, the malodorous tunnels were large enough to enable a man to crawl into them on his hands and knees. The ships that had come generations ago from distant ports to the rotting Salem wharves had brought strange cargoes.

Masson wondered sometimes at the extraordinary size of these burrows. He recalled certain vaguely disturbing legends he had heard since coming to ancient, witch-haunted Salem; tales of a moribund, inhuman life that was said to exist in forgotten burrows in the earth. The old days, when Cotton Mather had hunted down the evil cults that worshipped Hecate and the dark Magna Mater in frightful orgies, had passed; but dark gabled houses still leaned perilously towards each other over narrow cobbled streets, and blasphemous secrets and mysteries were said to be hidden in subterranean cellars and caverns, where forgotten pagan rites were still celebrated in defiance of law and sanity. Wagging their grey heads wisely, the elders declared that there were worse things than rats and maggots crawling in the unhallowed earth of the ancient Salem cemeteries.

And then, too, there was this curious dread of the rats. Masson disliked and respected the ferocious little rodents, for he knew the danger that lurked in their flashing, needle-sharp fangs; but he could not understand the inexplicable horror which the oldsters held for deserted, rat-infested houses. He had heard vague rumors of ghoulish beings that dwelt far underground, and that had the power of commanding the rats, marshalling them like horrible armies. The rats, the old men whispered, were messengers between this world and the grim and ancient caverns far below Salem. Bodies had been stolen from graves for nocturnal subterranean feasts, they said. The myth of the Pied Piper is a fable that hides a blasphemous horror, and the black pits of Avernus have brought forth hell-spawned monstrosities that never venture into the light of day.

Masson paid little attention to these tales. He did not fraternize with his neighbors, and, in fact, did all he could to hide the existence of the rats from intruders. Investigation, he realized, would undoubtedly mean the opening of many graves. And while some of the gnawed, empty coffins could be attributed to the activities of the rats, Masson might find it difficult to explain the mutilated bodies that lay in some of the coffins.

The purest gold is used in filling teeth, and this gold is not removed when a man is buried. Clothing, of course, is another matter; for usually the undertaker provides a plain broadcloth suit that is cheap and easily recognizable. But gold is another matter; and sometimes, too, there were medical students and less reputable doctors who were in need of cadavers, and not over-scrupulous as to where these were obtained.

So far Masson had successfully managed to discourage investigation. He had fiercely denied the existence of the rats, even though they sometimes robbed him of his prey. Masson did not care what happened to the bodies after he had performed his gruesome thefts, but the rats inevitably dragged away the whole cadaver through the hole they gnawed in the coffin.

The size of these burrows occasionally worried Masson. Then, too, there was the curious circumstance of the coffins always being gnawed open at the end, never at the side or top. It was almost as though the rats were working under the direction of some impossibly intelligent leader.

Now he stood in an open grave and threw a last sprinkling of wet earth on the heap beside the pit. It was raining, a slow, cold drizzle that for weeks had been descending from soggy black clouds. The graveyard was a slough of yellow, sucking mud, from which the rain-washed tombstones stood up in irregular battalions. The rats had retreated to their burrows, and Masson had not seen one for days. But his gaunt, unshaved face was set in frowning lines; the coffin on which he was standing was a wooden one.

The body had been buried several days earlier, but Masson had not dared to disinter it before. A relative of the dead man had been coming to the grave at intervals, even in the drenching rain. But he would hardly come at this late hour, no matter how much grief he might be suffering, Masson thought, grinning wryly. He straightened and laid the shovel aside.

From the hill on which the ancient graveyard lay he could see the lights of Salem flickering dimly through the downpour. He drew a flashlight from his pocket. He would need light now. Taking up the spade, he bent and examined the fastenings of the coffin.

Abruptly he stiffened. Beneath his feet he sensed an unquiet stirring and scratching, as though something were moving within the coffin. For a moment a pang of superstitious fear shot through Masson, and then rage replaced it as he realized the significance of the sound. The rats had forestalled him again!

In a paroxysm of anger Masson wrenched at the fastenings of the coffin. He got the sharp edge of the shovel under the lid and pried it up until he could finish the job with his hands. Then he sent the flashlight's cold beam darting down into the coffin.

Rain spattered against the white satin

lining; the coffin was empty. Masson saw a flicker of movement at the head of the case, and darted the light in that direction.

The end of the sarcophagus had been gnawed through, and a gaping hole led into darkness. A black shoe, limp and dragging, was disappearing as Masson watched, and abruptly he realized that the rats had forestalled him by only a few minutes. He fell on his hands and knees and made a hasty clutch at the shoe, and the flashlight incontinently fell into the coffin and went out. The shoe was tugged from his grasp; he heard a sharp, excited squealing, and then he had the flashlight again and was darting its light into the burrow.

It was a large one. It had to be, or the corpse could not have been dragged along it. Masson wondered at the size of the rats that could carry away a man's body, but the thought of the loaded revolver in his pocket fortified him. Probably if the corpse had been an ordinary one, Masson would have left the rats with their spoils rather than venture into the narrow burrow, but he remembered an especially fine set of cufflinks he had observed, as well as a stickpin that was undoubtedly a genuine pearl. With scarcely a pause he clipped the flashlight to his belt and crept into the burrow.

It was a tight fit, but he managed to squeeze himself along. Ahead of him in the flashlight's glow he could see the shoes dragging along the wet earth of the bottom of the tunnel. He crept along the burrows as rapidly as he could, occasionally barely able to squeeze his lean body through the narrow walls.

The air was overpowering with its musty stench of carrion. If he could not reach the corpse in a minute, Masson decided, he would turn back. Belated fears were beginning to crawl, maggot-like, within his mind, but greed urged him on. He crawled forward, several times passing the mouths of adjoining tunnels. The walls of the burrow were damp and slimy, and twice lumps of dirt dropped behind him. The second time, he paused and screwed his head around to look back. He could see nothing, of course, until he had unhooked the flashlight from his belt and reversed it.

Several clods lay on the ground behind him, and the danger of his position suddenly became real and terrifying. With thoughts of a cave-in making his pulse race, he decided to abandon the pursuit, even though he had now almost overtaken the corpse and the invisible things that pulled it. But he had overlooked one thing: the burrow was too narrow to allow him to turn.

Panic touched him briefly, but he remembered a side tunnel he had just passed, and backed awkwardly along the tunnel until he came to it. He thrust his legs into it, backing until he found himself able to turn. Then he hurriedly began to retrace his way, although his knees were bruised and painful.

Agonizing pain shot through his leg. He felt sharp teeth sink into his flesh, and kicked out frantically. There was a shrill squealing and the scurry of many feet. Flashing the light behind him, Masson caught his breath in a sob of fear as he saw a dozen great rats watching him intently, their slitted eyes glittering in the light. They were great misshapen things, as large as cats, and behind them he caught a glimpse of a dark shape that stirred and moved swiftly aside into the shadow; and he shuddered at the unbelievable size of the thing.

The light had held them for a moment, but they were edging closer, their teeth dull orange in the pale light. Masson tugged at his pistol, managed to extricate it from his pocket, and aimed carefully. It was an awkward position, and he tried to press his feet into the soggy sides of the burrow so that he should not inadvertently send a bullet into one of them.

THE ROLLING THUNDER of the shot deafened him, for a time, and the clouds of smoke set him coughing. When he could hear again and the smoke had cleared, he saw that the rats were gone. He put the pistol back and began to creep swiftly along the tunnel, and then with a scurry and a rush they were upon him again.

They swarmed over his legs, biting and squealing insanely, and Masson shrieked horribly as he snatched for his gun. He fired without aiming, and only luck saved him from blowing a foot off. This time the rats did not retreat so far, but Masson was crawling as swiftly as he could along the burrow, ready to fire again at the first sound of another attack.

There was a patter of feet and he sent the light stabbing behind him. A great grey rat paused and watched him. Its long ragged whiskers twitched, and its scabrous, naked tail was moving slowly from side to side. Masson shouted and the rat retreated.

He crawled on, pausing briefly, the black gap of a side tunnel at his elbow, as he made out a shapeless huddle on the damp clay a few yards ahead. For a second he thought it was a mass of earth that had been dislodged from the roof, and then he recognized it as a human body.

It was a brown and shriveled mummy, and with a dreadful unbelieving shock Masson realized that it was moving.

It was crawling towards him, and in the pale glow of the flashlight the man saw a frightful gargoyle face thrust into his own. It was the passionless, death's-head skull of a long-dead corpse, instinct with hellish life; and the glazed eyes swollen and bulbous betrayed the thing's blindness. It made a faint groaning sound as it crawled towards Masson, stretching its ragged and granulated lips in a grin of dreadful hunger. And Masson was frozen with abysmal fear and loathing.

Just before the Horror touched him, Masson flung himself frantically into the burrow at his side. He heard a scrambling noise at his heels, and the thing groaned dully as it came after him. Masson, glancing over his shoulder, screamed and propelled himself desperately through the narrow burrow. He crawled along awkwardly, sharp stones cutting his hands and knees. Dirt showered into his eyes, but he dared not pause even for a moment. He scrambled on, gasping, cursing, and praying hysterically.

Squealing triumphantly, the rats came at him, horrible hunger in their eyes. Masson almost succumbed to their vicious teeth before he succeeded in beating them off. The passage was narrowing, and in a frenzy of terror he kicked and screamed and fired until the hammer clicked on an empty shell. But he had driven them off.

He found himself crawling under a great stone, embedded in the roof, that dug cruelly into his back. It moved a little as his weight struck it, and an idea flashed into Masson's fright-crazed mind: If he could bring down the stone so that it blocked the tunnel!

The earth was wet and soggy from the rains, and he hunched himself half upright and dug away at the dirt around the stone. The rats were coming closer. He saw their eyes glowing in the reflection of the flashlight's beam. Still he clawed frantically at the earth. The stone was giving. He tugged at it and it rocked in its foundation.

A RAT WAS APPROACHING—the monster he had already glimpsed. Grey and leprous and hideous, it crept forward with its orange teeth bared, and in its wake came the blind dead thing, groaning as it crawled. Masson gave a last frantic tug at the stone. He felt it slide downwards, and then he went scrambling along the tunnel.

Behind him the stone crashed down, and he heard a sudden frightful shriek of agony. Clods showered upon his legs. A heavy weight fell on his feet and he dragged them free with difficulty. The entire tunnel was collapsing!

Gasping with fear, Masson threw himself forward as the soggy earth collapsed at his heels. The tunnel narrowed until he could barely use his hands and legs to propel himself; he wriggled forward like an eel and suddenly felt satin tearing beneath his clawing fingers, and then his head crashed against something that barred his path. He moved his legs, discovering that they were not pinned under the collapsed earth. He was lying flat on his stomach, and when he tried to raise himself he found that the roof was only a few inches from his back. Panic shot through him.

When the blind horror had blocked his path, he had flung himself desperately into a side tunnel, a tunnel that had no outlet. He was *in a coffin*, an empty coffin into which he had crept through the hole the rats had gnawed in its end!

He tried to turn on his back and found that he could not. The lid of the coffin pinned him down inexorably. Then he braced himself and strained at the coffin lid. It was immovable, and even if he could escape from the sarcophagus, how could he claw his way up through five feet of hard-packed earth?

He found himself gasping. It was dreadfully fetid, unbearably hot. In a paroxysm of terror he ripped and clawed at the satin until it was shredded. He made a futile attempt to dig with his feet at the earth from the collapsed burrow that blocked his retreat. If he were only able to reverse his position he might be able to claw his way through to air ... *air....*

White-hot agony lanced through his breast, throbbed in his eyeballs. His head seemed to be swelling, growing larger and larger; and suddenly he heard the exultant squealing of the rats. He began to scream insanely but could not drown them out. For a moment he thrashed about hysterically within his narrow prison, and then he was quiet, gasping for air. His eyelids closed, his blackened tongue protruded, and he sank down into the blackness of death with the mad squealing of the rats dinning in his ears.

American author Henry Kuttner (1915–1958) wrote prolifically for the pulps, comics and television, and employed a variety of pen names. "The Graveyard Rats" was his first sale to Weird Tales*, appearing in the March 1936 issue.*

WE ALSO LIKE CREEPY SCIENCE FICTION!
DON'T MISS BLACK INFINITY, NIGHTMARE ABBEY'S "SCI-FI SISTER"!

SNOW

By HELEN GRANT

"**I** THINK IT'S THIS—" BEGAN JONATHAN, AND VANISHED.

There was a *crump* of falling snow, and Calum was suddenly, shockingly alone. He gasped, his breath visible for an instant in the freezing air before it melted into the surrounding mist. A chasm had opened mere inches from the toes of his boots, where the cornice had collapsed. Hundreds of feet below, snow was still rushing down the slope. Jonathan was nowhere to be seen. He hadn't screamed; he hadn't finished his sentence. He just wasn't there anymore.

Calum took a breath, drawing freezing air into his lungs.

"Jonathan!" he yelled. "Jonathan!"

Silence.

"No," he muttered. "No, no." He squeezed his eyes shut for a moment, feeling the wetness at the corners of them. When he opened them again, God hadn't taken it back. Jonathan was still gone.

Calum looked at the rim of snow inches from his feet, and the dizzying view below it. His head swam, but he managed to take a step back. Then he took another. When he judged he was far enough from the edge that he was safe—probably—he fumbled for his phone, thinking he could call for help.

With heavy mitts on, he couldn't wrestle the phone out, so he slipped the right one off. His hands were shaking and the pocket was a tight fit; useless panic welled up and he tore at it, swearing. The phone shot through his fingers, described an arc in

the air and dropped into the snow.

Calum was going to lunge after it, but he stopped himself in time. He could see where the phone had entered the snow—he could see the hole—but it was too close to the edge. If he stepped forward, he *might* be able to retrieve it, or he might crash through what remained of the cornice, like Jonathan had.

"No," he said aloud. "Leave it."

When he was very stressed he did that: he talked to himself. He tried to persuade himself round to a sensible point of view—to rationalise.

"You can't do anything for him," he told himself. "You have to get yourself down safely. You don't need your phone for that."

He tried to quash the thought that actually he might need it, not just for calls but for the mapping software: it was Jonathan who knew Beinn a'Chaorainn—Jonathan who was now presumably lying at the bottom of it, under a tonne of snow.

"Retrace your steps," he said. "Simple."

But it wasn't. When he turned his head, all he could see was snow vanishing into thick mist. He thought about tracking the footprints they had made on the way up, but once you got away from the edge the ground was a frozen sea of small rocks pushing up through the snow; it was hard to pick anything out. He turned, and turned again, and now he wasn't even sure which way they had come from. The shock of what had happened to Jonathan was making clear thinking impossible. He still had that irrational feeling that if he could only rewind a few minutes—if he could ask Jonathan...

Standing still, he could feel the cold seeping into his fingers and toes. He had to get moving again. He picked the likeliest direction and started to walk, slowly and carefully. The memory of Jonathan's instantaneous disappearance hobbled him; every time he placed a boot in the snow he half-expected the same to happen.

The mist seemed to be thickening treacherously. After he had stumbled on a little further, it seemed to him that the ground was sloping more than it ought to, if he was where he had thought he was. The drop flashed through his head again and he lost his nerve completely.

"Help me," he whispered, and then he shouted it. "Help me! Somebody! Anybody!"

The sound was deadened by the mist. Calum stood still and stared into it, straining his eyes. He saw nothing—nothing—and then he thought he *did* see something: a thin, dark patch that wavered and flickered.

Please God, he thought. *Let it be someone.*

The dark patch coalesced into a human form, indistinct but definitely there; definitely not his imagination.

It occurred to him that they hadn't seen anyone else on the hill that day. There'd been no other cars parked where they'd left theirs. Earlier, before the mist had become so impenetrable, he'd looked back downhill and seen nobody following. So far as he knew, they'd been alone.

Briefly, hope flared: perhaps it was Jonathan, who'd clawed his way up from some unseen ledge?

Then the figure became more clearly defined and he saw that it wasn't. He was pretty sure it was a woman.

She strode towards him swiftly and confidently, becoming more solid with every step. These were not the movements of a woman who feared a misstep like the one that had taken his friend. Someone with years—probably decades—of experience in the hills, he thought, and when he saw the gear she was wearing, which was of good quality but a little outdated now, his opinion was confirmed. Then she came right up to him, and he was surprised to see that she was young.

Within the circle of the faux fur-trimmed hood her face was very pale and perfect, with brilliantly blue eyes and strongly-defined, regular features. Wisps of fair hair escaped from the hood.

"Thank God," said Calum. "I thought I was alone up here. My friend—Jonathan—fell through the cornice back there. I'm afraid he might be hurt, or—"

He couldn't quite bring himself to say it. He looked behind her, expecting to see someone else, a mountaineering partner, but couldn't see anyone.

She shook her head, the hood not moving with her so that the effect was a little peculiar, reminding him of an owl.

"You're not alone now."

"You're part of a group?" he said hopefully.

"It's just me."

He gaped at her. "You came up here *on your own?*"

"I know this hill very well," she said. "I've spent a lot of time here." She spoke levelly and he couldn't tell whether she was offended at his question.

"Well," he said, "Thank God you're here. Can I borrow your mobile?"

"I don't have one," she said. "But I can guide you down, if you like."

No phone? Up here, in these conditions? It was on the tip of Calum's tongue to ask her whether she was completely nuts, but he remembered that he was the one in trouble here; she seemed at ease, sure of her ground. She wasn't even shivering, though he was.

"Please," he said.

She nodded. "Follow me. Stay close."

"Thank you," he said, fervently.

As she turned away her voice floated back to him. "You're welcome. But I'd like you to do something for me."

"Anything," he said, meaning it, grateful for human company as much as for the assistance.

"Come back and find me," she said. She glanced back at him with those luminous blue eyes. "When the snow has gone, come back to the hill and find me."

"Alright," he said, a little confused. Was she coming on to him or something?

"Promise?" she pursued.

"I promise," said Calum, startled. He was about to ask something else, but she was already ahead of him, moving briskly and easily over the snowy stones. He had to keep going, never quite catching up with her, but not falling so far behind that he lost her in the mist.

It was hard to keep track of time: he was tired, cold, and shocked, and he kept reliving what had happened to Jonathan in his head. His feet moved mechanically; his breathing sounded loud in his ears. He was rather glad the girl didn't want to talk to him while they descended; he was trying to get things straight in his head, to think what to do first when they got to the bottom. The mist still pressed close about them.

The light began to fade: it was winter after all, and the days were short. The sun was invisible, a vaguely lighter patch in the endless grey, but he sensed the tone of the light deepening. Still he walked downwards, dog tired and sick at heart, stumbling a little now.

At long last the mist began to thin, and then suddenly he was out of it altogether. It was nearly twilight, and he was almost at the patch of forest he had to pass through to reach the car.

Calum stopped and put his hands over his face.

"Thank you, thank you," he muttered. He was too tired to properly feel relief, but he had the sensation of someone who had been pulled at the last minute from drowning.

He took his hands away and the girl had gone.

Calum turned his head this way and that. Nothing. He turned right round and looked back up the track into the mist and the gathering gloom. There was that flicker again—a figure disappearing back into the grey obscurity.

Is she really going back up there?

It was impossible. It was getting dark. But he was too exhausted to think about it. Probably she knew some other way back to wherever she was going; probably heat and lights and a dram of something warming awaited her at the other end.

All the same, he wished he could have thanked her.

He trudged through back to the car, where he took off his mitts, stowed his rucksack in the boot and changed into shoes he could drive in. Then he drove to the nearest village to call for help.

IT WAS A LONG NIGHT. The Mountain Rescue team went up with avalanche poles and transceivers, but Calum knew without asking that there was little or no hope of finding Jonathan alive. Nobody said the pair of them were idiots for attempting what they had in these conditions, with the prevailing forecasts. They didn't have to. It was perfectly obvious to Calum, as he sat shivering in the driver's seat of the car that had come up with Jonathan sitting next to him, cheerfully scrolling through maps. He wondered what he would say to Jonathan's family.

He told the rescuers about the girl who'd helped him, thinking perhaps they might know her—she was clearly so familiar with the hills hereabouts. Nobody seemed very interested.

"Oh, aye," one of them said, after he had finished describing her. That was all. He had the impression nobody believed him. She hadn't stuck around, after all; maybe she hadn't been there in the first place.

Calum thought about his stumbling walk down the mountain, with the girl always ahead of him, always visible, although he never caught up with her. Over the months that followed, he thought about it quite often, although these memories were intermixed with horrible flashbacks to the moment when Jonathan had disappeared. One moment he had been there, the next he had been gone. Calum agonised over it—whether there was something he, or they, could have done differently. Whether they should have gone at all. Sometimes he thought he remembered Jonathan crying out as he fell; other times, he knew he hadn't. It was all fuzzy in his head and he doubted himself.

He began to doubt his memories of the girl, too. Perhaps he *had* imagined her.

Perhaps she was the embodiment of something within himself, some drive towards survival that he had externalised. As for the promise she had extracted from him—what did it even *mean*?

More time passed, and he forgot about it altogether, though he didn't go back to the Laggan area for a very long time.

AMBER WAS FOUR YEARS younger than Calum, and beautiful: she had warm brown eyes and light auburn hair to match her name. She was also tough, athletic, and a passionate mountaineer. He was completely infatuated.

He hadn't *stopped* going into the hills after the accident, but he hadn't been out in snow again that winter, and he'd been a lot more cautious ever since. It was one thing to know, in an intellectual sense, that accidents happened, and not just to other people; it was something else to have your friend die in front of you. Calum knew he'd never attempt Beinn a'Chaorainn again.

Then Amber came along, and pretty soon he was out every weekend, living for those summit selfies where their faces were pressed close together, both of them grinning, with her looking like a goddess and him bursting with happiness.

He didn't tell her about Jonathan at first, because he didn't want to introduce a downer into their conversations, or spend ages explaining the details of what had happened. Then it felt too late; the moment had passed. So when they were sitting in the pub one night and she suggested doing Creag Meagaidh, from which you could actually *see* Beinn a'Chaorainn, he didn't have a good reason to say no.

He took a moment to sip his pint, so that he could think about what to say. It was February, and there was snow; the conditions were similar to the way they had been that day he had gone out with Jonathan, and the location was very close. He knew he wouldn't be able to stop himself thinking about his friend, not when the scene of his death was actually within sight.

Then he thought: *perhaps this is good. I have to face it sometime.*

So he said, "Yes," and when Amber smiled at him, the corners of her eyes crinkling, he knew he'd made the right decision.

THIS TIME, he made sure that clear weather was forecast for the entire day *and* the day after: no mist, no sleet, just sunshine.

Usually Amber had to turf him out of bed in the morning, but this time he surprised her by getting up first, well before dawn. He was determined that they would get onto the hill at first light—that there would be zero chance of running out of daylight. He had everything packed—lunch, water, crampons, ice axes, spare clothes, bothy bag—while she was still wandering about with a sleepy expression, a mug of coffee in her hand.

"Keen," she remarked, yawning.

"Yeah," he said, hesitated, and then left it at that.

They left the car in a little parking area on the main road, and began the walk in just as the sun was rising, the first rays illuminating the rugged landscape ahead.

For a while neither of them said much; they were looking about them and getting into their stride, and the terrain was difficult, requiring concentration. But then Amber became talkative. First she mused about the good conditions, and how lucky they were, and then—of all things—she started on the topic of accidents.

Calum couldn't think what had prompted this. Normally she had no morbid interest in that sort of thing, but now he couldn't get her off the topic. She was from the area—her family still lived in Spean Bridge—so she had heard about a lot of local incidents: the climbers caught in an avalanche on the very mountain they were ascending, for example. Then, to his horror, she pointed towards Beinn a'Chaorainn.

"Over there, on Beinn a'Chaorainn," she said, "a guy went right through a cornice. That was a few years back."

This was the moment when Calum could have said: *That was us—me and my friend Jonathan. He was the one who fell.*

But he just couldn't do it. Struck dumb, he listened to Amber describing how far the man had fallen, and how grisly it must have been for the rescuers who retrieved the body.

He tried to fix his attention on something else—the rough ground underfoot, overlaid with snow, the lightening sky ahead, anything. But Amber continued, relentless, and he couldn't help hearing.

"Thing was," she said, "it wasn't just him they found." She looked at him, squinting in the low sunshine.

"It wasn't?" Surely she must hear how rimed with horror his voice was?

"No." She shook her head. "When they were on the way up, looking, they found a hand. Well, not a whole hand, exactly. Carpals and phalanges, held together with rotting ligaments."

"Where was...?"

"The rest of the body?" She shrugged. "They don't know. I mean, obviously there *was* one. Nobody loses a *hand* on a hill and doesn't mention it. But that was all they found. They said it was possible the body was somewhere else entirely—an animal or bird could have carried the hand off and dropped it far away. They think it was a woman, from the size and proportions of the bones, but that's all."

"Shit," said Calum.

"Yeah."

After that, thankfully, Amber fell silent for a while. They walked on for a bit, up Creag na Cailliche and then along the side of a dry-stone dyke. They stopped for hot squash from a flask and a few squares of dark chocolate. It was cold—Calum could feel that when they stopped—but the air was very still, and it was utterly clear and bright. Looking up, he couldn't even see clouds. It was not at all like the day he and Jonathan had climbed Beinn a'Chaorainn. He said to himself again that this was *good*; he was replacing bad memories with positive ones. If only Amber hadn't brought it all up again...

He shook his head. They hoisted their packs back onto their backs and set off again. Snow crunched underfoot and their breath made little clouds. Amber sang quietly for a while, pure, high notes, and he smiled to himself, loving her.

Eventually they reached the great white expanse of plateau with the summit cairn, and Amber took the obligatory selfie in front of it. Sometimes they asked other people to photograph them together, but today they were the first up, and the only ones on the plateau. Calum glanced back downhill, and far in the distance he saw someone else coming up, a single dark speck against the white. They were far too far away to be of any use—if he and Amber waited for them to get here, they'd freeze.

He watched them for a minute, frowning. It looked as if they were on their own. Well, it wasn't unknown to meet single hillwalkers, even in snowy conditions, but it felt unwise to do it; if you broke an ankle or fell down a gully, who would know? Memory stirred uneasily and he recalled the girl he had met—or thought he had met—that day on Beinn a'Chaorainn. She'd been alone too. He rubbed his hands together, trying to get the blood flowing. Perhaps, he thought, he was the one who was out of step. Too cautious.

After that, they walked east to look at the corrie, keeping a safe distance from the edge.

Amber photographed various snowy perspectives, and then she drifted back to him.

"I have to pee."

"There's no cover up here," he pointed out. "Unless you go behind the cairn, which is a bit scuzzy."

"I'll just go over there," she said, gesturing. "You can turn your back."

"I've seen it all before," he pointed out, but he turned his back anyway, grinning, and looked towards Stob Poite Coire Ardair. He spent some time studying its mighty snow-covered flanks and whistling quietly to himself, until he began to think that Amber was taking her time.

It didn't seem quite gentlemanly to turn right round and look, but he twisted his head to the side and said, "Amber?" quite loudly.

At the same moment he became aware that something was drifting past his right shoulder. It was a thin tendril of mist. He blinked, thinking he was seeing things; the forecast was for perfectly clear fair weather. But no; his eyes were not deceiving him.

He did turn right round then, and saw to his horror that there was thick white mist moving quite rapidly across the plateau. It was almost upon him, and then it *was* upon him, all around him, cutting out the view completely. It was so sudden that he was disorientated.

"Amber?" he shouted, but his voice had a strange dead quality, all its resonance absorbed into the mist. "Amber!"

The whiteness that enveloped him was impenetrable, blending into the white snow underfoot so that he might have been floating in it. On every side it was featureless. He held out his hands in their thick mitts, just for the relief of something to focus on.

Calum filled his lungs, and shouted Amber's name again, as loudly as he could. Then he listened. He thought he heard *something* in reply, but it sounded muffled and far off. She wasn't *that* far away, surely?

Then he saw a flicker of movement in the mist and relief flooded through him.

"Oh, thank God," he said. "I thought we'd lost each other. This isn't what the forecast said. It was supposed to be clear."

She came closer, a female figure moving purposefully, becoming more clearly defined with every step.

"Amber—"

It wasn't Amber.

He thought he'd forgotten what she looked like, but he recognised her instantly: the fur-trimmed hood, the brilliantly blue eyes, the wisps of blonde hair.

She was angry.

Involuntarily, Calum took a step backwards.

She came right up to him, and the rage on her face frightened him.

"You promised," she spat. "I led you off the hill and you *promised* to come and find me. Why didn't you?"

"I'm sorry," stammered Calum. "I didn't think—"

"Sorry?!" She almost shrieked it, right into his face, so close that he flinched away. "I *saved* you. And you didn't come back." Her fists were raised now, but she didn't touch him. "You didn't come."

"I didn't know it was so important," he protested feebly.

"It was a *promise*." She glared at him. "Do you think I want to stay up here, month after month, year after year? Do you think I *like* it, slowly decaying in some stinking gully while the birds shit on me and peck off any bit they like? Do you?"

"No," said Calum, his eyes round with horror.

"I'm falling apart," she said. "Some miserable creature took one of my hands. Now if they find me, they won't even be able to bury all of me. And you—you couldn't be bothered to come back. Even though you *promised*."

Calum backed away; he couldn't help it. And she came on, shaking her fists in his face, never touching him but always threatening to touch.

On all sides the mist pressed in on them, seeming to throb with her anger.

"Please—" said Calum, not knowing what he was pleading for.

"No," she said. "You *promised*."

Calum kept backing up. They were locked into a horrible *pas de deux*: him backing, her following, the mist swallowing everything else. One step, one step more. The air seemed subtly different: a little colder, a little emptier...

Sensing something wrong, sensing that he was on the brink of something, Calum stopped.

At that moment, she flew at him, shrieking, and he saw her suddenly as she really was. He lurched backwards, and fell.

The drop was almost sheer. Calum plummeted, the breath screaming out of his lungs. Then he landed with a great *crack* that sent shock waves of pain through his body. The agony was so intense that for a while he couldn't even open his eyes. Incoherent oaths seeped from between his clenched teeth. He cried and gasped.

When he did open his eyes, he wanted to close them again immediately. He was caught, broken, halfway down the cliff. The mist had cleared and he could see the great blue sheets of ice that loomed above him, sheer, unclimbable, glossy gouts of frozen water. The upper edge of the cliff might as well have been a million miles away.

He tried to shift, to relieve the pain, and instantly stopped; he could feel how unstable his position was. Another inch and he would fall the rest of the way, which he now saw yawning below him—a drop hundreds of feet down another smooth wall of ice.

His jacket had ripped open and already he could feel the cold sinking its claws into him. If he lay here for very long, he would freeze to death.

Amber, he thought, but it was hopeless; even if she called someone right away, they wouldn't get here in time.

Calum looked up again, and thought he saw the dark speck of a head looking down from the top of the cliff. He couldn't tell at this distance whether it was Amber or the girl, but he didn't have long to think about it.

His teeth were chattering. It was cold— so cold.

Helen Grant writes Gothic novels and short supernatural fiction. Her latest novel Too Near The Dead *(Fledgling Press, 2021) was listed among the Guardian's best recent fantasy, horror and science fiction in August 2021.*

Helen's short stories have appeared in Weird Tales, Supernatural Tales, All Hallows *and anthologies including* Egaeus Press' *acclaimed* Crooked Houses, *Swan River Press's* Uncertainties 2 *and Black Shuck Books'* Ars Gratia Sanguis (Great British Horror 6). *Joyce Carol Oates has described her as "a brilliant chronicler of the uncanny as only those who dwell in places of dripping, graylit beauty can be." A lifelong fan of M.R. James, she has spoken at two M.R. James conferences.*

Setting is very important in Helen's work; she is often inspired by the typography or history of places in which she has lived. "Snow," set in Scotland, is no exception. The precise setting of the story was suggested by her husband Gordon, a climber and mountaineer of forty years' standing.

AWAKE in the HANDS of SOLITUDE

by Kurt Newton & John Boden
Art by Allen Koszowski

CYRIL VON FOERSTER LIFTED THE PALE FLAP OF SKIN NEAR THE TRANSVERSE CARPAL LIGAMENT AND PLACED THE MICRODISC ON THE EXPOSED MEDIAN NERVE. He then flushed the area with saline. Almost immediately the disc began to dissolve like a lozenge. Cyril resealed the skin with a single butterfly strip. Then he waited. The forefinger was the first to twitch. Then the thumb. Then the middle, ring and pinky, curling in unison like a trio of ballerinas taking a bow. Cyril couldn't help but smile again, even though this was hardly the first time he had performed this feat.

"Hello, my lovely." Cyril's voice was barely audible in the basement laboratory, a moth's wings batting in a chamber where footsteps echoed like horse's hooves. There was nothing wrong with Cyril's vocal cords; they were simply atrophied from lack of use. Living alone made conversation unnecessary.

But he wasn't alone. Not anymore. He had *them*.

Cyril stroked the hand, imprinting his electrochemical signature on the newly-created companion. "You don't know how special you are," he said, his voice adding an additional imprint. "Years of trial and error. And now you're here. But you need your rest."

He lifted the slender, pink appendage and placed it in a sterile glass container the size of a glove box, and slid the container onto his lap. Gripping the container with one hand, he thumbed the controls of his motorized wheelchair, backing away from the work bench. He pivoted, then rolled several feet before stopping in front of a transparent storage cabinet. The door opened with a vacuumed whoosh. Cyril placed the container in the cabinet with all the others. He had arranged the shelves beforehand to accommodate her, placing her center stage. She would be his crowning achievement, if the new programming proved correct.

There was a skittering at his feet. Cyril dropped his gaze.

On the floor, two hands wrestled with each other, fingers and wrists grappling for domination. Their nails clicked on the floor's surface.

"Boys?" Cyril's voice was like an off switch. The hands immediately disengaged. One hand scurried toward the pneumatic elevator and hopped across its threshold like a miniature kangaroo; the other chased close behind, keeping its wrist stub low to the ground, like a dog hanging its head in shame or embarrassment.

Cyril gazed upon his masterpiece once again. He felt an unaccustomed flutter in his chest. He took a deep breath, then followed the "boys" into the elevator. The door closed, and a gentle exchange of air pressure carried them aloft. Shortly thereafter, a motion sensor switched the basement lights off, leaving the cabinet aglow in the sterile dark.

THE SOFT HUM of the equipment blossomed and swirled in shadow.

Tap. Tap. (fingernail on box lid)

Thump. Thump. (fingerpad on box bottom)

Tap. Tap. Thump-tap-thump. Thump.

The new hand waited, then repeated the sequence. Then again. And again.

After the fourth repetition, she received a reply. It came from the shelf beneath her.

Thump. Thump. Thump. Tap. Tap. Thump. Tap. Tap.

If she had a mouth, she would have screamed. Especially when the same sentiment was then repeated by all of the other hands in the cabinet. Introductions and acknowledgement that she was indeed their superior. Their queen.

Skrissssssh. Skrissssssh. Skrissssssh. (slow drags of a nail across the surface of the lid) *No! No! No! This can't be!* She wanted none of it. Skrissssssh. Skrissssssh. Thump-thump-thump.

Her miniature tantrum was followed by an extended silence, a silence that was just as unbearable as the revelation of her new-found existence.

OUTSIDE, the sun had long ago submitted beneath night's fist. The shadows grew long until they stretched themselves to death. The windows of the grand manor darkened, giving the impression of an angry glare.

Chopin's Polonaise in A-flat major filled the evening with its leaping, forceful melody. Cyril was in the music room, relaxing after the day's work. The boys had been instructed to play something celebratory. During the spirited ending, in a lull between notes, the doorbell rang. The music ended abruptly.

Cyril wasn't expecting company. And ever since Camille died, and he'd begun his latest work, there were no servants to perform the mundane tasks, such as sending door-to-door salesmen on their way.

The door bell chimed again followed by a series of insistent knocks.

Cyril slid his body onto the seat of the wheelchair. The boys stood on their fingertips on the piano's keyboard, eager for the next directive. "Stay," Cyril told them, and the two flattened.

Cyril rolled to the front entrance's side window. A late model sedan was parked in the driveway. A man and a woman stood on the front step. Cyril unlocked the door, then reversed several feet. "Come in," he shouted.

The door opened. "Hello, Cyril. I hope you don't mind us dropping by. Was that you playing?"

The silence stretched like one of his equations and when it was broken it was by Cyril. "Yes. Who else would it be?" Cyril stared at the woman's face. The resemblance was uncanny. "Claudia. Nice to see you again." Claudia's husband was close behind. "Hello, Roger."

"Cyril." Roger nodded, clearly uncomfortable with the visit.

"Please, come in. What brings you here?" Cyril backed away to allow them entry.

Claudia was a lesser vision of her sister Camille, but a vision nonetheless. Her flowing chestnut hair and porcelain skin was as radiant as her sister's once was.

"There's been a desecration at the town cemetery," said Claudia.

"Oh, dear." Cyril looked at her dumbfounded.

"Camille's grave. Oh, my God, I thought you knew."

"How horrid," said Cyril. He led them into the sitting room. "Please. I'll make some tea?" He left for a moment, entering the kitchen to put the water on and prepare a tray. When he returned, Claudia was sitting on the divan while Roger paced about. Claudia commented on the artwork that hung on the sitting room walls.

"I see you still display Camille's water colors."

"She was an amazing artist. So talented," said Cyril.

Claudia nodded, remembering her sister's dreams of becoming the next Winslow Homer.

Cyril cleared his throat. "When you say desecrated, what exactly do you mean?"

Roger piped in then. "The grave was dug up and robbed."

"Roger!"

"Well, Claudia, tell him."

"Tell me what?" said Cyril.

Claudia's eyes met Cyril's with a peacefulness he knew all too well. "The Inspector said Camille's body had been mutilated."

Cyril had rolled up next to Claudia. "But who would do such a thing?"

"The authorities are investigating. But these things are usually the work of adolescents."

"Bloody pervert, if you ask me," said Roger.

"Roger, please." Claudia grabbed Cyril's hands. "The Inspector said nothing untoward was committed. Just the mutilation. Apparently, things like this have been going on for several years now at the cemetery. Likely the work of someone who is mentally deranged. I'm so sorry."

The tea kettle sounded. Cyril was deep in thought. He snapped out of his reverie and wheeled an about face. "I'll be right back."

While Cyril prepared the tea, Roger wandered about. He leaned into Cyril's study to have a look. An array of computer monitors displaying mathematical formulas and circuitry diagrams glowed in the waning light. Stacks of books and research papers cluttered the large ornate desk. Roger was about to have a closer look when he heard the clink of china. He returned to the sitting room.

"Here we are," said Cyril, and placed the silver platter on the coffee table. Cyril poured Claudia a cup of tea and proceeded to add the sugar and milk, just as she liked. Some things were similar between sisters. "Roger?"

"Oh, none for me, thanks," said Roger as he continued to pace.

Cyril positioned himself even closer to Claudia. Being in her proximity was intoxicating. "So, does the Inspector need me for anything?"

"He said he thought it best not to bother you, being the recluse that you are." Claudia rolled her eyes. Her crossed leg bounced lightly on her knee. Cyril smiled.

"But how can I be a recluse when I entertain such captivating company?"

Claudia blushed. Roger, although thick-headed at times, was not unobservant. He cleared his throat. "Claudia, dear, we should be going. We have a long drive ahead of us."

"That's not till tomorrow," she said.

"Are you staying in town?" asked Cyril.

"Yes," said Roger. "But we'll be leaving first thing in the morning."

Claudia placed the tea on the table and stood. "Well, I guess we should be going." She shot Roger a look.

"It was so nice of you to stop by," said Cyril. "I wish it had been under better circumstances."

"So do I," said Claudia.

Cyril escorted them to the front door.

"Goodbye, Cyril."

"Goodbye, Claudia. Safe travels."

Roger provided a cursory nod. He may have even grumbled under his breath, Cyril could not be sure. When they at last drove away, Cyril closed the door. He whistled. The boys came running and were at his feet. "I have a job for you," Cyril said. The two boys danced with excitement.

CYRIL'S CAR BACKED out of the garage, red lights illuminating the dark like lipstick in a bad dream about infidelity. The car came to a stop on the gravel drive. Its front wheels turned slowly, incrementally, then the car began to roll forward. Headlights flicked on. Inside: the figure of a man, too upright to be comfortable, head lolled against the head rest, as if asleep. The car rolled down the long sweeping drive to the driveway's entrance,

passing between the twin stone columns, and turned toward town.

It was a familiar dream.

There were hands at his feet, hands gripping the steering wheel even though his arms were limp at his side. All Cyril had to do was envision where he wanted to go and the car took him there. When he approached his destination, the car slowed and pulled onto the side of the road. He could see the motel in the distance, its sign flickering in the night like a cheap television set. The car door opened and he was suddenly on the ground. The smells of gasoline and tar flared his nostrils. He moved rapidly like a nocturnal animal on a scent trail. At last, he reached the motel and skirted around the building, listening for voices, stopping when he recognized the one he was after.

"There's something not right about that fellow."

"Oh, how my sister adored him. And he, her."

"That's what I'm afraid of."

"Afraid of what?"

"I saw the way he looked at you."

"Don't be ridiculous."

"There's something not right, I tell you. How does he manage alone like that? He must have help."

"He has a boy deliver groceries once a week. There is also a nurse that stops in for monthly check-ups. He is a brilliant man who likes his independence."

"You sound like you admire him."

"I do."

"Even after he killed your sister?"

"That's not what happened."

"Well, I don't trust him."

"You're jealous."

"And you can't look me in the eye and tell me you don't have feelings for him!"

After that, there was a long pause followed by the sound of a door slamming.

"I'm going out for a smoke."

WHEN ROGER STEPPED outside into the cool night air it was a welcome relief. He casually lit a cigarette. He couldn't help but think that his life was a sham. He was married to a woman who didn't love him, at least not to the degree he wanted. Perhaps he just wasn't successful or educated enough for her fine tastes. His lips tugged on the cigarette in anger. He heard the faint crackle of burning paper. He also heard the sudden rustle of something scurrying through the leaves. His eyes peered across the darkened landscape that surrounded the isolated motel.

What he saw were two rabbits bounding away, heading toward the road. Only these were like no rabbits he'd ever seen. If he was not mistaken, they appeared hairless and headless.

A chill ran up his spine and the cigarette dropped from his mouth. He bent to pick it up. If the strange sighting wasn't enough, there came the distant sound of a car door shutting, and an engine starting. It was really too dark to tell, but Roger thought he heard a car with its lights off slowly drive away.

THE DREAM BROUGHT Cyril home again, the car jockeying back into place in the carriage shed. The hands helping him into his wheelchair and navigating it inside, where he eventually arrived at his bedroom. The dream ended abruptly with a frenzy of doorbell rings and pounding on the front door.

Cyril awoke. It was the middle of the night. He slid out of bed into his chair and wheeled into the hallway. The pounding persisted, followed by several loud shouts. "I know you're in there, Cyril! I know what you've done!" Cyril turned the outside light on and opened the door.

"Roger? To what do I owe the pleasure?" The tone of Cyril's voice was anything but cordial.

"You know damned well why I'm here. You think you have everyone fooled. I saw you drive away from the motel." The look in Roger's eyes was both determined and scared. It made him look feral, desperate.

"You saw me drive away?" Cyril laughed. "Roger—have you been drinking? As you can clearly see, I can't walk let alone drive. Please, it's late."

Roger pointed his finger. "It was you. I checked the Bentley, in the shed. The engine's still warm."

"Go home, Roger. Sleep it off."

Roger shook his head, his eyes searching beyond Cyril into the depths of the mansion. "I don't know what you've got cooked up in there, and I don't know how you're doing it, but there's something not right. The desecrations at the cemetery ... somehow you're connected. I'm going to the authorities. I wonder what a search of your precious mansion will reveal?" Roger walked away then, his nerve heightened. He was acting like a man who felt he had finally one-upped his rival.

"I wouldn't do that, Roger." Cyril's eyes rolled up into his head and his hands began to dance on the wheelchair's armatures. Thump. Thump. Thump. Tap. Tap. Thump. Tap. Tap. The boys came running, followed by a half dozen others. Moments later, they poured from the mansion's entrance like rats escaping a fire. Only they were running to put a fire out. They caught up with Roger just as he slipped behind the driver's wheel of his car. Roger flailed and screamed as he attempted to fight them off, but each scream became more and more muffled, until he no longer made a sound.

Cyril sat in the doorway, feeling it all, experiencing it all, contorting and spasming as if suffering a violent seizure. Then the boys were climbing up onto his lap, their fingers twitching, seeking approval, while the others waited at his feet, waiting for their master's voice.

Cyril regained his composure. Sweat beaded on his brow. "Good boys." He stroked the one hand, then the other. Tap tap. Tap tap. "Now, we have some work to do."

The boys scrambled off his lap with renewed excitement, dancing in place like children about to burst.

HOURS LATER, the boys arrived home dirty and torn. There were briar scratches on their skin and blisters on their fingertips. They had "walked" nearly two miles through thick underbrush, nearly drowned in a woodland stream, and once had to hide in a hollow stump to avoid being plucked up by an owl.

Cyril had sensed it all. Just as he had sensed/directed the boys to drive Roger's car back along the route that led to the motel, finding the proper spot to drive off the road—through a guide rail and down into a ravine.

Cyril took the boys to the basement and patched them up with antibiotic cream and matching band-aids. They ran off to play as soon as Cyril said the magic words: "All better." As he was about to head upstairs, to prepare for the inquiries that were sure to follow come morning, Cyril heard a thumping from inside the cabinet. It was Camille, she was out of her container and raised on her hind wrist, tapping on the glass with her fingers.

Cyril wheeled over to the cabinet and opened the door. Camille leapt onto his chest and slapped his face. He felt an immediate flush of shame. The boys stopped mid-play to observe. Camille's fingers flexed with anger.

"I take it you disapprove?" said Cyril, quickly recovering from the embarrassment of such a public display. "But why am I surprised? You were always prone to emotional outbursts." He stared at her, the next generation microchip proving his hypothesis of total autonomy. He smiled then as she continued her demonstrative behavior, clicking and stomping her fingers. Her skin even turned red with rage. At last, she calmed, sitting with her back to him.

Cyril needed to keep in mind that he couldn't reprimand her the way he could the others. Camille appeared to be able to employ the best of both worlds: symbiosis and independence. She also must have sensed what was happening when Roger needed to be stopped. And as a free thinker, she also needed to react in the only way she knew how—the way the old Camille would have if she were still alive. It was truly an amazing thing to watch, and Cyril felt an intense love for this new Camille, and an unparalleled pride with both his accomplishment and her seeming rebirth.

"Camille?"

She didn't turn. She didn't even acknowledge.

Cyril smiled again. "Camille, please. I'm sorry you had to experience this awful business. But we are under siege. The world outside will not understand what I've done and why." He reached out and stroked her back with his finger. "I did it for you Camille. I did it for us."

She turned then, spinning on her wrist. She flexed her fingers like a spider and tapped out a Morse code message that he could not misinterpret.

I HATE YOU! I HATE WHAT YOU HAVE DONE! I WOULD RATHER DIE THAN BE WITH YOU!

She pointed to her container. She wanted to go back.

When Cyril lifted her up he could feel her recoil in his grasp. She curled up in the corner of her container and proceeded to spasm with a subtle shuddering of muscle and tendon, as if sobbing.

Cyril gently closed the cabinet door and wheeled toward the elevator, deep in thought. It's just the shock of her newfound surroundings, her newfound existence, Cyril assumed. She'll be more amenable once she realizes the rare and beautiful opportunity that has been bestowed upon her.

Cyril whistled and the boys scrambled to get into the elevator before the door closed.

IN THE STUDY, bathed in the glow of the computer screens, Cyril dozed in his chair. His jaw hung open and a thin ribbon of saliva connected it to his shoulder. In his dreams there were hands. So many hands. Slender and sleek and gnarled and calloused. They danced and slapped and poked and pulled. He smiled in his slumber, as he fell back into a pile of hands that rubbed and massaged his face and chest. A pair of hands, lowered a crown onto his head, made of finger bones and sinew. The hands marched to the edge of the room, lining like soldiers. They extended their index fingers and held them above the floor. Cyril sat up and straightened his crown. He stood and adjusted his coat and slacks. He smiled as the first hand, Hers, began to tap her finger upon the floor. It was followed by the next and the next until it was a drumming wave that grew and squeezed his lungs like a small bird in a simpleton's grip. He knelt and looked at Her. He smiled and like a scorpion's tail, she thrust her thumb into his eye. The other hands rushed him then and began pinching and scratching his flesh.

Cyril awoke slick with sweat and flushed

with desire. Exhausted, he wheeled himself to bed.

TAP. TAP. CLICK-CLICK. (the silence broken at last)

Camille sent her message to the rest of group. *We need to leave.*

There came a murmuring from the other containers, specimens collected over the last several years, prototypes: a seamstress, a carpenter, a pastry chef, a dentist. A series of successive thumps and finger snaps followed.

But we can't leave. He is our master.

He is not mine. And I am not his. We need to leave before—

Before what?

Before he is taken away.

Taken away? To where? By whom?

People. People who won't like what he has done.

What has he done?

He created us.

There was a long pause that was eventually broken by a response both loud and in unison that shook the cabinet: *We will stop them!*

The murmuring persisted but Camille was able to block it out, just as she was able to block Cyril from reading her thoughts. She was indeed on her own, and she needed to end this, even if it meant ending herself in the process.

THE FOLLOWING MORNING two policemen arrived.

Did Roger visit the night before?

Did Roger call to say he was going to visit?

Did Roger hint at anything that might explain why he was out on the road at that hour of the evening?

Cyril answered their questions as best he could, with as much concern and sadness such an unfortunate event required.

At last, as Cyril was seeing the policemen to the door, he said this: "Perhaps it's nothing, but during Roger and Claudia's visit, Roger did appear to be a bit jealous."

"How so?" asked one of the officers.

"As her brother-in-law, I've known Claudia for over twenty years, and we chatted it up as if it were old times. I think we even held hands at one point. I believe Roger may have felt a bit put out by this. Perhaps Roger was on his way here to settle some kind of score?"

"Was there a score to settle?" the other officer asked.

"Absolutely not. Though my wife may be dead, I am still in love with her. There is no other woman for me."

The officers regarded the wheelchair from which Cyril spoke and nodded. "Thank you for your time, Mr. Von Foerster."

No sooner had the policemen gone, Claudia arrived by taxi. Cyril showed her to the sitting room, offering her tea and sugar cookies, but all Claudia could do was sob. At last, Cyril offered her a box of tissues.

Claudia sat clutching Cyril's hands with hands that were hauntingly familiar. He felt terrible for Claudia. If she felt even a fraction of what he felt when Camille had died, there was no consoling her, no words she needed to hear, because there were no words to describe the loss of a loved one. It is as if a piece of one's heart is torn from the chest and the gap it leaves cannot be filled.

"Claudia?"

"Yes, Cyril?" She looked at him with eyes glistening.

"Is there someone you would like for me to call? Someone you can stay with?"

"Roger's parents are in transit, but they won't arrive until tomorrow." She looked at Cyril with utter despair, a boat cast adrift by the vagaries of the ocean current.

"You are welcome to stay here," said Cyril. "I am unconcerned with appearances. You should not be alone. Let me show you to your room."

Cyril led Claudia to the base of a grand stairway where he paused, gazing upward at the majestic second floor balcony. After the accident he chose not to have the elevator access the second floor. There was no need.

"Sorry, I can't take you all the way, but there are several bedrooms from which to choose," he said. "There are fresh linens in the closet. There is also food in the kitchen should you get hungry. Please, make yourself at home."

"Thank you, Cyril." Again, Claudia gripped his hand in thanks, her skin warm to the touch. Cyril felt a sudden blossoming of emotions, but it was quickly scythed through by a wave of panic and fear. Tap. Tap. Thump. Thump. Tap-tap. Tap-tap.

"Cyril? Cyril! Speak to me!"

The seizure was brief but enough to cause Claudia alarm.

"I'm fine," Cyril said. He cleared his throat and wheeled away, breaking their connection. "I'm sorry but there is some work I need to attend to."

"See you at dinner?" Claudia offered, but Cyril had already disappeared into the depths of the mansion.

Claudia scaled the grand stairway, her mind numb from the day's events. She realized she was tired, after all, and sleep was likely the best elixir her body needed.

WHEN CYRIL REACHED the laboratory all of the hands were obediently at home in their respective containers—even the boys. All except one.

Click-click. *She is gone*, said one.

We asked her to stay, said another.

To help us fight, said another.

She is ungrateful, said still another.

Cyril looked at the empty container and nodded. His admiration for her, however, was outweighed by his need to stop her from leaving. *No, not ungrateful*, thought Cyril. *Scared. Scared of what will become of us. What will become of her. We must find her before it's too late!*

Cyril opened all of the containers and set them free. They spilled out of the cabinet like clumsy spiders, clamoring over each other to be first to the elevator.

THAT EVENING a summer storm raged across the region. Rain pelted the earth in sheets, and thunder shook the mansion to its very foundation. Claudia awoke to a darkened room, the power having quit at some point, surrendering to the violent weather. She got up and tried to orient herself. She descended the stairs and wandered the hallways as lightning flashed like hordes of paparazzi gathered at the windows hoping to catch a glimpse of the grieving widow. The mansion was part museum, part

mausoleum. Claudia couldn't believe her sister had lived in such a place. When Camille was alive, she used to write letters describing how she would get lost in her own home. There were hallways leading to rooms that hadn't heard footsteps in years. These were the rooms Cyril and Camille's children were supposed to occupy.

"Cyril?" she called out. But there was no reply but the thunder.

At last, she happened upon Cyril's study, which was dark but for several computer monitors still on battery backup, casting a cool light where Cyril worked. Curious, she approached the large imposing desk and looked at what was on the screens. There were complicated-looking circuitry diagrams on one monitor; anatomical models on another. The models were of a human hand, 3-D mapping of the nervous system displayed like the fingers of a great river and all its tributaries.

As Claudia stood stunned at the discovery there came a scrabbling sound. At first, it was difficult to distinguish amid the lashing of the rain and rumblings of thunder, but it was enough to turn Claudia around in search of the noise. She was reminded of Mitzy, a miniature Yorkshire Terrier she and Roger once had. She always knew when Mitzy needed her nails trimmed by the little click-clacks they made on the hardwood floor.

A small white creature hopped up onto Cyril's desk and Claudia shrieked. She stepped back and nearly stumbled over Cyril's chair. But then the creature "stood up" in the light of the computer monitors and appeared to bow as if in greeting.

Claudia couldn't believe she was even considering that what she was witnessing before her to be real and not some phantasmagorical nightmare conjured by the stress of recent events. Because the creature before her wasn't a creature at all, but a hand. A human hand. A slender, feminine hand that was all too familiar.

"Camille?"

Camille tapped on the desktop and pointed. Tap-tap. Thump-thump.

"I don't understand," said Claudia, drawing closer, wanting to reach out, but afraid to.

Camille tapped again, more urgently, pointing to a place in the dark of the room. She tapped so hard blood oozed from a split fingernail.

"*Claudia?*"

Cyril's voice cut through the darkness. His call was followed by several lightning flashes and a loud thunder crack. As the thunder subsided, she heard many click-clacks in the outer hallway, converging on the study. The hair on the back of her neck rose. She instinctively scooped up Camille's hand and held it close, as a flood of white rats preceded Cyril's wheelchair, as he slowly rolled into the room. "I see you've found her," he said. This was not the Cyril Claudia knew. The look in his eye was inhuman, deranged.

He whistled then, and the rats at his feet—which were, in fact, disembodied hands from the nearly two dozen corpses he'd desecrated—scrambled up his legs and onto his body, creating a grotesque sleeve of interwoven fingers and fists that lifted him upright, out of the chair. He took one teetering step forward and outstretched his hand. "Give her to me!" he said.

Claudia bolted. She ran to where Camille had pointed to in the dark. There was a pocket door in the study that led to a rear hallway, and Claudia pushed through it, slamming the door shut behind her. She ran, one hand clutching Camille to her chest, the other feeling her way along. The hallway led to the kitchen. Through the kitchen was the sitting room in which she and Roger sat with Cyril just days earlier. And just outside the sitting room was the front foyer. She didn't know how but she knew she had to leave, even if it meant running out into the storm. When she reached the front foyer Camille's finger stretched again, pointing to a place alongside the front door. Lightning flashed and Claudia spotted a glint of metal dangling from a leather fob: the keys to the Bentley.

But she had to hurry. The ambling footsteps of Cyril's circus troupe of grotesqueries was approaching. "Claudia? Where are you?" There was now a maniacal playfulness in Cyril's voice, as if surrender was inevitable.

Claudia grabbed the keys and unlocked the front door. The door swung from her grasp, sucked open by a sudden wind gust. Rain flew sideways, pelting her legs.

"Claudia, stop!" Cyril stood in the foyer. "Please, she is everything to me."

"She was once everything to me," said Claudia. She squeezed Camille's hand tight, and she felt Camille squeeze back.

"Get her!" Cyril shouted, and he collapsed as if his bones had been turned to gelatin. The hands that supported him had disengaged and now collectively swarmed toward Claudia.

Claudia ran for the carriage shed.

Cold rain soaked her hair and filled her shoes. Lightning flashed with a ferocity she had never experienced first hand. When she reached the car, the lead hand was literally nipping at her heels. It scrabbled up her leg and leapt onto her wrist as she reached for the car door handle, but she swatted it away as if it were a giant bug. She quickly opened the car door and tossed Camille inside. She then slid behind the wheel and slammed the door shut.

But the door wouldn't close; there were multiple fingers preventing it from sealing. Claudia held the door and slipped the key into the ignition, but the car wouldn't start. A warning chime told her that the door was ajar.

By now, the hands had swarmed the windshield and were throwing themselves against the glass. Claudia again tried to close the door, this time using both hands. She opened it briefly before slamming it shut. Severed fingers fell like pieces of rotted fruit, littering the carpet beneath her feet. She tried the ignition again and the engine came to life.

Claudia reversed the Bentley out the carriage shed, turning sharply and slamming the brakes. The car fishtailed on the rain-soaked drive. Most of the hands that were on the windshield slid off, and those that managed to hang on were quickly jettisoned when Claudia turned the wipers on.

The last image Claudia saw in the rearview mirror was Cyril lying in the mud of the driveway, arm outstretched as if pleading for her to stop, and then the hands blanketing him, lifting him up and carrying him back inside the mansion.

SIX MONTHS LATER.

Shortly after she fled the nightmare at Cyril Von Foerster's estate, Claudia bought a modest villa in her native country of France and retired there to contemplate the course of her life. Needless to say, Roger's death had provided her with a comfortable existence. The events of that night never made the papers. Claudia considered telling her story but quickly dismissed the thought. Who would believe her? Besides, she had someone she needed to protect.

But on this day, all of that was inconsequential. She had a new home, a new life, even a new name, changed from her former married name of McVane to LaFortune, a name chosen from her mother's side of the family from a few generations past. She had the fresh morning air and the beautiful French countryside. She sat on the veranda enjoying the moment, listening to the soothing scrape of a paint brush against canvas, and the gentle tap of that brush against a glass bowl.

"Oh, that is so beautiful," she said, admiring Camille's latest. "You never cease to amaze me."

Camille sat on a small table wielding a modified paint brush, shortened to accommodate her diminutive size. She was putting the finishing strokes on another in a series of water color landscapes. Claudia still didn't understand how Camille did it. She assumed it had something to do with their connection. Camille needed Claudia beside her in order to "see." Perhaps her advanced circuitry allowed her to absorb electrical signals the way a television converted a stream of transmissions into an image. All Claudia knew was this new series of paintings had caught the attention of a handsome young artist she'd become acquainted with, and a show was already in the works at a local gallery. Claudia still felt a bit uncomfortable as the face behind the paintings, but she felt life had dealt Camille an undeserving blow and she was entitled to every bit of glory her meticulous hand could create. In another life Claudia believed Camille would have been the talk of the town. It was the least she could do.

In fact, the show was tonight. But, right now, Claudia didn't want to think about that. Life was just too grand to ignore the moment right in front of her.

NOT FAR FROM Claudia's villa, a black sedan pulled over onto the side of the road. A man dressed in a wide hat and trench coat held a piece of paper in his hand. It was a flyer for one of the local art galleries advertising a show by a new artist by the name of Claudia LaFortune. Miss LaFortune wasn't pictured in the flyer but her watercolors were. Watercolors that looked remarkably familiar. Watercolors that bore the signature style that could only have been produced by one person. Or one hand.

The man smiled. "We've found her," he said.

There came a rustling from the back seat. A hundred fingers rose up onto the seat cushion and clung to the headrests.

With the help of several other hands guiding his movements, the man started the Bentley's engine and put the gear shift into drive. Tap-tap. Thump-thump.

She's coming home.

"Awake in the Hands of Solitude" originally appeared in the 2019 anthology Machinations and Mesmerism: Tales Inspired by ETA Hoffmann.

As a child, Kurt Newton was weaned on episodes of The Twilight Zone and The Outer Limits, and Chiller Theater (which showed many of the classic sci-fi horror movies of the '50s and '60s), laying the groundwork for his fertile imagination. His stories have appeared in numerous publications over the last twenty years, including Weird Tales, Weirdbook, Space & Time, Dark Discoveries, Vastarien, Nightscript, Black Infinity and Cosmic Horror Monthly. He lives in Connecticut.

John Boden lives a stone's throw from Three Mile Island with his wonderful wife and sons. He likes heavy metal and is known for his ferocious sideburns. A baker by day, he spends his off time watching old television reruns or writing unique fiction such as his collection, Dominoes; two novellas, Spungunion and Jedi Summer; and a variety of collaborative efforts including Detritus in Love, Out Behind the Barn, Rattlesnake Kisses and Cattywampus.

THE LAST SIGHTING OF BLACK DOG

BY TOM ENGLISH

For he was speechless, ghastly, wan,
Like him of whom the story ran,
Who spoke the spectre hound in man.
—Sir Walter Scott
The Lay of the Last Minstrel, Canto Sixth, XXVI

THE HAGGARD OLD MAN SITTING ALONE AT THE COUNTER OF MILLIE'S ALL-NIGHT DINER PAID NO ATTENTION as I quietly took the stool next to him. "Excuse me," I said softly, "My name's Carl Thatcher. Aren't you Sol Pruzhansky?"

He turned his head and studied me for several moments. "What the hell do *you* want? Why aren't you home in bed like everyone else?"

"I was hoping to talk with you. A friend of mine said you come here often."

"I'm an insomniac, Mister—what's your name again?"

"Thatcher," I said, extending my right hand. "Please call me Carl." He hesitated before giving it a reluctant shake.

"So what did you want to talk about?"

"I'm writing a book about the local history of Leyden Township."

"No kidding." He turned back to the counter.

"You wrote for the *Ledger*, I used to read your column."

"Congratulations," he said dully, staring into his half-empty cup of coffee.

"I understand you've lived in the historic district for close to four decades."

"With my wife. I moved out almost three years ago, right after Sofia passed away. Too many memories there." He took a sip of coffee. "I live in town now. Just down the street. But who cares?"

"I'm really sorry about your wife, Mr. Pruzhansky," I said. "I was hoping you could tell me about Black Dog."

His coffee cup clattered against the counter, sloshing the inky contents across the varnished wood. "Oh you were?" he huffed. He started to say something else but stopped.

He yanked several napkins from the dispenser and began mopping up the tiny puddle. "Hell, why not?" he said finally. "Maybe it'll do something to ease this damn depression. Did that friend of yours also tell you I suffer from clinical depression? That's why I don't sleep at night."

He motioned for the waitress sitting behind the counter at the far end to refill his coffee. "Black," he told her.

"*Black*," he then directed to me, his voice

shaking, "like all my nights without Sofia. Black like the bitterness that's eating me up inside.

"Black," he said again, slowly, "like a dog named Churchill."

I couldn't understand why Pruzhansky got so upset over an old dog story, especially one he'd written about dozens of times in his newspaper columns, but I quickly pulled out a small tape recorder. "May I? I was never very good at taking notes."

He shrugged. "Suit yourself."

"CHURCHILL WAS A STRAY; a big shaggy Newfoundland that wandered into downtown Leyden about twelve years ago. He was close to the size of a calf, with tangled fur that had never known the touch of a brush, and huge green eyes that sparkled with intelligence; a gentle brute, with an air of dignity that belied his scruffiness, and a strange magnetism that tended to draw out the best in people. He could bring a smile to the biggest grouch; brighten the day of the worst cynic.

"He used to roam the streets looking for handouts, coming and going as he pleased between the storefronts lining Monument Avenue. On any given day, had you cared to venture around to the back entrances of some of these establishments, you could have seen the owners feeding him—everything from half of the morning donut to a rib-eye steak dinner. It wasn't long before 'Black Dog' became the unofficial mascot of every shop and restaurant in town.

"Ever notice the sign above Cooke's Hardware? There's a silhouette of a black dog. And look at that," Pruzhansky said, nodding at the clock hanging above the diner's cash register: the clock face was adorned with the profile of a black dog.

"Churchill was a favorite with the shoppers, too, especially with their kids. He rarely allowed anyone to get close enough to touch him, except for kids, who were able to pet and even hug the dog.

"Most mornings you could see Churchill following a group of kids on their way to Harding Elementary School. Actually, I believe it was the kids who were following the dog—which wasn't a bad thing. Churchill was incredibly street smart. One time I watched him sit on the corner of a busy intersection and wait for the green light. Even then, he turned his head in both directions before trotting across the highway. It was uncanny. For a while, parents stopped walking their kids to school, confident their children were just as safe with Black Dog. Steve Fortunato once stood up at a PTA meeting and half-jokingly said he thought Black Dog was some kind of guardian angel sent to watch over the kids ... the way Nana watched over the Darling children in *Peter Pan*."

The old man paused to sip his coffee. "Unfortunately, Churchill had one big strike against him: he had no collar, no tags, no license. Leyden has stringent leash and license laws. So it wasn't long before the dog popped up on the radar of Animal Control and they officially branded him a 'nuisance animal.' It didn't matter. He was too fast for the local dogcatchers. Too fast and a whole lot smarter.

"Didn't stop them from trying, though. Repeatedly. But Churchill was pretty wily; he could tell the difference between the ice cream truck and a dogcatcher's van. When the former drove down the street, he greeted it along with the rest of the kids—and yes, he always got a free treat. I'd watch that old softy Joe Watkins stand at the back of his truck, holding a vanilla Popsicle and grinning ear to ear while the dog licked at it unhurriedly.

"It was a different story when the Animal Control officer drove around the block. In fact, the dogcatcher was lucky to get even a glimpse of the dog. Churchill seemed to have a sixth sense. He must have been able to hear the van—or smell the driver—long before it rounded the corner."

Pruzhansky laughed unexpectedly. "Sometimes Churchill decided to hang around and take in a little sport. He'd approach the truck, wagging that matted tail of his, just long enough for the guy to get out. That's when the fun started. Churchill always stayed close to the truck, and the guy would run circles around it trying to catch the dog. It was like a Keystone Cops routine, and it never failed to draw an appreciative crowd of spectators who cheered for Black Dog and howled with laughter at his red-faced pursuer.

"When the poor guy felt he'd suffered enough humiliation for one day and was about to leave, Churchill would lie down, as though he, too, had enough. This always served to rekindle the dogcatcher's hopes of success. The man would slowly approach the dog while making kissing sounds and uttering syrupy phrases totally out of character. But when he got within a hand's breadth of the animal, Churchill would bolt beneath the truck and exit running on the other side, his ears flapping in the breeze, his tongue waving from the corner of his mouth.

"The hunt for Black Dog never ended there. Those feeble attempts were simply viewed as skirmishes lost in what was to become a long and much publicized campaign against the town celebrity. I wrote about a few of them, including the time they baited and set coyote traps at strategic places where the dog had been seen. But Churchill never took the bait. He feasted at the back-doors of a dozen eateries, and he wasn't about to stick his head into a noose.

"I think that initially the dog was simply an embarrassment to the city, a highly visible emblem of the incompetence of the Department of Animal Control. But it wasn't long before things became political. Soon afterwards, the mayor decided to turn the city's problems with Black Dog into a personal vendetta.

"I realize now, despite his outward appearance of success, Jeff Brooks was miserable on the inside. His wife had left him for another man. His daughter was withdrawing into a world of Wicca websites and Internet chat groups. But he only had himself to blame; he was consumed with political ambitions—had his eye on the state senate for a while—and I guess his wife and kid just felt left out.

"Brooks was elected mayor at the un-heard-of age of thirty-one—and of a rapidly growing hub of manufacturing and tourism. He was also the head of a lucrative legal practice that allowed him to live quite comfortably. But after all his early triumphs he suddenly saw his world spiraling down in flames. He'd watched his helpmate walk out the front door, his child retreat further and further from her father; he'd read the gossip columns of his hometown newspaper, heard the door to his hopes and dreams slamming shut. He no longer felt he had control over his own life. You might even say Brooks felt ... trapped."

Pruzhansky shook his head. "Isn't it funny how we resent the freedom and happiness of others? Deep down, we hate to see anyone or any thing having a better time of it than we are. Black Dog, as the local news had officially dubbed him, was rapidly becoming a symbol of independence, of the carefree life ... in a society overburdened with concerns.

"Black Dog came and went as he pleased. He didn't need to answer to anybody because he didn't belong to anybody. We, on the other hand, all belong to something. Maybe it's our careers, or our pastimes. Or some unhealthy relationship we get trapped into. An expensive vacation home or a new sports car. We think we own these things, but in the end, they own us.

"Black Dog symbolized what we all long for: no problems, no worries, no sadness." Pruzhansky leaned closer against the counter and ran his hand through his thinning hair. "No wonder someone wanted him picked up."

I nodded slowly, remembering the words of an old Chris Rea song: ...*No one knows that black dog better than I; When I see his running I can see me, teeth in the collar and he's tearing it free....*

"Churchill eventually worked his way up to the Old North End, the historic neighborhood where Sofia and I lived. When I saw him wandering our local sidewalks and gardens I was thrilled. *Despite* what followed his arrival, despite all the pain and emptiness I now feel, I'm honest enough to admit that I loved that mangy hound.

"I'd already written eight columns about him, in which I championed the dog's freedom. I had also made the field supervisor of Animal Control the butt of a long-running joke. That's the sort of thing that sells newspapers, and my column was *very* popular—

that is, with everyone but Mayor Brooks. Jeff never missed an opportunity to criticize my articles. And he got plenty of opportunities—the man lived next door to me."

"I knew Brooks had lived in the historic district," I said, "but I didn't realize just how close."

"Close enough for Sofia to try and reach out to the daughter, Abby. Close enough for the father to become a real pain in the ass." Pruzhansky smirked. "Close enough for me to see how aggravated Brooks got, when he pulled back the curtains each morning just in time to see Black Dog taking a crap on his well-manicured lawn!"

I tried hard not to smile. The old man's recollections of a simple local legend had veered unexpectedly into deeply personal and sensitive territory.

Pruzhansky absently ran his fingers around the rim of his coffee cup. "The first appearance of Black Dog in the historic area was at Leyden Parish, an old Anglican church. It's part of the Episcopal Diocese now, overseen by the Reverend Craig Reynolds. The dog came scratching at the door of the rectory late one evening ... a clear, warm night in May ... not a cloud in the sky. But the dog was cold and dripping wet.

"Reynolds didn't give this a second thought; it *had* been raining earlier that day. He knelt and looked into the dog's luminous green eyes and said, 'Hello, Stranger. What brings you to these parts?' He brought his unexpected guest inside, found an old towel and dried the dog's tangled coat.

"That night, Churchill—or rather *Stranger*, I should say—slept before the fireplace in Reynolds' room. The next morning, however, the dog was gone. But again, Reynolds didn't make much of this. Leyden Parish employed a full-time grounds keeper to maintain the gardens, and twice a week Mrs. Cuthbert went in to clean both the church and the rectory. Reynolds assumed one of them had let the dog out. And when he took his morning walk through the gardens, he spotted Stranger lying peacefully amid the gravestones and monuments on the east side of the church.

"What was remarkable was that a six-foot wrought iron fence surrounded the cemetery, and the gate had been closed and locked the night before. Reynolds was about to unlock the gate and bring Stranger out when a voice behind him said, 'Give me a minute to get my gloves on.' It was an Animal Control officer walking briskly up the path, holding a short pole topped with a noose. A can of Mace clung to his belt.

"Reynolds said, 'That won't be necessary, the dog's not disturbing anything.'

"The man tucked the pole under his arm and pulled on his gloves, saying 'Doesn't matter, he's got no license.'

"'Who called you?' Reynolds asked.

"'A tourist. Said a dog had got locked in the cemetery. It's a real stroke of luck. We've been trying to catch this one for months. You open the gate and stay out here until I get the noose around him.'

"'I hope you're not going to spray something in the dogs face,' Reynolds said, unlocking the gate slowly. 'He's very gentle. Let *me* go in and get him.'

"The man walked through the gate and shut it behind him. 'Against regulations,' he said. 'You gotta stay out here.'

"Reynolds jokingly told me, later that week, he had to do some serious repentance for entertaining mean thoughts about 'troublesome tourists and daft dogcatchers.' But he needn't have worried. After several minutes of pursuing Stranger between the tombstones, the man finally cornered the dog in a tight space near the back of the fence, between a thick hedgerow, an ancient oak, and a statue of Saint Francis of Assisi. Stranger plopped down on the wet grass a few paces from the fence and waited patiently while the man removed the Mace from his belt. Then suddenly, the dog sprang up and bounded across the fence.

"Reynolds said Stranger had cleared the spiked rail at the top of the fence with ease. A six-foot fence, mind you, and flat-footed—no running start!

"Stranger ran toward the church, and Reynolds met the dog at the front door. 'Okay, Houdini,' he laughed, 'Get inside, quick!' So Stranger padded in and promptly made himself at home on one of the antique pews.

"When the dogcatcher came to the

church door, he found it locked. When he knocked, Reynolds greeted the man but refused to let him enter. 'I'm afraid you have no jurisdiction here,' the Reverend said, grinning. 'The dog has claimed the right of sanctuary.'"

I smiled. "That's a wonderful anecdote."

"Yeah, but the guy from Animal Control was pissed. He made some calls, and it wasn't long before Mayor Brooks heard about it," Pruzhansky said. "You won't believe this, but later that day the sheriff came around to the rectory and served Reynolds with an arrest warrant. Brooks pushed to have the Reverend charged with 'contributing to a nuisance animal.'

"That bit of stupidity made the evening news. And of course, I wrote a scathing column about it. Brooks and various councilmen received dozens of irate phone calls. Steve Fortunato formed a 'Friends of Black Dog' committee, printed up some T-shirts, and marched in front of City Hall with a group of school kids. A few days later, the city dropped the charge, and Jeff Brooks visited the Reverend to apologize."

"Nuisance or not, the dog's a stray," Brooks explained to Reynolds. "I can't allow it to continue running wild. I have a responsibility to uphold city ordinances regarding these matters. And the citizens of Leyden have a responsibility to do their part in upholding the law. But when it comes to this dog I'm not getting any help."

"Laws are important, Jeff," Reynolds said, "But what about the higher law of love?"

Brooks realized the conversation was about to become theological, and simply said, "Again, Reverend, I apologize for singling you out to make a point. I know now I went too far. I guess I'm a little zealous when it comes to my work."

Reynolds put a hand on the man's shoulder and said, "Apology accepted. However, I do wish you were as zealous in your church attendance."

"I've been tied up on several projects," Brooks hedged. "Just not enough hours in the day."

"For your daughter's sake, I hope you can make some time soon. Abby used to stop by on her way home from school. I enjoyed our conversations. I believe she enjoyed them, too."

"You know how kids are, Reverend," Brooks said. "Abby's in high school now. She's probably meeting lots of new friends."

"I'd rest easier if I could be sure of that. My understanding is that she spends an inordinate amount of time indoors on the Internet."

"I bet Pruzhansky's nosy wife told you that," Brooks said irritably. "Just because Abby's doing a little research on Wicca doesn't mean she's going to hell, Reverend."

"Of course not," Reynolds said. "I'm actually not overly concerned about her research. But I am concerned she's spending too much time on social media. Believe it or not, I can fully understand Abby's curiosity about the supernatural. It's perfectly normal. Kids need to believe there's some magic still left in this troubled world of ours. However, I do think she could benefit from a little positive influence in her life. We have some excellent youth activities on Friday nights. I think Abby would enjoy the fellowship."

Pruzhansky took several gulps of lukewarm coffee. "Abby never made it to any of those church activities," he said. "Brooks never made any time for his daughter, and Black Dog never had any reason to leave the area.

"Obviously, none of this ever saw print. After all, I was writing about the colorful adventures of a carefree dog, not the troubled lives of a broken family. Hell, who wants to read about that?"

I nodded slowly.

"Churchill started making the rounds in the historic section of our neighborhood. The old folks adored him. When they were outdoors grilling, he was the guest of honor. When they threw a dinner party, the next morning the dog feasted on fancy hors d'oeuvres.

"My wife was crazy about him. When he finally came around to our backdoor, Sofia let out a little yelp. She'd never actually seen Black Dog until that morning. She brought out a pan of water and held it while the dog drank."

* * *

"ARE YOU CRYING?"

"He reminds me of my little Sasha," Sofia said, wiping her eyes. "Let's adopt him."

"I doubt we could keep him for very long. Besides, it wouldn't be fair. He's a free spirit. Black Dog belongs to everyone."

"Maybe he's a free spirit, but he doesn't seem to be in a hurry to leave us," she said. "Let's call him Spyridon.*"*

"That's no name for a dog! I want to call him Churchill.*"*

"Solomon Pruzhansky, where on earth did that *name come from?"*

"Winston Churchill suffered from deep depression. He often referred to it in his writings as his black dog.*"*

"You can't name a dog after such a great man."

"If Churchill could call his melancholia Black Dog, *then I can call this black dog* Churchill.*"*

"CHURCHILL NEVER ALLOWED Sofia to get *too* close. It was as though the dog was purposely keeping his distance ... until after...." Pruzhansky's voice trailed off.

"Often, when Sofia was gardening, and her back was to him, Churchill would quietly approach and brush against her. But when Sofia turned to him, the dog would walk away. I think that really saddened my wife, she wanted so much to be able to embrace him, to bury her face in that unkempt fur.

"Abby had also taken to Black Dog. That must have stuck in Brooks' craw. 'Look at him,' he said one day, while his daughter played on the lawn with Churchill. 'Acts like he owns the place.'

"'I think he's good for Abby; she seems rather gloomy these days,' I told him, as I watched the dog and girl play tug-of-war with a faded beach towel. 'I've never seen her having so much fun.'

"'I hate the sight of him,' Brooks said. 'He keeps me awake all night with that incessant barking of his.'

"That wasn't the first time Brooks had complained about the dog's barking, nor was it the last. And I always thought it strange, because Churchill didn't bark. At least, I'd never heard him bark ... or howl. I think Churchill was too dignified for that. Can't

say the same for Brooks; he was constantly yapping about something.

"Case in point, when he heard the dog was greeting sightseers who came to visit Leyden Church, or view the old homes along Magnolia Lane, Brooks said Black Dog was scaring away the tourists; that if it didn't stop, Churchill would succeed in destroying the town's tourism industry. Fortunately, none of the Historical Society's board members paid Brooks any mind.

"I'm sure the complaint about the dog barking was simply another excuse to get rid of Churchill. Or maybe he *had* heard barking. But it must have been some other dog in the neighborhood. Funny thing, though, our houses were pretty close together, divided by only a small grape arbor and a rose garden. And I never heard anything. I also knew, according to Reverend Reynolds, that the dog usually slept outside his door in the churchyard.

"As I watched Churchill frolicking with Abby, I asked Brooks, 'Instead of disliking the dog so much, why don't you try to get know him?'

"'I haven't been able to get anywhere near the brute,' he said.

"'Ha,' I said, 'I think you're scared of the dog.'

"'No, I'm not,' he said.

"But when I whistled to Churchill, Brooks quickly made an excuse about having to make some phone calls, and walked briskly up the steps and into his house. A few days later, Brooks paid another visit to Reverend Reynolds. Seems the mayor had been having nightmares. Or maybe they weren't nightmares."

"THERE'S SOMETHING not natural about that dog," Brooks told the Reverend. "For instance, Black Dog was full grown when he strayed into Leyden. A vet once told me the dog appeared to be about four to six years old. That was eight years ago. Does the dog look any older to you now?"

"No," Reynolds said, "but would he?"

"Newfoundlands have a life-expectancy of about fifteen years. That's if they get proper care. Black Dog has to be at least twelve by now. But there's no grey about the

muzzle. And he hasn't slowed down a bit. Animal Control still can't catch him."

"Stranger has stayed active all his life," Reynolds said. "It's kept him healthy. Just yesterday I watched him chase down a grown rabbit."

Brooks grimaced. "Tore it apart, huh?"

"No, Jeff, he actually let it go—after he sniffed it and nuzzled it about the ears. There's no aggression in Stranger, he just likes to play."

"I wish I had your confidence." Brooks said, before growing silent.

"What's bothering you, Jeff, is it Abby?"

"Reverend, you once said you deal in the supernatural. Well, there's something ... not natural about this dog."

"ACCORDING TO REYNOLDS, the mayor had gone white as a sheet. Brooks explained to him that every night before turning in, he was careful to lock and double-check all the doors and windows in the house. It was an obsession of his, in fact. And the night before, he had taken all his usual security measures. He was positive no one or no *thing* could have got in.

"Brooks went to the den to look over some city budget reports, and sat down in a corner, across the room from the fireplace. Before long, seated in an overstuffed wing chair, with the sound of the logs crackling softly in the grate, Brooks had nodded off, with papers strewn across his lap. He told the Reverend that a little after midnight he awoke from an unpleasant dream—something he couldn't remember the next day, but which had a very unsettling affect.

"He sat up in his chair and squinted at the fireplace. The flames had died out, and with the glare of the floor lamp behind him, he was unable to make out anything in the gloom at the opposite end of the room. But as his eyes began to slowly adjust he realized something was blocking his view of the grate. Otherwise, he should have been able to see the embers glowing amid the ashes.

"Brooks suddenly realized he could smell the unpleasant odor of wet dog hair, and he started to make out the shape of the thing crouching before the hearth. He said it was the silhouette of a huge animal, completely black except for two luminescent green eyes staring at him unblinkingly.

"Brooks was too scared to call out, too scared to move even an inch. He sat frozen in his chair all night long, fighting to keep his eyes open. He told Reynolds he'd watched the black dog for what seemed hours, until he could no longer focus and fell asleep again. When he awoke, the sun was pouring through the windows and the dog was gone."

"INTERESTING," Reverend Reynolds said, "but you could have been dreaming the whole night."

"This was no dream," Brooks huffed.

"I'm sure there's a simple explanation, though."

"I've heard things about black dogs. Myths, legends—call them what you want—about spectral dogs that hang around old churchyards."

"I'm familiar with all the legends. Churches were often thought to be liminal places, thresholds to the spirit world," Reynolds said, "because the veil separating life and death was thought to be thin there. The same was said of ancient lanes and trackways, crossroads and even the former sites of gallows.

"But if the veil between the material world and heaven is thinner here," Reynolds continued, "it's due to the spirituality of those who attend The Eucharist Service."

"I understand that seeing a black dog is a portent of death," Brooks said.

"If that's true then we're all in for it," Reynolds quipped.

"BROOKS GOT PRETTY aggravated at Reynolds' reluctance to take the business seriously. But the Reverend did share a few legends he'd picked up in his studies on the supernatural. One in particular, about an incident that took place in Peel's Castle, on the Isle of Man. It involved a large black dog with coarse fur that had been seen during the day in various parts of the structure. No one knew where the dog had come from; he didn't belong to anyone in the castle.

"At the end of each day, after the fortress gate had been locked, the sentries would return to the guardroom located just inside the great entrance. When the candles were lighted and a fire was burning on the hearth, the dog would walk silently out of the dark passage and lie down before the fire. All through the night the dog would watch the sentries, not straying an inch from his station before the hearth, his eyes glowing green in the candlelight.

"Night after night the dog held this strange, mute vigil. At daybreak, he would get up and disappear back down the passage. The sentries were terrified of the dog, sensing the creature was not mortal. When the dog was in the room they would speak in hushed tones. They would avoid using coarse words or saying anything bad about anyone.

"The sentries used to take turns carrying the large iron key to the Captain of the Guard each night after locking the gate; but after the first appearance of the black dog, none of the men cared to walk down the dark passageway alone. When the hour came to carry the key to their leader, two men would always go together.

"There was one man, however, who decided to defy the dog. He'd had too much to drink, and began to boast that he wasn't afraid to walk down the passage alone. To show his bravery, he declared that he alone would deliver the key, even though it wasn't his turn. And he dared the dog to stop him.

"He boasted, 'I'll know whether you be dog or devil.'

"His friends tried to stop him, but the man grabbed the key and hurried out into the gloomy passageway. The black dog, who on previous nights had never stirred from his place before the fire, got up slowly and followed the sentry into the darkness. The dog was never seen again after that night, but the next morning the sentry was found dead. There were no wounds on the body, no signs of violence. Apparently, the man had died of fright.

"Reverend Reynolds asked Brooks, 'Do you consider yourself a type of sentry, Jeff?'

"'Yes, I do,' Brooks said. 'As the Mayor of Leyden, I feel it's my duty to watch over the people.'

"'That may well be, but Stranger is no *Cu Sith*.'

"Responding to the blank look on Brooks' face, Reynolds added, 'Devil dog. It was a name for the spectral hound that haunted the Highlands.'

"But Brooks had taken the Reverend's ghost story far too seriously. 'Come on, Jeff,' Reynolds said. 'It's a beautiful day, the sun is shining, we're standing here next to the house of God—how can you entertain such dark fantasies. You know, it's superstitions like these that contribute to *big-black-dog syndrome*.'"

"HAVE YOU EVER heard of it?" Pruzhansky asked me. "It's a proven fact, black dogs are the last to be adopted from animal shelters. For one thing, they don't photograph well, so they don't look very appealing in those signs that get posted in supermarkets and laundromats. And most people think black dogs look aggressive. I certainly don't think so, but for some reason, most people tend to equate *black* with *mean*. I'm sure that hundreds of years of superstition helped foster that prejudice.

"When people go to the pound looking for a pet, they usually want a puppy, or a dog that's not too big, with brown or blond or reddish fur. They look away as they hurry past the black dog's cage—trying hard not to look into the dog's sad eyes, knowing the animal will probably end up being put to sleep."

The old man shook his head. "What were the chances of a huge black dog like Churchill being rescued from the pound? But I'm sure Brooks didn't have a clue about such things. He just didn't like dogs—or any pets, for that matter. And that was a big disappointment to his daughter.

"One Saturday, when Brooks was working at the office, Sofia saw the backdoor to his brick colonial swing open and Abby bound out with Churchill dancing around the teenager.

"'Abby,' Sofia exclaimed. 'Does your father allow you to have the dog inside?'

"The girl shook her head. 'But he's not here.'

"'That's no reason to disobey your father.'

"'What does he care?' Abby asked. 'He's

never around. And he never lets me have anything I want.'

"Sofia and I learned later that Abby had pleaded with her father to allow her to adopt the dog. He refused, of course. So Abby shut herself up in her room. She cried for a while, and then went back to the Internet.

"I WISH YOU DID HAVE A DOG," Sofia said. "Maybe he could pull you away from those horrible websites. If only there were other children in the neighborhood, for you to play with, instead of just a bunch of old retirees."

"I have friends!" the girl said, fidgeting.

"In chat rooms? You don't know those people, Abby. You need real friends, children your own age."

"These people understand me. They share my interests."

"In Wicca? I wish you wouldn't dabble in those things. It's not safe. I know. When I was a little girl in New York, I—"

"SOFIA NEVER FINISHED her story that day. Brooks drove down the long driveway leading to the detached garage on the far side of the house. 'I better go now,' Abby said, and she disappeared around the corner of the house. Although my wife couldn't see what took place between Abby and her father, see could certainly hear it. Brooks was yelling about something, as usual. This time, Abby was yelling back."

Pruzhansky stopped here. "I apologize for taking up your time, Mr. Thatcher. None of this ever saw print and I have no business telling it to you now. I'm not usually this garrulous; chalk it up to boredom."

"I'm a prudent fellow, Mr. Pruzhansky. I've never written anything that could hurt anyone," I said. "But I'm also a very curious fellow. If there's more to this story, I'd really like to hear it." I reached over and shut off the tape recorder. "Please, just to satisfy my own curiosity."

The old man pointed to his empty cup, and the waitress stood up unenthusiastically and removed the glass carafe from its warming element. "Sofia was right about so many things. Abby was one of them. She did need friends her own age. *Real* friends.

"She thought she'd found one, too; a

young man she'd met at an online forum operated by a company that sold herbs, incense, polished rocks." Pruzhansky grunted. "A lot of New Age bullshit that was guaranteed to bring peace and contentment. Or to transport you to higher levels of consciousness.

"The young man told Abby his name was Shawn; that he had just turned eighteen; that he was a senior at Ridgecrest High, about an hour away in Paigeville. He arranged to drive down and meet Abby one Saturday afternoon. They were going to take in a matinee and have an early dinner. Shawn even promised he'd have Abby home by eight o'clock.

"I wonder if Brooks was even paying attention when his daughter asked for permission. His mind was probably on other things, as usual.

"When Shawn arrived that Saturday, he drove up the narrow lane leading to the Brooks' home, a long driveway that curves around through a grove of mature oaks, to an old carriage house that Brooks used as a garage. Abby greeted the young man cheerfully, and invited him into the kitchen for a soda. While they chatted, Shawn learned her father had got a phone call and had left hurriedly to attend an *emergency* campaign meeting in the next town. Brooks had told Abby to have fun and not expect him back for several hours.

"Upon hearing this, Shawn said he'd left something in his car, and went out to get it. Now, Magnolia Lane is not a very busy street. There's no 'through traffic' allowed, and despite an occasional tourist or jogger, it's very quiet. Most of the historic houses are set back a couple hundred feet from the road. And in the case of Brooks' house, you couldn't even see it from the street, due to the grove of trees.

"I think I mentioned earlier that Sofia and I weren't able to see Brooks' garage from our garden, because it was on the opposite side of his house. The Millars lived on the other side of Brooks, but their view of the driveway and carriage house was obscured by a row of overgrown boxwoods.

"Abby's visitor must have taken all this in. He stood by his car for a couple minutes before pulling it into the carriage house. When he returned, he had a deck of Tarot cards and asked if he could predict Abby's future."

Pruzhansky shifted uncomfortably. "Abbey says she still has nightmares about what happened afterward. According to the police report, the man's real name was Wilson Haines and he was twenty-seven. Two years earlier, Haines had been charged with stalking a teenage girl in another state. He had driven two hours to get to Leyden that day, with only one thing on his mind.

HAINES FANNED THE Tarot deck and asked if they could sit on the couch. Abby took him down the hallway to the den, where he began to lay down cards on the coffee table. He kept asking her to sit closer to him, and when she did, he started to fondle her.

Abby quickly pulled away. She stood, and asked if they could go to the movies like he promised. Haines laughed. He grasped the girl's hand and said, "But I haven't seen your bedroom yet."

Abby twisted free and tried to run out the door. Haines caught her arm and spun her around. "What are you afraid of, little girl," he said. "Look at me, I'm not scared."

He seized her by the lapels and tore her blouse open, sending the buttons flying across the room. Abby started crying, tried to close up her blouse, but Haines grabbed both her wrists and forced her to the floor. She screamed and Haines slapped her as hard as he could.

Abby was dazed by the blow. For a moment she stopped struggling. Haines was starting to unfasten her jeans when he glanced up and saw something that made his blood run cold.

Through the open door he could see a shape silhouetted against the light pouring through a window at the end of the hall. A huge black dog was lumbering up the passage toward him, moving noiselessly but purposefully, its head lowered, its teeth bared. Two green eyes burned in the dog's massive head.

"HAINES FELL BACK in terror. He didn't seem to notice when Abby rolled over and crawled

from the room. She was dizzy and her cheek was bleeding, but she managed to get to her feet. She staggered out the backdoor and through the rose garden. She was hysterical when she got to our house.

"Sofia took the girl upstairs while I dialed 911. I knew the police would never get there in time to catch the man, so I hurried outside to get a look at the license plate before he could drive off. But Haines' car was still inside the carriage house, and I realized he hadn't come out yet.

"I'm not the world's bravest man, Mr. Thatcher, nor the strongest. I wasn't exactly in a hurry to go inside Brooks' house. I walked slowly up the back steps, gripping the handrail—expecting Haines to charge through the door at any second, knocking me over to get to his car. But I found the man curled up in the corner of the den, exactly where Abby had left him.

"When the police arrived, they asked Haines why he hadn't tried to leave before they got there. He said he had wanted to, but he couldn't. The mayor's watchdog had held him in the corner of the room."

Pruzhansky cleared his throat. "To their credit, the police were very discreet about the whole business, but Brooks still wanted to get Abby away. They moved to a more suburban neighborhood, and when his term as mayor was about to end last year, Brooks decided not to run again. He told me he wanted to concentrate on Abby ... and his legal practice. I understand he's even working with troubled kids now."

"That's a great story," I said. "Churchill was a real hero, then."

Pruzhansky stared at me for a moment. "Mr. Thatcher, when I found Haines cowering in that corner, he was the only living thing in the room besides me.

"After the police left I went back inside Brooks' house to look for the dog. I searched upstairs, looked under the beds. I walked around the house calling the dog's name. I even walked a few houses down the street looking for Churchill. Not only was the dog nowhere to be found, but no one has seen him since."

"So Haines was the last to see the dog?"

"In essence," the old man said slowly.

"Now I wish I hadn't made that promise," I joked. "I wanted to write about the *last* sighting of Black Dog."

Pruzhansky didn't seem to be listening. "When I couldn't find Churchill, I walked back to Brooks' house to lock it up—Brooks wasn't back yet, and Sofia had gone with Abby to the Emergency Room. Before I left again, I remembered having seen a little trail of water that ran the length of the hallway. I wasn't sure where it had come from, I had assumed something got spilled during the struggle that afternoon, but I decided I'd mop it up before leaving.

"It wasn't urine," Pruzhansky said, interpreting my expression. "Not dog, not human.

"Before bed that night, I told Sofia what Haines had said to the police: about Churchill being in the room; about how—if it were true—the dog had protected Abby. Sofia grew quiet after that, pensive. When I mentioned the trail of water in the hall, she began to cry. She told me something that night, something so painful she'd never been able to talk about it until then."

"WHEN I WAS a little girl," Sofia said, "I lived with my aunt, Raisa Zaslovsky. My mother had died about four months after we immigrated to America. She had grown ill on the passage over, so after we arrived in New York we moved in with Raisa. My aunt tried to make my mother well again, but her condition seemed to quickly worsen.

"After my mother died, my Aunt Raisa let me have a small black dog. I can't tell you what kind of dog he was—probably a mutt. He had wandered up the steps of our apartment building and was sitting there waiting for me when I came home from school. I was so lonely in Manhattan, and I begged Aunt Raisa to let me keep him. When she finally agreed, I was overjoyed. She helped me bathe the dog, and that night Sasha slept at the foot of my bed.

"But Sasha's days were numbered. My aunt had made the acquaintance of a Madam Dupree, a psychic medium who had become very popular in the thirties. My aunt was obsessed with the occult, and Madam Dupree began paying us frequent visits. Things started out simply, reading palms and tea leaves. But soon, my aunt started talking about séances and contacting my dead mother.

"I've always heard that dogs are able to perceive things we can't—they're very sensitive to the supernatural. Maybe they have more sense than we do, too.

"Sasha didn't get along with the psychic. Every time Madam Dupree visited, Sasha would crouch in the far corner of the room and carefully watch the woman. He wouldn't take his eyes off her until she'd leave, and during the entire visit a low growl would rumble deep in his throat.

"One night my aunt wanted me to sit with them for a séance. I didn't want to. I was afraid, and I ran to my room. Several times Raisa and Madam Dupree tried to come upstairs and bring me down, but Sasha stationed himself at my bedroom door. Whenever either of them reached the landing, he'd start barking violently. And if they persisted in approaching my door, he'd rear up, bearing his teeth and growling viciously.

"The next day I hugged Sasha's neck and went to school. When I got home Sasha was gone. My aunt told me the dog was getting too big to keep in an apartment, and that she'd given him away. I got hysterical. I started crying and screaming, begging her to let me go and get my dog back. But my aunt refused to tell me where she'd taken Sasha. She kept telling me it was for my own good.

"I cried all night. The next morning, I was too sick to go to school. I stayed indoors for days, watching at my window, praying that my Sasha would return to me.

"When I did go out, I learned from the lady next-door to us what really happened to Sasha. Madam Dupree had come while I was at school. She talked my aunt into having the dog put down. She had brought some kind of opiate with her, something that would knock the dog out. Together they mixed it into Sasha's food.

"After Sasha fell asleep, Dupree had a man come around. He put Sasha into a burlap sack and carried it—" Sofia wiped the tears streaming down her checks. "The man dropped the bag into the river."

PRUZHANSKY'S LIPS TIGHTENED, and for several

moments he sat silent. "My wife passed away in her sleep that night. I woke up next to her ... the way I had for forty-three years. But when I leaned over to kiss her, her lips were like ice.

"She was only five years older than me. She was only sixty-eight, for god's sake! She was still active and healthy and sharp!"

He closed his eyes and shook his head. "I think her Sasha finally returned for her.

"That night, at the Brooks' home, that was the last sighting of Black Dog. No one has reported seeing him since. But sometimes, when I'm able to fall asleep, I have dreams about the dog. In my dreams, he's running free with my Sofia, in a beautiful world where there's no pain. And when I awaken, I pray that someday he'll return for me ... to guide me back to her."

He squeezed his eyes tightly shut, deepening the furrows of age and grief that creased his cheeks. But the tears escaped, falling silently upon the counter.

I stood quietly, reached in my pocket and placed two twenties on the counter next to the old man's elbow. Then I picked up my recorder and slipped away, leaving him there, alone with his own private Churchill, the black dog of his bittersweet memories.

💀 💀 💀

According to Tom English, many of the story elements in "The Last Sighting of Black Dog" are true—*people, places, and certain events; and Churchill, in particular, who is based on a legendary black dog roaming the historic area near his home.*

Tom is an environmental chemist who loves watching old movies, reading vintage comics, and writing supernatural stories. His work has appeared in magazines and print anthologies such as Haunted House Short Stories *and* Detective Thrillers Short Stories *(both from Flame Tree Publishing); and* Gaslight Arcanum: Uncanny Tales of Sherlock Holmes, *to name a few. Tom also edited* Bound for Evil: Curious Tales of Books Gone Bad, *a 2009 Shirley Jackson Award finalist for best anthology; and has written five inspirational books with his wife, Wilma Espaillat English, including* Spiritual Boot Camp for Creators & Dreamers, *which the* BookLife Prize *praised as "uniquely thorough, well-written, persuasive, and inspiring."*

He resides with Wilma, surrounded by books and beasts, deep in the woods of New Kent, Virginia.

THE MAN IN
THE RUBBER MONSTER SUIT

BY GREGORY L. NORRIS
ART BY ALLEN KOSZOWSKI

THE IRONY WAS, THAT MORNING STARTED OUT BRIGHT AND SUNNY, TELEGRAPHING THAT THE DAY TO FOLLOW MIGHT BE KINDER THAN THE DOZEN OR SO BEFORE IT. But by the time Miles met the man in the rubber monster suit in the back alley outside Soundstage 17, all the color had evaporated from the morning, which took on the pale white of the man's T-shirt, the black of his pants and scuffed shoes, and the gray pallor of his skin. It was like Miles Johan Tebbs had found himself living inside one of the low budget black and white creature features the studio had contracted him to write—two scripts down, one to go.

"Meet the monster," said Carson, director of the second of Mile's three mutant offspring.

The middle child, *Horror From the H-Bomb*, presently occupied the big soundstage stained in shadows at his back. Within its cavernous walls, both the live-action and monster effects were being produced. It wasn't Miles's favorite of the three scripts; *The Abomination* was better, he felt, in terms of story, while *The Fiend Outside Your Window*, though presently stalled on his typewriter back at the bungalow provided by the studio, had the potential to be more than its two predecessors combined.

The monster's name was A. J. Vocks. Vocks was lean to the point of brittle—one stiff gust of the Santa Anna winds might snap him in two, Miles thought while extending his hand. Malnourished, pallid, the man's skin reminded him more of the underside of a mushroom than anything healthy on a living human being, and his repulsion rose at the notion of touching it. Too late, their hands connected, and any illusions Miles had dreamed up of spongy flesh ended. Vocks shook with the kind of strength that could shatter the bones of lesser men. When he attempted to break the connection, Vocks held on for another painful second or so, a disquieting look on his face, and Miles wondered if he'd be able to type once his visit to the soundstage ended and he was back in the box-shaped prison of that drab, loaned place.

Their eyes connected, which was almost as unpleasant as the handshake. Sweat slicked the man's face. If he looked, Miles was sure the armpits of Vocks's white T would bear sallow yellow stains. He did, but the marks of perspiration were colorless.

Vocks was perfect for the role, an actor whose face would never be shown, likely never known beyond call sheets and the film's end credits. The ideal man to fill the rubber monster suit. A true horror, whether or not as a result of the H-bomb.

"I've heard good things about you, Vocks," Miles lied, because that's what you did in Tinseltown. You smiled and shook hands with everyone in the cult you were introduced to, even its monsters.

Carson patted Miles's shoulder. "I'll meet you both inside. Miles, it's a good day to be on set—we're filming the big night battle scene."

Carson then scratched at the paunch hanging over his belted slacks and suddenly wasn't there anymore. The background noise fell even farther distant. It was a gray, still morning in Hollywood, and this next part of the script lacked all dialogue.

"So, what makes you so high and mighty at the typewriter?" Vocks eventually asked.

The question—sounding more of an accusation—caught Miles off guard. "I don't know. What makes you think you're so good at being a monster?"

Vocks flashed a humorless grin that showed teeth, the gesture more snarl than actual smile. "Me? Oh, I know all about being the monster. You'll see."

The snarl flattened. Vocks grumbled something under his breath, which unleashed a shiver down Miles's spine despite the new day's relative warmth. On his next shallow sip of breath, Miles caught the man's rank smell, something unnatural that stunk of factories, of war. He realized it was the lingering odor of the rubber monster suit upon Vocks's sweaty skin, which might have contributed to the man's pale appearance.

A LONG HOUR LATER, the stage was lit, all precautions had been followed, and Miles was seated among Carson, the script supervisor, and half a dozen onlookers—studio suits, likely some of the bigger wigs who'd invested in the public's hunger for radioactive horrors and moving pictures that went bump in the night.

Action played on the monitor, though as Miles sat and pondered the blank sheet rolled into the typewriter back at his borrowed lodgings, very little was actually happening. Water sloshed in the pool meant to represent Pearl Harbor on the darkest night in human history. The gunboats rigged to rain hellfire on the monster as it came striding out of the waves looked like toys.

In a far corner, the absence of color deepened, as though A.J. Vocks—the question of what the man's first and middle names were chased Miles—had transformed the real world into the same black and white film stock being used to record his long stride in from Stage Left.

Miles waited, pondering the stalled script, obsessing over it. His mind drifted. He would return from the set with good intentions, but the very nature of being around people would drain him of his creativity, and most likely he'd sprawl across the sofa and waste what remained of his afternoon by napping. There would be takeout in the night's plans. The brown sauce from egg foo yong might land on the clean page when he finally got to it, smudged in the shape of his thumbprint. He'd grow frustrated, turn on the TV until the station signed off with the National Anthem. Such was the habit lately. He'd fallen into a cycle. Yes, *The Fiend Outside Your Window* was his best work ever, but Miles was in a rut as a result. A sensation he equated with having a belly full of broken glass boiled in his guts. Sweat broke on his forehead. He dabbed at it with his handkerchief and glanced back at the screen feeding in images from that dark corner of the soundstage where a strange man in a rubber monster suit was about to stride across Pearl Harbor.

An unexpected breeze cooled Miles's face. Fans turned to simulate the churning of the water, a fake tsunami recreated in miniature within the soundstage's walls. Only when Miles looked, the image on the screen had jumped out of cathode ray tubes and beyond the glass. Or he had fallen past the edges of the console, into the action. Either way, the fake representation of Hawaii now towered around and above him, and the fake palm trees had renounced their plastic scale to become realistic trunks and fronds being whipped about, shredded. Even his view of the harbor was three-dimensional. The pool, only two feet deep and filled with chlorinated water, now stretched all the way to Asia and smelled saline, of the Pacific.

Gunboats manned the harbor. The air crackled with a tenseness that set off Miles's heartburn. It wasn't true—either the stress of getting through *Fiend* had overtaken him, or he was asleep. Likely on the sofa in that sterile environment back in En Cerito, tortured by the knowledge that he'd already peaked; the script was his best work and, ironically, his last. Not real. None of it. An illusion born of defeat. Only as he wiped the rain and sea spray off his face, the realness persisted. And if these things were true, so was the rest of it, warned a voice from inside his mind.

Boom.

Thunder sounded in the distance from somewhere beyond the dense fog. No telltale of lightning flashed. Another clap followed.

Boom.

It wasn't thunder, the same voice taunted. No, those were the footsteps of a giant. And they were coming closer, closer.

The monster appeared, a gray ghost beyond a filter of gauzy fog; a horror spawned by the H-bomb tests in the Pacific. Miles knew the monster stood at over 400 feet tall; he had written a line of dialogue pretty much stating that fact somewhere around the second plot point in the script. He was a mere five-nine in his loafers, rooted on a patch of grass gazing at the edge of the world, as a radioactive giant strode toward him.

Its eyes glowed white in the darkness. Though devoid of pupils, the monstrous eyes locked upon him and burned through his physical body, into his soul. Its reptilian mouth formed the lizard's version of a smile, as though hungering for the tiny morsel of flesh his body promised. He hadn't written the horror as craving human blood; its reasons for attacking Pearl Harbor were left vague through both rewrites. It was a monster—destroying entire cities was what monsters did in this new Atomic Age.

Electricity crackled around him and prickled over his skin. Right as the gunboats opened fire and the night sky transformed to a hellish impersonation of daylight between the flashes, Miles's bladder let go.

He screamed. The cannonade and the roars from the horror as hot steel drilled into its hide of scales smothered his voice.

Run, damn it—run! his inner voice urged.

Run, yes, into the heart of the naval base. Only the giant monster would pursue him no matter where Miles went. And his body was paralyzed from below the knees on down, despite the warmth surging into his new loafers.

Wake up, Miles!

The battle intensified. The deafening blasts grew far beyond the cheap flashes of gunpowder from toy boats that would be enhanced in post-production. The fierceness of the attack lit the sky, shook the earth— much like the H-bomb that had given life to the giant horror ambling toward him. His baby, Miles realized. It was coming for the father who'd created it.

Boom. Boom.

He screamed again. A hand grabbed hold of him. It was the monster's, ready to crush him, Miles was sure. But when he blinked, it was only Carlton Carson's.

"What the hell, Miles?" the director demanded.

Miles glanced around the soundstage. The nightmare had shrunk in scope, back to within the dimensions of the television screen. The gunboats had ceased firing, and the horror stood frozen, waiting. All of the studio suits' eyes were aimed at him. The urine running down his thighs was real.

"Uh," Miles stammered. The screams were real, too, judging by the rawness of his throat and the ice thawing atop his flesh, the latter the lingering chill of a man's worst nightmares playing out at just after eleven in the morning.

On his way out of Soundstage 17, he cast a glance back at the screen. Vocks had removed the head of his rubber monster's suit and, grinning, seemed to be staring through the feed, right at Miles.

THE BUNGALOW ON En Cerito Drive was an oblong box at the top of a long flight of steps. The studio owned dozens exactly like it. Gone were most of the citrus groves upon the very slope that Miles's loaned home occupied. A dusty, desert smell infused the air.

A sympathetic wardrobe lady had gotten him into clean slacks and underwear. Miles parked his car, another studio loan, at the base of the stairs and started the long climb up to his temporary home. The illusion of a day painted in strokes of black and white persisted wherever he looked.

The inside of the bungalow had bottled the day's building warmth. Miles pushed open the biggest of the windows in what passed for the living room en route to the kitchen. The orange trees were gone, but orange juice in a glass bottle chilled in the icebox. He had vodka, too—despite the threat posed from Senator McCarthy over what one chose to drink or believe. In the end, he settled for a tall glass of water with plenty of cubes.

Miles carried the sweating glass past the sofa, which attempted to seduce him through the promise of a nap, to the folding card table upon which his typewriter sat. The device of torture was bold black, the blank sheet clutched in its teeth crisp white. Miles sipped and then sweated like the glass. *The Fiend Outside Your Window* tormented him into looking away. The sofa. A nap first, and then he'd attempt to write past the stalled scene. Anything to put the bizarre sequence of events at the soundstage out of his head.

He drained the glass and set it beside the inert typewriter, which seemed reluctant to spit out another page covered in words, kicked off his shoes, and stretched out on the sofa. The cushions exuded a stale smell of cigarettes; ghostly reminders of all the writers who'd sweated out words for the studio before him, translating the dark fruit grown in grey matter into three-act structures held together by brass brads. Who could say what other monsters had been released into the world from this very room?

Miles, who didn't smoke, not yet, drew in an ashy breath and attempted to doze.

Boom.

His eyelids shot open like shades drawn too quickly. White sunlight poured into the gray room through the black window frame. The black typewriter sat atop the scuffed gray tabletop, a blank white sheet tucked into its hinged jaw. It was only the gallop of his heart, Miles told himself. Or the leftovers from his hallucination within Soundstage 17, an echo that had jumped past his skull to terrorize his ears.

Boom.

This time, the glass did a little shimmy on the top of the folding card table.

Footsteps, those of a giant, approached the bungalow.

Miles's heart attempted to jump out of his chest and into his throat. He choked it down, along with a dry swallow, and rolled off the sofa, onto the patch of drab beige carpet on the floor. Like all else, the carpet had renounced its color and hovered somewhere between sepia and gray. It trembled beneath his cheek as yet another monstrous footfall shook the world.

A shadow swept by the nearest window. Miles gazed up in time to see something tall breeze past, out of sight, around the corner.

"No," he gasped. The word sounded gray to his ears and tasted ashy on his tongue.

The vast dark presence appeared at the next window in line. Miles scrambled up and into the corner between walls and windows right as a giant's eye peered in, its scope reduced in size by the empty glass on the card table. The dusty desert smell changed into the dense stink of sweat and rubber he remembered from the morning.

"I know you're in there," said A.J. Vocks, the man inside the rubber monster suit, his voice booming through the closed window glass. "Let me in, Miles."

Boom. Boom. Footsteps.

Miles shifted to the next of the room's boxy corners, matching the giant's maneuvers around the building.

"Standing out here makes me feel like the monster in your latest opus, *The Fiend Outside Your Window.*" Vocks chuckled, and the house swayed.

Terror surged through Miles's blood. He held his breath. The last sip of air turned volcanic in his lungs along with the foul mix of Vocks's sweat and molded rubber.

"Miles?" the giant taunted. "Please open a window and let me come in."

The shadow shifted. A sharp *ping* ripped through the air. Severed electrical lines, Miles realized. Vocks had snapped through the wires with ease and little pain, according to his movements, which now put him near the sofa.

Miles hurried over to that corner, praying to whatever deity or saint would take his call that Vocks didn't see him.

This wasn't possible! A dream, a nightmare suffered through in the waking world, just like what he'd experienced inside Soundstage 17. All of it, the result of being stalled on the third script, the best writing of his life. He'd peaked, he knew. Anything after what was already there would pale. Pressure, that's all. *Wake up! Wake up—*

Miles remembered pushing the big window open, the one with the view into the city's growing sprawl. The one where shadows now lurked, and the stink of rubber poured in, too thick to breathe, reminding him of a tire fire at the dump, a boyhood memory in the town that was his old home at the opposite coast of America. He envisioned the power lines severed, spitting sparks and current, the hillsides clear cut of citrus trees and terraced in bungalow boxes collapsing under the weight of the giant's footfalls.

"Miles," Vocks cooed in a slippery bellow. "I know you're in there. I can see you."

Miles tipped his head in the direction of Vocks's voice. The gigantic eyeball framed in the window was aimed his way. A gargantuan finger pushed against the screen. The entire window and its casing began to collapse into the room.

Miles moved between the behemoth's finger and glass, and pushed back with all of his strength. Right before the glass shattered, he saw Vocks's mouth, that grinning snarl fixed upon his lips. The giant's teeth chattered behind his sinister smile, as though hungry to devour him!

It was, Miles thought, so like the absent, mad clack of the typewriter keys, spitting out word after word onto the blank page. If he woke from the nightmare in time, if he lived past this moment with the fiend outside the window reaching in, salivating for his flesh, he promised the gods and saints that he would go straight back to the blank white page stuck in the black typewriter, and exorcise fear and monsters alike.

Raised on a healthy diet of creature double features and classic SF TV, Gregory L. Norris writes regularly for numerous short story anthologies, national magazines, novels, and the occasional episode for TV or film. Gregory novelized the NBC Made-for-TV classic by Gerry Anderson, The Day After Tomorrow: Into Infinity *(as well as a sequel and a forthcoming third entry into the franchise for Anderson Entertainment in the U.K.), a movie he watched as an eleven-year-old sitting cross-legged on the living room floor of the enchanted cottage where he grew up. Gregory won HM in the 2016 Roswell Awards in Short SF Writing. He once worked as a screenwriter on two episodes of Paramount's* Star Trek: Voyager. *Kate Mulgrew,* Voyager's *"Captain Janeway," blurbed his book of short stories and novellas,* The Fierce and Unforgiving Muse, *stating, "In my seven years on* Voyager, *I don't think I've met a writer more capable of writing such a book—and writing it so beautifully."*

In late 2019, Gregory sold an option on his modern Noir feature film screenplay, Amandine, *to the new Hollywood production company Snark-hunter LLC, owned by actor Dan Lench, a devotee of Gregory's writing. In late 2020, Snarkhunter optioned Gregory's tetralogy Horror film based upon four of his short stories,* Ride Along. *That same month, his short story "Water Whispers" (originally appearing in the anthology* 20,000 Leagues Remembered), *was nominated for the Pushcart Prize.*

Gregory lives and writes at Xanadu, a century-old house perched on a hill in New Hampshire's North Country with spectacular mountain views, with his rescue cat and emerald-eyed muse.

Read his fond remembrance of Kolchak: The Night Stalker, *also featured in this issue, and follow his further literary adventures at:* www.gregorylnorris.blogspot.com

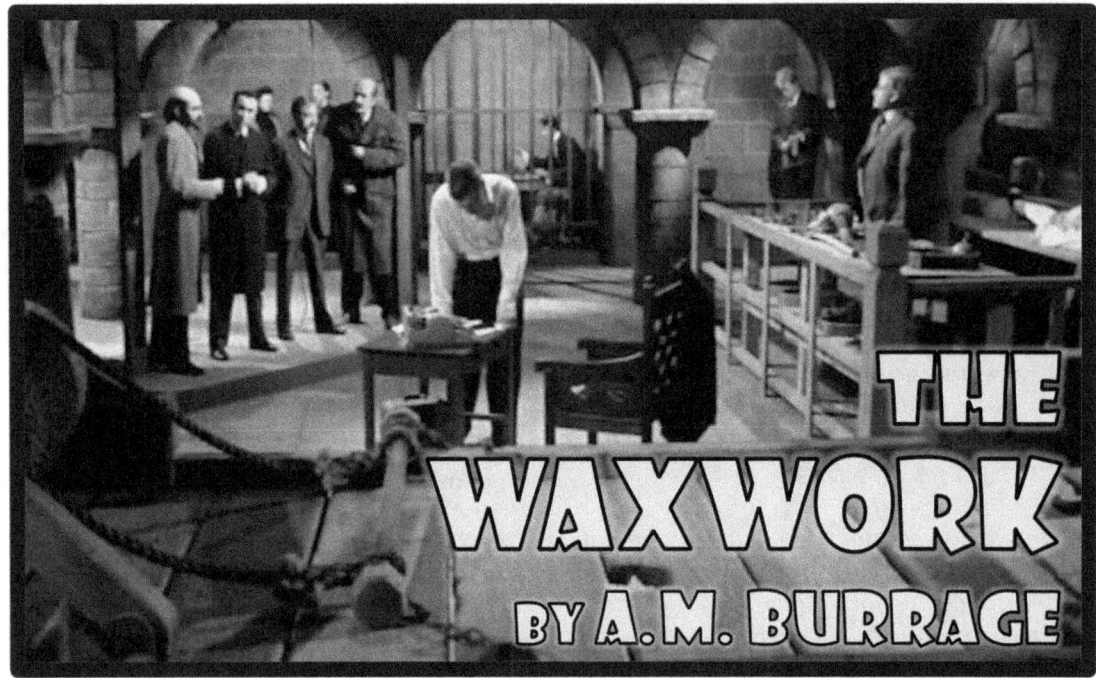

THE WAXWORK

BY A.M. BURRAGE

WHILE THE UNIFORMED ATTENDANTS OF MARRINER'S WAXWORKS WERE USHERING THE LAST STRAGGLERS THROUGH THE GREAT GLASS-PANELED DOUBLE DOORS, THE MANAGER SAT IN HIS OFFICE INTERVIEWING RAYMOND HEWSON.

The manager was a youngish man, stout, blond and of medium height. He wore his clothes well and contrived to look extremely smart without appearing overdressed. Raymond Hewson looked neither. His clothes, which had been good when new and which were still carefully brushed and pressed, were beginning to show signs of their owner's losing battle with the world.

He was a small, spare, pale man, with lank, errant brown hair, and although he spoke plausibly and even forcibly he had the defensive and somewhat furtive air of a man who was used to rebuffs. He looked what he was, a man gifted somewhat above the ordinary, who was a failure through his lack of self-assertion.

The manager was speaking.

"There is nothing new in your request," he said, in fact we refuse it to different people —mostly young bloods who have tried to make bets—about three times a week. We have nothing to gain and something to lose by letting people spend the night in our Murderers' Den. If I allowed it, and some young idiot lost his senses, what would be my position? But your being a journalist somewhat alters the case."

Hewson smiled.

"I suppose you mean that journalists have no senses to lose."

"No, no," laughed the manager, "but one imagines them to be responsible people. Besides, here we have something to gain; publicity and advertisement."

"Exactly," said Hewson, "and there I thought we might come to terms."

The manager laughed again.

"Oh," he exclaimed, "I know what's coming. You want to be paid twice, do you? It used to be said years ago that Madame Tussaud's would give a man a hundred pounds for sleeping alone in the Chamber of Horrors. I hope you don't think that we have made any such offer. Er—what is your paper, Mr Hewson?"

"I am freelancing at present," Hewson confessed, "working on space for several papers. However, I should find no difficulty in getting the story printed. The *Morning Echo* would use it like a shot. 'A Night with Marriner's Murderers.' No live paper could turn it down."

The manager rubbed his chin.

"Ah! And how do you propose to treat it?"

"I shall make it gruesome, of course; gruesome with just a saving touch of humor."

The other nodded and offered Hewson his cigarette-case.

"Very well, Mr Hewson," he said. "Get your story printed in the *Morning Echo*, and there will be a five-pound note waiting for you here when you care to come and call for it. But first of all, it's no small ordeal that you're proposing to undertake. I'd like to be quite sure about you, and I'd like you to be quite sure about yourself. I own I shouldn't care to take it on. I've seen those figures dressed and undressed, I know all about the process of their manufacture, I can walk about in company downstairs as unmoved as if I were walking among so many skittles, but I should hate having to sleep down there alone among them."

"Why?" asked Hewson.

"I don't know. There isn't any reason. I don't believe in ghosts. If I did I should expect them to haunt the scene of their crimes or the spot where their bodies were laid, instead of a cellar which happens to contain their waxwork effigies. It's just that I couldn't sit alone among them all night, with their seeming to stare at me in the way they do. After all, they represent the lowest and most appalling types of humanity, and—although I would not own it publicly—the people who come to see them are not generally charged with the very highest motives. The whole atmosphere of the place is unpleasant, and if you are susceptible to atmosphere I warn you that you are in for a very uncomfortable night."

Hewson had known that from the moment when the idea had first occurred to him. His soul sickened at the prospect, even while he smiled casually upon the manager. But he had a wife and family to keep, and for the past month he had been living on paragraphs, eked out by his rapidly dwindling store of savings. Here was a chance not to be missed—the price of a special story in the *Morning Echo*, with a five-pound note to add to it. It meant comparative wealth and luxury for a week, and freedom from the worst anxieties for a fortnight. Besides, if he wrote the story well, it might lead to an offer of regular employment.

"The way of transgressors—and newspaper men—is hard," he said, "I have already promised myself an uncomfortable night, because your Murderers' Den is obviously not fitted up as a hotel bedroom. But I don't think your waxworks will worry me much."

"You're not superstitious?"

"Not a bit." Hewson laughed.

"But you're a journalist; you must have a strong imagination."

"The news editors for whom I've worked have always complained that I haven't any. Plain facts are not considered sufficient in our trade, and the papers don't like offering their readers unbuttered bread."

The manager smiled and rose.

"Right," he said, "I think the last of the people have gone. Wait a moment. I'll give orders for the figures downstairs not to be draped, and let the night people know that you'll be here. Then I'll take you down and show you round."

He picked up the receiver of a house telephone, spoke into it and presently replaced it.

"One condition I'm afraid I must impose on you," he remarked, "I must ask you not to smoke. We had a fire scare down in the Murderers' Den this evening. I don't know who gave the alarm, but whoever it was it was a false one. Fortunately there were very few people down there at the time, or there might have been a panic. And now, if you're ready, we'll make a move."

Hewson followed the manager through half a dozen rooms where attendants were busy shrouding the kings and queens of England, the generals and prominent statesmen of this and other generations, all the mixed herd of humanity whose fame or notoriety had rendered them eligible for this kind of immortality. The manager stopped once and spoke to a man in uniform, saying something about an arm-chair in the Murderers' Den.

"It's the best we can do for you, I'm afraid," he said to Hewson. "I hope you'll be able to get some sleep."

He led the way through an open barrier and down ill-lit stone stairs which conveyed a sinister impression of giving access to a dungeon. In a passage at the bottom were a few preliminary horrors, such as relics of the Inquisition, a rack taken from a mediaeval castle, branding irons, thumb-screws, and other mementoes of man's one-time cruelty to man. Beyond the passage was the Murderers' Den.

It was a room of irregular shape with a vaulted roof, and dimly lit by electric lights burning behind inverted bowls of frosted glass. It was, by design, an eerie and un-comfortable chamber—a chamber whose atmosphere invited its visitors to speak in whispers. There was something of the air of a chapel about it, but a chapel no longer devoted to the practice of piety and given over now for base and impious worship.

The waxwork murderers stood on low pedestals with numbered tickets at their feet. Seeing them elsewhere, and without knowing whom they represented, one would have thought them a dull-looking crew, chiefly remarkable for the shabbiness of their clothes, and as evidence of the changes of fashion even among the unfashionable.

Recent notorieties rubbed dusty shoul-ders with the old "favorites." Thurtell, the murderer of Weir, stood as if frozen in the act of making a shop-window gesture to young Bywaters. There was Lefroy, the poor half-baked little snob who killed for gain so that he might ape the gentleman. Within five yards of him sat Mrs. Thompson, that erotic romanticist, hanged to propitiate British middle-class matronhood. Charles Peace, the only member of that vile company who looked uncompromisingly and entirely evil, sneered across a gangway at Norman Thorne. Browne and Kennedy, the two most recent additions, stood between Mrs. Dyer and Patrick Mahon. The manager, walking around with Hewson, pointed out several of the more interesting of these unholy notabilities.

"That's Crippen; I expect you recognize him. Insignificant little beast who looks as if he couldn't tread on a worm. That's Armstrong. Looks like a decent, harmless country gentleman, doesn't he? There's old Vaquier; you can't miss him because of his beard. And of course this—"

"Who's that?" Hewson interrupted in a whisper, pointing.

"Oh, I was coming to him," said the manager in a light undertone. "Come and have a good look at him. This is our star turn. He's the only one of the bunch that hasn't been hanged."

The figure which Hewson had indicated was that of a small, slight man not much more than five feet in height. It wore little waxed moustaches, large spectacles, and a caped coat. There was something so ex-aggeratedly French in its appearance that it reminded Hewson of a stage caricature. He could not have said precisely why the mild-looking face seemed to him so repellent, but he had already recoiled a step and, even in the manager's company, it cost him an effort to look again.

"But who is he?" he asked.

"That," said the manager, "is Dr. Bourdette."

Hewson shook his head doubtfully.

"I think I've heard the name," he said, "but I forget in connection with what."

The manager smiled.

"You'd remember better if you were a Frenchman," he said. "For some long while that man was the terror of Paris. He carried on his work of healing by day, and of throat-cutting by night, when the fit was on him. He killed for the sheer devilish pleasure it gave him to kill, and always in the same way—with a razor. After his last crime he left a clue behind him which set the police upon his track. One clue led to another, and before very long they knew that they were on the track of the Parisian equivalent of our Jack the Ripper, and had enough evidence to send him to the madhouse or the guillotine on a dozen capital charges.

"But even then our friend here was too clever for them. When he realized that the toils were closing about him he mysteriously disappeared, and ever since, the police of every civilized country have been looking for him. There is no doubt that he managed to make away with himself, and by some means which has prevented his body coming to light. One or two crimes of a similar nature have taken place since his disappearance, but he is believed almost for certain to be dead, and the experts believe these recrudescences to be the work of an imitator. It's queer, isn't it, how every notorious murderer has imitators?"

Hewson shuddered and fidgeted with his feet.

"I don't like him at all," he confessed. "Ugh! What eyes he's got!"

"Yes, this figure's a little masterpiece. You find the eyes bite into you? Well, that's excellent realism, then, for Bourdette practiced mesmerism, and was supposed to mesmerize his victims before dispatching them. Indeed, had he not done so, it is impossible to see how so small a man could have done his ghastly work. There were never any signs of a struggle."

"I thought I saw him move," said Hewson with a catch in his voice. The manager smiled.

"You'll have more than one optical illusion before the night's out, I expect. You shan't be locked in. You can come upstairs when you've had enough of it. There are watchmen on the premises, so you'll find company. Don't be alarmed if you hear them moving about. I'm sorry I can't give you any more light, because all the lights are on. For obvious reasons we keep this place as gloomy as possible. And now I think you had better return with me to the office and have a tot of whisky before beginning your night's vigil."

THE MEMBER OF the night staff who placed the arm-chair for Hewson was inclined to be facetious.

"Where will you have it, sir?" he asked, grinning. "Just 'ere, so as you can 'ave a little talk with Crippen when you're tired of sitting still? Or there's old Mother Dyer over there, making eyes and looking as if she could do with a bit of company. Say where, sir."

Hewson smiled. The man's chaff pleased him if only because, for the moment at least, it lent the proceedings a much-desired air of the commonplace.

"I'll place it myself, thanks," he said, "I'll find out where the draughts come from first."

"You won't find any down here. Well, good night, sir. I'm upstairs if you want me. Don't let 'em sneak up behind you and touch your neck with their cold and clammy 'ands. And you look out for that old Mrs. Dyer; I believe she's taken a fancy to you."

Hewson laughed and wished the man

good night. It was easier than he had expected. He wheeled the arm-chair—a heavy one upholstered in plush—a little way down the central gangway, and deliberately turned it so that its back was towards the effigy of Dr. Bourdette. For some undefined reason he liked Dr. Bourdette a great deal less than his companions.

Busying himself with arranging the chair he was almost light-hearted, but when the attendant's footfalls had died away and a deep hush stole over the chamber he realized that he had no slight ordeal before him. The dim unwavering light fell on the rows of figures which were so uncannily like human beings that the silence and the stillness seemed unnatural and even ghastly. He missed the sound of breathing, the rustling of clothes, the hundred-and-one minute noises one hears when even the deepest silence has fallen upon a crowd. But the air was as stagnant as water at the bottom of a standing pond. There was not a breath in the chamber to stir a curtain or rustle a hanging drapery or start a shadow. His own shadow, moving in response to a shifted arm or leg, was all that could be coaxed into motion. All was still to the gaze and silent to the ear. "It must be like this at the bottom of the sea," he thought, and wondered how to work the phrase into his story on the morrow.

He faced the sinister figures boldly enough. They were only waxworks. So long as he let that thought dominate all others he promised himself that all would be well. It did not, however, save him long from the discomfort occasioned by the waxen stare of Dr. Bourdette, which, he knew, was directed upon him from behind. The eyes of the little Frenchman's effigy haunted and tormented him, and he itched with the desire to turn and look.

"Come!" he thought, "my nerves have started already. If I turn and look at that dressed-up dummy it will be an admission of funk."

And then another voice in his brain spoke to him.

"It's because you're afraid that you won't turn and look at him."

The two Voices quarreled silently for a moment or two, and at last Hewson slewed his chair round a little and looked behind him.

Among the many figures standing in stiff, unnatural poses, the effigy of the dreadful little doctor stood out with a queer prominence, perhaps because a steady beam of light beat straight down upon it. Hewson flinched before the parody of mildness which some fiendishly skilled craftsman had managed to convey in wax, met the eyes for one agonized second, and turned again to face the other direction.

"He's only a waxwork like the rest of you," Hewson muttered defiantly. "You're all only waxworks."

They were only waxworks, yes, but waxworks don't move. Not that he had seen the least movement anywhere, but it struck him that, in the moment or two while he had looked behind him, there had been the least subtle change in the grouping of the figures in front. Crippen, for instance, seemed to have turned at least one degree to the left. Or, thought Hewson, perhaps the illusion was due to the fact that he had not slewed his chair back into its exact original position. And there were Field and Grey, too; surely one of them had moved his hands. Hewson held his breath for a moment, and then drew his courage back to him as a man lifts a weight. He remembered the words of more than one news editor and laughed savagely to himself. "And they tell me I've got no imagination!" he said beneath his breath.

He took a notebook from his pocket and wrote quickly.

"Mem.—Deathly silence and unearthly stillness of figures. Like being bottom of sea. Hypnotic eyes of Dr. Bourdette. Figures seem to move when not being watched."

He closed the book suddenly over his fingers and looked round quickly and awfully over his right shoulder. He had neither seen nor heard a movement, but it was as if some sixth sense had made him aware of one. He looked straight into the vapid countenance of Lefroy which smiled vacantly back as if to say, "It wasn't I!"

Of course it wasn't he, or any of them; it was his own nerves. Or was it? Hadn't Crippen moved again during that moment when his attention was directed elsewhere. You couldn't trust that little man! Once you took your eyes off him he took advantage of it to shift his position. That was what they were all doing, if he only knew it, he told himself; and half-rose out of his chair. This was not quite good enough! He was going. He wasn't going to spend the night with a lot of waxworks which moved while he wasn't looking.

...Hewson sat down again. This was very cowardly and very absurd. They *were* only waxworks and they *couldn't* move; let him hold that thought and all would yet be well. Then why all that silent unrest about him? —a subtle something in the air which did not quite break the silence and happened, whichever way he looked, just beyond the boundaries of his vision.

He swung round quickly to encounter the mild but baleful stare of Dr. Bourdette. Then, without warning, he jerked his head back to stare straight at Crippen. Ha! he'd nearly caught Crippen that time! "You'd better be careful, Crippen—and all the rest of you! If I do see one of you move I'll smash you to pieces! Do you hear?"

He ought to go, he told himself. Already he had experienced enough to write his story, or ten stories for the matter of that. Well, then, why not go? The *Morning Echo* would be none the wiser as to how long he had stayed, nor would it care so long as his story was a good one. Yes, but that night watchman upstairs would chaff him. And the manager—one never knew—perhaps the manager would quibble over that five-pound note which he needed so badly. He wondered if Rose were asleep or if she were lying awake and thinking of him. She'd laugh when he told her that he had imagined....

This was a little too much! It was bad enough that the waxwork effigies of murderers should move when they weren't being watched, but it was intolerable that they should *breathe*. Somebody was breathing. Or was it his own breath which sounded to him as if it came from a distance? He sat rigid, listening and straining, until he exhaled with a long sigh. His own breath after all, or—if not, Something had divined that he was listening and had ceased breathing

simultaneously.

Hewson jerked his head swiftly around and looked all about him out of haggard and haunted eyes. Everywhere his gaze encountered the vacant waxen faces, and everywhere he felt that by just some least fraction of a second had he missed seeing a movement of hand or foot, a silent opening or compression of lips, a flicker of eyelids, a look of human intelligence now smoothed out. They were like naughty children in a class, whispering, fidgeting and laughing behind their teacher's back, but blandly innocent when his gaze was turned upon them.

This would not do! This distinctly would not do! He must clutch at something, grip with his mind upon something which belonged essentially to the workaday world, to the daylight London streets. He was Raymond Hewson, an unsuccessful journalist, a living and breathing man, and these figures grouped around him were only dummies, so they could neither move nor whisper. What did it matter if they were supposed to be lifelike effigies of murderers? They were only made of wax and sawdust, and stood there for the entertainment of morbid sightseers and orange-sucking trippers. That was better! Now what was that funny story which somebody had told him in the Falstaff yesterday?...

He recalled part of it, but not all, for the gaze of Dr. Bourdette urged, challenged, and finally compelled him to turn.

Hewson half-turned, and then swung his chair so as to bring him face to face with the wearer of those dreadful hypnotic eyes. His own eyes were dilated, and his mouth, at first set in a grin of terror, lifted at the comers in a snarl. Then Hewson spoke and woke a hundred sinister echoes.

"You moved, damn you!" he cried. "Yes, you did, damn you! I saw you!"

Then he sat quite still, staring straight before him like a man found frozen in the Arctic snows.

Dr. Bourdette's movements were leisurely. He stepped off his pedestal with the mincing care of a lady alighting from a 'bus. The platform stood about two feet from the ground, and above the edge of it a plush-covered rope hung in arc-like curves. Dr. Bourdette lifted up the rope until it formed an arch for him to pass under, stepped off the platform and sat down on the edge, facing Hewson. Then he nodded and smiled and said "Good evening."

"I need hardly tell you," he continued, in perfect English in which was traceable only the least foreign accent, "that not until I overheard the conversation between you and the worthy manager of this establishment, did I suspect that I should have the pleasure of a companion here for the night. You cannot move or speak without my bidding, but you can hear me perfectly well. Something tells me that you are—shall I say nervous? My dear sir, have no illusions. I am not one of these contemptible effigies miraculously come to life: I am Dr. Bourdette himself."

He paused, coughed and shifted his legs.

"Pardon me," he resumed, "but I am a little stiff. And let me explain. Circumstances with which I need not fatigue you, have made it desirable that I should live in England. I was close to this building this evening when I saw a policeman regarding me a thought too curiously. I guessed that he intended to follow and perhaps ask me embarrassing questions, so I mingled with the crowd and came in here. An extra coin bought my admission to the chamber in which we now meet, and an inspiration showed me a certain means of escape.

"I raised a cry of fire, and when all the fools had rushed to the stairs I stripped my effigy of the caped coat which you behold me wearing, donned it, hid my effigy under the platform at the back, and took its place on the pedestal.

"I own that I have since spent a very fatiguing evening, but fortunately I was not always being watched and had opportunities to draw an occasional deep breath and ease the rigidity of my pose. One small boy screamed and exclaimed that he saw me moving. I understood that he was to be whipped and put straight to bed on his return home, and I can only hope that the threat has been executed to the letter.

"The manager's description of me, which I had the embarrassment of being compelled to overhear, was biased but not altogether inaccurate. Clearly I am not dead, although it is as well that the world thinks otherwise. His account of my hobby, which I have indulged for years, although, through necessity, less frequently of late, was in the main true although not intelligently expressed. The world is divided between collectors and non-collectors. With the non-collectors we are not concerned. The collectors collect anything, according to their individual tastes, from money to cigarette cards, from moths to matchboxes. I collect throats."

He paused again and regarded Hewson's throat with interest mingled with disfavor.

"I am obliged to the chance which brought us together tonight," he continued, "and perhaps it would seem ungrateful to complain. From motives of personal safety my activities have been somewhat curtailed of late years, and I am glad of this opportunity of gratifying my somewhat unusual whim. But you have a skinny neck, sir, if you will overlook a personal remark. I should never have selected you from choice. I like men with thick necks … thick red necks…."

He fumbled in an inside pocket and took out something which he tested against a wet forefinger and then proceeded to pass gently to and fro across the palm of his left hand.

"This is a little French razor," he remarked blandly. "They are not much used in England, but perhaps you know them? One strops them on wood. The blade, you will observe, is very narrow. They do not cut very deep, but deep enough. In just one little moment you shall see for yourself. I shall ask you the little civil question of all the polite barbers: Does the razor suit you, sir?" He rose up, a diminutive but menacing figure of evil, and approached Hewson with the silent, furtive step of a hunting panther.

"You will have the goodness," he said, "to raise your chin a little. Thank you, and a little more. Just a little more. Ah, thank you! … Merci, m'sieur … Ah, merci … merci…."

OVER ONE END of the chamber was a thick skylight of frosted glass which, by day, let in a few sickly and filtered rays from the floor above. After sunrise these began to mingle with the subdued light from the electric bulbs, and this mingled illumination added a certain ghastliness to a scene which needed no additional touch of horror.

The waxwork figures stood apathetically in their places, waiting to be admired or execrated by the crowds who would presently wander fearfully among them. In their midst, in the centre gangway, Hewson sat still, leaning far back in his arm-chair. His chin was uptilted as if he were waiting to receive attention from a barber, and although there was not a scratch upon his throat, nor anywhere upon his body, he was cold and dead. His previous employers were wrong in having credited him with no imagination.

Dr. Bourdette on his pedestal watched the dead man unemotionally. He did not move, nor was he capable of motion. But then, after all, he was only a waxwork.

"The Waxwork" first appeared in Burrage's 1931 collection Someone in the Room, *as by "Ex-Private X." The story was adapted for television in 1950, for* Lights Out; *in '52, for* Suspense, *(as "The Return of Dr. Bourdette"); and again in '59 for* Alfred Hitchcock Presents. *Chances are, the story also helped inspire episodes of other anthology series, such as Boris Karloff's* Thriller *("Waxworks," 1962) and* The Twilight Zone *("The New Exhibit," 1963). The photos illustrating this reprint are taken from the* Alfred Hitchcock Presents *adaptation of the story.*

Although Alfred McLelland Burrage (1889–1956) also wrote romance and historical fiction, as well as numerous stories for British boys' magazines, he is chiefly remembered today for his English ghost stories, which American editor and bibliographer E. F. Bleiler praised as "intelligent, well crafted and imaginative."

Classic Macabre by
Robert Bloch
Catnip

With Purr-fect Art by
Allen Koszowski

RONNIE SHIRES STOOD BEFORE THE MIRROR AND SLICKED BACK HIS CURLY HAIR. HE STRAIGHTENED HIS NEW SWEATER AND STUCK OUT HIS CHEST. NOT BAD! HAD TO WATCH THE WAY HE LOOKED, WITH GRADUATION ONLY TWO WEEKS AWAY AND THAT ELECTION FOR CLASS PRESIDENT COMING UP. If he could get to be class president, then next year in high school, he'd swing a little weight maybe. Go out for second team or something. But he had to look sharp—

"Ronnie! Better hurry or you'll be late!"

Ma came out of the kitchen, carrying his lunch. Ronnie wiped the smile off his face. She walked up behind him and put her arms around his waist.

"Darling—I only wish your father were here to see you—"

Ronnie wriggled free. "Yeah, sure. Say, Ma."

"Yes?"

"How's about letting me have another buck, huh? I got to get some things today."

"Well, I suppose. But try to make it last, son. This graduation costs a lot of money, seems to me."

"I'll make it up to you someday, Ma." He watched her as she fumbled in her apron pocket and produced a wadded dollar bill.

"Thanks. Be seeing you." He picked up his lunch and ran outside. He walked along, smiling and whistling, knowing Ma was watching him from the window.

Then he turned the corner, halted under a tree, and fished out a cigarette. He lit it and sauntered slowly across the street, puffing deeply. Out of the corner of his eye he watched the Ogden house just ahead.

Sure enough, the front screen-door banged and Marvin Ogden came down the steps. Marvin was fifteen, one year older than Ronnie, but smaller and skinnier. He wore glasses and stuttered when he got excited, but he was valedictorian of the graduating class.

Ronnie came up behind him, walking fast.

"Hello, Snot-face!"

Marvin wheeled. He avoided Ronnie's glare, but smiled weakly at the pavement.

"I said hello, Snot-face! What's the matter, don't you know your own name, jerk?"

"Hello—Ronnie."

"How's old Snot-face today?"

"Aw, gee, Ronnie. Why do you have to talk like that? I never did anything to you, did I?"

Ronnie spit in the direction of Marvin's shoes. "I'd like to see you just try doing something to me, you four-eyed little—"

Marvin began to walk away, but Ronnie kept pace.

"Slow down, jerk. I wanna talk to you."

"Wh-what is it, Ronnie? I don't want to be late."

"Shut your yap."

"But—"

"Listen, you. What was the big idea in History exam yesterday when you pulled your paper away?"

"You know, Ronnie. You aren't supposed to copy somebody else's answers."

"You trying to tell me what to do, you sucker?"

"N-no. I mean, I only want to keep you out of trouble. What if Miss Sanders found out, and you want to be elected class president? Why, if anybody knew—"

Ronnie put his hand on Marvin's shoulder. He smiled. "You wouldn't ever tell her about it, would you, Snot-face?" he murmured.

"Of course not! Cross my heart!"

Ronnie continued to smile. He dug his fingers into Marvin's shoulder. With his other hand he swept Marvin's books to the ground. As Marvin bent forward to pick them up, he kicked Marvin as hard as he could, bringing his knee up fast. Marvin sprawled on the sidewalk. He began to cry. Ronnie watched him as he attempted to rise.

"This is just a sample of what you got coming if you squeal," he said. He stepped on the fingers of Marvin's left hand. "Sucker!"

MARVIN'S SNIVELING FADED from his ears as he turned the corner at the end of the block. Mary June was waiting for him under the trees. He came up behind her and slapped her, hard.

"Hello, you!" he said.

Mary June jumped about a foot, her curls bouncing on her shoulders. Then she turned and saw who it was.

"Oh, Ronnie! You oughtn't to—"

"Shut up. I'm in a hurry. Can't be late the day before election. You lining up the girls?"

"Sure, Ronnie. You know I promised. I had Ellen and Vicky over at the house last night and they said they'd vote for you for sure. All the girls are gonna vote for you."

"Well, they better." Ronnie threw his cigarette butt against a rosebush in the Eisners' yard.

"Ronnie—you be careful—want to start a fire?"

"Quit bossing me." He scowled.

"I'm not trying to boss you, Ronnie. Only—"

"Aw, you make me sick!" He quickened his pace, and the girl bit her lip as she endeavored to keep step with him. "Ronnie, wait for me!"

"Wait for me!" he mocked her. "What's the matter, you afraid you'll get lost or something?"

"No. *You* know. I don't like to pass that old Mrs. Mingle's place. She always stares at me and makes faces."

"She's nuts!"

"I'm scared of her, Ronnie. Aren't you?"

"Me scared of that old bat? She can go take a flying leap!"

"Don't talk so loud, she'll hear you."

"Who cares?"

Ronnie marched boldly past the tree-shadowed cottage behind the rusted iron fence. He stared insolently at the girl, who made herself small against his shoulder, eyes averted from the ramshackle edifice. He deliberately slackened his pace as they passed the cottage, with its boarded-up windows, screened-in porch, and general air of withdrawal from the world.

Mrs. Mingle herself was not in evidence. Usually she could be seen in the weed-infested garden at the side of the cottage; a tiny, dried-up old woman, bending over her vines and plants, mumbling incessantly to herself or to the raddled black tomcat which served as her constant companion.

"Old Prune-face ain't around!" Ronnie observed, loudly. "Must be off someplace on her broomstick."

"Ronnie—please!"

"Who cares?" Ronnie pulled Mary June's curls. "You girls are scared of everything, ain't you?"

"*Aren't,* Ronnie."

"Don't tell me how to talk!" Ronnie's gaze shifted again to the silent house, huddled in the shadows. A segment of shadow at the side of the cottage seemed to be moving. A black blur detached itself from the end of the porch. Ronnie recognized Mrs. Mingle's cat. It minced down the path towards the gate.

Quickly, Ronnie stooped and found a rock. He grasped it, rose, aimed, and hurled the missile in one continuous movement.

The cat hissed, then squawled in pain as the rock grazed its ribs.

"Oh, Ronnie!"

"Come on, let's run before she sees us!"

They flew down the street. The school bell drowned out the cat-yowl.

"Here we go," said Ronnie. "You do my homework for me? Good. Give it here."

He snatched the papers from Mary June's hand and sprinted ahead. The girl stood watching him, smiling her admiration. From behind the fence the cat watched, too, and licked its jaws.

II

IT HAPPENED THAT AFTERNOON, after school. Ronnie and Joe Gordan and Seymour Higgins were futzing around with a baseball and he was talking about the outfit Ma promised to buy him this summer if the dressmaking business picked up. Only he made it sound like he was getting the outfit for sure, and that they could all use the mask and mitt. It didn't hurt to build it up a little, with election tomorrow. He had to stand in good with the whole gang.

He knew if he hung around the school-yard much longer, Mary June would come out and want him to walk her home. He was sick of her. Oh, she was all right for home-work and such stuff, but these guys would just laugh at him if he went off with a dame.

So he said how about going down the street to in front of the pool hall and maybe hang around to see if somebody would shoot a game? He'd pay. Besides, they could smoke.

Ronnie knew that these guys didn't smoke, but it sounded bigshot and that's what he wanted. They all followed him down the street, pounding their cleats on the side-walk. It made a lot of noise, because every-thing was so quiet.

All Ronnie could hear was the cat. They were passing Mrs. Mingle's and there was this cat, rolling around in the garden on its back and on its stomach, playing with some kind of ball. It purred and meeowed and whined.

"Look!" yelled Joe Gordan, "Dizzy cat's havin' a fit 'r something, huh?"

"Lice," said Ronnie. "Damned mangy old thing's fulla lice and fleas and stuff. I socked it a good one this morning."

"Ya did?"

"Sure. With a rock. This big, too." He made a watermelon with his hands.

"Weren't you afraid of old lady Mingle?"

"Afraid? Why, that dried-up old—"

"Catnip," said Seymour Higgins. "That's what she's got. Ball of catnip. Old Mingle buys it for her. My old man says she buys everything for that cat; special food and sardines. Treats it like a baby. Ever see them walk down the street together?"

"Catnip, huh?" Joe peered through the fence. "Wonder why they like it so much. Gets 'em wild, doesn't it? Cats'll do anything for catnip."

The cat squealed, sniffing and clawing at the bail. Ronnie scowled at it. "I hate cats. Somebody oughta drowned that damn thing."

"Better not let Mrs. Mingle hear you talk like that," Seymour cautioned. "She'll put the evil eye on you."

"Bull!"

"Well, she grows them herbs and stuff and my old lady says—"

"Bull!"

"All right. But I wouldn't go monkeying around her or her old cat, either."

"I'll show you."

Before he knew it, Ronnie was opening the gate. He advanced toward the black tom-cat as the boys gaped.

The cat crouched over the catnip, eyes flattened against a velveteen skull. Ronnie hesitated a moment, gauging the glitter of claws, the glare of agate eyes. But the gang was watching—

"Scat!" he shouted. He advanced, waving his arms. The cat sidled backwards. Ronnie feinted with his hand and scooped up the catnip ball.

"See? I got it, you guys. I got—"

"Put that down!"

He didn't see the door open. He didn't see her walk down the steps. But suddenly she was there. Leaning on her cane, wearing a black dress that fitted tightly over her tiny frame, she seemed hardly any bigger than the cat which crouched at her side. Her hair was gray and wrinkled and dead, her face was gray and wrinkled and dead, but her eyes—

They were agate eyes, like the cat's.

They glowed. And when she talked, she spit the way the cat did.

"Put that down, young man!"

Ronnie began to shake. It was only a chill, everybody gets chills now and then, and could he help it if he shook so hard the catnip just fell out of his hand?

He wasn't scared. He had to show the gang he wasn't scared of this skinny little dried-up old woman. It was hard to breathe, he was shaking so, but he managed. He filled his lungs and opened his mouth.

"You—you old witch!" he yelled.

The agate eyes widened. They were bigger than she was. All he could see were the eyes. Witch eyes. Now that he said it, he knew it was true. Witch. She was a witch.

"You insolent puppy. I've a good mind to cut out your lying tongue!"

Geez, she wasn't kidding!

Now she was coming closer, and the cat was inching up on him, and then she raised the cane in the air, she was going to hit him, the witch was after him, oh Ma, no, don't, oh—

Ronnie ran.

III

COULD HE HELP IT? Geez, the guys ran too. They'd run before he did, even. He had to run, the old bat was crazy, anybody could see that. Besides, if he'd stayed she'd of tried to hit him and maybe he'd let her have it. He was only trying to keep out of trouble. That was all.

Ronnie told it to himself over and over at supper time. But that didn't do any good, telling it to himself. It was the guys he had to tell it to, and fast. He had to explain it before election tomorrow—

"Ronnie. What's the matter? You sick?"

"No, Ma."

"Then why don't you answer a person? I declare, you haven't said ten words since you came in the house. And you aren't eating your supper."

"Not hungry."

"Something bothering you, son?"

"No. Leave me alone."

"It's that election tomorrow, isn't it?"

"Leave me alone." Ronnie rose. "I'm goin' out."

"Ronnie!"

"I got to see Joe. Important."

"Back by nine, remember."

"Yeah. Sure."

He went outside. The night was cool. Windy for this time of year. Ronnie shivered a little as he turned the corner. Maybe a cigarette—

He lit a match and a shower of sparks spiraled to the sky. Ronnie began to walk, puffing nervously. He had to see Joe and the others and explain. Yeah, right now, too. If they told anybody else—

It was dark. The light on the corner was out, and the Ogdens weren't home. That made it darker, because Mrs. Mingle never showed a light in her cottage.

Mrs. Mingle. Her cottage was up ahead. He'd better cross the street.

What was the matter with him? Was he getting chicken-guts? Afraid of that damned old woman, that old witch! He puffed, gulped, expanded his chest. Just let her try anything. Just let her be hiding under the trees, waiting to grab out at him with her big claws and hiss—what was he talking about, anyway? That was the cat. Nuts to her cat, and her too. He'd show them!

Ronnie walked past the dark shadow where Mrs. Mingle dwelt. He whistled defiance, and emphasized it by shooting his cigarette butt across the fence. Sparks flew and were swallowed by the mouth of the night.

Ronnie paused and peered over the fence. Everything was black and still. There was nothing to be afraid of. Everything was black—

Everything except that flicker. It came from up the path, under the porch. He could see the porch now because there was a light. Not a steady light; a wavering light. Like a fire. A fire—where his cigarette had landed! The cottage was beginning to burn!

Ronnie gulped and clung to the fence. Yes, it was on fire, all right. Mrs. Mingle would come out and the firemen would come and they'd find the butt and see him and then—

He fled down the street. The wind cat-howled behind him, the wind that fanned the flames that burned the cottage—

* * *

MA WAS IN BED. He managed to slow down and walk softly as he slipped into the house, up the stairs. He undressed in the dark and sought sanctuary between the bedsheets. When he got the covers over his head he had another chill. Lying there, trembling, not daring to look out of the window and see the glare from the other side of the block, Ronnie's teeth chattered. He knew he was going to pass out in a minute.

Then he heard the screaming from far away. Fire engines. Somebody had called them. He needn't worry now. Why should the sound frighten him? It was only a siren, it wasn't Mrs. Mingle screaming, it couldn't be. She was all right. He was all right. Nobody knew....

Ronnie fell asleep with the wind and the siren wailing in his ears. His slumber was deep and only once was there an interruption. That was along towards morning, when he thought he heard a noise at the window. It was a scraping sound. The wind, of course. And it must have been the wind, too, that sobbed and whined and whimpered beneath the windowsill at dawn. It was only Ronnie's imagination, Ronnie's conscience, that transformed the sound into the wailing of a cat....

IV

"Ronnie!"

It wasn't the wind, it wasn't a cat. Ma was calling him.

"Ronnie! Oh, Ronnie!"

He opened his eyes, shielding them from the sunshafts.

"I declare, you might answer a person." He heard her grumbling to herself downstairs. Then she called again.

"Ronnie!"

"I'm coming, Ma."

He got out of bed. Went to the bathroom, and dressed. She was waiting for him in the kitchen.

"Land sakes, you sure slept sound last night. Didn't you hear the fire engines?"

Ronnie dropped a slice of toast. "What engines?"

Ma's voice rose. "Don't you know? Why, boy, it was just awful—Mrs. Mingle's cottage burned down."

"Yeah?" He had trouble picking up the toast again.

"The poor old lady—just think of it—trapped in there—"

He had to shut her up. He couldn't stand what was coming next. But what could he say, how could he stop her?

"Burned alive. The whole place was on fire when they got there. The Ogdens saw it when they came home and Mr. Ogden called the firemen, but it was too late. When I think of that old lady it just makes me—"

Without a word, Ronnie rose from the table and left the room. He didn't wait for his lunch. He didn't bother to examine himself in the mirror. He went outside, before he cried, or screamed, or hauled off and hit Ma in the puss.

The puss—

It was waiting for him on the front walk. The black bundle with the agate eyes. The cat. Mrs. Mingle's cat, waiting for him to come out.

Ronnie took a deep breath before he opened the gate. The cat didn't make a sound, didn't stir. It just hunched up on the sidewalk and stared at him.

He watched it for a moment, then cast about for a stick. There was a hunk of lathe near the porch. He picked it up and swung it. Then he opened the gate.

"Scat!" he said.

The cat retreated. Ronnie walked away. The cat moved after him. Ronnie wheeled, brandishing the stick.

"Scram, before I let you have it!"

The cat stood still. Ronnie stared at it. Why hadn't the damn' thing burned up in the fire? And what was it doing here?

He gripped the lath. It felt good between his fingers, splinters and all. Just let that mangy tom start anything—

He walked along, not looking back. What was the matter with him? Suppose the cat did follow him. It couldn't hurt him any. Neither could old Mingle. She was dead. The dirty witch. Talking about cutting his tongue out. Well, she got what was coming to her, all right. Too bad her scroungy cat was still around. If it didn't watch out, he'd fix *it*, too. He should worry now.

Nobody was going to find out about that

cigarette. Mrs. Mingle was dead. He ought to be glad, everything was all right; sure, he felt great.

The shadow followed him down the street.

"Get out of here!"

Ronnie turned and heaved the lathe at the cat. It hissed. Ronnie heard the wind hiss, heard his cigarette butt hiss, heard Mrs. Mingle hiss.

He began to run. The cat ran after him.

"Hey, Ronnie!"

Marvin Ogden was calling him. He couldn't stop now, not even to hit the punk. He ran on. The cat kept pace.

Then he was winded and he slowed down. It was just in time, too. Up ahead was a crowd of kids, standing on the sidewalk in front of a heap of charred, smoking boards.

They were looking at Mingle's cottage—

Ronnie closed his eyes and darted back up the street. The cat followed.

He had to get rid of it before he went to school. What if people saw him with her cat? Maybe they'd start to talk. He had to get rid of it—

Ronnie ran clear down to Sinclair Street. The cat was right behind him. On the corner he picked up a stone and let fly. The cat dodged. Then it sat down on the sidewalk and looked at him. Just looked.

Ronnie couldn't take his eyes off the cat. It stared so. Mrs. Mingle had stared, too. But she was dead. And this was only a cat. A cat he had to get away from, fast.

The streetcar came down Sinclair Street. Ronnie found a dime in his pocket and boarded the car. The cat didn't move. He stood on the platform as the car pulled away and looked back at the cat. It just sat there.

Ronnie rode around the loop, then transferred to the Hollis Avenue car. It brought him over to the school, ten minutes late. He got off and started to hurry across the street.

A shadow crossed the entrance to the building.

Ronnie saw the cat. It squatted there, waiting.

He ran.

That's all Ronnie remembered of the rest of the morning. He ran. He ran, and the cat followed. He couldn't go to school, he couldn't be there for the election, he couldn't get rid of the cat. He ran.

Up and down the streets, back and forth, all over the whole neighborhood; stopping and dodging and throwing stones and swearing and panting and sweating. But always the running, and always the cat right behind him.

Once it started to chase him and before he knew it he was heading straight for the place where the burned smell filled the air, straight for the ruins of Mrs. Mingle's cottage. The cat wanted him to go there, wanted him to see—

Ronnie began to cry. He sobbed and panted all the way home. The cat didn't make a sound. It followed him. All right, let it. He'd fix it. He'd tell Ma. Ma would get rid of it for him. Ma.

"Ma!" He yelled as he ran up the steps.

No answer. She was out. Marketing.

And the cat crept up the steps behind him.

Ronnie slammed the door, locked it. Ma had her key. He was safe now. Safe at home. Safe in bed—he wanted to go to bed and pull the covers over his head, wait for Ma to come and make everything all right.

There was a scratching at the door.

"Ma!" His scream echoed through the empty house.

He ran upstairs. The scratching died away.

And then he heard the footsteps on the porch, the slow footsteps; he heard the rattling and turning of the doorknob. It was old lady Mingle, coming from the grave. It was the witch, coming to get him. It was—

"Ma!"

"Ronnie, what's the matter? What you doing home from school?"

He heard her. It was all right. Just in time, Ronnie closed his mouth. He couldn't tell her about the cat. He mustn't ever tell her. Then everything would come out. He had to be careful what he said.

"I got sick to my stomach," he said. "Miss Sanders said I should come home and lay down."

RONNIE LAY IN BED and dozed as the afternoon shadows ran in long black ribbons across the bedroom floor. He smiled to himself. What a sucker he was! Afraid of a cat. Maybe there wasn't even a cat—all in his mind. *Dope!*

"Ronnie—you all right?" Ma called up from the foot of the stairs.

"Yes, Ma. I feel lots better."

Sure, he felt better. He could get up now and eat supper if he wanted. In just a minute he'd put his clothes on and go downstairs. He started to push the sheets off. It was dark in the room, now. Just about supper-time—

Then Ronnie heard it. A scratching. A scurrying. From the hall? No. It couldn't be in the hall. Then where?

The window. It was open. And the scratching came from the ledge outside. He had to close it, fast. Ronnie jumped out of bed, barking his shin against a chair as he groped through the dusk. Then he was at the window, slamming it down, tight.

He heard the scratching.

And it came from *inside the room!*

Ronnie hurled himself upon the bed, clawing the covers up to his chin. His eyes bulged against the darkness.

Where was it?

He saw nothing but shadows. Which shadow moved?

Where was it?

Ronnie didn't know. All he knew was that he lay in bed, waiting, thinking of Mrs. Mingle and her cat and how she was a witch and died because he'd killed her. Or *had* he killed her? He was all mixed up, he couldn't remember, he didn't know what was real and what wasn't real anymore. He couldn't tell which shadow would move next.

And then he could.

The round shadow was moving. The round black ball was inching across the floor from beneath the window. It was the cat, all right, because shadows don't have claws that scrape. Shadows don't leap through the air and perch on the bedpost, grinning at you with yellow eyes and yellow teeth ... *grinning the way Mrs. Mingle grinned.*

The cat was big. Its eyes were big. Its teeth were big. It crouched there, hunching to spring.

Ronnie opened his mouth to scream.

Then the shadow was sailing through the air, coming at him, at his face, at his open mouth. The claws were fastened in his cheeks, forcing his jaws apart. And the head dipped—

Far away, under the pain, someone was calling.

"Ronnie! Oh, Ronnie! What's the matter with you?"

Everything was fire. Ronnie lashed out and suddenly the shadow went away and he was sitting bolt upright in bed. His mouth worked but no sound came out. Nothing came out except that gushing red wetness.

"Ronnie! Why don't you answer me?"

A guttural sound came from deep within Ronnie's throat, but no words. There would never be any words.

"Ronnie—what's the matter? *Has the cat got your tongue?*"

"Catnip" first appeared in the March 1948 issue of Weird Tales.

During a career that began with the pulp magazines of the 1930s and stretched across seven decades, prolific American novelist and screenwriter Robert Bloch (1917–1994) wrote close to three dozen novels, scores of television and film scripts, and hundreds of short stories. Although he began by emulating the works of Lovecraft, Bloch quickly moved on, becoming a master of the macabre specializing in tales of crime and psychological horror. He is best known today for his novel Psycho, *which was filmed in 1960 by director Alfred Hitchcock. The box-office popularity of* Psycho *prompted a rash of similarly-themed movies, spawning a cinematic subgenre.*

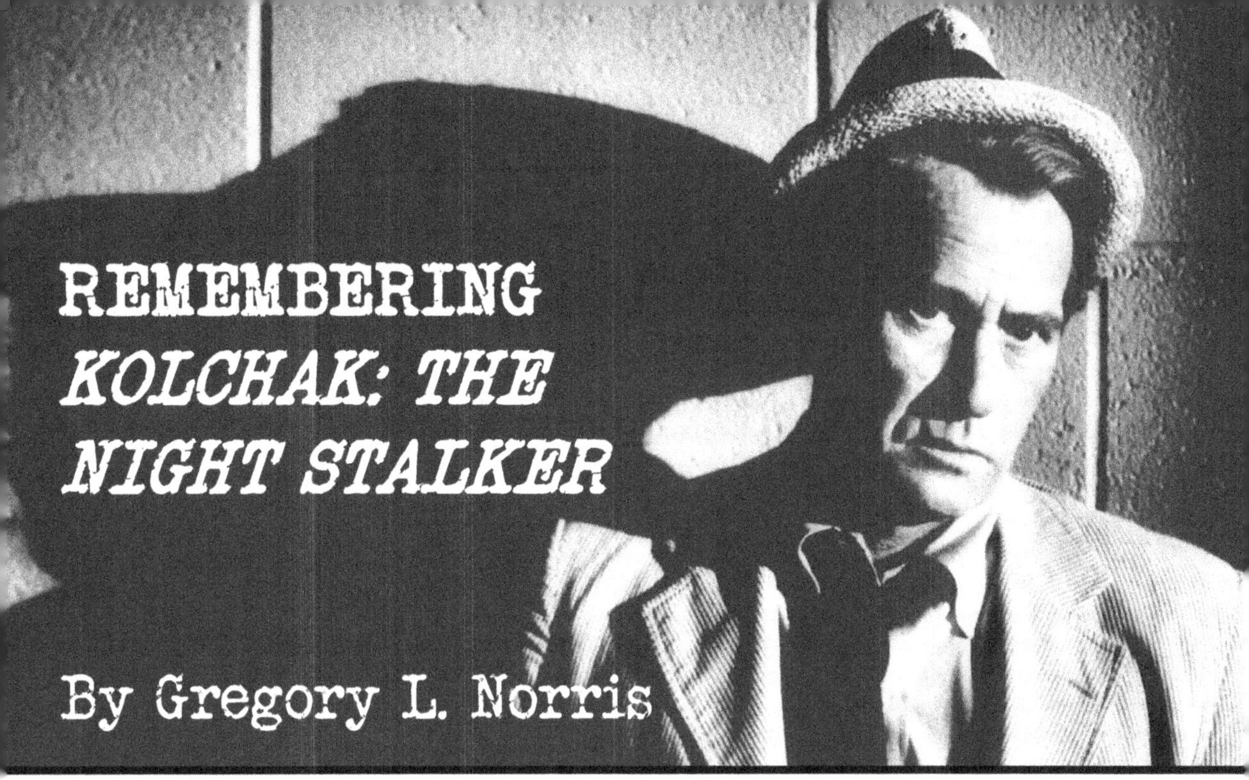

REMEMBERING KOLCHAK: THE NIGHT STALKER

By Gregory L. Norris

A MAN ENTERS THE CHICAGO OFFICES OF THE INDEPENDENT NEWS SERVICE—INS FOR SHORT. CLAD IN A RUMPLED SEERSUCKER SUIT, TENNIS SHOES, BUTTON-DOWN SHIRT, UNKNOTTED BLACK TIE, AND A STRAW HAT WITH A BLACK AND BURGUNDY BAND, HE LOOKS LIKE HE'S SLEPT IN HIS CLOTHES. IT'S DARK OUT, THE HOUR LATE. THERE'S NOBODY ELSE AROUND. *The man whistles a catchy tune to himself as he proceeds to his desk, third one in line beyond the swinging bullpen doors. It's time for investigative newshound Carl Kolchak to report on the latest gruesome and unnatural crimes to terrorize the Windy City.*

Kolchak pours a coffee—black, whips his hat at the hook, misses, and takes a seat at his desk. He rolls a blank white sheet into his manual typewriter and goes to work. Words appear in a mad frenzy as his fingers pound keys, all of them telegraphing the otherworldly and horrifying nature of the story he's uncovered. From somewhere nearby in the deserted newspaper offices, a frisson of wrongness emanates. Alerted to it, Kolchak looks up. The overhead lights dim, bathing him in shadow. The wall clock freezes.

The electric fan dies. Kolchak whips around, eyes wide and unblinkingly filled with terror while aimed at something the viewer doesn't yet see—something not of this sane and normal world.

AND WITH THAT, each Friday at 10 p.m. during a single season in 1974–75, TV audiences followed Carl Kolchak into the shadows and watched him stalk the night in search of the truth while pitted against a host of supernatural villains.

THE STORY OF *Kolchak: The Night Stalker* began with an unpublished vampire novel manuscript written by Jeff Rice that had attracted the attention of famed author Richard Matheson, revered for his work on *The Twilight Zone* and such Horror classics as *I Am Legend* and *The Legend of Hell House*. At the time, the ABC television network and it's "Movie of the Week" was a cinematic treasure trove responsible for such outstanding efforts as *The House That Would Not Die*, *Crowhaven Farm*, *Don't Be Afraid of the Dark*—which pitted Kim Darby against a trio of evil gremlins in a spooky old manor—and the brilliant

Barry Atwater and Darren McGavin, in *The Night Stalker*.
Opposite page: Matheson at the Movies.

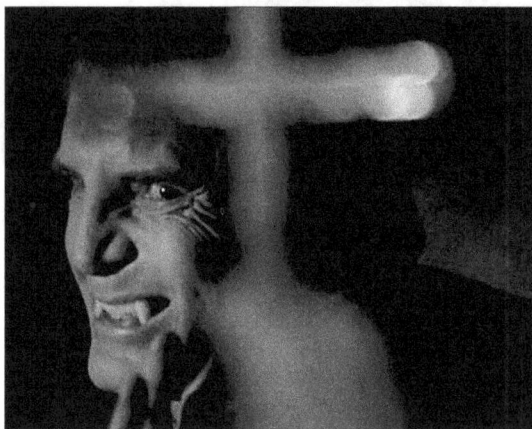

A Cold Night's Death, among others. Produced by Dan Curtis, fresh from his five-year run on the dreamy daytime gothic soap *Dark Shadows*, *The Kolchak Papers* was adapted into *The Night Stalker,* in which a Las Vegas reporter suspects a vampire is behind a series of grisly murders.

Starring Darren McGavin, who'd briefly stalked the nights of a different city in the title role of *Mickey Spillane's Mike Hammer*, *The Night Stalker* premiered on January 11, 1972 and earned the highest ratings of any made-for-TV movie until that point and was soon packaged for theatrical distribution overseas. The movie, which also featured Simon Oakland as reporter Carl Kolchak's long-suffering editor Tony Vincenzo and Barry Atwater in an unforgettable performance as Janos Skorzeny, the vampire, concluded with Kolchak staking Skorzeny through the

heart, and afterward being run out of Vegas by authorities eager to cover up the truth, thus setting the stage for a sequel, *The Night Strangler*.

Scoring another ratings coup, *The Night Strangler* ran on January 16, 1973 without commercials and finds a transplanted Kolchak in the Pacific Northwest as another series of grisly, unexplained murders rocks Seattle, Washington. Kolchak bumps into Tony Vincenzo once more, and the assignment that results leads to deeply buried secrets—literally and figuratively—in the underground city of Old Seattle, which rests mostly intact beneath modern pavement. The killer (played by *The Six Million-Dollar Man*'s future boss, Richard Anderson) has committed similar murders every twenty-one years since the Civil War and must do so again to create a magic elixir based on human blood that prolongs his life. Kolchak follows the story down, down to a forgotten world both sinister and stunning in its depiction—whole streets bathed in a perpetual, foggy false night by the city built over rooftops, and elegant

rooms draped in cobwebs and populated by skeletons of the long dead. As happened in Vegas, Kolchak eliminates the killer right as the police swarm in, and he's given the boot. Before the closing credits roll, Kolchak and Vincenzo are seen driving out of Seattle, headed toward New York City where, presumably,

Underground Seattle,
from *The Night Strangler*
Bottom: Richard Anderson as the strangler, before and after.

more mayhem is fated to ensue.

But the two make it only as far as Chicago.

ACCORDING TO A 2004 interview, the late Dan Curtis confirmed that a third Matheson screenplay entry into the franchise had been planned, titled *The Night Killers*. But the network decided instead to go to a full series commitment, and in 1974 *Kolchak: the Night Stalker* was produced with McGavin once more in the lead role and Oakland as his boss, the two relocated to the iconic Old Colony Building in downtown Chicago, home to the INS.

Joining Kolchak and Vincenzo in their weekly pursuit of the day's—and night's—news were Jack Grinnage as Kolchak's

dandified foil, Ron Updyke; Ruth McDevitt as self-help columnist Emily Cowles (and, in the pilot episode, "The Ripper," an elderly busybody instrumental in helping Kolchak corner the monster in his lair); and, early on in the series' run, Carol Ann Susi as Monique Marmelstein, niece of one of the newspaper's corporate bigwigs. (Decades later, Susi would provide the grating voice of Howard Wolowitz's mother on *The Big Bang Theory*.) A revolving door of morgue attendants and irate police captains came and went from one episode to the next.

In order, Kolchak encountered and prevailed against Jack the Ripper, a zombie, hostile alien visitors with a hankering for bone marrow, a female vampire (one born in Vegas tied in to the original *The Night Stalker* movie), a werewolf, an arsonist doppleganger, a dog possessed by the devil —classic 70s fare, an evil Native American Diablero, a swamp monster, a powerful Native American demon, a cannibalistic Hindu demon, a murderous android run amok, a flesh-eating caveman, a haute couture witch, a headless biker, a succubus, an Aztec mummy, a murderous black knight, Helen of Troy who sucked the life out of the young and beautiful, and a reptilian sentry. Twenty episodes in all were produced before McGavin, tired of the monster-of-the-week format and concerned regarding script quality, asked to be freed from his contract. Three

Clockwise from top left: INS offices; *Kolchak* promo depicting "Demon in Lace"; McGavin with Ruth McDevitt; and with Jack Grinnage and Simon Oakland.

Clockwise from top left: "The Spanish Moss Murders"; Kolchak on the trail of "Mossy"; "Horror in the Heights"; and "Bad Medicine" with Richard Kiel.

additional scripts had been ordered in which Kolchak faced off against a supernatural femme fatale ("Eye of Terror"), a monster in West Virginia coal mining country ("The Get of Belial"), and a cursed painting ("The Executioners").

Standouts include "The Spanish Moss Murders," in which a legendary childhood monster, Pére Malfait, is raised through a sleep study experiment and goes on a rampage to kill all who threaten its existence. Another excellent—and chilling—effort is "Horror in the Heights," in which the city's aging Jewish population is terrorized by the Hindu demon-spirit Rakshasa, which strips its victims' flesh off their bones and is a harbinger of the End of Days—bold storytelling for any decade, not just the time.

"If I had to pick just one episode, gun to my head, I guess I'd have to go with 'Demon in Lace' because it is probably the most Lovecraftian of the bunch. And the monster of the week in this one is really

creepy—as in right out of an issue of *Creepy* Magazine," says Jason McCuiston, frequent contributor to *Black Infinity* and author of the novel *Project Notebook* and the *The Last Star Warden* series, of the succubus episode which involves a cursed stone tablet returned from the Iraqi desert. "A close second has to be 'Zombie' because of that scene where Carl is in the back of the hearse trying to sew up the zombie's mouth and it wakes up. Scarred me for life!"

Among *Kolchak: The Night Stalker*'s impressive guest stars are a young Erik Estrada in one of his earliest roles, *One Life to Live*'s Phil Carey, a pre-*James Bond* Richard Kiel as the Diablero, and Tom Skerritt (*Alien*) as a shapeshifting, rising politician possessed by the devil. Comic Phil Silvers and former *The Three Stooges* funnyman Benny Rubin both appear in one of the spookiest episodes of the series' run, "Horror in the Heights," and Lara Parker, Angelique from *Dark Shadows*, got to roll out her patented witch's cackle one last time in "The Trevi Collection."

The series, though groundbreaking for its time, also suffered from its 70s vibe in that some peripheral characters tended to play out as stereotypical during their brief appearances on screen. But it also succeeds beautifully for that same vibe in terms of cinematography—slow motion sequences and freeze frames conveying the utter horror of the moment from a time before the modern—and tired—use of jump scares.

the rock-solid determination to get to the bottom of the story, no matter what."

And, of course, there's McGavin's star power in a role made unforgettable fifty years on and counting.

"Well, I believe *Kolchak: The Night Stalker* is one of, if not the very first horror-adventure series on TV. It's the grand-daddy of *Werewolf, Friday the 13th: The Series* (if anyone else remembers those), *The X-Files*, *Supernatural*, and their ilk," adds McCuiston. "*The Twilight Zone* and its imitators had introduced weekly horror to the TV audience, but these were anthologies: one-and-done stories. And while shows like *Star Trek* and *The Wild, Wild West* had dealt with horror elements in the occasional episode, Kolchak was the first everyman hero we followed into old cemeteries, abandoned houses, and urban decay on a weekly basis. And that every-man quality is probably the hallmark of the series. Carl wasn't an FBI agent, a gunslinger, or even a muscled-up pro-fessional monster hunter. He was a bow-legged guy with a camera, a recorder, and

THE FINAL EPISODE of the series, "The Sentry," aired on March 28, 1975. From there, two episodes were repackaged to-gether and released as *The Demon and the Mummy*. *Kolchak: the Night Stalker* played in syndication and does so to this day.

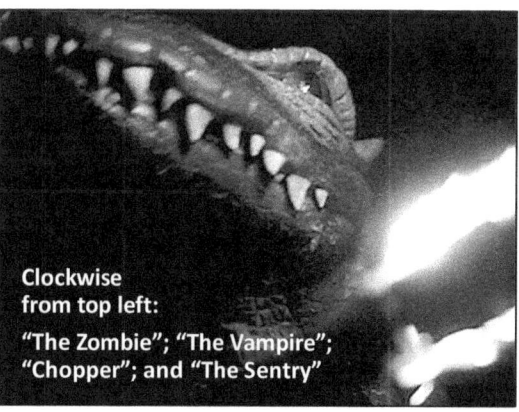

Clockwise from top left:
"The Zombie"; "The Vampire"; "Chopper"; and "The Sentry"

McGavin with Tom Skerritt, in "The Devil's Platform" and (below) Lara Parker, in "The Trevi Collection"

Chris Carter, creator of *The X-Files*, openly credits Kolchak's adventures as the inspiration behind his hugely successful franchise. In 1998, Carter approached McGavin to dust off his seersucker suit and reprise the role in an episode that would have matched FBI agents Mulder and Scully with Carl Kolchak. McGavin declined, but Carter still paid homage by casting him as Arthur Dale, father of the X-Files, in the episode "Travelers."

In 2005, the Alphabet Network produced the inferior *Night Stalker*, a remake that only ran for six episodes that fall season. Gone was the frenetic pace and energy of the original, instead replaced by a watered-down canvas whose only similarities to the source material were in a bad splice of McGavin's Kolchak standing in the newsroom alongside new series' star Stuart Townsend, the title character's name, and that of Kolchak's boss,

The truth is out there. Getting it printed is the problem. Editor Tony Vincenzo (Simon Oakland) often found Kolchak's facts hard to believe.

Anthony Vincenzo (Cotter Smith). Whereas McGavin's Kolchak was frumpy and likeable, Townsend's was a brooding, vapid, and unsympathetic pretty boy.

Numerous comics, graphic novels, and anthologies have continued the Kolchak story, beginning in the early 2000s, which also include adaptations of two of the unproduced original scripts, "The Get of Belial" and "Eye of Terror." To celebrate the half-century mark since the original made-for-TV movie first aired, editor James Aquilone is releasing *Kolchak: The Night*

CONTINUED AFTER NEXT PAGE

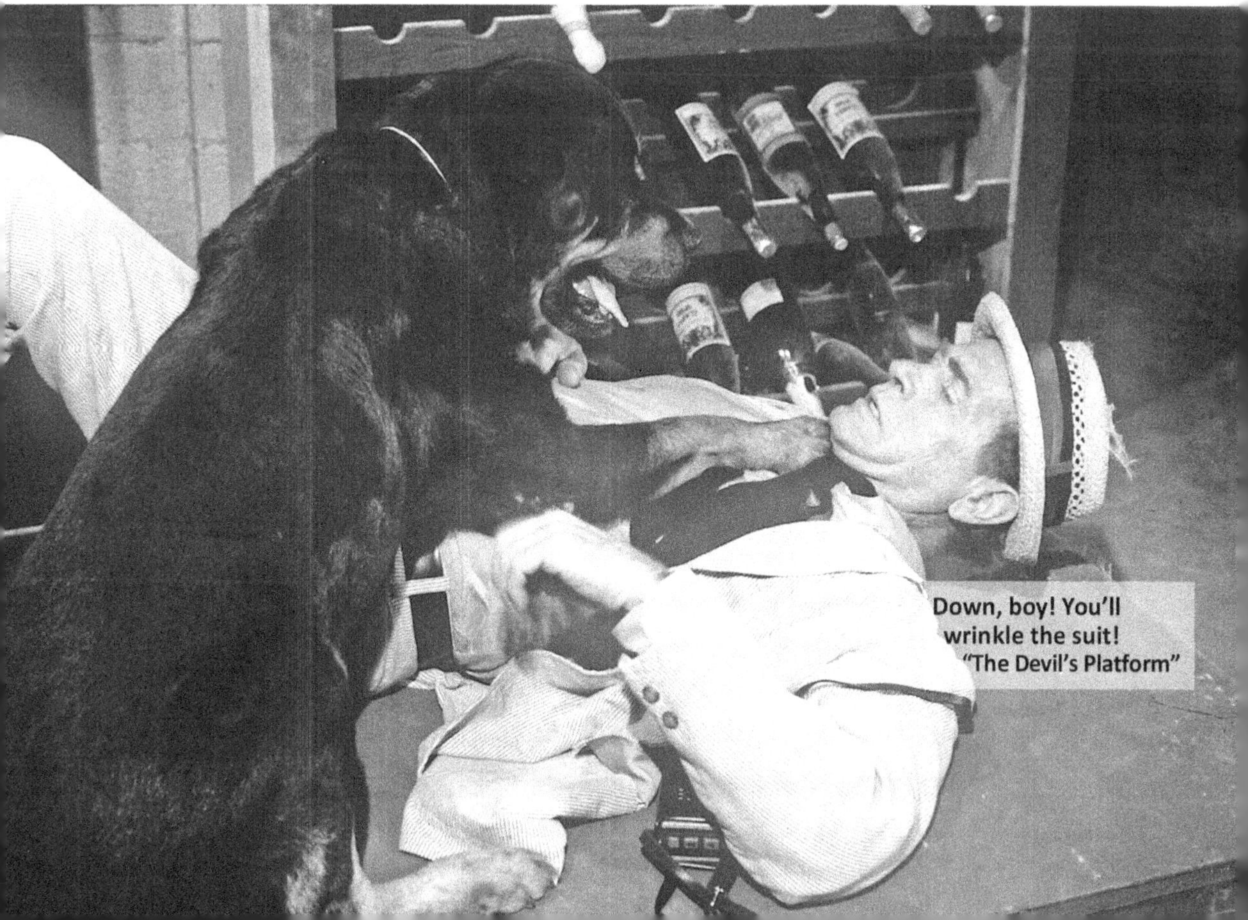

Down, boy! You'll wrinkle the suit! "The Devil's Platform"

The Strangler and the Stalker!
Promo for *The Night Strangler*.

Stalker 50th Anniversary Prose Anthology to commemorate the series' milestone.

Though rumors of a big screen adaptation continue to circulate with no firm commitment—in 2012, Disney announced a re-imagining that reportedly was to star Johnny Depp, the legacy of *Kolchak: The Night Stalker* endures.

"I believe it's because the show had heart," says McCuiston. "Darren McGavin was giving his all in every take and you can see that on the screen. I mean, the guy wasn't exactly a kid when this show was filmed and yet that's actually him shimmying up the sides of houses and crawling through windows and climbing fences. He

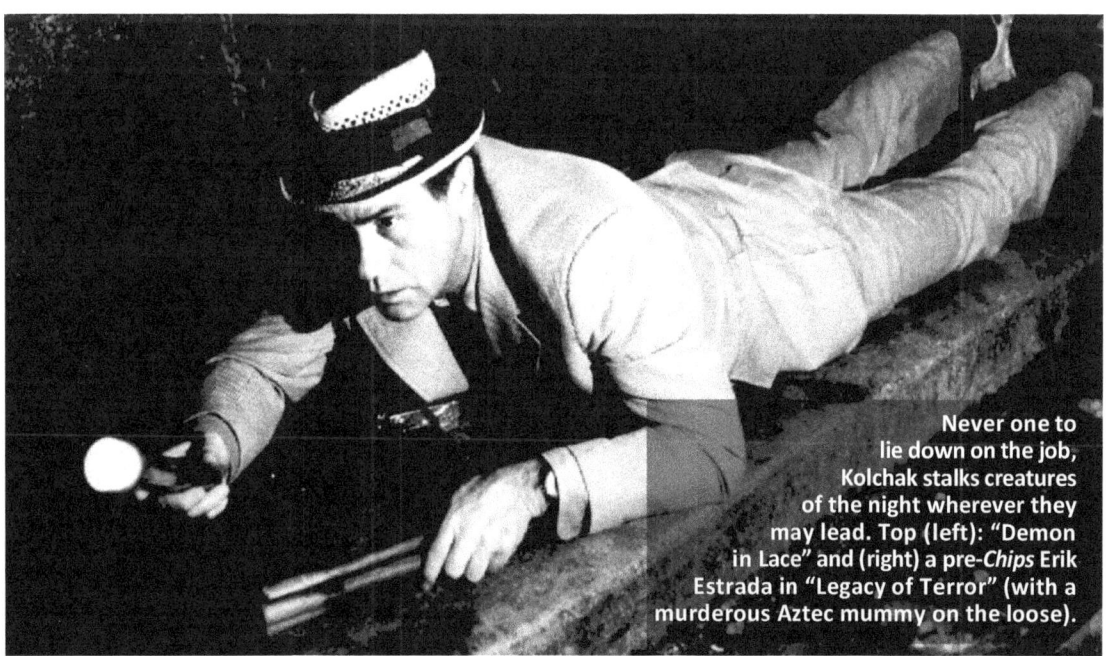

Never one to lie down on the job, Kolchak stalks creatures of the night wherever they may lead. Top (left): "Demon in Lace" and (right) a pre-*Chips* Erik Estrada in "Legacy of Terror" (with a murderous Aztec mummy on the loose).

Just keep telling yourself ... it couldn't happen here.

similar to those that dominate modern TV. But I think a lot of today's shows have traded that intensity of telling a really good, tight story in a single 40- to 50-minute block for these meandering and often self-indulgent plotlines that span an entire season. In a word, they just don't have the heart of *Kolchak: The Night Stalker*."

was a charismatic force of nature and a consummate professional, and I believe the other cast members raised their own game because of that. Most of the characters were only in one or two episodes, but they were always portrayed as living parts of Kolchak's world. And the epic interactions between McGavin and Simon Oakland—another master of his craft—are always a highlight of every episode. I know that by the time the show was done, McGavin was getting tired of the 'monster-of-the-week' format and wanted broader story arcs

KOLCHAK FINISHES TYPING and pulls the sheet of paper out of his typewriter. He scans what he's written, laughs, and then crumples the sheet into a ball and pitches it into the trash. He slings his camera and tape recorder by their straps onto his shoulder and grabs his seersucker coat from the hook, dislodging a framed photograph in the process. Straw hat on head, he ambles across the dark INS newsroom, switches off the light, and stalks out, into the night.

Give Me Back My Name

By David Surface

WHEN ROB WOKE, THE ROOM WAS PITCH-DARK WITH NOTHING FOR HIS EYE TO HOLD ONTO. HIS BRAIN FLASHED THROUGH A SERIES OF OTHER BEDROOMS HE'D SLEPT IN, OTHER HOUSES, APARTMENTS AND MOTEL ROOMS, each one quickly dissolving into the next, while he lay still and waited for the objects around him to become clear. The familiar shape of a bureau to his right. The solid rectangle of a framed picture on the wall. Carrie's body breathing next to his.

He lay there for a moment longer, letting the relief of knowing where he was soak into him, then got out of bed and went downstairs to start the coffee.

This was his favorite part of the day, the quiet in-between time before anything had started, when it felt like he was the only person in the world. He enjoyed this morning ritual, filling the kettle, striking a match, lighting the blue flame on the stovetop, and setting the kettle on it. Then the patient waiting for the flame to do its work while the blackness outside the windows turned blue.

The coffee was ready and waiting in the two big mugs by the time Carrie came downstairs, bleary-eyed and carrying her big shoulder-bag stuffed with students' homework. She took the mug from his hand, dropped into one of the kitchen chairs and took a deep and grateful sip.

"God, that's good…" she whispered.

"Ready for another big day at school?" he smiled. Carrie rolled her eyes.

"Yeah … I gotta tell the kids a ghost story today."

"Really? I thought you liked ghost stories."

"I do. But the school wants me to keep telling the same one every year. You know, where the dead woman keeps saying, *Give me back my golden arm.*"

"You mean the one where you're supposed to yell at the end and make everyone jump?"

"Yeah. The husband steals his wife's golden arm, and at night he hears her calling, *Give me back my golden arm… Give me back my golden arm…* It's so stupid. I mean, who has a golden arm?"

"I don't know…" he said, "Will the kids even think that's scary? A golden arm?"

"Yeah," Carrie said, "Maybe I should update it or something. *Give me back my iPhone Six!*"

After Carrie left, Rob went out and raked the front yard to let the cold October air wake him up. He spent the rest of the morning washing the dishes from breakfast, then sweeping and dusting. He liked to keep moving when he was alone. It kept his mind focused and sharp.

At twelve, he took a break to eat lunch and check his email and saw a message from a job he'd applied for. *We'd like you to come in for an interview,* the email said, *after you've agreed to submit to a routine background check.* He deleted the email without responding, stood up and went back to cleaning the house.

Rob had dinner on the table as usual when Carrie got home from school. Pasta primavera with marinara sauce and crusty bread. They ate while Carrie told Rob about her day.

"So, how did the ghost story go? Did you scare the hell out of those poor defenseless children?"

Carrie took another sip of wine before she answered. "Oh sure. Scarred them for life. *Give me back my golden arm...* Actually, I think I saw a couple of them jump at the end.*"

"What does a ghost need with a golden arm?" he asked. "I mean, it's not like she can go out and *spend* it or something, because she's dead, right?"

"I don't know," Carrie shrugged. "Maybe it's like … the principle of the thing. You know. You take something from me, now you have to give it back."

They were clearing the table after dinner when she asked him.

"So, have you heard back from that security job yet?"

"Nope," he said. "Not yet."

"Jeez," Carrie said, "What's taking them so long? Are they doing one of those background checks or something? They probably just want to make sure you're not a serial killer," Carrie grinned. "You're not a serial killer, are you?"

"No," he managed a wry smile, then bent down and kissed her on the forehead. "I'm not a serial killer."

Rob usually made sure to look at all the requirements before applying for a job. Every time he found one that required a background check, he'd cross it off his list and move on to the next. He must have missed this one—he'd have to be more careful next time.

A simple job—that's what he'd told Carrie he needed. One where he could work in peace and quiet without anyone breathing down his neck. And as usual, she'd agreed. *People should do what they're good at,* she'd said. He was good at being alone. Low profile jobs were the best. Construction. Maintenance. Security. Carrie didn't seem to mind. It was one more reason he felt safe with her.

You must have been a shepherd in a former life, she'd said once. He'd smiled but felt the sting. His former life was gone. In fact, it wasn't even his life anymore.

WHEN HE'D LEFT the house that morning twenty years ago, he hadn't known he was going to disappear. He was just going to go for a long drive to clear his head after another terrible fight with Ann. He was twenty-three years old back then, their divorce was almost final, and the future was a horrifying void. The legal bills and demands for support confused and terrified him.

They can't make you give what you don't have, a friend had told him. What his friend hadn't said was what they could do to him. He was stunned when he understood how bad things really were, but it made a terrible kind of sense. Ever since he was a child, Rob had been haunted by the feeling that something bad was going to happen to him one day. Something he didn't have the power to stop. Now he knew what it was. He was going to prison. Not today, not tomorrow. But someday. It was going to happen.

By the time he realized how far he'd driven, he'd gone nearly two hundred miles. The landscape around him had started to change, the look of the trees and houses. Even the sky seemed different. It was the feeling of *newness* that overcame him. He could feel his old life falling away, like the pieces of a cocoon he was shedding. Ann's anger, the divorce proceedings, the lawyer bills. The threat of prison. They were all there in his rearview mirror, like storm clouds gathering, but it was a storm that was happening somewhere behind him. He could outrun it.

I could just keep going. That was the thought that rose in his mind and took hold of him. It was true. He could just keep going. And he did.

He'd done none of the things he should have done first to make disappearing easy. The fake IDs and social security number, the new name. He had to learn about all of it on the run. He'd thrown his cell phone into a river—he knew enough to do that—then found a library that would let him use the computer. It amazed him that he could go online and find a complete set of instructions for how to assume a new identity. It had been written for women escaping dangerous, abusive husbands or boyfriends. He was surprised and reassured by how much of it applied to him. You didn't have to be a bad person to disappear, he realized. It was something that happened to good people too.

He spent three days in a dusty cubicle, just taking notes in a spiral notebook. When his eyes and his brain got tired, he'd look out the library window at the bright green lawn outside, and the orderly white houses. Once, the door to one of the houses opened and a man stepped outside. Rob watched the man walk to his mailbox and get his mail. An older man with graying hair, he was reasonably trim and fit and wore what looked like a blue track suit. Rob watched the man flip through his mail, then turn and walk back into his house, his movements unhurried and confident. The thought crossed Rob's mind that this was how he'd like to look one day. An unhurried, confident man with attractively greying hair and no worries.

Twenty years later, that's exactly what he was.

He'd never told Carrie about Ann. Or his real name. That was one of the rules for disappearing. *Do not tell your new partner about your former life, no matter how much you are tempted.* He'd felt tempted for a brief while, after they'd been together for about seven years, but the feeling had passed. After all, he was a new person now. The old one no longer existed.

One night, they were sitting outside after dark, drinking and talking. Carrie was worried about her sister who'd just separated from her husband. "I really hate it," Carrie said. "It's so sad. They used to be such good friends."

"Yeah, well, that's how a lot of marriages start out," Rob said. "You think you're *such good friends* with someone. Then one day you don't even know who they are...." He felt himself starting to go down into a familiar spiral, but stopped himself. He was more drunk than he'd realized. When he looked up, Carrie was staring at him, her eyes growing wide with shock.

"Rob...were you...? Oh my God. You were married before. You were, weren't you?"

He froze. A sudden panic twisted in his chest, like a wild animal caught in a trap. He wanted to lie, but he knew it was too late. She'd seen him.

"Yes. I'm sorry. But ... it was a long time ago. I was just a stupid kid. It only lasted a few months."

It was dark outside, but he could see her face turn pale. "Jesus, Rob, why didn't you tell me?"

"I don't know. I guess ... I guess it was just too painful."

"Why? What happened?"

"She died." The words surprised him. He didn't know he was going to say them, but once he did, he just kept going. "It was cancer. Ovarian."

He could see her struggling with what he was telling her. "I'm ... I'm sorry," she finally said. "That must have been awful."

It killed him, how quickly she'd turned from shock to sympathy. She believed him. Relief rushed through him, mixed with shame. He hated to lie to her, but he did it to protect her. To protect them both and their life together.

Carrie waited a moment, giving him some time, he supposed. Then she asked quietly, "What was her name?"

For a second, he almost said *Ann.* There was no reason not to. Then, almost before he knew it, the caution he'd drilled into himself took over.

"Hannah."

He saw the impact that hearing the name

made on her. The name made it real. He could almost she her flinch. Now it was his turn to wait and give her a moment. When he thought she looked ready, he continued.

"I'm sorry I never told you. I just ... I mean, it was a long time ago. It was a really hard time, and I guess ... I guess I just didn't want to think about it. I'm sorry." He was pushing his luck, he knew, but he asked anyway. "Forgive me?"

She looked at him for a long time before answering, and for a moment he was afraid she'd seen through him. Then she sighed.

"I guess I'll have to, won't I?"

That night he dreamed that he murdered Ann. All the planning and plotting he'd done in real life to erase his marriage, to erase *her,* came into play in his dream, and he moved through it like some kind of faceless killer, perfectly executing every detail of her death in the most cold-blooded, methodical way. In his dream, there was a box he had to put her body into. The box was too small to hold her body, so he started folding her in half, then again, and again, breaking her down and pushing the parts together until they fit. The box was made of clear plexiglass, so he could see the different parts of her inside, pressed up against it—a whorl of long brown hair, one flattened cheek, the fingers of one hand splayed against the glass like a starfish. He didn't want anyone to see, so he took the box out into the middle of the ocean and dropped it in where it sank without a trace. Instead of waking up with his heart pounding or in a cold sweat, he woke feeling oddly satisfied and accomplished. Almost proud.

HE BEGAN TO NOTICE Carrie acting strangely, a little preoccupied and distant. He knew she must be thinking about "Hannah" and the story he'd told her. Of course, it made sense—how could he expect her *not* to think about it? He supposed it would take a while for her to get used to the idea that he'd had another wife before her. Eventually, the thought would lose its rawness, and become part of the fabric of the past. Knowing she was alive somewhere would only make it worse. Carrie would dwell on it for months, maybe years. It was better to say that

"Hannah" was dead. He'd actually done her a favor.

Then the thought occurred to him—how did he know that Ann *wasn't* really dead? It was possible. After all, it had been twenty years—a lot could happen in twenty years. Cancer. Car crashes. All kinds of things. Why shouldn't one of them happen to her?

He began to think of Ann as *gone*. Truly gone. At first, he felt a twinge of the old regret, but that faded, and he almost came to believe that it was true. Not only that, but that he'd somehow *made* it true. By telling that lie, it was the same as if he'd killed her.

One day, Carrie asked if she could talk to him about something. She never asked if she could talk to him unless it was something difficult and important. This time she seemed nervous, more nervous than usual. He stroked her arm and told her it was okay, she could ask him anything, while he braced himself for whatever she was going to say.

"I just wanted..." She stopped herself and then started again, "I was wondering ... if you can tell me ... if you don't mind telling me ... about Hannah. Where is she buried?"

He froze. Of all the things she could have asked him, this was one he did not expect. He struggled to find something quick to say.

"Idaho," he blurted out. He was going to say Indiana, but that felt too close. Idaho was farther away. Idaho was perfect. He watched Carrie take in this piece of new information.

"Because..." she began again, "If you ... if you ever wanted to visit there ... I mean, visit *her* ... for any reason, you should do that. I mean, there's no reason for you not to do that now. If you want to. Right?"

The awfulness of it, her selflessness, how good she was trying to be for him, hit him like a blow. He closed his eyes, waiting to recover from it. He thought of what it must look like to her, that he was overcome. He was, but not in the way she thought.

"Thank you," he said, "But ... I don't ... I mean, it's been so long...."

Carrie stepped forward, put her hand on his shoulder and gently rubbed him. "That's okay," she said. "Just ... if you ever want to. Whenever you're ready."

For the rest of the night, he felt shaken. The lies he'd had to tell Carrie over their years together had actually been very few. His name, where he was from, not much else. His marriage to Ann had always been a lie of omission. He'd simply never brought it up, and Carrie had never asked. Until now.

Why hadn't he just denied it? That would have been the end of it. But part of him knew that Carrie would always have that doubt in her mind. Saying yes had been his way to get around that. Now it felt like a crack was forming in the ice under his feet. And every question she asked and every answer he gave felt like a hammer blow, making the crack spread faster.

The next night, Carrie asked him, "Did you and Hannah … did you have any children?"

"No," he said. He gave a silent prayer of thanks—not for the first time—that at least this much was true. Then he remembered. When he and Ann were first married, they'd bought a cute stuffed dog as a "pet" because they couldn't afford a real one. Sometimes he thought it was a substitute for the child they hadn't had yet. They'd lie in bed and tease each other with it, making it talk in funny voices, playing together like children. A few years later when their fighting had become ugly and violent, when he was packing to leave, he'd found that stuffed dog in the closet, preserved carefully in a white shoebox wrapped with a gold ribbon. It was the only time that he'd actually wept, falling to his knees on the floor with the toy in front of him, sobbing like a parent grieving the death of a child.

THE NEXT DAY they drove out to the country to pick up some garden supplies. On the way home, the traffic slowed down to almost a standstill, and they crept along at five miles an hour. "What's the hold up?" Rob grumbled. He craned his neck to see if he could spot construction signs or police lights ahead, but the long line of cars disappeared around a curve; whatever was causing the holdup was hidden.

Something on the right side of the road caught his eye. It was one of those little shrines made of tinfoil and painted wood. It seemed like he saw them everywhere lately. All those names and brief sentimental messages. *Kristal – Forever In Our Hearts.* Crosses with artificial flowers, sometimes real ones, held in place with twisted wire.

"I don't understand why anyone would want to do that," he said. "I mean, why would you want to commemorate the spot where someone was killed? That's horrible."

"Well, they do it on battlefields, don't they?" she said. "Like Gettysburg and Antietam."

The traffic crept forward slowly, then stopped. He glanced over at the little shrine again, the typical white-painted cross with fake flowers and some kind of stuffed animal tied to it. As they got closer, he could see it was a stuffed dog. He noticed the eyes, sad and droopy, the large brown pupils turned upward in a look of supplication, like a saint at prayer in an old painting. They were the same eyes that their stuffed dog had. His and Ann's.

He looked closer. It was the same toy. The same one.

Panic flooding his brain, he pulled the car over onto the shoulder, pushed the gas pedal to the floor and sped alongside the other cars toward the exit far ahead, gravel crunching and spitting under the tires.

"What are you doing?" Carrie yelled, but he kept going until he pulled off the highway and eased the car onto a two-lane road.

"Why the hell did you do that?" Carrie asked. "What's wrong with you?"

He knew he should tell her something, offer some kind of explanation. But he couldn't.

When he thought about it later, he realized how foolishly he'd behaved. That toy dog he'd seen by the side of the road—they must have made hundreds of them. Maybe thousands. There was nothing strange about it. Nothing at all.

That night he told Carrie he needed to go for a walk. She looked up for a moment, her eyes red from the onions she was chopping. "It's going to rain, isn't it?"

"I don't know … maybe," he said, heading for the door. "I'll make it quick."

"Supper's at seven, okay?" he heard her call out behind him. He headed down the driveway to the street, turned left and started walking as fast as he could. All the stress and anxiety he'd felt building since his talk with Carrie, it was all chemical, he knew. Just hormones. Fight or flight. It would fade in time. Everything would fade in time. Carrie's shock over finding out he'd been married before. Any lingering suspicions she might have. They would all get worn away under the steady, grinding pace of their daily lives. No matter how upsetting something might seem at first, there was nothing that time wouldn't take care of.

He'd only gone a couple of blocks when he felt a cold drop hit his forearm. He took a quick glance up at the sky, saw heavy gray clouds rolling in, then started walking faster to beat the rain and to get his heart rate up to clear the poisons out of his system.

It seemed like more cars than usual were speeding past him. People on their way home from work, he guessed. Not too many people out walking like him. Just the old man across the street who never smiled, trimming his hedges. A young boy with a backpack getting home late from school. A woman standing in the middle of the street.

He paused and peered ahead at the woman, wondering what she was doing there. At first, he thought she must have dropped something while crossing the street, but she didn't appear to be looking for anything. She was just standing there on the white line in the middle of the road, staring straight ahead in his direction. She was too far away for him to get a good look at her face, but there was something familiar about the outline of her body and the way she was standing that made him feel uneasy.

As he watched, the woman tilted her head to one side as she looked at him, the way Ann used to do. A cold feeling crept up inside of him. *It can't be,* he thought. *She's dead.* It took him a second to remember that wasn't true. Still … how could it be her? It wasn't possible. He felt frozen in place like an animal seen by a predator. He didn't dare to move or breathe.

He heard the rain before he saw it, the sharp popping in the leaves of trees, slow at first, then faster, more cold drops hitting his arms and neck. He saw the old man put his clippers aside and hurry indoors, but the woman didn't move. She was still standing in the middle of the street with the rain falling all around her. His own shirt was already wet and clinging to his skin, but from a distance it looked like the woman's hair and clothes were still dry.

The hiss of car wheels in the rain came fast from around the sharp curve behind him, and he stepped out of the way as a red SUV blew past, spraying water as it hurtled toward the woman. He braced himself for the terrible thud, for the sight of the broken body flying through the air. But when he looked again, the car was speeding on its way around the bend, and the woman was still standing in the center of the street. Still looking in his direction.

That was when she began to walk toward him.

He turned and started walking toward home, not looking back. When he couldn't stand it any more, he broke into a run and didn't stop until he burst in through the kitchen door, wet and breathless. Carrie was still standing at the oven, stirring the onions. She looked up, an alarmed expression on her face.

"Jesus … what happened to you?"

"Nothing…" he panted, "Just trying to get out of the rain.…"

He waited till she wasn't looking, and locked the door behind him.

LATER, HE FOUND Carrie at her desk, peering intently at her laptop screen.

"What town did you say Hannah was buried in?"

He'd just come to ask if she wanted a cup of tea or something, but her question stopped him cold.

"What are you doing?" he asked, trying to keep his voice as normal as possible.

"I just want to see where it is."

Why? That was what he wanted to ask. But he didn't. If he asked *why,* she'd know he didn't want to tell her. Still, he had to say something.

"Carlton." It was the first name that popped into his mind. A half-second later he realized it was the name of his high school

English teacher. He listened to her fingers clicking busily on the keys, then pause.

"It's not here."

"Well ... it was a really small town," he said, hoping that would sound reasonable. Her fingers clicked some more. Then she leaned back and frowned at the computer.

"I can't find it."

"Really? That's weird." He didn't know what else to say. Then he remembered why he'd come into the room. "You want me to get you some tea?"

She looked up at him, still frowning. "Yeah," she finally said. "That would be nice...."

LEAVES BEGAN TO pile up in the yard and choke the gutters that overflowed like waterfalls, but he stayed in the house. There was plenty of work to do indoors, he told himself. The truth was that he didn't feel safe outside. It reminded him of how he'd felt when he'd first come here years ago, when every person on the street looked at him a little longer than he thought they should, and every police siren went right through him like a knife. He felt that way now.

"I've been thinking about going to visit my aunt in Portland," Carrie said one night.

"I didn't know you had an aunt in Portland."

"Yeah. I thought we could go out there for a visit. You know, see some of the sights. It's really beautiful out there."

He felt an alarm go off somewhere inside his body. "I don't know... You know I don't like to fly." He didn't really mind flying. What he didn't like was having his ID checked so many times. He'd done it before when he had to. But there was no point in pushing his luck.

"No," she said, "I thought we could drive."

"To Portland? How long a trip is that?"

"Only three days. There's a lot of pretty land between here and there. I mean..." she paused and put her hand on the back of his. "You seem a little stressed. I think maybe you could use it, right? A little time away from here...?"

And just like that, he felt a door open somewhere inside him. *A little time away from here*. Thunder rumbled somewhere in the distance. He could hear the rain tapping at the windows again, trying to get in.

"Sure," he said, taking the hand she'd offered into his. "That sounds nice."

THE FIRST FIVE HUNDRED MILES *are the longest.*

That was the joke that came into his head as they crossed the state line from Iowa into Nebraska. He didn't say it, because he was afraid that she might see what he was seeing—the long days and nights he'd spent on the road twenty years ago when he'd left his old life behind. It unnerved him, how much it looked the same. The same flat, colorless fields. The same ribbon of blacktop stretching all the way to the horizon.

Carrie liked to stop at odd little restaurants and shops she found along the way where they'd sample the coconut creme pie and buy corny postcards. He could tell she was trying to make this a fun trip to relieve some of the pressure of whatever had been bothering him. But to him, her efforts felt stiff and forced. There was something else on her mind. He couldn't tell what it was, but he didn't want to ask. He just wanted to get through this trip and then make it back home.

The next morning after breakfast, Carrie insisted on driving. He'd driven most of the way yesterday, she pointed out, so it was only fair. He agreed, reluctantly. He liked to drive, it was true, but more than that, he didn't like being driven by someone else, sitting in the passenger seat with nothing to do.

When they crossed the state line into Idaho, Rob felt a stir of some nameless anxiety in his chest, but couldn't figure out what it was. Carrie, who was usually talkative in the car, had been unusually quiet. About an hour after they crossed into Idaho, he was surprised when she took an exit off the interstate onto a smaller state route.

"Where are you going?" he asked. She said nothing, but he could feel her gathering her words, trying to find the right ones.

"We're going by Carlton," she said. "I just thought ... since we're so close, we might as well drop by there. Just for a minute."

Carlton? He tried to remember where

he'd heard that name—then it hit him. It was the name of the town where he'd told her his first wife was buried. The one he'd made up.

There is no Carlton, he wanted to say. *It doesn't exist.* Instead, he did his best to swallow the panic rising inside him, and tried to control his voice.

"Why … why do you want to go there?"

"I just thought…" she stopped to swallow and take a breath—clearly, this was difficult for her. "I just thought we should stop, just for a minute, and … pay our respects. To your wife. To Hannah."

His mind went blank for a second, then the urge to rage at her, to jump out of the car or take the wheel from her hands, all overtook him.

"Jesus, Carrie. I can't…" he began, trying to summon up the anger he needed to distract her and throw her off. "I can't believe you're just doing this without telling me. Why the hell… why would you do this without telling me? Without talking with me about it first? What if I don't *want* to do this? Did you ever think about *that?*"

"Of course I thought about that," she said, her voice rising. "I know you don't want to do this, Rob, but I think you should. I think you need to. Ever since you told me…." She stopped, and he realized she was trying not to cry. "Ever since you told me about Hannah, about you and Hannah, you haven't been the same. There's something wrong, Rob. I don't know what it is, but I can tell. Something's wrong. And, I don't know, maybe I'm wrong, maybe I don't have the right. Maybe I'm crazy, but I just think if we do this, it might help you. It might help both of us."

That was when he understood. This had been her plan all along. To fix him. To fix the two of them. It was horrible. What would she do when she realized that the town wasn't there?

He was trying to summon up the courage to tell her the truth, when a road sign appeared in the distance and moved past them.

CARLTON.

His mind went blank as he read the letters. What was happening? How was this possible? Could there be a real town with the same name he'd made up? What were the odds? Had he seen the name somewhere before and forgotten it?

He heard the *click click click* of the turn signal and felt the pull of the car as she slowed down and turned off onto the exit.

He stared out the passenger window at the broad, empty streets lined with old buildings and chain stores. When Carrie pulled over at a market, he thought she was going in to use the bathroom, until she emerged a minute later holding a small bouquet of yellow flowers. His heart hurt when he saw them.

THEY TURNED OFF the main street and made two more turns. Then he saw the cemetery.

Carrie drove the car through the iron gates and proceeded to roll through the rows of headstones as if she knew where she was going. He pictured them searching through the headstones for hours, then finally giving up. He'd tell her that he wasn't sure it was the same cemetery, that *it was so long ago.* She'd understand. She wouldn't be happy, but she'd believe him. And that would be the end of it.

Carrie finally parked the car and turned off the engine. She sat for a moment, then looked at him, her eyes full of concern. "Are you ready?" she said quietly. He realized his heart was beating very quickly. He felt dizzy and short of breath. She would probably take it for emotion. He nodded, then they both got out and started walking. Carrie held the bouquet of yellow flowers in her hand.

He quickly scanned the cemetery and tried to gauge how big it was. He was trying to calculate how long it would take before she gave up, when she stopped suddenly, and a strange little sound came from her throat.

There to the right of them, no more than four feet away, was a shiny headstone engraved:

HANNAH MARTIN.

Rage—that was the first thing he felt. A wave of rage surging through his veins. Who was doing this? And why? It was horrible, some kind of cruel, sadistic joke. He looked wildly around as if there might be a camera crew hiding behind a tree, recording his terror and humiliation. But the cemetery was empty—they were the only people there.

He looked back at Carrie, half-expecting to see an evil grin on her face—*is she in on this?* She was staring solemnly down at the grave. She looked up at him and he was stunned to see tears glittering in her eyes. Then she held out the little yellow bouquet toward him.

"Do you want to...?" she said in a soft whisper. He stared in horror at the yellow flowers and shook his head. "It's okay..." she said softly, then stepped forward herself and leaned down to prop the little bouquet up against the gravestone. At that moment, he would not have been surprised to see them vanish or burst into flame. She stood with her hands folded respectfully in front of her, still gazing down at the grave. He tried to imagine what was going on in her mind, but couldn't—his own mind felt like it had exploded and was a jumble of fragments now, jagged pieces that couldn't connect.

He became aware that she was saying something. From the tone of her voice, he could tell it was a question, but he didn't quite understand it. She had to say it twice before the words made sense to him.

"Are you ready?"

Ready? Ready for what? She stepped back and nodded toward where they'd parked the car and he understood.

"I mean..." she said, "We can stay a little longer ... if you want to."

"No...." It was the first word he'd been able to speak. He turned and started walking back toward the car, his mind still spinning. A touch on his arm made him jump; it was her, of course. She'd come up to walk silently beside him, one hand resting gently on his right arm, like they were leaving a funeral.

The drive to the motel was long and mostly silent. Carrie drove. This time he was glad. He didn't feel quite capable of driving yet. His mind was still in a turmoil. What was happening to him? Had he seen the name of that town on a map or in a book somewhere, forgotten that he'd seen it, then had it echo back to him when he needed it? And the other name. The one on the gravestone. How

was that possible? How many Hannah Martins could there be in the world? He knew that a Google search usually turned up a long list of even the strangest name. How strange was it, really, to find a gravestone with Hannah's name? Then he remembered—there was no Hannah Martin. It was the name he'd invented when he needed something to tell Carrie, the way he'd invented a new name for himself when he'd first disappeared years ago. *Robert Martin.* For years it felt fake on his lips. Now it was who he was. For a terrifying moment he couldn't remember what his real name used to be.

"Are you okay?"

At first he wasn't sure if he'd heard her correctly. He turned and saw her glancing over at him with a concerned look on her face.

He tried to answer but couldn't. His mind had stopped working. They drove along in silence for a moment. He could feel her gathering her words again.

"I know..." she started, "I know that was hard for you. I just thought it was something we needed to do. You and me."

You and me. Rob and Carrie Martin. There was no Rob Martin, but that was who he was now. And what about her? Half of her name real, the other half not. He wondered if she could feel it.

The motel was a few flat buildings scattered at the edge of the highway. It was right out of an old movie, with its near-empty parking lot and old purple neon sign with one letter burnt out. It looked, he thought, like the kind of place that a person might come to end their life.

He got out of the car and squinted at the single harsh floodlight above that was surrounded by a halo of moths and other insects swirling round and round endlessly. Looking around, he felt as though he'd been here before. It was the kind of place he'd stayed at back when he'd first gone on the run, holed up in a musty room with the shades drawn, cutting up his driver's license and credit cards, shedding the last traces of his old life.

They opened the door to their room, the smell of mildew covered with a thin veneer of disinfectant rolled out to meet him, and the anxious feeling of being trapped rose up inside of him. For a moment he wanted to turn and leave, ask her to find someplace else. But he was so exhausted by everything that had happened today, he wasn't sure if he could even make it back to the car. All he wanted was to lie down, close his eyes and turn off the panicked thoughts that were still racing through his mind. He took a deep breath and walked inside.

It was worse than he'd imagined. The awful striped wallpaper, the ugly brown carpet worn thin by decades of lonely, pacing feet. As he looked around the room, a terrible feeling stirred inside him. He knew this room. He'd been here before. Twenty years ago, when he was first on the run. But that was in another state. Like the name of the town, and the name on the gravestone, it wasn't possible. *Motel rooms look the same,* he told himself.

Then he saw it—the jagged tear in the ugly wallpaper, there in the same place near the cheap digital clock. The torn place looked like the shape of a hand. Twenty years ago, he'd spent hours looking at it, afraid of what it might do if he turned out the light. He couldn't wait to turn out the lights so he wouldn't have to look at it.

Carrie was already in bed. He locked the door, snapped off the lights so he could no longer see the awful striped walls, but the smell of rot and chemicals was still there, hovering all around him in the dark. He closed his eyes and breathed deeply, trying to put himself to sleep. To hurry the morning light when they could leave this place.

"Rob..." she said, her voice in the dark startling him. It took her a long time to speak again. At first he thought it was because she couldn't tell if he was still awake. For a moment, he thought of pretending to be asleep, but there was something in her voice that told him she wasn't going to let this go; she was going to keep going until she'd said whatever she had to say.

"I'm glad I know about Hannah now. I wish you'd told me a long time ago, but that's all done now, and I'm glad I know." She paused again, but only for a moment. "If ... if there's anything else, anything you haven't told me, you can tell me about that too. It doesn't matter what it is. You can tell me. You know that, don't you?"

Lying on his back, he shut his eyes tight against the dark, against the feeling rising inside his chest. He could feel her waiting.

"And if you don't want to tell me..." she continued, "Whatever it is, whatever the reason. If you don't want to tell me, if you never tell me, that's alright too. Rob? Do you know what I'm saying?"

He dug his fingers into the sheets, clutching them tightly like he was trying to stop himself from falling. After a while, he heard her sigh and roll over, and a few minutes later, her steady, even breathing.

He'd been exhausted, but now a nervous energy flooded his veins. He got up as quietly as he could and slipped into the bathroom to relieve himself. He didn't turn the light on, but even in the dark, he could see that the toilet seat was metal, like in an army barracks. Or a jail cell.

She knows, he thought. Or, if she doesn't yet, she's close to it.

Moving back into the bedroom, he felt too wired to go back to bed. He watched Carrie breathing long enough to make sure she was really asleep. Then he pulled on his pants and shoes and stepped outside, taking care to close the door quietly.

The night was colder now, the stars sharper and more distinct in the black sky above, and he could feel his pulse quicken to pump warmth to all the parts of his body. Somewhere a generator or an electric light was humming; the steady sound almost felt like it was coming from inside of him. It was on a night like this when he'd left, twenty years ago.

He could do it now. If he wanted to. He could get in the car and just start moving the way he had back then. Part of him was repelled by the thought, but the simple fact of it, the fact that he *could*, called to him.

He didn't have to leave, he told himself. He could just go for a drive. Just a short drive, to clear his head. He'd be back in an hour, maybe two. She didn't have to know.

He started to walk toward the car when he noticed a figure standing across the parking lot in the space between two of the buildings. It was a woman, he could tell, silhouetted by another light somewhere behind her. He kept expecting her to move, but she didn't. She was just standing there, facing in his direction. He realized she was watching him, and a cold, trapped feeling rose inside of him.

The woman slowly cocked her head to one side like a curious, hungry bird, and he knew who she was.

What do you want? he wanted to scream. Before he could, she was flying toward him like the ground rushing toward someone falling, her face flooding his vision, so huge that he couldn't make it out, but he knew it, like he knew the voice howling inside of him like a raging wind that nothing can stop or keep out.

Give me back my face.

Give me back my name.

Give me back my life.

💀 💀 💀

David Surface is the author of the collection Terrible Things *from Black Shuck Books. His stories have appeared in* Shadows & Tall Trees, Supernatural Tales, Nightscript, The Tenth Black Book of Horror, Phantom Drift, Morpheus Tales, Twisted Book of Shadows, Uncertainties III, *and* The Best Horror of the Year, *Volume 13. A YA supernatural suspense novel co-written with Julia Rust,* Angel Falls, *is forthcoming from Haverhill House Publishing's YAP imprint in 2022. David is also the author of the newsletter* STRANGE LITTLE STORIES. *To learn more about David and his writing, visit davidsurface.net*

VICTORIANS

BY JAMES DORR

THE FIRST THING I REMEMBERED OF MY EARLY CHILDHOOD WAS THE FOG. I MUST HAVE BEEN ONLY FIVE YEARS OLD WHEN I LEFT THE HOUSE THAT I HAD BEEN BORN IN—BEYOND THAT MY MIND WAS STILL PRETTY MUCH BLANK—and I would not have returned even now, more than thirty years later, except that I had finally married. Her name was Amelia and I had met her in Chicago, but now I traveled home alone. I had determined to open the house first and, only after it had been restored to a livable condition, to send for my bride.

I crested a hill and, just as the road hooked down toward the river and to the town I would find across it, I caught my first glimpse of the house my father had been born in too—the house he had died in and that my mother had fled from just after, never to come back. That, at least, was what they had told me after I had been taken away, to another state, to be raised by a cousin on my mother's side.

The fog, a persistent feature of autumn during those first years of my life, had always been thickest nearest the river. Above it, however, under a pale late afternoon sun, I could just make out the eight-sided top of the great central tower—the Queen Anne tower that dominated so many Victorian homes of its age—as well as the tips of three of the highest pinnacled chimneys. Memory came back in driblets and pieces. I knew that when I approached the next day to take possession, I would recognize below them the sharply peaked hip roof, broken at angles by the main gables that clutched the tower within the ell they formed at their crossing. The tower itself, with its latticed, oval, stained glass windows, would soar a full story over even the tallest of these, a clear rise of nearly seventy feet from its base to the scale-shingled dome that crowned it.

Memories continued to come back unbidden. I followed the road down a series of switchbacks until the top of the double lane iron bridge I knew I would find loomed out from an ever increasing fog. By now I had lost sight of my parents' home altogether, but in my mind I could hear the voice of a young attorney reading a will.

The will specified that the house would be mine, but only after I had gotten married.

The young attorney, a Stephen Larabie—really no more than a clerk at the time—explained to me what my older cousin protested seemed an unusual provision. "Your father," the lawyer said, "fully expects you not to marry until you've tasted somewhat of the world, just as he did. But at the same time you must eventually take on the obligations of manhood, as well as its pleasures, and settle down. The house, that you will not obtain until you do so, is intended to be a reminder."

My cousin who, in that I was a minor, had been court appointed to speak for my interests, had laughed at that. "You mean young Joseph"—he gestured toward me—"is being told that he has permission to sow his wild oats when he gets a bit older, but, until he's grown out of such urges, to stay out of town. In other words, not to keep out of trouble, but just out of scandal."

The lawyer cleared his throat. "Something like that, yes. I doubt you knew Joseph's father well—as you do know, he was always reclusive and rarely visited even immediate family members after his own marriage—but he, like his house, was quite Victorian in his nature."

"You mean that he was a hypocrite, don't you?" my cousin asked.

I remember now that the lawyer had glanced in my direction to see if I had understood anything of what he and my cousin were saying, but I had already begun to play with his pens and inkwell.

"Some people claimed that of him, yes. At least that he might at times have followed a double standard." He cleared his throat a second time. "In any event," he said as he stood up, having come to the end of his papers and seemingly anxious to usher us out, "the will specifies that this firm will keep the house in trust until Joseph is ready."

And now I was ready, by my father's will. The firm, now owned by Stephen Larabie, had apparently kept an eye on my own various comings and goings as well as the house. And so, three days after Amelia and I had returned from our honeymoon, I received the telegram that had brought me back to this place, at best still scarcely half-recollected, that yet had so overshadowed my first years.

So ran my thoughts now as I reached the bridge and, turning my lights on low, carefully picked my way across it. Fortunately, the fog seemed less thick on the river's town side and, even though it was starting to get dark, I found the hotel I had made reservations at with surprisingly little trouble. Since I was tired from a full day's drive, I checked into my room and showered and changed first, then decided to have a couple of drinks and something to eat in the small restaurant I had earlier spotted just off the lobby.

When I sat down, the hostess smiled at me, and somehow I found that I couldn't help thinking how much the opposite, and yet, in terms of the abstract of beauty, how much the same she was as Amelia. Where, for example, my own wife was blonde and her figure slender, the restaurant hostess was every bit as buxom and dark. Where Amelia was quiet, the hostess appeared, as other customers came to be seated, almost too vivacious. And afterward, when she winked at me while I took out my card to pay the bill, I learned that even her name was much like my wife's, and yet unlike it, as well.

Her name was Anise.

When I returned to my room later on, I placed my wife's picture on the dresser and went to sleep quickly. The first thing next morning, I looked up Attorney Larabie's office.

As soon as I strode in through the door, I was struck by how quickly my mind recalled the tiniest details of my visit, some thirty years past, down to and including the stain on the wood floor where I had dropped one of the young lawyer's pens. The man who confronted me now, however, must have been fifty-five or sixty.

"Mr. Parrish?" he said, extending his hand. "Mr. Joseph Parrish?"

I nodded and accepted his handshake.

"Are you Stephen Larabie? I got your telegram...."

"Yes," he said, before I could add more. Still gripping my hand, he pulled me over to a table and sat me down, then produced a thick sheaf of papers. "Couple of things I'll need you to sign first," he continued. "That'll most likely take up the whole morning so, unless you have some objection, I thought we might have a quick lunch after that and then take a look at the house together."

I nodded, wondering somewhat distractedly if lunch would be at the hotel restaurant and, if so, if the hostess, Anise, would be on duty for that meal as well. I shook the thought away and soon enough became lost in contracts and deeds instead. Lunch, in fact, turned out to be a quick affair at a hamburger place just outside of town, on the way to the bridge. And then, as river fog started to thin, giving some hope of a clear if not wholly sun-filled afternoon, we found ourselves on the steep and winding road up the cliff on the other side.

Larabie turned to me while I was driving. "How much do you remember of your father?" he asked. "Or, for that matter, of your mother?"

"Very little," I had to confess. I searched my memory and nothing came, yet I had the feeling that if I just waited—waited until I was inside the house that they had lived in...

"You do know, at least, that your father was murdered?"

Larabie paused, reacting, perhaps, to what I imagined was my blank expression. I had no such memory.

"That's what the police said in any event," he finally continued after some seconds. I *did* remember that when, with my cousin, I had been in his office before, the younger Larabie had struck me as being every bit as taciturn about giving out excessive information.

"Did they catch the man who did it?" I asked. Again, attempt to recall as I might, I had no memory—at least not yet—and hence no real feeling one way or the other. But I was beginning to have a foreboding.

"Figured it was probably a drifter," Larabie answered, his voice sounding thoughtful. "A lot of people were moving from town to town those days—mostly farmers who'd been foreclosed on. Big farms forcing out smaller holdings. And you've got to realize that this was a small town. People generally disliked sharing local troubles with outsiders. So the police just poked around a little outside the house—set up a few roadblocks—but they never did catch him."

"M-my mother wasn't murdered too, was she?" It had suddenly occurred to me what he might have been trying to hint at and, while I didn't really remember her any more than I did my father, the thought of my mother's death by violence somehow *was* shocking.

"Oh no," he said quickly. "In fact it was her who phoned the police. Figured she must have been out when it happened and had you with her, but came home just after. Sort of a lucky reversal for her, though, that that's the way it worked out." He hesitated for a moment.

"What do you mean?"

"It was your father who usually went out while she and you were the ones left behind." He hesitated again, then frowned. "I may as well tell you, your father was somewhat of a ladies' man. Good looking man even in his late thirties, just like you, and everyone knew it—except maybe her. Used to be a whorehouse where the hotel is now and some said he spent more time in that than he did in his own house."

"Really?" I asked. I was about to ask him more when we reached the crest of the hill we were climbing. The road widened and, just at that moment, a ray of sun burst through the clouds overhead. The house could now be seen suddenly rising, dominating the next ridge over, in all its flamboyant, old-fashioned splendor.

As we approached, it loomed higher and higher, the light glinting off the gingerbread scroll work that framed the huge front third-story gable. I pulled up into its curving driveway, got out of the car and let my eyes wander—below the trim of the gable, in shadow, the arch of a balcony pointed yet higher to the great tower, half impaled by the slant to its right, and the cast-iron finialed crest of the main hip roof behind it. And yet above that, thrust to the sky, the three major chimneys—the tallest one crowned with a wired, glass-balled spire that was meant to catch lightning, my new memory prompted—added their own bursting streaks of color. An almost blood-colored patterned-brick red, when the sun struck full on it, that, in the jumbled gray and white of friezes and rails of the building below them, was matched alone by the stained-glass red of the tower's downward spiraling ovals.

I walked, as if in a dream, to the house— apparently long-repressed memories came back of the tower windows lighting a second and third-story staircase before it curved backward up into the attic. Others of diamond-panes in the front parlor. I scarcely noticed Larabie's presence until we stood on the broad front veranda.

"You'll notice we kept the property up for you, Mr. Parrish," the lawyer said. "Painted it most recently only last summer, in fact." He pulled a notebook out of his pocket, along with a large, old-fashioned iron key. "You'll notice we nailed up the lower-floor windows with furring strips—this far from town why take any chances?—but, once we're inside, the smaller fireplaces you'll see sealed off were boarded up in your grandfather's time. After they put in the central gas heating."

I nodded dumbly. Yes. I remembered. One of the lesser, back left chimneys went down to the basement. I watched as he twisted the key in the door, only half noticing that it opened with hardly a squeak. I smelled the fresh oil—they had, apparently, kept up the inside as well as the outside—not just of hinges, but of the darkly polished woodwork that surrounded us as we stepped into the shallow, box-like reception hall.

"Just a moment now, Mr. Parrish." Larabie spoke in almost a whisper. He handed me the first of the keys, then produced a second. He twisted it in a smaller lock across from the entrance we had just come through, then pushed back the double sliding doors that opened the wall to the huge, oak paneled, main staircase hall.

"Your mother went with this house, Mr. Parrish," Larabie said as he stood aside to let me look. To try to remember. Second only in size to the large formal dining room, the hall, with its stairs angling up to the right and around the back wall, was the dominant feature of the first floor. "Your mother was frail, white-skinned and slender, with pale blonde hair," the attorney continued. "There were times when she would descend, the white of her clothes standing out as well from the dark wood around her, and look the perfect Victorian lady. Times when I'd come here on legal business...."

I nodded. I saw. I remembered my mother on that staircase, saw in her now, in retrospect, the thin, almost sickly Romantic ideal that would have held sway not so much in her time here, but generations before when the house had been first constructed. I longed now to climb the stairs—now I remembered how she would pause at the corner landing, letting me dash to her so we could go to the main hall together. But first I had to know something more.

I turned to Larabie.

"You told me just before we came to the top of the cliff that my father was murdered. But not my mother...."

"No, Mr. Parrish. She was the one who called the police—I think I may have said that already—but, when they arrived here, they came through the sliding doors, just as we did, and the only person they found in the hall was you. You told them your mother had gone away. That was all you would tell them. But when they asked you about your father, you pointed, silently, to the rear archway that leads to the kitchen."

More memory came back—the memory of blood. Of *wanting* to forget what I....

"Under the circumstances," I heard the attorney continue, as if at a distance, "no one blamed your mother. For leaving you that way. She must have been so horribly frightened—and she did keep her wits about her long enough to make sure help came. She had always been such a frail woman...."

Incongruously, I thought of my wife then—fragile and pale. The bride I would send for who, people might say, would fit comfortably in with this house as well. Then—stark contrast—of yet another detail I suddenly found I remembered. My father had been murdered in the kitchen, had almost staggered out past the pantry, past the back stairs and into the service hall when he had fallen.

An axe in his back.

I must have begun to look Victorian-pale myself. I felt the attorney's hand on my shoulder. Now I remembered the men in uniform, blood being cleaned up in the kitchen later by neighbors, my own panic at missing my mother. My wondering when I would see her come down the main staircase again.

"Mr. Parrish?" Larabie's voice was very low. "Mr. Parrish—perhaps you'd like to come out for some fresh air?"

I shook my head slowly. "No," I answered. "Everything does look in order, however, so why don't *you* wait outside if you'd like to. I just want do a little exploring on my own, to get an idea of how much work it'll take before Amelia—before Mrs. Parrish and I can move in."

Larabie nodded. "Upstairs, you'll find we pretty much left everything alone. May be dusty, though. Didn't even put drop cloths down much above the second floor."

"I think you've done an excellent job with what I've seen so far," I assured him. I took a deep breath, then looked at my wristwatch and glanced toward the front door. "I shouldn't be any more than an hour...."

I waited, gazing up at the main staircase until I heard the outside door close, then turned to the back hallway and the kitchen.

On my left, I passed the downstairs parlor first and then the dining room, noting the bay window in the latter—the first-story bulge that jutted out onto the side veranda, forming the base of the four-story tower. Once in the kitchen, I took a deep breath. I saw, at least in my mind's eye, the stains. I thought for some reason of the ink I had spilled myself on Larabie's floor as I imagined my mother calling me, saw her standing over the sink, the door that led to the yard and the woodshed behind the house still yawning open, her hands red with blood.

My mother's hands. *Why?*

I watched as she washed them, then followed a trail of water stains this time—pale, clear drops diluting a deeper red—back toward my father. It circled, minced, avoided expanding pools of crimson as it reached the telephone in the hallway, then returned to the door by the pantry that led to the back stairs. The stairs my mother would never use because, as she used to say, "It isn't proper."

The stairs that rose toward the outside wall, then curved and spiraled up through the tower until they angled back into the attic.

A child's "secret passage."

I followed the trail.

I heard my mother's voice. "Joseph," she said, as we climbed the spiral, "you must forget everything that you've seen. It's only a game, like the games your father played down in the village. Games I might have been told about, but had never believed until he came home, more drunk than usual, early this morning." We reached the top, where the stairs straightened out again for their final climb up to the attic, and the sun suddenly shone through the windows, filling the tower with spotlights of blood red. "While he was sleeping," my mother continued, "I thought of a game too."

My mother had always used the front staircase. The back stairs were dusty. And one had to stoop to get from the attic into the tunnel beneath the front gable. But this was different—this was a game.

I straightened up, bumped my head, realized I stood in the attic myself now.

I had trouble breathing the stuffy air. I leaned against a rough brick column—the front parlor chimney, my memory told me—and felt the flange where it thrust through the roof brush against my shoulder. I blinked my eyes, hard, to clear my vision and, when I opened them up again, I saw what still looked like a pool of blood.

Again a memory—a recognition. I was already within the front gable. The red that I saw was the light of the sun, spilling out from a second low arch where the gable roof met the tower's final top level. I heard my mother's voice warning me to be sure to brush my pants carefully before, once the game we would play was ended, I went back downstairs. I saw my mother kneeling next to me as we crawled through the final tunnel.

We came to a child's hidden pirate castle. A room of oval stained-glass windows that served as portholes, of worn-out sheets and ropes carefully hung from the open beams of the dome roof above as a ship's sails and banners.

I helped my mother build a tower within the great tower's uppermost room, helped her make a stair-like heap of the boxes and trunks I'd dragged in for years from the main attic proper as pirate treasure.

"Now you must help me with one thing more," she said when we were finished. She climbed to the top and began to pull on the ropes that hung toward her. "Hold my legs. That's right. And now I want you to promise me that everything that has happened today will be our secret. Do you promise, Joseph?"

"Yes, Mother," I said. The memory was clear now.

"I want you to think of this as a game. Like playing pirates. Do you understand?"

"Yes, Mother," I said again.

"Good. Now your mother must walk the plank—just like in a game. As soon as you feel me move my feet, I want you to push me off these boxes and knock them over, just as if you were a real pirate captain pushing me off the plank. I want you to go downstairs after you've done that, without looking back. Some men will come later and all you must tell them is that your mother went away. Do you promise, Joseph?"

I had promised.

I blinked again. I stood alone in the tower

now. Raising my eyes to the dome above me, I gazed at my mother, her flesh long since shrunken into a parchment against her body, still hanging in the red light of the windows just as I had left her.

And somehow, for no reason whatsoever, I thought of Amelia who so resembled her, walking down the front, formal staircase. Amelia, my bride, also somewhat reclusive, who I was sure, as soon as the house was cleaned and ready, would come to love it and make it her own.

And then, without willing to, I thought as well of the restaurant hostess. I could not help it.

Of dark, round-curved Anise who lived in town and would be waiting.

"Victorians" first appeared in the 1997 anthology Gothic Ghosts, *published by Tor Books.*

Indiana author James Dorr's most recent book is a novel-in-stories from Elder Signs Press, Tombs: A Chronicle of Latter-Day Times of Earth. *Working mostly in dark fantasy/horror with some forays into SF and mystery, his* The Tears of Isis *was a 2013 Bram Stoker Award® finalist for Superior Achievement in a Fiction Collection, while other books include* Strange Mistresses: Tales of Wonder and Romance, Darker Loves: Tales of Mystery and Regret, *and his all-poetry* Vamps (A Retrospective). *He has also been a technical writer, an editor on a regional magazine, a full-time non-fiction freelancer, and a semi-professional musician, and currently harbors a Goth cat named Triana. An Active Member of SFWA and HWA, Dorr invites readers to visit his blog at:* jamesdorrwriter.wordpress.com

FIDDLEHEADS

BY DOUGLAS SMITH

THE FIDDLEHEADS WERE BACK.

Andy Pembleton saw the ferns as he walked in the wooded ravine behind the house where he lived with his Mom. It was the same day he had his idea.

His idea to find his little brother.

Nothing had been growing in the ravine yesterday. But now the ferns had already pushed their curled heads two inches above the forest floor, peeking bright green through the gray corpses of last fall's dead leaves.

Andy stared at the patch of new life at his feet. The fiddleheads always meant spring was finally back. But they also meant the anniversary of losing his little brother.

Ever since Martin had gone missing nearly two years ago, not a day went by in which Andy didn't want him back the way that only a twelve-year old boy can want something. But lately, his longing for the only friend he'd ever known had grown into an almost physical pain.

Walking in the ravine helped him feel better. The town kept talking about putting paved trails in back here, but they never had.

He was glad because it kept the woods his private place, a place of secret paths and hidden glades that only he knew. A place where he could be alone.

He sat on the ground in front of the patch of new fern heads, ignoring the damp that seeped through the butt of his jeans. The days were getting warmer, and the wet earth smelled of new life and old rot. Life and death were all mixed up together in here.

Of all things in the ravine, he liked the fiddleheads best. The ferns fascinated him in a way he could never figure out. Maybe it was how fast they grew. They'd be fully grown in less than a week and would stand taller than Andy, and he was big for his age.

Maybe that was it. The fiddleheads showed how fast things could change. How fast things could come into this world.

How fast they could disappear from it, too.

Reaching down, he snapped off the head of one of the ferns. He pulled it, unwinding it, then let it curl back into the shape that gave the fern its name. He remembered when Dad first showed the ferns to him and Martin.

But Martin was gone now, and Dad didn't live with them anymore. Just the fiddleheads were left from that memory.

He heard Mom calling him for lunch, from the patio door of their house. He sighed and got up, reluctant to leave his special place, but feeling a little better. He stuck the fiddlehead he'd broken off into his pocket, and turned to leave the ravine.

Then he saw the little mound where Patches, the family cat, was buried. His stomach tightened. Fiddleheads were growing on top of the mound, death and life mixing there as well. He'd be glad when the fiddleheads were high enough to hide the spot.

Turning his back on the grave, he walked home.

THAT EVENING, sitting at the cluttered kitchen table, over a supper of hamburger stew and Kraft Dinner, Andy decided he'd try to tell Mom how he was feeling lately.

He could still talk to her sometimes, though not the same way as before Martin disappeared. She didn't spend as much time with him, either. Since Dad left them, she had to work in the day and at night, and often weekends too. But sometimes Andy wondered if being around him reminded her too much of Martin.

"Mom?"

"Uh huh?" Mom said, not looking up as she shook some pepper on her stew.

"I…" he began, wondering if he should tell her. "I still miss Martin," he finished, all in a rush.

Mom put the pepper shaker down and sat very still.

He wished he hadn't said anything, but he couldn't stop now. "I mean, I mean I miss him more than ever lately. Even more than when he … when he went away."

Mom looked out the window, and for a moment, he didn't think she was going to answer him. Then she turned back and even smiled in a sad kind of way. "We'll always miss him," she said. "But what you're feeling, it'll get better."

He thought he knew what she meant, and it made him angry. "Because we'll forget him, you mean."

Mom shook her head. "No. We'll never forget. Not ever."

He believed that Mom wished that she *could* forget Martin, and that made him even angrier. He felt as if he was going to cry.

Mom tried smiling again. "We won't forget. It just … it just won't hurt so much."

He didn't want it to stop hurting. He just wanted Martin back. "Why am I even sadder now?"

Mom stopped smiling and got up from the table. She started to clear the dishes. "Because when Dad … when your father left, it made us remember all over again when Martin left us too."

Dad had left last fall. Mom blamed a lot of things on Dad since then. He shook his head. "I think it's because this is when Martin went away. Next week."

Mom was silent for a moment. "Yes," she said finally. "Yes, it was." He knew that she was trying to forget, not remember. But he'd never forget May 2. It was only three days after Martin's birthday. Or what would be his birthday if Martin were still here to celebrate it.

Mom scraped what was left on her plate into the garbage. "He would have been nine years old," she said, as if she was talking to herself.

"He's *going to be* nine years old," he almost shouted, and his voice broke a bit.

Mom put her plate in the sink. She stared at him, and he could feel his heart pounding. Finally, she turned on the water. "Yes," she said softly. "You're right. Martin's going to be nine."

He finished his dinner in silence. Martin had disappeared on his birthday outing, and he knew that Mom didn't like to talk about that day. His real birthday had fallen on a Wednesday that year, and Martin had wanted his party on the following weekend instead, so that they could all go to Canada's Wonderland. The family had just moved to Toronto from Vancouver, and Martin had never been to the theme park.

Thinking about that day always confused him. It held both some of his favorite memories, along with the worst thing that had ever happened to him. And it had started the changes between Mom and Dad. He knew they both blamed each other for not watching Martin more closely, for not seeing him wander off. For losing him. Sometimes he blamed them both, too.

But mostly, he blamed himself.

After dinner, he went up to the little bedroom that he used to share with Martin. He still thought of it as "their" room—his and Martin's. Pulling out his memory box from underneath their bunk bed, he sat down on the worn brown rug and opened the cardboard shoebox.

A picture lay on top. In it, he and Martin were on a roller coaster at Wonderland, their arms raised over their heads as the coaster began a long drop. They were laughing.

They were happy.

That had been before he and Martin had argued. He didn't know for sure if that had made Martin run off, but he always blamed himself.

Other kids made fun of Andy, for being behind a grade and in a special class. Martin had never done that. But that day at Wonderland, he and Martin had stood watching a play with some characters from TV in it.

"They look different than on TV," Andy said.

Martin looked up at him. "They're just actors in costumes, Andy. Not even the real ones from the show."

Andy liked that show and was happy to actually get to see the characters. What Martin was saying spoiled everything.

"No, they aren't. They're real," he said.

Some kids around them snickered, and Andy felt his face get hot. Then, for the first time ever, Martin looked at Andy the way kids at school did.

"Andy," Martin said, "don't be so *stupid*!"

He spun around and stepped towards Martin, towering over him, his fists clenched. "Don't you ever call me that!" he yelled. "I'm not stupid. Don't say that!"

Eyes wide, Martin backed up a step, bumping into another kid. All of the kids had become really quiet, then a little girl started to cry.

He grabbed Martin's hand. "C'mon. Let's go."

Martin pulled his hand away, but followed Andy back to where Mom and Dad were waiting. The adults just smiled, unaware of the argument. He didn't speak to Martin, didn't even look at him again, for the rest of the day.

So he hadn't noticed when or how Martin disappeared. He just knew that he had yelled at Martin that day, and later his brother was gone...

He jumped as he felt a hand on his shoulder. Mom knelt beside him on the floor. He hadn't heard her come in. She gave him a hug, something she didn't do that much anymore, then she took the picture out of his hand and stared at it.

"I wonder what he'd look like today?" she said.

He shifted so that her arm came off his shoulder. "You mean what he *looks* like."

"Yes. Yes, that's what I meant," Mom said, but he knew it wasn't.

Suddenly, thinking about her question, he felt confused. "What do you mean? Martin will look like Martin."

Mom shook her head. "Look at you in this picture. See how much you've grown? How different you look? It's been two years..." Mom's voice trailed off, then she tossed the picture in the box, face down. She stood up. "Martin would ... *will* have grown and changed too, Andy." She went back downstairs.

He picked up the picture again, staring at himself in it, not at Martin as he usually did. He had to admit that he did look different now—taller, wider shoulders, hair darker and longer. And a face that was, well, different.

He reached into his pocket and pulled out the fiddlehead from the ravine. He thought about how fast they grew, how fast they changed.

That's when he got his idea.

THE NEXT MORNING, walking in the ravine, thinking about his idea, he noticed that the fiddleheads had grown even taller. They were now at least six inches high and had already unfurled rows of feathery arms below their curled tips. He swore he could see them growing, moving, like people rising and stretching from an earthy sleep.

Sunlight sneaking through the trees high overhead painted the fiddleheads in ever shifting shapes of sun and shade, making the new ferns look as if they were dancing. He stared at the patterns of light and dark.

Light and dark. Light and dark.

Life and death. Light and dark.

Andy reached into his pocket and pulled out the Child Find flyer that the police had distributed when Martin disappeared. Andy stared at the face on the flyer, taken from a photograph that Dad had snapped that fateful day. A picture of Martin then.

But not the way he would look *now*, Mom had said.

He stared at the fiddleheads.

Things grew. Things changed.

The police and the missing child agencies were looking for the *wrong* Martin. If they were still looking for him at all—the police detective never returned Andy's phone calls, and Mom wouldn't even call them to follow-up anymore.

At first, he had wondered why Martin didn't come home himself. He didn't think that Martin would still be angry with him. Martin must miss him as much as he missed Martin. He figured that Martin had run off and gotten lost that day and was still lost, or had bumped his head and forgotten things, like on TV shows.

So he would search for Martin, for a kid around town who looked like how Martin might look now—taller, darker hair, thinner and, well, different. He just felt sure that he'd know Martin when he saw him again. He'd bring the kid here, where no one else came, and show him their house from the ravine. If the kid recognized it, then he'd be Martin, and he and Andy could march up to the front door and surprise Mom.

It would be great. Everything would be good again. Maybe Dad would even come home.

Feeling better than he had in a long time, he turned to leave the ravine, to go over to the mall and start looking.

Something moved off to the right. He turned. The fiddleheads swayed in a breeze he couldn't feel. They parted, and he saw Patches' grave again.

He swallowed. Yeah, things grew, things changed.

But things died too.

The sunlight flickered through the trees, playing over the fiddleheads dancing beside the grave. Light and dark. Life and death. He stared at the little grave. Soon the fiddle-heads would hide it, and he wouldn't have to think about it anymore.

He walked out of the ravine. The fiddle-heads seemed higher already.

THINGS WEREN'T GOING like Andy had figured. The kid looked around the ravine, acting scared now.

"Where are your games?" the kid re-peated, his voice even louder this time.

"Quiet," Andy said in a loud whisper.

"No!" yelled the kid. He looked like he was going to cry.

It had been easy to get this kid to come here. Andy had seen him sitting on a bench in the mall, playing with his handheld game player, and had told the kid that he had lots of game cartridges he was giving away. Finding a boy who fit what Martin might look like now had been harder. Andy had thought this kid did, but he wasn't so sure anymore. The kid said his name was Billy not Martin, and he hadn't recognized Andy or the house. He didn't know any of the things that Martin should know.

Billy began trying to edge past him, to-wards the path they'd come in on. "I don't think you have any games."

"Yes, I do," Andy said, stepping in front of him.

Billy shoved at him. "Let me go. I'm going home."

"No. You can't," Andy said, standing his ground.

Billy was crying now. "I'm telling my parents. I want to go home. Let me go." Billy tried to push by him again.

Trying to leave him. Like Martin. Like Dad.

Andy, bigger and stronger, grabbed Billy and threw him to the ground, landing on top of him. Billy started to scream, so he shoved a hand over Billy's mouth and another hand around Billy's neck. The screams turned to gurgling sounds. Billy started to punch at his face.

Trying to hurt him. Like Martin. Like Dad.

Andy started to cry. This had all gone wrong. He just wanted to find Martin. He just wanted to have his family back. He just wanted to stop feeling all alone.

He twisted his face away from Billy's punches, and something moving to his right caught his eye.

The fiddleheads swayed in the breeze, back and forth, back and forth. They parted. He saw Patches' grave.

It had been late October that day. Dad had just left, and Andy was missing him and Martin really badly, missing the family he once had. He had sat in the ravine sur-rounded by fiddleheads that stood brown and withered like tiny skeletons. Dead and gone.

Gone like Dad. Gone like Martin.

Patches, a black and white stray, had followed him and crawled into his lap. Andy had sat there that day, stroking its fur, tracing the white and black patches with his finger.

White and black. Light and dark. Life and death.

It had felt good to have Patches with him, something warm and alive, something that hadn't wanted to leave him.

Like Martin had left. Like Dad had left. Leaving him. Hurting him.

Andy had started to cry that day. He was tired of being hurt. No one would hurt him again. No one would leave him again.

Patches squirmed in his lap. Trying to leave him. Andy grabbed him and pushed him down. The cat hissed, trying to claw Andy. Trying to hurt him, trying to leave him.

Sobbing, Andy squeezed his hands hard. Something cracked, and Patches lay still in his lap.

After a while, Andy's sobs stopped. Billy's noises had stopped too. Beneath him, Billy lay really still.

He stood up, shaking. He stared at the body but didn't really feel anything except being scared and wanting to puke. He looked around.

The fiddleheads still stood parted, showing where he'd buried the cat. Putting his hands under Billy's arms, he dragged the boy through the ferns, away from the path, and dropped him there. Then he fell to his knees and threw up, retching and coughing. Wiping his mouth on his sleeve, he got up and stumbled out of the ferns on shaky legs. He looked back.

The fiddleheads were slowly rising back into place. They seemed even taller now, thicker too, like they were trying to help him hide the...

Like they were trying to help him.

Broad and full, the ferns reached out to touch each other, forming a feathery green wall, hiding his secrets for him. Andy couldn't see anything behind them. Not Patches' grave. Not Billy.

The fiddleheads whispered on the wind, telling him that it was okay, that he was only trying to do something good, that he was just trying to find Martin.

Things die, Andy, they said, *but things come back, too. We die each fall, but each spring, we come back. Martin will come back too. You just have to keep looking*, they whispered, *just have to keep looking*.

The fiddleheads swayed, back and forth, back and forth, and Andy stood watching, swaying with them, listening as they whispered to him. After a while, he turned his back on the ferns and walked home.

The fiddleheads were right. He would just have to keep looking.

"Fiddleheads" first appeared in the 2013 anthology Chilling Tales Two: In Words, Alas, Drown I.

Douglas Smith is a multi-award-winning author described by Library Journal as "one of Canada's most original writers of speculative fiction."

Doug has been published in twenty-seven languages and thirty-five countries. His books include The Wolf at the End of the World, Chimerascope, Impossibilia, Playing the Short Game: How to Market & Sell Short Fiction, *and the upcoming YA urban fantasy trilogy,* The Dream Rider Saga (The Hollow Boys, The Crystal Key, *and* The Lost Expedition).

Doug is a three-time winner of Canada's Aurora Award and has been a finalist for the Astounding Award, CBC's Bookies Award, Canada's juried Sunburst Award, and France's juried Prix Masterton and Prix Bob Morane.

His website is www.smithwriter.com and he tweets at twitter.com/smithwritr

THE SWAMP DEVIL

By Jason J. McCuiston

FRANCIS TURNED AT THE SHARP CRACK OF A PISTOL SHOT. Looking up from the tracks they'd followed all morning, he shielded his eyes against the bright August sun. Oscar's distant figure rode straight for him, galloping across the untended field as if the Devil himself were at his heels.

"*Dragoons!*" Oscar shouted. His chestnut gelding leapt a split-rail fence dividing the field from a muddy lane edging a tract of marshland. More shots followed, plumes of smoke just visible beyond the field. "The Green Horse, Colonel! Dragoons!"

"Everyone into the swamp!" Francis said. His thirty militiamen moved as one to guide their horses into the tree line. The puzzling tracks led into the fen at any rate. "Form a line as soon as you're under cover!" Francis remained mounted in the open.

At least now I know why a gun crew would willingly go in there, rather than stay on the road. The mere sight of one of Tarleton's Raiders would terrify a six-man detachment of raw Continental recruits, goading them into such recklessness.

"Are you positive?" Francis asked as soon as Oscar reined in beside him. The question was force of habit, an excuse to make certain of the man's well-being. Francis never doubted Oscar's judgment or his word.

"Yes, sir," Oscar said, wiping sweat from his dark brow. "The Butcher of Waxhaw, himself. And at least two-hundred light horse with him!"

Francis frowned at the sudden pain in his ankle when the first green-jacketed riders appeared at the opposite end of the field, a good fifteen hundred yards away. *General Gates is massing near Camden with thousands of men, yet he sends me and my thirty best out to look for one lost wagon of powder and a single gun! And now we're all that stand between his unprotected flank and the British Legion! Blast the man!*

"I see ol' Bloody Ban's tufted hat from here, Colonel!" Jedidiah Plunkett shouted from somewhere in the tree line. "Want me and Martha to put one between his eyes?"

Francis smiled at the old fire breather's boast, wondering if he and his Kentucky rifle might not be able to do it even at this distance. "Not yet, Jed." He watched Tarleton bring his Dragoons into an organized canter across the open field. "We'll wait 'til they cross the fence, then give them something to think about.

"We don't have all day to play with these fellows, and we've still got a cannon crew to find." Francis doffed his tricorn, wiped sweat from his brow, and stretched his aching back in the saddle. The pain in his ankle flared, but he ignored it.

He waited until he was certain that the British commander could see him, then raised his hat and gave a cheery wave before turning his horse and leading Oscar into the swamp. As expected, the Dragoon bugler sounded the charge a moment later.

Francis gave Jedidiah a nod and his line of concealed men unleashed a single, thunderous volley before remounting and hurrying deeper into the woods. He did not look back, knowing that the Dragoons had probably lost nearly a dozen horses, and possibly half as many men in the fusillade. He smiled at the thought.

An inhuman howl sounded somewhere deep in the swamp, echoing weirdly through the pitch pines, birch, and Spanish moss. The smile died on Francis's lips. Sudden cries and flapping wings filled the wood as scores of frightened birds took flight.

Then all was silent.

Despite the summer heat and stifling humidity, Francis's skin went clammy and cold. He had lived in and around these parts his entire life and he had never heard of anything that could make such an unnatural sound as that demonic howl...

AT THE EDGE of the shadowed tree line, Banastre Tarleton reined in his bloodied troops.

"We've lost eight horses and six men wounded, one killed, sir," Captain MacNee said at his side. "I believe that was Colonel Francis Marion, a leader of the rebel militia. Should we pursue?"

The young British lieutenant colonel removed his helmet and examined the black plume, clipped short by a rifle ball. "No, Captain. This sounds like just the sort of trap into which he'd wish to lure us. We have no idea how many sharpshooters he has hidden in there. Besides, we have our orders to join Lord Cornwallis at Camden.

"As for this damned old fox, the Devil himself could not catch him in that swamp..."

FRANCIS FELT AN oppressive weight on his shoulders, a tingling on the back of his neck. Something rather unsettling. Something that made a part of him want to go back into the sunlight and face two hundred angry Dragoons rather than whatever was making these dismal wetlands its home. *This is foolishness. I've not been ... afraid since the shipwreck when I was a boy. Now, I'm a grown man, armed with musket, pistol, and tomahawk, and surrounded by thirty of the best fighting men in the Carolinas!*

Another throb of pain in his ankle made him wince. *I'm just out of sorts because of this blasted leg! Thanks to it, I was absent when Charleston fell, and even now I'm all but helpless when not in the saddle. Doddering old man! So easy for Gates to cast aside...*

"What do you reckon that howl was, Colonel?" Oscar quietly asked, his dark eyes scanning the shadows in the tall sycamores and the brackish undergrowth. The smell of rotting vegetation and stagnant water was all but overpowering.

Francis swatted a mosquito from his face. "Probably a wounded animal. Perhaps those Jersey boys stumbled upon a bear and, in their surprise, sent it off with some lead in its hide."

"Didn't sound like no bear I've ever heard of," Jedidiah grumbled. "Maybe the Cherokee have slipped back into this here swamp to fight for the redcoats. Coulda been one o' their calls. Maybe even signalin' an ambush."

Francis scowled. "There are no Cherokee in this part of the Carolinas. At least none with a will to fight." *Captain Moultrie and I made certain of that nearly twenty years ago.* The thought brought guilt, and Francis spurred it away with a kick to his horse's flanks.

"Maybe freed slaves, then," Jedidiah persisted. "Sounded like the work of heathen savages to me!"

Francis did not need to look to know that Oscar was giving the frontiersman a load of stink eye. And deservedly so, if for no other reason than the comment reminded them all of the less-savory acts they had been forced to commit in recent days. Acts he feared they would repeat in the days to come.

They followed the wagon tracks deeper into the marsh. The preternatural silence grew more and more oppressive, broken only by the tinkle of harness, the soft tread of hoof on damp earth, and the drone of insects. No birds chirped or sang. The creaking of the tall birch and cedar trees in the slight breeze rumbled like distant thunder.

Francis was about to call a halt for rest when one of the scouts cried out, "Here! We've found them!"

He guided his horse along the solid ground at a trot, Oscar and Jedidiah following close behind. When he reached the scouts and their find, the sight was anything but what he had expected. The roaring drone of thickly swarming flies was his only warning.

Instead of a few frightened and lost Continental soldiers and perhaps a lame draft horse or a mired caisson, he looked upon an open-air abattoir. The ammunition cart and the four-pound galloper were indeed there, but the wheels of both had been shattered so that the caisson and the iron cannon barrel lay awkwardly on the muddy ground. Francis took in the details of the salvageable munitions, but his mind reeled at the carnage surrounding them.

The gun crew's muskets were broken, shattered or snapped in half, their bayonets bent. Blood everywhere. Entrails. Severed limbs. So many he could not be certain how many men and horses had been slaughtered in this place.

Jedidiah whistled. "Sure looks like the handiwork of pissed-off savages to me, Colonel."

Francis scowled. "Not likely. Probably an animal attack. Look for spoor."

Jedidiah shrugged, dismounted to search the area. Francis thought to send Oscar back to the rest of the troops before they arrived on the scene, but a gasp from behind told him it was too late. He turned to see the balance of his force lead their horses into the clearing. He could see on their faces a growing, uncharacteristic fear. These were battle-hardened men who had never shirked in the face of danger, nor when called upon to do the darkest of deeds. Yet every mother's son of them could see that there was something wholly unnatural about whatever had happened here.

"Harry, you and William help Jed look for tracks," Francis said in even tones. He had been a soldier long enough to know that inaction was the first assault on discipline. "Bean, you and your boys see what powder and shot can be salvaged here. The rest of you, form a perimeter and start digging a grave."

There was the merest hint of hesitation, but the men went to work before he had to speak again. Francis watched them for a moment, then walked his horse over to examine the remains. Even without dismounting, he could see that Jedidiah's estimation was wrong. These men and animals had not been hacked apart by swords or tomahawks. They had been torn to pieces with brutish strength and feral claws. *It has to be a bear.*

"Colonel," Oscar whispered at his knee. "Jed's found something."

The man's manner put a knot in Francis's gut. He hurried his horse over to where the old sharpshooter leaned against a birch tree, smoking his pipe, looking pensive. "What is it, Jed?"

"Hell if I know, Colonel." The older man plucked at his pipe's stem. "I've tracked and hunted damn near everything that draws breath in these here parts, and I ain't never seen nothing like this."

Francis followed Jed's gaze to the tip of his boot. A long, three-toed print sank near two inches into the soft soil. Four feet away, another partial print led into the scum-covered black water of the swamp. "Whatever made that print…"

"Is about seven or eight feet tall and weighs as much as two men," Jedidiah finished. "And judging by that stride, it can cover a hell of a lot of ground in a hurry."

Francis pursed his lips. "Cover them up. Not a word. It was a bear attack. Am I clear?" *This swamp is several miles long, and we'll need to keep to it unless we want to face those Dragoons in open country. I can't have my men fearing some "Swamp Devil" for the duration.*

Frightened men are beaten men.

Oscar and Jedidiah, the only two witnesses to the weird spoor, nodded. Francis sensed reluctance on both their parts as they scraped the tracks clean with their boots. "Good. Now we've got a funeral service to conduct and a gun to salvage."

Following the impromptu burial, the men gathered up what they could from the smashed caisson and the gun carriage. The iron galloper now rested on an improvised litter drawn behind Harry and William Tanner's horses. The small force had not ventured much further into the swamp before Francis heard the first whispered speculation:

"You reckon it was ghosts that got 'em? Maybe some o' the Loyalists we hanged?"

"Nah. I think them escaped slaves used hoodoo to conjure up some kinda demon."

"I'll bet it was a Cherokee curse. Y'know this ground is soaked with their blood."

Francis contemplated calling a halt to address the rumors, but hated the idea of telling a bald-faced lie to his men. They trusted him, and in that trust lay the greater part of their loyalty and service. He could not endanger that for the sake of a few campfire tales. In truth, he did not know what had killed those men and horses, and therefore had no grounds to dismiss their stories, farfetched as they might be.

As the talk continued it grew more fanciful and ridiculous, and was soon accompanied by laughter. If fear had been the progenitor of the speculation, it was now replaced by the men's need to one-up each other in the realm of tall tales. Just as the sunlight began to fall in the west, one of Bean's boys started singing "The Unquiet Grave" in a deep baritone. The song was a melancholy love story with a ghost, but the Bean boy sang it with an ironic up-tempo which made the others join in and improvise with increasingly bawdy and humorous verses.

"That's enough," Francis said when the song had reached its raunchiest point. "We'll set up camp here for the night." The cannon and powder had slowed their progress considerably, as it forced them to keep to dry ground instead of wading their horses through the shallows. He reckoned they had only covered three or four miles since leaving the site of the massacre. But with dusk fast approaching, he could not afford to plunge deeper into the swamp. Especially as they had come upon a sizeable bit of high ground ideal for a campsite.

An hour later, Francis leaned against his saddle beside a fire, his bare foot elevated on a stack of firewood and wrapped in one of Oscar's poultices. The ankle had swollen so badly that they nearly had to cut his boot off. Oscar crouched at the fire, boiling a willow-bark tea. Bean's boys moved through the camp dispensing hard bread, smoked meat, and ale. Nearly a dozen small campfires fought against the darkness descending upon the swamp. Jedidiah and the Tanner brothers walked the perimeter as the first watch.

"What about that business today, Colonel?" Wayland Bean said in a hushed tone, seated across the fire from Francis. "You know as well as I do that it was no Indian attack or even angry freed slaves. That was—"

"A bear attack," Francis said. "I'll grant you, the average swamp bear is not the largest nor most ferocious of the ursine family, but that does not preclude the possibility of the occasional aberration."

Bean frowned, took a sip from his tin cup. He did not believe it was a bear attack, but obviously did not wish to press the issue. "The gun is slowing us down. We should spike it, drop it in the swamp, and make haste to Camden with the ammunition. One four-pounder is not going to make a difference in Gates's campaign."

Francis flicked a huge palmetto bug from his knee. Bean was scared and was trying to get out of the swamp as soon as possible. If not for his own sake, then for the sake of his four sons riding in the troop. "Our orders are to return with the gun, Wayland. We have it now, so all that remains is to get it back to Gates. What he does with it after that is entirely up to him."

Gates already detests me. I am not about to fail in such a simple mission and give the man further reason to marginalize me and my command. Not when we were all that opposed the British control of the Carolinas in the weeks following Monck's Corner and Waxhaw.

Bean did not like the answer, but he accepted it. He nodded and rose, bidding Francis a good night. When they were alone, Francis asked Oscar, "What do you think?"

Oscar was quiet for a moment, carefully ladled out the tea into Francis's mug. "I think … that there's something not *right* in this swamp. I felt it as soon as we entered the tree line. Before we even heard that terrible howl… Listen, Colonel. Do you hear that?"

Francis raised his chin and listened. The swamp was silent save for the sound of crickets and cicadas. "Hear what?"

"Exactly," Oscar said. "Only bugs. Normally, this time of year, you couldn't hear yourself think for the tree frogs trying to out-sing the chuck-will's widows. It's too quiet out there, Colonel."

Francis sipped the bitter tea and frowned. "Surely you don't think there's something … *supernatural* behind all this. I thought you were a good Christian, Oscar."

Oscar gave him a wry smile. "The Bible's full of tales of supernatural things, Colonel. That's what scares me. We could be in here with one of the 'rulers of the darkness of this world' that St. Paul speaks of in Ephesians."

A scream cut through the night. A pair of musket shots. A horrific roar.

Francis spilled his hot tea with a curse. "Help me to my feet!"

There were more shots and more screams before he could hobble to the other end of the camp. By the time he reached the scene, the rest of his men were pointing rifles and muskets into the night or waving useless torches. Useless in revealing the intruder, but not in revealing its gruesome handiwork.

The flickering yellow flames glistened on the blood-slicked things that used to be the brothers Harry and William Tanner.

Or at least most of them.

"Where's the rest of Harry?" a shaky voice asked.

Something hot and wet fell on the back of Francis's neck. He looked up. In the boughs of the twisted ash tree hung Harry's broken upper torso, the innards dangling like obscene Christmas tinsel a dozen feet off the ground.

"Get him down from there," Francis said.

Nobody moved.

Sharp pain lanced up Francis's leg. He was about to shout for his order to be obeyed when Jedidiah, kneeling over William's ravaged body said, "Will's not dead!"

Oscar helped him to the wounded man. "Will," he said into the ruined face. "Who did this? What did this?"

The young man stared into the night, his mouth working for several seconds before words finally tumbled out. "It was the Devil," he said in a choking voice. "Those damned red eyes..." He coughed, blood rushing over his broken teeth. His last words echoed through the swamp, obscuring his death rattle: "It was *the Devil!*"

"We'll bury them. Then we're leaving this swamp at first light. Saddle your horses and load your guns. Nobody sleeps tonight."

The night lasted an eternity. Several times shots rang out, but they were false alarms. Still, Francis could not shake the feeling that they were being watched by something outside their little ring of fire. Watched by something with red eyes.

It's getting bolder. One thing to ambush six men distracted by a mired wagon. Another entirely to attack a wary party of thirty, even at night. No animal would do such a thing. At least one not driven mad by pain and disease. But those wounds...

The heat and humidity came before the dawn. And with them came the mosquitos. Francis hadn't been able to get his boot over his swollen ankle, so the little vermin feasted on his exposed foot. As soon as the eastern horizon took on a vague greyish shape, he called everyone to mount up. "And secure the cannon!"

"You don't mean we're still going to try and get that blasted thing out of here, Colonel!" Bean said. His face was drawn, his eyes bloodshot. Clearly, he had spent the night imagining that it had been two of his sons slaughtered beneath the ash tree. "I thought you said we were leaving this swamp today."

"So I did, Master Bean," Francis said, walking his horse close to the man. "And so we are. But we are going to complete our mission. In fact, have two of your boys carry the galloper today."

Bean's face went red and twisted. He was about to balk, but Francis leaned from the saddle and whispered, "You know what I'm apt to do to punish insubordination in the face of danger, Bean. Please don't make me do it."

Bean's eyes filled with cold hatred, but his jaw set and he gave a harsh nod. "Yes, Colonel." Turning to his sons, he said, "Jaimie, Matt, get that litter and gun."

Francis watched to make certain the task was done, and done well, then he signaled the men to move out. The swamp was still dark, but with the use of torches, they were able to make slow progress away from the camp that was now a graveyard. At full sunup, he told Jedidiah to take point to see if he could find a quicker route through the marshland. The old hunter spurred ahead without a word.

There was no singing this morning.

The whispers, and they were few, which Francis overheard were not of tall tales or bawdy songs. They were the whispers of demoralized men questioning their leader and his judgment. Questioning their chances of survival. He had not heard such whispers since his youth as a fresh lieutenant in the Crown's war against the Cherokee. He had forgotten what it felt like not to have the full support of the men under his command. He had forgotten how isolated it made him feel.

The sharp crack of a rifle shot. Then another, muffled blast.

Both from somewhere up ahead. "Jed!" Francis put a spur to his stallion and raced past the column of men. He heard Oscar's chestnut galloping right behind.

"Jed!" Francis called. He caught the faint tang of burnt powder in the air and guided his horse in that direction. "Jed! Where are you?" He splashed across a black rill and up a muddy bank thick with white-studded buttonbush. *"Jed!"*

"Over here, Colonel," came the reply. "I'm fine!"

Francis and Oscar cleared a stand of close-trunked beech to find Jed smoking his pipe and reloading Martha. At his feet lay the corpse of a massive, shaggy-coated bear. Jedidiah looked up and smiled. "Seems it was a bear after all, Colonel." The old hunter knelt and held up the dead animal's fore-paw. "Look, only three toes."

Francis breathed a sigh of relief. "It certainly is the biggest swamp bear I've ever seen."

"And mad," Jed confirmed. "The old bastard came on even after I put a ball in its skull. Fortunately, my pistol found its heart. Otherwise you'd be digging another hole in this here swamp for me."

Francis laughed and wiped sweat from his face. "Thank God we're not. And thanks to you, we'll not be digging any more holes while we're here. Oscar, spread the word that Jed has killed the culprit of last night's unpleasantness."

"Yes, sir."

Despite the improved spirits and the re-stored faith in his command, Francis could do nothing about the terrain they had to trav-erse. Again the cannon and ammunition pre-vented them from making good time through the swamp. The further northwest they went, the softer and wetter the ground be-came until there was nothing poking above the green-slimed water but tall sycamores, felled trees covered in Spanish moss, beaver dams, and the occasional muddy island. When it became apparent that they could not cross the marsh without getting the powder wet and the possibility of losing the cannon, Francis called a halt at the water's edge.

"We'll camp here tonight. Jed, take a cou-ple men and scout around the edges of this mire to see if you can find a way through. Bean, you and your boys set to building a raft. If we need to, we'll float the munitions across to solid ground." The orders were car-ried out with alacrity, if not enthusiasm, and Francis was soon seated against a cedar tree with his injured foot up again. Oscar changed the dressing while the rest of the men hobbled the horses and set up camp.

"Looks like the swelling's gone down from the ankle," Oscar said. "But your foot is all ate up, Colonel."

"Damned mosquitos." Francis swatted another away as it made an unnerving assault on his inner ear. He watched Oscar closely for a moment. "You don't think that bear was the attacker, do you?"

Oscar didn't look up from the fresh bandage. "Neither do you. We've been doing this too long, Colonel, not to know when we're being stalked. And you know as well as I do that whatever killed them Tanner boys last night has been stalking us all day."

Francis sighed and leaned back against the tree trunk. *Night is coming soon and there is a good chance so is this* thing, *whatever it may be.*

"We'll post a double guard," he said, rub-bing the sweat from his eyes. "It may raise the men's suspicions, but at least we won't get caught with our pants down again."

Only, they were.

Francis woke to the screaming of horses and the thunder of panicked hooves. He jumped to his feet before he remembered his broken ankle. Grinding pain shot up his leg, numbing his mind with white fire for a moment. When it passed and the breath-taking ache allowed him to think, he saw the camp in chaos. There were shouts, gun-shots, splashing water, and that hellacious roar he had dreaded. He drew his pistol and tomahawk from his belt, and struggled to stand against the cedar tree.

In the darkness, he saw dimmed camp-fires and blazing torches waving frantically against the night. A muzzle-blast sparked like lightning and was gone. "Oscar!" Francis called. "Oscar! Where are you?"

"The horses!" Oscar shouted as he ran to Francis's side. "The horses were scattered, Colonel! The men are in a panic!"

"Form a box!" Francis demanded, trying to impose order on the situation. But he could see that the men were isolated in small groups of twos and threes. A few men ran singly through the darkness, eyes wide with terror. Francis grabbed one of these as he passed and tossed him to the turf at his feet. He squinted and saw that it was one of Bean's boys. The young man was covered in blood. He was missing his left arm above the elbow, but did not seem to notice.

Francis knelt beside the boy and snatched up his belt to use as a tourniquet. "You're all right, son," he said, trying to calm the young man who was clearly in shock. "It'll be all right."

The cedar tree exploded behind him. Oscar screamed.

Francis turned to see a towering nightmare. The thing stood half-again as tall as Oscar. Its thick arms spread wide, ending in long claws that glistened in the flickering firelight. The fire's yellow glow revealed the scaly outline of the beast's hide, glimmering like hellfire in its red eyes.

With one sweep of its massive arm, it sent Oscar careening into the darkness. Francis raised his pistol and fired. The creature howled and vanished in the haze of smoke. Francis tucked the empty weapon into his sash, dragged the Bean boy to his feet, ignoring the shards of broken glass moving in his ankle. "Come on, son. We've got to be going."

He shouted orders at the men fleeing into the swamp, but all semblance of discipline was gone. The Swamp Devil had seen to that. One hand wrapped around the staggering youth's waist and the other brandishing his tomahawk, Francis plunged into the benighted wilds with the rest of them. *Hopefully we can find some form of shelter and keep safe until dawn.* The notion brought a wave of guilt as he thought about his men. Jed, Bean and the rest of his boys… and Oscar.

"Poor, poor Oscar," he moaned as he splashed into the waist-deep black water. The thought of a copperhead or water moccasin was the furthest thing from his mind at the moment. *What is that thing? Is it in fact some demon come to punish me for my sins against the Cherokee? Is it avenging those runaways and Loyalists we hanged? Is this my fault? Are my men dying because of me? Did Oscar die because of me?*

Though it took a while for his eyes to adjust to the gloom, he did not slow his dogged pace. Between his near-crippled leg and the burden of his injured soldier, it was all he could do to stay upright as he trudged painfully through the fetid water. Isolated screams and gunshots echoed in the eerie silence of the swamp. Eventually, even these stopped.

"You're fine, son," he whispered to the senseless boy, "Just stay with me. You'll be all right." He did not know how many times he said the words as he wandered blindly through the swamp that night. "You're Jack, right? Bean's youngest? Your mother is a Cherokee, isn't that so? Well, don't you worry, son. I'll get you back to her. Don't you worry at all. Just stay with me. Everything is fine."

But when the blackness finally turned to grey and silver, he looked to see that Bean's son was already gone. The boy's blue eyes were glassy, staring into infinity from a bone-white face. Francis hauled the body up onto a clutch of felled sycamores. He took a deep breath and closed the youth's vacant eyes. Bowing his head, he whispered, "I'm sorry, son. Rest in the Lord."

Something popped and hissed behind him.

Francis turned, his tomahawk raised. In the pale light of dawn, he saw the shimmer of a Will O' the Wisp above a small grassy island just before it faded. A sudden rage replaced the fear gnawing at his gut, the guilt in his soul. He looked into the morning gloom and shouted at the top of his lungs, "I'm here, you Devil! *Come and get me!*"

Francis did not wait long before his challenge was answered. He was thankful it was just long enough.

With resounding cracks and splashes of splitting and falling trees, the swamp came alive. The moss-covered beast rushed through the undergrowth in a near-straight line. It howled and hissed, slashing saplings and vines, splashing through the foul water. It came on as fast as any horse at the charge.

But Francis was ready. "Come on, you bastard! Come and get me!"

At the edge of the thicket, it stopped. Tendrils of mist rose from the black water and a heavy silence fell. The monster stared at Francis. He stared back into its unholy eyes. The sun was rising and he could see the thing clearly for the first time. His stomach knotted as he beheld the abomination—part man, part lizard or serpent, or alligator.

And there was indeed something of man in it. He could see a cruel intelligence in its glowing red eyes and in the manner in which its saurian head rocked back and forth on its broad shoulders, sniffing the fetid air.

"What are you waiting for?" Francis roared, splashing the slime-coated water with his tomahawk. "Are you scared of me?"

The thing lowered its head and roared. The hellish sound echoed long and loud through the swamp. Then the creature stalked into the water and came for him.

Francis stood in front of Jack Bean's corpse, raising his tomahawk in challenge. He held one end of his unwound bandage in his other hand. As soon as the monster neared the small grassy island, he tugged on the improvised rope.

There was a flash and a roar of thunder.

He had tied the other end of the bandage to the trigger of his flintlock pistol, which he had shoved barrel-first into the gas pocket he had spotted at dawn. The flint sparked the swamp gas just as the creature reached it, causing an explosion.

Francis smashed into the downed trees, knocked flat by the force of the blast. Bells rang in his ears and acrid smoke burned his eyes and nose. When he could again see through the fading haze, the beast stood not a dozen paces away. Its saurian head lowered, forked tongue flicking from its fang-lined maw. A blackened streak ran across its scaly chest, a smear of blood trickling from the wound. Its baleful eyes studied him.

Francis laughed. "Well, I've given you my best shot." He hauled himself back to his feet and raised the tomahawk. "Let's get this over with, then. But I'll not make it easy for you."

He thought he heard thunder and the creature stood to its full height. Then it turned and raced back into the swamp. Francis frowned, confused, before hearing the crack of a rifle. The shot was followed by a salvo of musketry and the woods where the creature had vanished turned into a hailstorm of lead and splinters.

"You all right, Colonel?" Jed called.

Francis turned to see his men—most of them. In the darkness, he had nearly crossed the length of the mere. He laughed and gave them a wave. "I'm fine," he said. Looking at the dead man beside him, his face fell. "I'm afraid Bean's youngest didn't make it."

Oscar trotted his horse into the shallows and Francis's smile returned. The man's left arm was in a bloodstained sling, but other than that, he appeared fine. "Neither did Bean, Colonel. But his other boys kept the gun and the powder safe. We've accomplished our mission…"

Nearly a mile away, Lt. Colonel Banastre Tarleton lowered his spyglass and sat ashen-faced in the saddle. He and Captain MacNee were atop a low rise that provided a perfect vantage into the northern edge of Scape Ore Swamp. "Something wrong, sir?" the captain asked.

"It appears I was wrong, MacNee," Tarleton said, gaping at what he had just seen. "The Devil *did* catch that old fox. And apparently, he just let the bastard go."

☠ ☠ ☠

"The Swamp Devil" was featured as the May 24, 2019, episode of the podcast Tales to Terrify. *This is the story's first appearance in print.*

Jason J. McCuiston has studied under the tutelage of best-selling author Philip Athans. His stories of fantasy, horror, SF, and crime have appeared in numerous anthologies, periodicals, web-sites, and podcasts, including Black Infinity Magazine *and* StoryHack Action & Adventure. *His debut novel, the sci-fi/noir thriller* Project Notebook *is available from Amazon and Audible. He has published two illustrated collections of pulp-style sci-fi action and adventure featuring* The Last Star Warden *with Dark Owl Publishing. Connect with him at www.facebook.com/ShadowCrusade*
You can find most of his publications on his Amazon page at www.amazon.com/-/e/B07RN8HT98

THE HUNTING GROUNDS

BY STEVE DUFFY

ONCE SHAY CAME BACK FROM AFGHANISTAN TO VALLEJO, THE URGE TO LEAVE IT ALL BEHIND TOOK HOLD OF HIM AND THERE WAS NO WAY HE COULD SHAKE IT. THE ARMY, THE DESERT, WHATEVER, HAD USED HIM UP AND ALTERED HIM, irreversibly it seemed, and his old life was not a compromise he found bearable any longer. Within a month he'd sold up his possessions and headed north, living from day to day, not stopping anywhere for long. Everywhere he went there were people, some meaning well, some not caring to understand him, some damaged in more fundamental ways than him. All through his wandering he dreamed of a place where he might truly be alone, somewhere he might hope to find himself and nothing else.

He camped for a while near Mount Shasta, lying out under the stars at night and dreaming of the ground shaking beneath him, California crumbling into the sea in dust and rubble. When the subduction failed to manifest and the plates failed to shift, he headed up into Oregon with a group of travelling new-agers. They were looking for a place to spend the End Times, they said; Shay found them insufficiently serious in their motivations. After spending a few days at their compound in the Umpqua National Forest he hit the road again, ending up in a ragged tent city in the Springwater Corridor of East Portland. Shay's paper trail led to the ticket counter in PDX, where he booked a one-way flight to Anchorage, Alaska; this was in the month of April, when the starflowers and the fairybells were coming into bloom in the kindly lands along the Columbia River.

His movements from then on were trackable only by ATM withdrawals and a handful of charges on his plastic: camping stores and gunsmiths, supermarkets, train tickets. Proceeding first by railroad and then by thumb, he was heading deep into the interior, for his jumping-off point, wherever that might be. He told himself he'd know it when he saw it.

On the road west of Fairbanks, around the start of June, the way led through a broad valley studded with skinny young conifers. All at once there came a break in the low wooded hills, a notch that opened up a long vista to high distant peaks topped with everlasting snow, and the urge took him there and then, irresistible. He asked the trucker he was riding with to stop and let him off. "Son," the trucker said, the first words he'd spoken in the sixty miles they'd driven together, "are you a fool?"

"This is where I'm headed," he told the trucker. "I just recognized it now." The trucker shrugged, and watched him climb down from the cab. Shay set out in the direction of the mountains, not bothering to look at his maps. In a very short time he was out of sight of the road, and there was nothing moving on the road that might have seen him disappear between the trees. The brief immensity of the boreal summer enfolded him: he walked on in a sort of awe, like the first saint of a new religion.

SHAY HIKED FOR five days, crossing neither roads nor trails, and on the morning of the sixth he came out on the far side of a long stretch of forest. Below the ridge where he stood, the ground sloped away to a wide river plain of marsh and meadow sparsely sown with low brush and quaking aspen, round green hills on the farther bank and bare mountains rising beyond in what seemed an illimitable distance. The sky was perfectly, blankly blue, unscored by contrails, cloudless and gigantic. He felt as if the scene corresponded to some ideal he'd been holding in his head without knowing it, something inaccessible to the conscious mind but instantly recognizable once encountered. Aloud, he said, "This must be the place," and laughed at the clichéd perfection of it all.

A little way down the uneven slope at his feet there rose a weird protrusion, smooth and regular. Approaching it he realized it was a capped stovepipe, the only manmade thing in that landscape. For a moment Shay's heart sank: he felt as if some other explorer had already planted a flag in Eden and annexed it in the name of progress. He circled around below the stovepipe, and saw that it belonged to a sort of dugout shelter, recessed into the side of the hill with the springy turf for a roof. Only the front elevation was visible: a triangular frontage with a door and two shuttered windows. The porch was all grown up with moss and weeds, the rough planking weathered down into an almost natural state.

Shay pulled up the undergrowth from around the doorstep. It looked as if the cabin had been uninhabited since last year at least; probably much longer. At some point the planks had been painted inside and out with what looked like Alaskan native designs, though the colors were all but worn away. He was glad that the place hadn't been built by anyone from outside, as he was already beginning to think of the rest of the world.

Heaving the door open on its leather hinges, he saw that inside the cabin was a potbelly stove, a raised platform for a bed, a few tools hanging from hooks on the walls, and—incongruous yet somehow reassuring—an old wooden rocking chair and a guitar. Someone had chosen this place, maybe a long time ago, he thought. That person had summered here at least, had looked out on the same valley and the same hills and peaks; probably someone like Shay himself, and this notion pleased him. He liked the idea of walking in the footsteps of those who had gone before, who had trodden lightly on the land. He picked up the guitar: the top E string was broken and it was crazy out of tune, but after a few minutes he was able to get a melody going. Shay decided to stay here for the summer at least.

It was a fine season, perpetual daylight and the weather clement for the most part. He set lines along the riverbank and took his fill of trout and Coho salmon; he shot game when he could get it, moose and caribou, and he had traps for rabbit all along the valley. There were mushrooms and berries, cattails and fiddleheads too, and down near the river he found Eskimo potato plants. These last showed signs of having been cultivated once; they were planted in straight rows, with the rotted remains of wooden beds around them to raise them clear of predation. The river water was sweet and fresh and glacier-cold, and to drink it was to take in the untainted essence of the wild. There were fewer no-see-ums and mosquitoes than he'd expected, and after a while what few there were ceased to bother him much. It was as if he was slipping undetectable through the world, as if his tenancy of the cabin was as natural to the valley as the presence of the animals and the birds.

Now and again Shay saw bears on the hills, over on the far side of the valley. They seemed to keep to their own side of the river, and he didn't want to shoot them for game, or for any other reason. One evening when he went to fetch water, a big grizzly was drinking on the farther bank. The two of them faced each other for a minute, maybe longer, before the bear turned and loped back into the trees. He thought back to Afghanistan, the dim figures he'd tracked in his gunsight, the blurs of motion seen through thermal imaging. There had been a point where to pull the trigger had been the most natural thing in the world, and after that a point in which lowering his rifle and clicking off the goggles had been the only thing to do. For a long time after, he'd dreamed of those luminous green ghosts, rising from the night all electric, sinking back into impenetrable shadow, re-emerging closer, ever closer. He'd come a long way to leave them behind, but here in the valley he felt sure they could no longer find him.

When the midnight sun turned to dusk again he would lie on the hillside above the cabin, watching the stars as they turned in their great wheel around Polaris. Some nights, unearthly shrouds of aurora would surge and ripple across the sky in the green phosphor of night vision. These, he knew, were the signs of coming fall, an end to endless summer and the eternal now. What came next? He set himself no concrete deadlines—for a long time he'd lost count of the days and months—telling himself that before the first snows fell he could hike back to the road, hit the nearest town for supplies, maybe rent a room there if the forecast for winter was harsh. He told himself the cabin would still be there if he abandoned it for a season and came back in the spring. At the same time, the thought of staying put, of weathering it out here in the valley, was a wicked temptation. *People die up here*, he thought, and then: *but people die everywhere. At least up here they live.* It went to the heart of what Shay had come here for, and in the end he just gave up trying to decide, leaving it to the weather and the equinox to make his decision for him.

AT THE CLOSE of a day in which the wind had carried a thin sharp edge of chill down from the mountains, Shay was sitting outside his cabin skinning a brace of hare for his evening meal when he saw, coming down the ridge alongside the river, the first human being he'd seen since he jumped down from the truck. He tensed up, seeing that the figure was dressed in camo and carrying a rifle slung over his shoulder, then relaxed a little as his features came into view. It was an Alaska Native, a big-set man who might have been any age between fifty and eighty. Beneath his Stetson his hair was long and grey and loose, and he looked as if he belonged in the valley just as much as anything he'd seen all summer.

Shay stuck his knife in the turf and rose to his feet as the man approached, lifted a hand, open palm. The stranger looked at him for a while, returned the gesture and said, "How you doin'?" His voice was deep and resonant, not unfriendly but noncommittal.

"Good," Shay said and then, feeling for a basis on which to proceed, "Is this your cabin?"

The stranger looked at the open door, then back at him, and seemed to think about the question. Eventually he said, "I use it every once in a while, is all. It was built long before my time. You can stay here if you want."

Shay felt a great sense of relief. "I was just getting a meal ready. You want some?"

"That'd be good." The stranger unslung his backpack and rifle and settled down on the doorstep of the cabin. "Name's Isaac."

"Hey, Isaac," Shay said, and introduced himself. His own name felt weird in his mouth, difficult to shape, like a word from some language that nobody spoke any more, Hittite or Minoan.

"You been here long?" Isaac asked.

"Since the start of summer."

"I see you mended the place some." It was true: Shay had cleaned the planking of moss, and replaced the broken panes in the windows with little louvered slats of wood.

"I did," he said, "but I don't have a string for that guitar."

Isaac nodded gravely. "You learn to do without," he said.

After the meal, they sat out on the hillside and watched the sun touch the tops of the high mountains with cold fire. They didn't talk much; Isaac still hadn't asked what Shay was doing here, for which he was grateful. A flock of sharp-tailed grouse rose as one from their stamping ground down in the valley and took flight above them. Isaac watched them circle overhead and said, "You don't got a shotgun?"

"No," Shay said. "I tried some ground snares down by the lek there, didn't have much luck."

"But you got a rifle, though?" Isaac indicated the large spread of antlers Shay had fixed above the door to the cabin.

"Yeah," he said, "running short on ammo now, though. Guess I should stock up on a few things before winter."

"You don't want to be here by then," Isaac said. He looked at him as if to emphasize the point, and Shay saw his face crease up in a grimace. "This isn't a place to winter."

"I haven't made my mind up yet," Shay said, not wanting to contradict him, but feeling again that mulish impulse to stay and see what came of it.

"I can't tell you what to do," Isaac said. "You come too far to be told. But I say don't do it."

"It can be hard, I guess," he conceded, not wanting to contradict him.

"It's not that." Isaac was giving Shay his undivided attention now. "Yes, it's hard. A man thinks he can make it if he's prepared; well, maybe he can, maybe he can't. Most men can't. A man like you might, all things being equal. But there are other things, things you won't be prepared for."

"The loneliness?"

"It's not that. It's the opposite."

"Are there other people who come here?" That might be enough of a reason to pull out for the winter at least. "Is this a hunting ground for any of the nations? Tanana? Ingalik?"

"No," Isaac said. "No, these lands beyond the river, they don't belong to any of the people."

"So I'm free to stay here?"

"I didn't say these lands weren't claimed," Isaac said, no louder than a whisper, only it was a low rumble in his chest. He turned away and began rolling a cigarette.

"Are there other people come here, then?" Shay asked. "Outsiders like me, out-of-staters?"

"Yes and no," Isaac said, after thinking about it for a while. "People like you, no. Outsiders—" He started to say something, but after another pause he let it drop, licking the cigarette paper instead. "I say pull out now, before the snow comes, that's all." He held out the tobacco pouch.

"I don't know," Shay said, passing up the offer. "So are there others like you who come here, to the cabin?"

"I'm the last now," Isaac said. "There were guys before me, I guess someone will do it after I'm gone. Each year when the fall comes I walk the boundaries. There are lodges like this all around the rim. Takes me a month or so, I'm back in town when the snow comes."

"Boundaries of what?"

"All that land across this river here," Isaac was not exactly answering the question, he noticed; "I start up north a ways, swing around back down to here, on the southern edge of the grounds."

"Is that a tribal thing?" He didn't understand.

"I guess," Isaac said, and lit his cigarette with a battered brass Zippo.

"I don't know," Shay said. "I can't be with people for long, you know?"

"I know," Isaac said, and it sounded like he really did. "I walk this trail because I learned how to be with myself. That other life, it's not for everyone. But you got to do it," he insisted, and again there was an earnestness in his voice, a directness. "Just hang it out in town till spring comes. You look like a tough guy, you can hack it."

Again Shay said, "I don't know." He

tilted his head back, saw the stars pricking holes in the deep blue dome above, the thick scatter of the Milky Way. "I used to look at the stars when I was out on night patrol in the desert," he said. "There's nothing so remote. So far away."

"I know," Isaac said, his eyes still on his cigarette. "The old folks used to say they tell a story."

"Oh yeah?"

"They had stories for everything, back then. You saw those paintings in the cabin, the pictures on the walls?" Shay nodded. "You can see the stars in them, they're part of the story they tell. Now, those pictures were there before I ever came here—I had to learn how to read them. I didn't build this lodge, you know?"

"So what is the story?"

"It's the story of the early times," Isaac said. "The first times, the coming of the people to the North. And you ask those old folks, they'd say the story goes around and around to you and me right here, right now. It's a circle: there isn't any end to it."

Just then, Shay's attention was caught by movement across the valley. By now the dusk was deep, but his eyes were attuned to it and he was able to make out a herd of caribou, maybe a dozen, galloping across the lower slopes and making for the trees. "Bear?" he said, knowing that Isaac would have seen it too.

"I don't think so," Isaac said. "Watch now." The two of them sat and watched, but no grizzly broke cover in the wake of the pack.

"I guess they were just spooked for no reason," Shay said.

"You'll see a lot of that." Isaac's face was set and unreadable. "Animals acting weird. Birds too, you won't see so many birds from now on. Insects will be everywhere, or nowhere at all. It'll be quiet, but a different quiet, like a dead quiet. And at night you'll see some stuff, maybe."

"What stuff?"

"I mean this is the changing season. Things will be different over in the hunting grounds."

Shay wasn't following. "How do you mean, different?"

"Everything will be different," Isaac repeated. He got to his feet, stretched. "I been walking all day. I'm tired."

"You should take the bed in the cabin," Shay said, aware that he was offering Isaac only what was already his by right. Still he didn't really understand what the old man was trying to tell him, wasn't sure if he was just throwing up smoke.

"I'll take the rocking chair," Isaac said. "One of us should keep watch."

WHILE IT WAS still night, Shay came suddenly awake out of deep sleep and a vague, unresolved sort of dream. There was a figure bending over him, and he lurched upright. The dark silhouette resolved itself into Isaac, crouching at the side of the bunk with a blanket around his shoulders. "Sorry," he said quietly. "But I want you to see this."

Shay got up and followed Isaac outside. The dawn was still some hours off, the starlight already carrying the cold glitter of the coming winter. "What?" he asked.

"Check out the caribou," Isaac said, and when Shay strained to see across the valley, he took him by the shoulder and reoriented him facing northwest. "Up there, the stars. You call it the Big Dipper."

Shay searched for Ursa Major, the great bear slumped across the sky. He blinked, wondering if his eyes were still blurred by sleep.

"There's old coyote, he stands still." Isaac was speaking as if to a child. "There's the lynx—hey, look, see the meteor?" Isaac pointed out the transient streak of light that split the constellation's zigzag. "Now where's the caribou?"

It was the damnedest thing. He couldn't make out the Big Dipper. There was something like the shape, only turned all around, crooked, wrong somehow. But how could the stars be wrong?

"I can't..." He fumbled for words. Eventually, he was forced to put it in the simplest and most idiotic way. "The stars aren't the same."

"The stars will be different now," Isaac said, as if it was the most natural thing in the world, foreordained and inevitable. "That's how it begins."

"How what begins?"

Now it was Isaac's turn to search for the words. Eventually, he said, "Come back in the cabin." He tapped Shay's solar-powered camping lantern. "Is that thing charged?"

Shay clicked it on, and the interior of the cabin was filled with an unnatural moonglow. In it Isaac's face looked older than it had in the gentle light of autumn, lined and weathered.

"Good enough," Isaac said. "Now look at these pictures." He pointed where to look among the designs on the walls, and Shay followed as he spoke.

"This is what they tell. This here—" he indicated a face—"is the first of the people, the first man to set foot in the hunting grounds. The stars show it's summer. This is Bear, and he says, greetings, brother. The man says, greetings to you, brother, are these your lands? And Bear says, these lands belong to no one but Inupasugjuk. Who is that, says the man, I never heard that name. Inupasugjuk, says the bear, the giant, the hunter, his name is a secret, and he comes with the fall. He was here before any of the animals, always hungry, waiting forever for his chance to hunt something down and kill it. Waiting for man most of all, because man tastes the best—man's fear makes the meat taste sweet to him. He is as tall as the highest mountain, as strong as the thunderstorm, and he is terrible. And although he is so big, he'll hide in plain sight, and you'll never see him until he is upon you."

Isaac was pointing to a grotesque snarling face in the paintings, a bald head and a mighty beard set low beneath the shoulders of a hulking body. In place of teeth, it had tusks. He glanced to see if Shay was following, and continued:

"Then how shall I know when he is coming, says the man? Bear says, he leaves no track, so you must look up in the sky. Because when he is hunting, even the stars scatter like birds. Look in the sky, smell for his spoor on the wind, and watch the other animals. All of them will warn you in their own voices. And the souls of the ones he has eaten, they will dance in the sky when he is near, and the name of those dancers is *aksarnirq*, the dancing dead."

Isaac indicated the designs around the head of the creature. "Those dead souls, you call them the aurora," he said. "Now look at the stars."

Studded in the folds of the aurora were little black asterisks. "Not white," Isaac said. "Black. Black stars. That means the stars are different. That's his sign."

Shay was frowning, trying to take it all in. Finally he said, "Do you … do you believe all this? What the bear said? That thing, whatever you called it?"

"Talking bear?" Isaac looked at him sternly. "Do I look like a child to you?"

"But—"

"You don't get it, do you? Like those stars—do you believe there's a real big dipper up in space? Course you don't. You're not an idiot. Me, I don't believe there's a caribou up there either, or a lynx. All of this—" he gestured at the paintings—"all of this is just a way of telling the story, it's not our way, it's their way, and that story might mean something different to us than what it meant to them. This is how the dead speak to us—in stories, in riddles, in things we can't remember and things they can't explain. Look, forget this," and he grasped Shay by the shoulders and manhandled him back out of the cabin, "forget all that old-time story stuff I told you. Look up. See how it's all going crazy. See how it just isn't normal anymore. How can you stay in a place where the stars aren't right? Take your damn chance and get out."

Shay and Isaac stood for a long time under the stars, staring at each other. Eventually Isaac released his grip, turned away in what might have been frustration or just plain resignation, and took up his seat in the rocking chair again. Shay stood out there for a while longer, then went back into the cabin. When he switched off the camping lantern, the shapes on the walls seemed to retain some of the pale light, and even when he closed his eyes the face of Inupasugjuk swam in the blood-red blurs and phosphene swirls of his retinal field.

Isaac set off early the next morning, without waiting for Shay to wake. He was heading for the western end of the valley, where the river took a turn between high hills and flowed northwest through a flattened, barren flood plain. Two leisurely days' hike took him to the last of the lodges along the perimeter, situated at the top of a low bluff facing east toward the hunting grounds. A great-horned owl was perched on its roof: it regarded him unafraid as he drew near, then flapped its massive wings and took to the air as silently as a ghost.

While there was still daylight Isaac went down to the river for water. He sniffed at it suspiciously, tasted it from his palm and spat it out. In his pack he carried water purification tablets; he added them to the water in his bottle, and after an hour or so drank from it with a grimace. All along the river, he now saw, were the belly-up bodies of dead trout, luminous with rot in the twilight, floating downstream from the hunting ground to the sea.

He spent the night in the lodge, alternately dozing and tracking the stars as they slipped in their courses, slow as the hour hand on a clock, reassembling with exquisite sluggishness into strange new constellations. Before sunrise the *aksarnirq* rose above the high slopes, and Isaac watched them undulate across the horizon. For a moment in the pale predawn he thought he saw a shape silhouetted against the aurora, something far-off and immense, as if a mountain had reared up for a moment then hunkered back down below the peaks.

The traps he'd set the night before yielded only a single hare, but when he cut it open the meat was black and stinking. He threw it away in disgust, and chewed on moose jerky from his pack before boarding up the lodge ready for the coming storms. With one last look back at the hunting grounds, he started out southwest, aiming to hit the highway in about a week. As he walked away, the owl glided back and took up its roost on top of the lodge once more.

The first four days led over easy ground. He made good time along a long straight animal trail densely tracked with hoofprints and fringed with chewed-on saplings. Now he was relieved of the necessity to keep watch, he could settle in his sleeping bag and in theory at least, sleep the night

through. In practice, though, his thoughts kept turning to Shay. Had he done the right thing and cleared out? Isaac doubted it. Some people just had the look of the lost about them—people who don't know what they're looking for until it finds them—and in Isaac's judgement Shay was one of them. On the morning of the fifth day, he sat cross-legged for a long time and thought it over, while overhead the cirrocumulus banked up in long white rows that told of winter on the way. He closed his eyes and tried to picture the scene back there in the valley. Aloud he said, "Goddamnit," and got to his feet. He repeated the curse two or three times, first with increasing emphasis then in resignation, and set out back the way he'd come.

The weather had turned now, chill winds with the sting of sleet and rain lashing down from the Arctic straight into Isaac's face. His old bones had the unremitting ache of winter in them, but he trudged on resolutely, knowing that time was of the essence, trusting to luck that he'd make it there before it was too late, for Shay, for himself, for everything. With some trepidation he turned off the trail and struck out over wooded country: it was a more direct route to where he was headed, and the trees sheltered him from the worst of the weather, but the going was that much harder. He walked for as long as there was light, and shot whatever he could whenever he could for provisions. He forced himself not to think about what he might find in the valley.

At one point he heard pounding hooves, far off at first then closer, and he crouched in the lee of a rock outcrop for cover. A herd of caribou came stampeding through the forest, bellowing in fear, shouldering the young saplings aside, snagging themselves in the lower branches of the bigger trees, twisting and wrestling clear, some actually breaking their antlers loose and pounding on with the broken spreads swinging and jouncing from their bloodied heads in a way that made Isaac sick to watch. After the herd had thundered off into the setting sun, there was only the sound of the wind, but it carried on it the stink of corruption.

He hit the river early on the fifth day of

his detour, some way downstream from the valley. The clouds were sitting right on top of the mountains now, wreathing the peaks in impenetrable shade. If you looked long enough, you could fancy there was movement inside that misty shroud, dim gigantic figures looming in the iron-grey murk. Isaac kept his eyes on the ground in front of him.

The weather worsened by the hour. When the afternoon was turning dark in the teeth of the massing storm clouds, he finally came in sight of the cabin. The snow came swirling hard and heavy on the roaring northern wind as he scrambled up the bluff.

The cabin door was banging open and shut. Isaac dodged inside and leaned hard on it against the gale, kicking the chock into place to hold it. The noise of the storm was almost as loud inside as it had been outside; the stove was out, and the frigid clamminess of winter earth had settled around the cabin like the chill of a fresh-dug grave. On the bed lay Shay, and at first Isaac thought he'd come too late. There was no color in his sunken cheeks, and he looked wasted, skeletal, as if he'd lain there since June and all that had come to pass after that had been nothing but a deathbed dream. All the tan of the summer, and of the desert before it, had leached out of him in a matter of days, and his skin was the color of old newsprint blown in the wind.

Isaac bent over Shay. He slapped his cheeks, softly at first, with no reaction, then harder, until he came around. He stared at Isaac, trying to focus; his eyes looked too large for his hollowed sockets. "Get up," Isaac told him, heaving him up into a sitting position that Shay could barely sustain. "Get up, you've got to get up now."

"Brother Bear told me..." Shay's voice was a croak, parched as dry leaves blown from the branches. "No—you told me, right? I'm all messed up." He coughed, a racking rattle that sounded like the clatter of bones in his chest. "The thing that lives in the hunting grounds... yeah, that was you told me about that. It's all messed up in my head."

Isaac picked up the water bottle by the bed, held it to Shay's lips then threw it into a corner when he saw the ditch-brown color of the water. He gave him to drink from his own bottle, then searched through Shay's backpack for all the clothes that would fit on him. He dressed Shay layer by layer like a scarecrow, and said "Okay, we're gonna make for the road, you and me. Away from here, at least," he added, suppressing the thought in his mind that Shay would be lucky to last a day on the trail.

"I don't know, man," Shay said, setting off another paroxysm of coughing. "He marked me, man—I mean, I looked at him, you know, and he set his mark on me."

Isaac stopped, bent to Shay's eye level. "Say what?"

Shay rasped in a couple more breaths, then said in almost a whisper, "That one. You know his name. Set his damn mark on me, man." As if he was sharing some great and awful secret. "Water's bad, game's gone bad... first time I saw him I fell and hit my head, dizzy, can't see straight—I tell you, man, he is all I see now. Just him and nothing else. Night vision, you know what I'm saying, night vision. I bear his mark."

Isaac waited no longer. "Come on," he said, reshouldering his pack and heaving Shay to his feet. For a moment they reeled in an awkward do-si-do, Shay tottering, Isaac clasping him tight under his armpits. Isaac managed to get him shoulder to shoulder, braced him with one strong arm and kicked the chock away from the door. "Come on," he urged again, as if all his words, all his explanations, had been blown away in the face of the numinous. With Isaac bearing the greater part of Shay's weight, they staggered out into the stinging snow.

For a moment they fought for balance, and while Shay steadied himself, Isaac glanced across the valley, in the direction of the hunting grounds. The far slopes were already white with snow, and across the valley floor he saw bears lumbering down out of the treeline, galloping toward the river. Isaac was about to set Shay down and reach for his rifle, when he saw that the bears were not coming after them, probably had no idea he and Shay were even there; rather, they were the hunted ones, scattering in a blind panic. The pack plunged into the water and thrashed across to the farther bank, and Isaac knew what had spooked them, sensed it rather than saw it, felt it in the bite of the blizzard and the darkness of the storm. He turned Shay around, grunted "Come on" one more time, and set off at a lurch toward the uncertain shelter of the trees. Behind them, out of the hunting grounds, a shadow dark as death slid across the hard driven snow, as slow as the shadows that mountains cast at evening, and every bit as relentless.

Steve Duffy lives and works in North Wales. His most recent collection of weird stories, Finding Yourself In The Dark, *was published by Sarob Press in 2021; he's currently in the process of putting together his next. Steve was the winner of the International Horror Guild's award for Best Short Story 2000, and in 2015 he received the Shirley Jackson Award for Best Novelette.*

"The Hunting Grounds" was inspired in equal measure by Algernon Blackwood's "The Wendigo," and by the real-life stories of Timothy Treadwell and Chris "Alexander Supertramp" McCandless.

"EVERYTHING GOOD DIES HERE":

REFLECTIONS ON JACQUES TOURNEUR'S
I WALKED WITH A ZOMBIE

By Justin Humphreys

Paul Holland: *It's easy enough to read the thoughts of a newcomer. Everything seems beautiful because you don't understand. Those flying fish, they're not leaping for joy, they're jumping in terror. Bigger fish want to eat them. That luminous water, it takes its gleam from millions of tiny dead bodies. The glitter of putrescence. There's no beauty here, only death and decay.*

Betsy Connell: *You can't really believe that.*

Paul Holland: *Everything good dies here. Even the stars.*

When *I Walked with a Zombie* comes up in print or conversation, there is no getting around its title. When I mention the film to people familiar with it, the title generally makes them perk up and rave about the movie itself. But when I mention it to neophytes and the uninterested, I'll usually get a raised eyebrow and a smirk—a stupidly dismissive snap judgment over that somewhat lurid name. The curse of producer Val Lewton's magnificent low-budget 1940s horror classics—of which this is one—was their titles: their sensationalism belied the films' quality, intelligence, and poetry. Lewton's *Cat People, The Body Snatcher, Curse of the Cat People,* and others were subtle and intense, shadowy, eerie, full of quiet dread, and defied horror cinema's stereotypes. In so doing, they redefined the genre. Arguably foremost among them, *I Walked with a Zombie* isn't just a great horror film, it's a truly great film, period.

I Walked with a Zombie has a hypnotic power like few other films I can think of, particularly in its dialogue-free passages. If you ever get the chance to see it on 35mm film in a theater, I strongly recommend going. I've seen it screened twice, and it *mesmerizes* audiences. I have watched as Tourneur's equally brilliant *Cat People* set smug, brainless, condescending 21st-century audiences laughing—which isn't hard since they frequently come to older movies to bully them. But *I Walked with a Zombie* held those same yokels silently enthralled, its transcendent power fearlessly *daring* the audience to try and find any lapse of artistic skill in it— because there are none.

effort to save Jessica. In so doing, simmering turmoil within the family leads to death and misery.

Based very loosely on an *American Weekly* magazine article by Inez Wallace, the film was initially scripted by Universal monster movie stalwart Curt Siodmak (*The Wolf Man, Frankenstein Meets the Wolfman*), and rewritten by Ardel Wray, with contributions from Val Lewton himself. How much of Siodmak's original remains is difficult to say, but it's telling that Siodmak would get surly when the film came up in interviews. Wray's involvement notably makes this one of the only truly great horror films of the 1940s written by a woman. The film has a distinctly feminine point of view, and its story and characters deliberately bear more than a passing resemblance to Charlotte Bronte's *Jane Eyre*. This last aspect wasn't

From left, Christina Gordon, Frances Dee, and Tom Conway. Below, Edith Barrett as Mrs. Rand.

I Walked with a Zombie centers on nurse Betsy Connell (Frances Dee), hired by a sugar planter, Paul Holland (Tom Conway), to care for his nearly-catatonic wife, Jessica (Christina Gordon), at their home on San Sebastian, a Caribbean island. Holland lives on his plantation with with his alcoholic half-brother, Wesley Rand (James Ellison), and his seldom-seen mother, Mrs. Rand (Edith Barrett). With her charge seemingly incurable by conventional medicine, Betsy turns to the local Voodoo practitioners in a last-ditch unusual, since Lewton's team frequently drew inspiration from classic art and literature. Arnold Bocklin's painting "Isle of the Dead" inspired Lewton's eponymous 1945 film, and that same painting hangs on a wall in *I Walked with a Zombie*; William Hogarth's "The Rake's Progress" similarly inspired Lewton's *Bedlam* (1946). Lewton and company's research into Voodoo is apparent throughout, as is the influence of William Seabrook's seminal study of the subject, *The Magic Island* (1929), right down to a character's name, "Ti-Joseph," carried over from Seabrook. This was a major shift from the crudeness of earlier Poverty Row zombie films like *King of the Zombies* (1941) and *Revenge of the Zombies* (1943). In 1943, countless audience members were probably

From left, Frances Dee, James Ellison and Tom Conway.

first introduced to terms like *hounfour* and *houngan* and names like Damballa and Papa Legba through this film. (That Lewton had a sense of humor is apparent in a throwaway gag in the opening credits, where the standard opening disclaimer playfully states its characters bear no resemblance to "Persons living, dead, or *possessed*.")

Its director, the great Jacques Tourneur, was already becoming a key member of Lewton's unit with *Cat People* (1942) and *The Leopard Man* (1943). Lewton's films' style had rapidly developed with these outstanding works, and, by the time he and Tourneur made *I Walked with a Zombie*, they had reached a new level of quiet sophistication. In a 1977 interview, Tourneur described Lewton as "an idealist" and himself as "very pragmatic, so we made a great team and worked well together ... It was a happy time in my life because he gave me a sense of poetry I sorely lack. The three films we made together had a feel that was very ... poetic which stayed with me afterwards." Tourneur would go on to make the film noir masterpiece *Out of the Past* (1947), and the supernatural horror masterpiece *Night of the Demon* (1957, aka: *Curse of the Demon*), among his many other notable credits. Among his many acolytes is Martin Scorsese, who called him

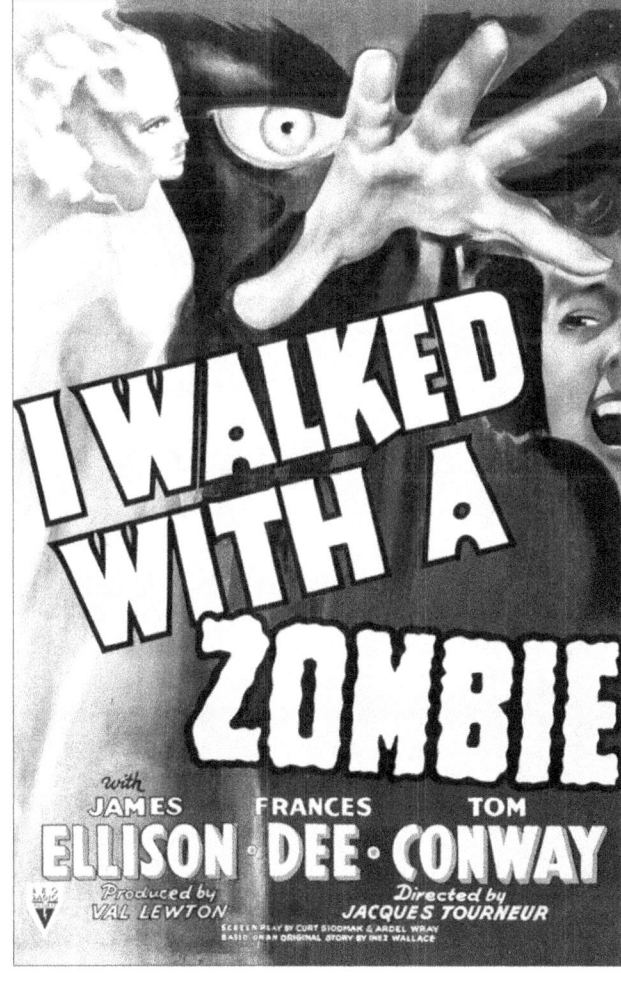

Jessica's Gothic tower.

arose from budgetary considerations: the more dimly-lit a movie was, the lower the electrical bills were and that much less set had to be dressed. *I Walked with a Zombie* is a vivid reminder that great films don't need money behind them, just imagination and skill. Aside from the scenes on the beach, almost all of it was filmed on studio sets. It's easily one of the most beautiful (largely) studio-bound "B"-films of the '40s.

Arguably the single most sublime sequence is Betsy and Jessica's moonlit walk through the cane fields to the

"One of those directors who renews your enthusiasm for movies."

High among *I Walked with a Zombie*'s other major contributors is cinematographer J. Roy Hunt. Hunt's brilliant chiaroscuro lighting gives the film a genuinely poetic, fairy tale quality. Some truly outstanding visual moments include the moment where Betsy blows out the lamp and suddenly the room is starkly lit only by the slits of light through the blinds and the staircase in Jessica's tower, a jagged shock of white erupting from the darkness. The accent here is on mood, not melodrama or simplistic shocks. The reliance on darkness in RKO's horror movies and film noirs

Betsy leads Jessica to the hounfour, hoping to find a possible cure there.

Voodoo ritual at the hounfour, and their first encounter with the zombie Carrefour (Darby Jones). Just prior to this showpiece is a gorgeous tracking shot over the Hollands' home, the family in characteristic poses, opening on Paul busying himself at his desk, then shifting over to Rand dissolutely smoking and drinking, and then to Betsy leading Jessica to see Alma the maid. The nighttime walk is a masterpiece of cinematography, editing, sound design, pacing, and suspense. Betsy and Jessica pass by markers along the way like a cow skull, a dead goat hung from a tree, and a gourd full of holes, whistling eerily, with the wind blowing past them all the while. The cane fields' silence gradually gives way to the sounds and music of the Voodoo rites.

Music is central to *I Walked with a Zombie*: the dirge the workers sing onboard the ship at the beginning and when they find the bodies at the end, the Voodoo song at the hounfour, and, most memorably, in Sir Lancelot's "Shame and Sorrow for the Family" (aka: "Fort Holland Calypso Song"). Sir Lancelot, a pioneering

Silent and statuesque, the vigilant zombie sentry Carrefour awaits at the crossroads.

calypso singer, performs the song onscreen, inadvertently tipping Betsy off to the Hollands' scandals and what common knowledge they are throughout the island. The filmmakers' thorough research into the Voodoo milieu shines through in details like these: calypso was originally used to spread news and gossip—sometimes coded—and to comment on island life. A ballad about the Holland family's turmoil fits the film perfectly, since the story's overall structure is akin to a murder ballad. Sir Lancelot's charm starkly contrasts with his song, and he has some of the film's funniest lines: "Apologize, that's what I'll

do. Creep in just like a little fox and warm myself in his heart." After Rand passes out, he eerily finishes his song for Betsy, seemingly to warn her.

Ironically, his song became a perennial calypso hit in a roundabout way. Initially released as a 78 under the title "Scandal in the Family," the original version—lyrics intact—was covered by various artists, including as a televised duet by Johnny Cash and Odetta. In 1962, calypso singer Lord Melody released a risqué comic version about a son trying to get his father's blessings to marry, only to find that all of his intendeds are actually his illegitimate half-sisters. In this alternate form, it's now a calypso standard with its roots in

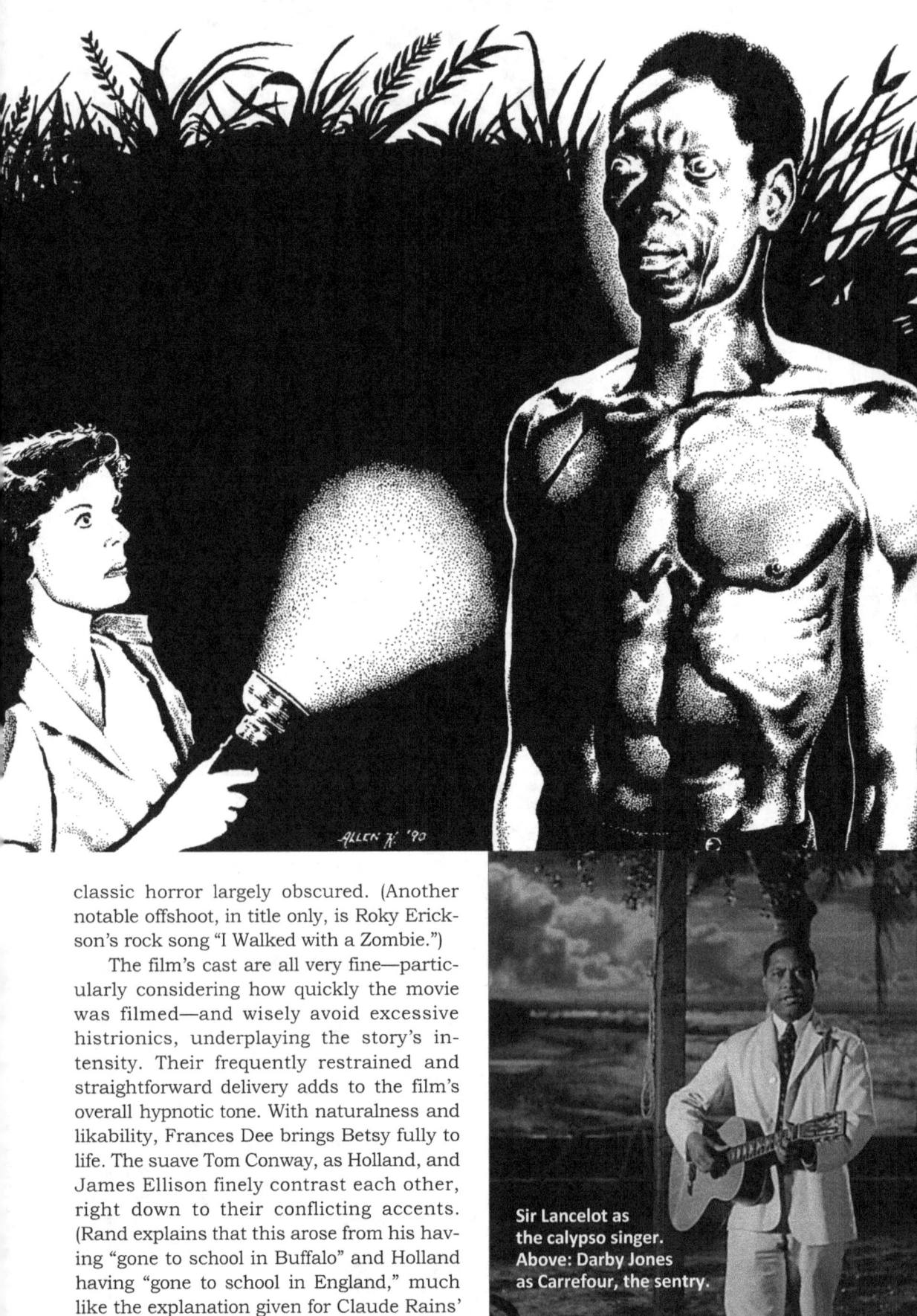

ALLEN K. '90

classic horror largely obscured. (Another notable offshoot, in title only, is Roky Erickson's rock song "I Walked with a Zombie.")

The film's cast are all very fine—particularly considering how quickly the movie was filmed—and wisely avoid excessive histrionics, underplaying the story's intensity. Their frequently restrained and straightforward delivery adds to the film's overall hypnotic tone. With naturalness and likability, Frances Dee brings Betsy fully to life. The suave Tom Conway, as Holland, and James Ellison finely contrast each other, right down to their conflicting accents. (Rand explains that this arose from his having "gone to school in Buffalo" and Holland having "gone to school in England," much like the explanation given for Claude Rains'

Sir Lancelot as the calypso singer. Above: Darby Jones as Carrefour, the sentry.

and Lon Chaney, Jr's wildly different father-son accents in *The Wolf Man*.) Conway is, as Rand describes him, "Strong, silent, and very sad. Quite the Byronic character"—every bit the romantic Gothic antihero. Ellison plays against Rand's alcoholism, forcing affability and cheerfulness which quickly fade when tensions inevitably arise, like how his smile vanishes when he hears Sir Lancelot singing about him and his family. The first Mrs. Vincent Price, Edith Barrett, is very good as Mrs. Rand, playing a woman decades older than herself with only minor makeup. In one of her very few film roles, Christina Gordon unforgettably plays the possessed Jessica, ever silent, her expression faraway, her nightdress wafting in the breeze. Darby Jones is memorable as the lanky zombie Carrefour—a role he semi-reprised in RKO's *Zombies on Broadway* (1945).

Like a zombie: Jessica does not bleed.

There are many misapprehensions about 1930s and 1940s cinema by writers who don't know those eras' films well, not least of which is the mistaken notion that *all* old movies are unfailingly racist. Take, for example, these quotes from Jamie Russell's zombie movie compendium, *Book of the Dead:*

"...The early films in the zombie genre—from *White Zombie* to *King of the Zombies* and *I Walked with a Zombie*—relied on a racist understanding of the black male Other as a symbol of horror (the zombie) ... These films styled the Caribbean as a terrifying land that contained the seeds of the white world's destruction." Although the earlier PRC zombie movies he mentions are inarguably loaded with racial stereotypes, lumping *I Walked with a Zombie* in with them is a major blunder, and an insult to the good work Lewton's unit did. Pseudo-

A doll dressed like Jessica is drawn by a string, to lure the catatonic woman to the hounfour.

academics love seeing racism where it isn't, and this kind of simpleminded reaction to an advanced film like *I Walked with a Zombie* is a reflection of its author's ingrained agendas, not of any accurate comprehension of the film's actual content.

With only minor scrutiny, it's obvious that *I Walked with a Zombie* respects its black characters, and, astonishingly, it's one of the only 1940s films I can think of that consistently, unequivocally treats slavery as an atrocity. A sense of sorrow and tragedy lingering on San Sebastian from its slavery

Theresa Harris as Alma.

days is established early on. During Betsy's initial conversation with the coachman, he explains how the Holland family first brought the slaves to San Sebastian. That memory is ever-present because of "Ti-Misery," the figurehead of St. Sebastian and his arrows from their slave ship, repurposed to adorn the fountain in their garden, with "a sorrowful, weeping look on his black face." The slaves were "chained to the bottom of a boat," the coachman continues, and their descendants now largely populate the island. When Betsy naively asks "They brought you to a beautiful place, didn't they?" he replies, half-polite, half-amused, "If you say, miss. If you say." He's actually echoing and continuing what Holland told her on the ship earlier—a warning of the grimness lurking behind the lush tropical façade.

Much is made of slavery's lasting impact on the locals. Holland himself acknowledges the figurehead and its significance: "That's where our people come from—from the misery and pain of slavery. For generations, they found life a burden. That's why they still weep when a child is born and make

Carrefour searches for Jessica. Below: after Jessica is found dead, Carrefour brings home her body.

merry at a burial ... I've told you, Miss Connell, this is a sad place." The film seems to say that the evil deeds of Holland's ancestors were so great and their residue so strong, that evil might be an underlying supernatural cause behind his family's internal collapse. The locals aren't truly endangering anyone—the terrible sins of his fathers are much more of an underlying threat. Even the film's closing prayer, spoken over the image of the slave ship's figurehead, points to a desire to heal the lasting wounds of slavery: "Ye, Lord, pity them who are dead, and give peace and happiness to the living."

It should be noted that, in contemporary reviews, the highly liberal magazine *The Nation* praised Lewton's films for their unstereotyped portrayal of black characters. In particular, actress/singer Theresa Harris played a key role in breaking away from crude movie caricatures in Lewton's, and others', work. Harris had already appeared in classics like *Baby Face* (1933) and *Jezebel* (1938), frequently as maids, and had shown a comic and musical flair in films like *Buck Benny Rides Again* (1940), where she plays Eddie "Rochester" Anderson's girlfriend. In her work at RKO in films like Lewton's *Cat People* and *Out of the Past* (1947), and elsewhere, including *Phantom Lady* and *Strange Illusion*, Harris flouted the caricatured "mammy" maids of the time. Although she was stuck playing menial roles, she made much of them, but this lack of opportunity or varied roles reportedly led to her leaving the industry. She remains sorely underrated. One of her most memorable lines in *I Walked with a Zombie* is her description of caring for Holland's wife—

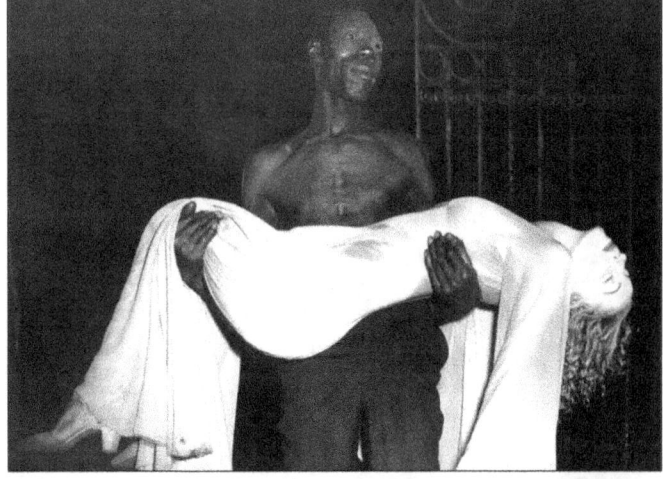

"It's just like dressing a great, big doll." It's an eerie bit of foreshadowing of the houngan preparing his Voodoo effigy of Jessica.

Getting back to the film's treatment of its black characters, *I Walked with a Zombie* isn't about "the Caribbean as a terrifying land that contained the seeds of the white world's destruction." If anything, the main characters are largely unafraid of Voodoo, including the elderly Mrs. Rand, and treat it as silly superstition. And rather than being nervous

about the island's black population, Holland expresses full awareness and guilt at the terrible cruelty that his ancestors inflicted on *their* ancestors. That the character Carrefour is startling and unsettling doesn't diminish the fact that he's ultimately fairly harmless and docile, and is easily shoo-ed away by an old woman. During the film's climax, when the houngan appears to draw Jessica out to be murdered—if that's the right word, in this case—by Rand, he might just be speeding-up the inevitable: in the previous scene, the unraveling Rand had tried to talk Betsy into poisoning Jessica.

In hindsight, *I Walked with a Zombie* remains one of the masterworks of American horror cinema, and arguably the greatest film about Voodoo ever made. Its artistic brilliance remains inspirational after endless viewings. Its low-key Gothic pressure-cooker atmosphere and genuine eeriness add up to authentic visual poetry. It ennobles the horror genre, and like the figurehead of St. Sebastian in the Hollands' garden, it grimly abides.

Justin Humphreys is a writer, film historian, curator, and consultant. He has published three books, including the Rondo Award-winning The Dr. Phibes Companion, *and he's currently completing producer/director George Pal's authorized biography,* George Pal: Man of Tomorrow, *with the Pal Estate's full cooperation. Humphreys has been the curator of Pal's Estate since 2011. Recently, he hosted two documentary shorts on the bestselling BluRay restoration of Pal's* The Wonderful World of the Brothers Grimm *(Warner Archive) and recorded audio commentaries for Pal's* Conquest of Space *(Imprint) and the Dr. Phibes double feature (Kino Lorber). He frequently appears on-camera or in audio commentaries for video labels including Criterion, Paramount, and Arrow. For more information about* George Pal: Man of Tomorrow, *follow the book's only authorized Facebook page:* www.facebook.com/GeorgePalManofTomorrowOfficialPage.

Humphreys also specializes in curating, cataloging, and brokering entertainment memorabilia—particularly props, costumes, scripts, and artwork. At Bonhams Auctions, he handled countless Hollywood treasures, including cataloging large portions of the estates of Natalie Wood, Maureen O'Hara, Charlton Heston, Tod Browning, and Harper Goff, as well as many of Rudolph Valentino's personal effects. In 2017, Humphreys cataloged the original Robby the Robot from Forbidden Planet, *which sold for $5.3 million, setting a world record for the most expensive movie prop to ever sell at auction.*

The Thing in the Cellar

By David H. Keller

IT WAS A LARGE CELLAR, ENTIRELY OUT OF PROPORTION TO THE HOUSE ABOVE IT. The owner admitted that it was probably built for a distinctly different kind of structure from the one which rose above it. Probably the first house had been burned, and poverty had caused a diminution of the dwelling erected to take its place.

A winding stone stairway connected the cellar with the kitchen. Around the base of this series of steps successive owners of the house had placed their firewood, winter vegetables and junk. The junk had gradually been pushed back till it rose, head high, in a barricade of uselessness. What was back of that barricade no one knew and no one cared. For some hundreds of years no one had crossed it to penetrate to the black reaches of the cellar behind it.

At the top of the steps, separating the kitchen from the cellar, was a stout oaken door. This door was, in a way, as peculiar and out of relation to the rest of the house as the cellar. It was a strange kind of door to find in a modern house, and certainly a most unusual door to find in the inside of the house—thick, stoutly built, dexterously rabbeted together with huge wrought-iron hinges, and a lock that looked as though it came from Castle Despair. Separating a house from the outside world, such a door would be excusable; swinging between kitchen and cellar it seemed peculiarly inappropriate.

From the earliest months of his life Tommy Tucker seemed unhappy in the kitchen. In the front parlor, in the formal dining-room, and especially on the second floor of the house he acted like a normal, healthy child; but carry him to the kitchen, he at once began to cry. His parents, being plain people, ate in the kitchen save when they had company. Being poor, Mrs. Tucker did most of her work, though occasionally she had a charwoman in to do the extra Saturday cleaning, and thus much of her time was spent in the kitchen. And Tommy stayed with her, at least as long as he was unable to walk. Much of the time he was decidedly unhappy.

When Tommy learned to creep, he lost no time in leaving the kitchen. No sooner was his mother's back turned than the little fellow crawled as fast as he could for the doorway opening into the front of the house, the dining-room and the front parlor. Once away from the kitchen, he seemed happy; at least, he ceased to cry. On being returned to the kitchen his howls so thoroughly convinced the neighbors that he had colic that more than one bowl of catnip and sage tea was brought to his assistance.

It was not until the boy learned to talk that the Tuckers had any idea as to what made the boy cry so hard when he was in the kitchen. In other words, the baby had to suffer for many months till he obtained at least a little relief, and even when he told his parents what was the matter, they were absolutely unable to comprehend. This is not to be wondered at, because they were both hard-working, rather simple-minded persons.

What they finally learned from their little son was this: that if the cellar door was shut and securely fastened with the heavy iron lock, Tommy could at least eat a meal in peace; if the door was simply closed and not locked, he shivered with fear, but kept quiet; but if the door was open, if even the slightest streak of black showed that it was not tightly shut, then the little three-year-old would scream himself to the point of exhaustion, especially if his tired father would refuse him permission to leave the kitchen.

Playing in the kitchen, the child developed two interesting habits. Rags, scraps of paper, and splinters of wood were continually being shoved under the thick oak door

to fill the space between the door and the sill. Whenever Mrs. Tucker opened the door there was always some trash there, placed by her son. It annoyed her, and more than once the little fellow was thrashed for this conduct, but punishment acted in no way as a deterrent. The other habit was as singular. Once the door was closed and locked, he would rather boldly walk over to it and caress the old lock. Even when he was so small that he had to stand on tiptoe to touch it with the tips of his fingers he would touch it with slow caressing strokes; later on, as he grew, he used to kiss it.

His father, who only saw the boy at the end of the day, decided that there was no sense in such conduct, and in his masculine way tried to break the lad of his foolishness. There was, of necessity, no effort on the part of the hard-working man to understand the psychology back of his son's conduct. All that the man knew was that his little son was acting in a way that was decidedly queer.

Tommy loved his mother and was willing to do anything he could to help her in the household chores, but one thing he would not do, and never did do, and that was to fetch and carry between the house and the cellar. If his mother opened the door, he would run screaming from the room, and he never returned voluntarily till he was assured that the door was closed.

He never explained just why he acted as he did. In fact, he refused to talk about it, at least to his parents, and that was just as well, because had he done so, they would simply have been more positive than ever that there was something wrong with their only child. They tried, in their own ways, to break the child of his unusual habits; failing to change him at all, they decided to ignore his peculiarities.

That is, they ignored them till he became six years old and the time came for him to go to school. He was a sturdy little chap by that time, and more intelligent than the usual boys beginning in the primer class. Mr. Tucker was, at times, proud of him; the child's attitude toward the cellar door was the one thing most disturbing to the father's pride. Finally nothing would do but that the Tucker family call on the neighborhood physician. It was an important event in the life of the Tuckers, so important that it demanded the wearing of Sunday clothes, and all that sort of thing.

"The matter is just this, Doctor Hawthorn," said Mr. Tucker, in a somewhat embarrassed manner. "Our little Tommy is old enough to start to school, but he behaves childish in regard to our cellar, and the missus and I thought you could tell us what to do about it. It must be his nerves."

"Ever since he was a baby," continued Mrs. Tucker, taking up the thread of conversation where her husband had paused, "Tommy has had a great fear of the cellar. Even now, big boy that he is, he does not love me enough to fetch and carry for me through that door and down those steps. It is not natural for a child to act like he does, and what with chinking the cracks with rags and kissing the lock, he drives me to the point where I fear he may become daft-like as he grows older."

The doctor, eager to satisfy new customers, and dimly remembering some lectures on the nervous system received when he was a medical student, asked some general questions, listened to the boy's heart, examined his lungs and looked at his eyes and fingernails. At last he commented:

"Looks like a fine, healthy boy to me."

"Yes, all except the cellar door," replied the father.

"Has he ever been sick?"

"Naught but fits once or twice when he cried himself blue in the face," answered the mother.

"Frightened?"

"Perhaps. It was always in the kitchen."

"Suppose you go out and let me talk to Tommy by myself?"

And there sat the doctor very much at his ease and the little six-year-old boy very uneasy.

"Tommy, what is there in the cellar you are afraid of?"

"I don't know."

"Have you ever seen it?"

"No, sir."

"Ever heard it? Smelt it?"

"No, sir."

"Then how do you know there is something there?"

"Because."

"Because what?"

"Because there is."

That was as far as Tommy would go, and at last his seeming obstinacy annoyed the physician even as it had for several years annoyed Mr. Tucker. He went to the door and called the parents into the office.

"He thinks there is something down in the cellar," he stated.

The Tuckers simply looked at each other.

"That's foolish," commented Mr. Tucker.

"'Tis just a plain cellar with junk and firewood and cider barrels in it," added Mrs. Tucker. "Since we moved into that house, I have not missed a day without going down those stone steps and I know there is nothing there. But the lad has always screamed when the door was open. I recall now that since he was a child in arms he has always screamed when the door was open."

"He thinks there is something there," said the doctor.

"That is why we brought him to you," replied the father. "It's the child's nerves. Perhaps foetida, or something, will calm him."

"I tell you what to do," advised the doctor. "He thinks there is something there. Just as soon as he finds that he is wrong and that there is nothing there, he will forget about it. He has been humored too much. What you want to do is to open that cellar door and make him stay by himself in the kitchen. Nail the door open so he can not close it. Leave him alone there for an hour and then go and laugh at him and show him how silly it was for him to be afraid of an empty cellar. I will give you some nerve and blood tonic and that will help, but the big thing is to show him that there is nothing to be afraid of."

ON THE WAY back to the Tucker home Tommy broke away from his parents. They caught him after an exciting chase and kept him between them the rest of the way home. Once in the house he disappeared and was found in the guest room under the bed. The afternoon being already spoiled for Mr. Tucker, he determined to keep the child under observation for the rest of the day. Tommy ate no supper, in spite of the urgings of the unhappy mother. The dishes were washed, the evening paper read, the evening pipe smoked; and then, and only then, did Mr. Tucker take down his tool box and get out a hammer and some long nails.

"And I am going to nail the door open, Tommy, so you can not close it; as that was what the doctor said, Tommy, and you are to be a man and stay here in the kitchen alone for an hour, and we will leave the lamp a-burning, and then when you find there is naught to be afraid of, you will be well and a real man and not something for a man to be ashamed of being the father of."

But at the last Mrs. Tucker kissed Tommy and cried and whispered to her husband not to do it, and to wait till the boy was larger; but nothing was to do except to nail the thick door open so it could not be shut and leave the boy there alone with the lamp burning and the dark open space of the doorway to look at with eyes that grew as hot and burning as the flame of the lamp.

That same day Doctor Hawthorn took supper with a classmate of his, a man who specialized in psychiatry and who was particularly interested in children. Hawthorn told Johnson about his newest case, the little Tucker boy, and asked him for his opinion. Johnson frowned.

"Children are odd, Hawthorn. Perhaps they are like dogs. It may be their nervous system is more acute than in the adult. We know that our eyesight is limited, also our hearing and smell. I firmly believe that there are forms of life which exist in such a form that we can neither see, hear, nor smell them. Fondly we delude ourselves into the fallacy of believing that they do not exist because we can not prove their existence. This Tucker lad may have a nervous system that is peculiarly acute. He may dimly appreciate the existence of something in the cellar which is unappreciable to his parents. Evidently there is some basis to this fear of his. Now, I am not saying that there is anything in the cellar. In fact, I suppose that it is just an ordinary cellar, but this boy, since he was a baby, has thought that there was something there, and that is just as bad as though there actually were. What I would like to know is what makes him think so. Give me the address, and I will call tomorrow and have a talk with the little fellow."

"What do you think of my advice?"

"Sorry, old man, but I think it was perfectly rotten. If I were you, I would stop around there on my way home and prevent them from following it. The little fellow may be badly frightened. You see, he evidently thinks there is something there."

"But there isn't."

"Perhaps not. No doubt, he is wrong, but he thinks so."

It all worried Doctor Hawthorn so much that he decided to take his friend's advice. It was a cold night, a foggy night, and the physician felt cold as he tramped along the London streets. At last he came to the Tucker house. He remembered now that he had been there once before, long ago, when little Tommy Tucker came into the world. There was a light in the front window, and in no time at all Mr. Tucker came to the door.

"I have come to see Tommy," said the doctor.

"He is back in the kitchen," replied the father.

"He gave one cry, but since then he has been quiet," sobbed the wife.

"If I had let her have her way, she would have opened the door, but I said to her, 'Mother, now is the time to make a man out of our Tommy.' And I guess he knows by now that there was naught to be afraid of. Well, the hour is up. Suppose we go and get him and put him to bed?"

"It has been a hard time for the little child," whispered the wife.

Carrying the candle, the man walked ahead of the woman and the doctor, and at last opened the kitchen door. The room was dark.

"Lamp has gone out," said the man. "Wait till I light it."

"Tommy! Tommy!" called Mrs. Tucker.

But the doctor ran to where a white form was stretched on the floor. Sharply he called for more light. Trembling, he examined all that was left of little Tommy.

Twitching, he looked into the open space down into the cellar. At last he looked at Tucker and Tucker's wife.

"Tommy—Tommy has been hurt—I guess he is dead!" he stammered.

The mother threw herself on the floor and picked up the torn, mutilated thing that had been, only a little while ago, her little Tommy.

The man took his hammer and drew out the nails and closed the door and locked it and then drove in a long spike to reinforce the lock. Then he took hold of the doctor's shoulders and shook him.

"What killed him, Doctor? What killed him?" he shouted into Hawthorn's ear.

The doctor looked at him bravely in spite of the fear in his throat.

"How do I know, Tucker?" he replied. "How do I know? Didn't you tell me that there was nothing there? Nothing down there? In the cellar?"

Weeks before its appearance in the March 1932 issue of Weird Tales, "The Thing in the Cellar" was published in the U.K. anthology Grim Death (1932), the eighth volume of Christine Campbell Thomson's Not at Night series.

The inventive American author and psychiatrist Dr. David Henry Keller (1880–1966) was one of the most popular and influential writers during the early years of pulp science fiction and fantasy. Keller concentrated on human emotions in his stories, and occasionally wrote under various pseudonyms, including Monk Smith, Jacobus Hubelaire, Cecilia Henry, Amy Worth, and Henry Cecil. Keller was also an early scholar of H.P. Lovecraft. His notable and frequently-reprinted story "The Thing in the Cellar" is a worthy tale of horror.

THE DEAD WAYS

BY LYNDA E. RUCKER

"SOME UNFORTUNATE SOUL FELL ON THE TRACKS," SAID THE MAN AT THE TICKET WINDOW. He pointed. "Rail replacement bus out the door to your left there."

"But—" Kate clenched her fists, pressing her nails hard into her palms, and turned away. There was nothing to be done. It wasn't his fault, after all. It wasn't anybody's fault. She asked, turning back, "How long will it—?" but he was already gone, the ticket booth empty as if he'd never been there.

Nothing was ever anybody's fault, but nothing ever went right as a result.

She grabbed the handle of her wheeled overnight case she'd not even had time to unpack—she'd only just arrived, they'd been having a drink at a hipster pub over the road called The Wild Hunt when she got the call from the hospital about her mother—and dragged it back over to where Andrew waited. She told him what the ticket man had said.

Andrew frowned. "Not the horrors of the rail replacement bus!" he said, and then perhaps sensing that it wasn't the moment for levity, "You could get a ticket for the next train to Victoria. It goes on a different set of tracks than the fast one to St. Pancras."

She dithered, and they checked, but the next one was running late and was still due to arrive at Victoria half an hour later than the one she'd booked, plus there would then be the Tube journey to St. Pancras. It was already getting late. It would be too late by the time she arrived at Peterborough for a hospital visit anyway.

"It'll be fine," she said. "I don't think it's a replacement bus all the way to London. I didn't ask."

They walked out the front entrance of the Margate train station. The sun was low over the sea, smearing the sky into one of its extraordinary sunsets, pink and orange against a canvas of darkening blue.

"I'm sorry," she said, and he said, "Call me as soon as you know something," and she said she would. When she got on the bus she asked the driver how far it was going but she couldn't understand his answer, not then or a second time, and she was too embarrassed to ask a third time, suddenly conscious of her American accent.

There was no one else on the bus. Kate hauled her case up to the top deck and sat at the front behind the big window. At least she could enjoy the view.

She took out her phone and started to tap out a message, then stopped and put it away before hitting "send." What did you say, after all? "On my way, if you regain consciousness and see this, don't die before I get there"?

No one else boarded that she saw. The driver pulled the door shut and they lumbered from the curb, heading up and away from the coast.

SHE SUPPOSED she ought to spare a thought for the aforementioned unfortunate soul who had ended up on the tracks, whether through misadventure or intent. And yet it wasn't really possible, given the circumstances. She had no room for it. You couldn't hold two tragedies in that way, not when one was immediate and personal and the other was abstract.

It had begun to rain, and in the steady patter against the glass she imagined a refrain: *Don't die, don't die, don't die.* She wondered if the person on the tracks had died. Maybe they had not. Maybe their fate was tied up in some inexplicable way with her mother's; maybe if her mother lived they would as well and vice versa. Or maybe it was the opposite: a life for a life. Kate wound the strap of her purse around her wrist, threaded her fingers through it and unthreaded them again. *Don't die.* This was impossible. She pulled her phone back out. She needed some music, a podcast. But the battery was drained. The phone sat unresponsive in her hand, a blank, black rectangle.

When had she stopped automatically tucking a book into her case wherever she went, even if she was only going out for an hour or two? When had she given up the reliable magic of words printed on a page and started depending on things that ran on batteries and invisible waves in the air? *I sound old,* she thought, followed by *and what's wrong with that.* She had always liked old things, even as a child: on visits to her mother's family here in England she had loved its ancient structures and roads aged not in decades but millennia, not like back home in Oregon where "old" meant a house built in 1900. There was a steadiness to old things. *We've got you,* they said to you. *We've been here before. We've seen it all. We know there is nothing new under the sun. We were here before anyone could imagine you and we'll be here long after you're forgotten.*

She loved the stories here, too, the old bits of folklore and the ancient rituals that still survived and everything that was lost as well, the silence of standing stones; the mute ridgeways; mounds and ley lines.

Kate pressed her forehead against the rain-speckled window in front of her. It was cool like her mother's hand had been when she was little and she had the flu that turned into pneumonia and she ended up in the hospital. She didn't really remember it, just in that you way you "remember" stories from your childhood only because you've been told them over and over—she only remembered that sensation, the cool touch amid searing heat. Kate said, "*Mommy,*" out loud because there was no one on the bus to hear, and that was when the tears came, hot like that fever, spattering like the rain.

SHE PULLED HERSELF together almost immediately. She couldn't afford to fall apart, not now anyway. She wondered what time it was. She thought about going downstairs and asking the driver but decided against it because it didn't matter, it wouldn't change anything.

The bus was traveling along a flat road, cultivated fields on either side of them though she had no idea what grew in them. She didn't recognize where they were, either, but then she wouldn't. She'd only been in London for a couple of years, it was only her second visit to Kent and she didn't have a car—you didn't need one—you could go everywhere by train. It was one of the things she loved, one of the things she had talked up along with the free healthcare and the pubs when she told everyone back in Portland that she was leaving for good this time. *America is broken,* that was the kind of thing she had said, because it was the kind of thing that people in Portland said. They all nodded and agreed that they envied her being able to just go like that.

But those weren't the real reasons. Her mother had gone back home nearly twenty years ago, as soon as Kate went off to college—America had never been home for her, not when her own family had been in the Peterborough area for hundreds, maybe thousands of years, farming amid the marshy fens. And the older she got, the more Kate found it was true for her as well. Maybe it was because her father—her American side—had been such an absent figure compared with her mother, who was always there and very real. She couldn't explain it, she really didn't belong anywhere, but she belonged more *here* than she did *there,* even if everyone marked her as an outsider the moment she opened her mouth.

The rain intensified; soon that and the growing dark would mean she couldn't see anything outside at all. She wondered if it was raining this hard back in Margate. *If I were home in London, if I hadn't gone to see Andrew today, I'd already be in Peterborough. I'd have been there in time to see her before visiting hours ended. If anything happens to her tonight...*

She couldn't finish the thought.

It had been so awkward with Andrew, everything was so tentative and new. You couldn't even call it a relationship, not yet. Right now it was just a "thing." She could see him trying to figure out what his role was at this nascent stage with such an unwelcome real-world event thrust upon them. Should he offer to accompany her? The very thought horrified her, and she deflected the unspoken question with movement and chatter. Like a teenager: *Mom! So embarrassing!* They would have a good laugh about it, she and Rosie. *Why do you call your mother Rosie?* Andrew had asked. *It's her name,* only it wasn't, her name was Margaret, but absolutely everyone had always called her Rosie. Who knew why? Who knew why families ever did these things? They just did. And then she started to tell Andrew another story, she didn't know why: Rosie was tiny because she had been struck by lightning when she was twelve and she never grew after that, and only after Kate was saying this did it strike her what a silly unlikely thing it was. Surely it wasn't true, though she'd always assumed it was.

She had the distinct feeling that whatever might have been delicately budding between the two of them had been nipped, the spectre of her mother's mortality an altogether too-heavy topic for their undefined "thing." She would message him the following day with an update and that would be it, really, perhaps a few more messages exchanged between them with dwindling frequency, neither of them mentioning trying to arrange another visit until finally some months later they might find themselves at the same event where they would smile and nod and if anyone asked she might say to them "oh, we were seeing each other for about five minutes last year," but she might not, it was that brief, so funny how things unfolded, with one twist of fate's wheel you might have three children and grow old together or you might never see one another again.

What a time to be alone with your thoughts. Before she got on the train from London she would try to grab a book at the station, maybe get a drink, too, calm her nerves. For now, she practiced breathing like her meditation app had taught her. Deep calming breaths. Observe your thoughts and emotions but don't get attached to them.

But she couldn't stop thinking about the man on the tracks. Why a man? Couldn't it just as well be a woman? A man for sure if it was deliberate, she thought. Women tended to die quietly, in their rooms.

The bus rocked gently, a motion somewhere between soothing and sickening. And there was something wrong with the engine—no, not the engine, something howling?

Her imagination getting the better of her. "My grandfather used to tell me there was a wild hunt in Peterborough," she'd said to Andrew a couple of hours earlier as they sat in the pub of the same name. "It was written about almost a thousand years ago but he swore he'd heard them once when he was a boy, the baying hounds and the hunters' horns and the unholy shrieking."

Andrew had laughed politely. "But you don't believe in that stuff, right," the correct reply clear from his tone.

But something *was* baying, she wasn't just imagining it. She looked behind her in case someone was back there after all, someone with their phone's speaker turned up loud. There was simply row after row of empty seats.

She thought about articles she'd read about people going mad at meditation retreats, but nobody had a psychotic break five minutes into a breathing exercise on a replacement bus, surely.

Still and all. Better safe than sorry. Maybe not the best stress reliever after all. She took out her phone, as though the battery might have spontaneously regenerated, and put it away again. She cupped her hands around her eyes and pressed them against the glass next to her.

There were low figures, like big dogs, running alongside the bus, keeping pace.

It was the dark. It must be the dark, and the rain, making shapes out of nothing. But when did it get so dark? The sun had just been setting a little while ago. She leaned forward, pressed her cupped hands against the glass in front of her and realized she couldn't see the headlights of the bus on the road before them, couldn't see anything at all.

At that moment the vehicle shuddered to a halt. Maybe something *was* wrong—but of course not; they had just come to another stop, and some passengers would get on, and soon she would be sorry that she no longer had the silence and the solitude that was tormenting her now. Someone would be watching something obnoxious on their phone without using earbuds, teenagers would have loud and boisterous conversations, a child would be crying.

But none of those things happened.

She was not sure how long she sat there, but eventually she got up and, tentatively, went down the stairs. The lower deck was empty as well. The front doors were open. "Excuse me," she said as she made her way up to the driver, but she needn't have bothered.

There was no one at the wheel.

This was silly. They were stopped to pick up passengers, and the driver had stepped out and was having a smoke. She would step outside too and speak to him. That would break the ice and she would ask him about the time and she would sit downstairs for the rest of the journey, which would be

entirely normal, and she could stop imagining things and ruminating over that which she had no control.

Kate stepped up to the door.

The paralyzing cold struck her there. It felt as though something had sucked her breath right out, replacing the air in her lungs with ice. The darkness was alive and would devour her if she let any part of her body pass beyond the safety of the bus, she was sure of it.

From the blackness beyond the doorway came the sound of horns, then a cacophony of howling, and an otherworldly shrieking, a shrieking that felt like all the sounds she had been wanting to make since the hospital had rung her and said her mother had been admitted. Kate closed her eyes and opened her mouth and shrieked with them, shrieked for all the fear and sorrow and loss and death in the world. The world was dark, the world was black, the world was gone.

KATE SHUDDERED AWAKE with a gasping breath and a cry. Her heart thudded in her chest. She looked hastily around, embarrassed, but she remained alone on the top level of the bus, which was trundling along in the dark, rain pattering against the windows.

She grabbed her case and dragged it along the aisle, meaning to go downstairs and sit near the driver, but at the top of the stairs, she stopped.

It was stupid and irrational, but she was afraid to go downstairs now. The remnants of the dream lingered. She pulled her case down the aisle and sank into the seat just behind the stairwell, leaned forward with her arms on the railing in front of her and put her head down.

When she raised it again, it was to stare at the CCTV feed above the stairwell, which showed the empty stairwell itself.

Surely they must be getting close to wherever they were going; even if it was all the way to London, the entire journey couldn't take more than a couple of hours. They had probably stopped and picked up some passengers while she was sleeping, too, and if she just went downstairs, she could ask one of them where they were and what time it was.

A hooded figure appeared in the CCTV footage, on the stairwell, moving with unnatural speed up the stairs.

Kate let out a cry, but the figure was gone.

She stood up and leaned over the railing. Nothing there, just a set of empty stairs.

She sat back again. The figure on the screen returned, and a moment later it came into sight, small and wearing a raincoat with a peaked hood. Kate made a noise that she turned into a coughing fit. The figure turned, and the face in the hood was a plump, grandmotherly one.

"You all right, love?"

Kate nodded.

"Awful weather out there," the woman said in a voice that suggested she was confiding something of great import. "I'm so unsteady on those stairs but I get sick sometimes when I'm riding down below. Better up here where you can see up front, don't you think?"

Kate, who still couldn't see anything at all out the front, nodded again.

"My husband, God rest his soul, was so terrified of heights he couldn't even go to the top deck of a bus. Forty years of marriage and it was always either me trying not to be sick down below or him sweating and swaying with his eyes shut up here." The woman looked toward the front and frowned. "View's not much better up here tonight, is it?"

Kate said, "Do you have the time?"

"Oh, I never wear a watch, love. Can't stand the things. You have to be careful about time, you know. It skips and scourges and scapes. It lies to you."

The woman made her way along the aisle and sank into the seat across from Kate.

Kate asked her, "Do you know where the bus is going?"

The woman looked into her face intently. In the dim light, her eyes appeared black. "All the way, I'd imagine."

"All the way to London? Really?"

The woman laughed. "London, oh no, I hardly think so. Not London. No, not there."

Kate tried again. "Where are *you* headed?"

The woman said, "Would you like something to eat, love?" She didn't appear to have any luggage with her nor even a handbag, so Kate wasn't sure where she had produced the cake wrapped in wax paper she was trying to pass across the aisle.

"No thank you. I don't want any," but the woman wouldn't stop, she just sat there holding the cake out, and she said, "The bus is going exactly where it needs to be going, as you are."

Something seemed to shift under the woman's raincoat. Kate had the idea for a moment that the coat hid wings, and the woman put her in mind of a crow, with her dark eyes darting all about.

"You really must eat something," the woman was saying, "it's going to be ever so long before we get there," but Kate was already on her feet, pulling her case along behind her.

"I have your husband's problem," she said. "I get sick up here. Excuse me." The bus was swaying from side to side now, it seemed as though it was being buffered by wind, but she went unsteadily to the head of the stairs and started down.

ON THE LOWER LEVEL, three seats were occupied.

A young man had taken the front left one. His blond hair spilled out of a hoodie. He smelled of piss and alcohol—even from some distance away—and had presumably passed out. An empty can of cider rolled monotonously back and forth near his feet.

Three seats back and on the opposite side of the aisle, an older man wearing a flat cap read an *Evening Standard*. And on one of the risers at the back, a goth girl, jet-black hair and tattooed sleeves, rings through her nose and lower lip, ignored the rest of them via big Bluetooth headphones clamped firmly on each ear.

Not the most promising collection of traveling companions, but refreshingly unexceptional. Kate took a seat opposite flat cap man and leaned toward him.

"Excuse me," she said.

The man rattled his paper, harrumphed in an ostentatiously irritated manner and looked over at her.

"Is the bus going all the way to London?"

The man regarded her for a moment. Then he raised one finger slowly to his lips and looked at her meaningfully.

"I—excuse me?"

The man frowned. He leaned forward as well, and spoke in a stage whisper.

"You don't want to wake that one there." He pointed at the passed-out youth. "You've got to stay quiet or we'll never get where we're going."

Kate didn't bother trying to keep the note of desperation out of her voice. "Where exactly *are* we going?"

"No. No." The man began shaking his head convulsively. "No." Both hands clenched and crushed the broadsheet. "You're going to wake him. You're going to wake them. You're going to start it all again."

Kate got up and moved toward the front of the bus. Behind her, the man said, "Don't do it. Don't do it," in a flat, wheezing voice that said he was absolutely certain nothing now could stop her from doing it.

There was a bulky shape on the other side of the driver's plexiglass. Then the shape turned toward her and it wasn't a man's face at all, it wasn't a man's head, it was the face of something feral with antlers on its head and its eyes were black like those of the woman upstairs, and behind her the passengers had begun barking and baying and she didn't dare look back at them, she didn't dare look at anyone, and the bus shook so hard it felt like it would disintegrate as it roared on through the night.

"Miss."

Someone was shaking her.

Kate started.

"Miss. You have to get off the bus."

The man had a heavy accent, Eastern European maybe. He was wearing heavy-duty gloves and holding a plastic bag half-full of rubbish.

She blinked. They were outside the glass edifice of St. Pancras Station. It was still raining, still night.

"What time is it?"

"I think it's about nine. Do you need any—"

But she was off the bus before he could finish, running for the lights of the station, holding her overnight case in front of her across her chest like a shield, into the great hall where she stood gasping and blinking and there was Starbucks and Pret A Manger and the banks of ticket machines and the big boards blinking with departures and arrivals, everything as it should be, everything normal and solid and real.

She caught her breath before taking the escalators up to the second level and the platforms where trains left for the southeast.

At the barriers, she said to one of the attendants, "Is there still a replacement bus running to Margate?"

The man shook his head. "Trains are running normally. There's no replacement bus."

"But there was," she said. "Earlier. From Margate to here." *I was on it*, she almost said, but didn't.

He shook his head. "Good service on all Southeastern lines today. No buses. There's road works next weekend, maybe you're thinking of that?"

"There was a man," she said. "A person. Someone fell on the tracks."

Now he was looking at her in a way that made her wonder how she must appear, was she wild-eyed, did she look crazy? "There's been no accident like that today on these lines." He'd probably seen and heard it all before. *I'm not crazy, though*, she wanted to say. Which was probably what they always said.

"I'm sorry," she mumbled.

Kate went back down the escalator. She needed to work out where the next train was leaving from, here or King's Cross, and get a ticket. She needed to get a sandwich.

But as people streamed past her, bound for the coast, bound for the Eurostar, bound for the northern moors and fells, the highlands, the remote islands, all the distant places, she no longer felt as though she was one of them. She was singularly unmoored, somehow marked, and they knew it. Groups parted to give her a wide berth as they approached her. No one really looked at her—of course, this was London, no one really looked at anyone—but this was different. She set her case down and stared at her hands, half-expecting that they would be translucent and was surprised to see she was solid as ever.

She followed a woman in a camel-colored coat holding a little girl's hand back out of the station because they reminded her of her mother and herself when she was little. They were quickly swallowed by the night. The sky was impossible, glittering with more stars than she'd ever seen in the city before. Little points of light were everywhere; from the sky, from the station, from the black cabs and buses and cars, a billion billion points of light knitting the trackless black, passages for the dying, signposts for the dead.

Lynda E. Rucker grew up writing stories in a house in the woods full of books and cats in the southeastern U.S. She has sold dozens of short stories to various magazines and anthologies including Best New Horror, The Best Horror of the Year, The Year's Best Dark Fantasy and Horror, Black Static, Nightmare, F&SF, Postscripts *and* Shadows and Tall Trees *among others. She has had a short play produced as part of an anthology of horror plays on London's West End, has collaborated on a short horror comic, and is a regular columnist for the UK horror magazine* Black Static. *In 2015, she won the Shirley Jackson Award for Best Short Story. Her first collection,* The Moon Will Look Strange, *was released in 2013 from Karōshi Books and her second,* You'll Know When You Get There, *was published by Swan River Press in 2016. In 2018, she edited the anthology* Uncertainties III *for Swan River Press. A third collection of short fiction is forthcoming in 2022.*

WE HOPE YOU RETURN TO NIGHTMARE ABBEY—

WE'RE DYING TO HANG OUT WITH YOU AGAIN.